SPY TANGO

Garrett Hutson

This book is a work of fiction. Aside from historical figures, the names, characters, events, and places depicted are the products of the author's imagination. Any resemblance to actual events, places, or persons living or dead is entirely coincidental.

Cover design by Steven Novak

For more information, or to book an event, please contact the author at www.garretthutson.com

ISBN 978-0-9982813-8-4 (paperback)
ISBN 978-0-9982813-9-1 (eBook)

For Henry, Alice, Eli, and Opal, who wait for me at the top of the basement stairs while I write.

1

Friday, March 15, 1940 – Barrio Belgrano, Buenos Aires, Argentina

The agent's jaunty step, and the tune he whistled as he strolled home for siesta, told his unseen observers that he was oblivious to their presence. He didn't glance around as he put his key in the lock, or he might have noticed the detectives in summer suits who crept from tree to tree on the opposite side of the street.

He removed his hat as he stepped through the door of the apartment building, and fanned himself. His blond hair clung to his head, damp with sweat.

He saw them when he started to close the door.

"Uno momento, señor," one of the detectives called, crossing the street. He held out his badge. *"Policía. Podemos hablar con usted?"*

Helmut Kortbein considered declining and slipping out the back, but instead he asked why they wanted to speak with him. His Spanish was good—he'd been in the country for fourteen years—and his German accent was not so unusual in this part of the city.

"We've been informed you are in possession of an illegal radio," one of the detectives said in Spanish.

He played dumb. "I own a radio, yes—but that is hardly illegal."

"Not that kind of radio," the other detective said. "Illegal broadcasts have been traced to this block. May we have a look inside your apartment, sir?"

He thought of the transmitter, stored inside an innocuous looking valise at the back of a closet. If they did more than a cursory search, they would find it.

Instinct kicked in. He slammed the door and bolted for the building's rear exit. He threw the door open and flew around the corner into the alley.

And ran straight into a trio of uniformed police officers.

Martin Schuller sipped his coffee under the shade of a large umbrella, at an outside table at the café on the corner of Avenida Cabildo in the *Barrio Belgrano*, watching the drama unfold a block down the side street.

When the police brought Helmut Kortbein out of the building in handcuffs, ignoring his shouting about false arrest, Martin looked through the window of the café and nodded.

FBI Special Agent Reginald Sloan sauntered through the door and paused to lean against the frame, keeping in the shade of an awning. "'Beware the Ides of March.'" He held a half-empty glass of beer in his hand, the local pale lager, and gestured toward the police. "Did they find the radio?"

"I haven't seen it yet," Martin said, looking back down the side street.

Sloan took a drink and watched. "Ricardo sent all the staff home, but said he'd stick around for a while. In case we need anything."

Martin glanced at his watch and nodded. It was two o'clock. Most of the city had already closed up for the afternoon, and wouldn't reopen for another two or three hours. It varied a little every day, unpredictable.

It was a great courtesy that the manager of the café was delaying his siesta for them. It was not the first time Ricardo Messini had done them a favor.

"There it is," Martin said, watching as a pair of police carried out an open suitcase, full of tubes and wires. A two-way radio.

"Good. That'll ensure a conviction," Sloan said, and raised his glass. "One more off the streets, thanks to you and me. Here's to maintaining the neutrality of the western hemisphere. Cheers."

Martin acknowledged the toast with a small nod and raised of his coffee cup.

Sloan took a seat at Martin's table.

"It's tough to be the investigator, but not be able to share the glory. It still frustrates me that we can't nab the bad guys ourselves, after we do all the investigation." He drained the last of the beer, and set down the empty glass a touch too hard. "It was our intelligence that got him, but no one will ever know."

A bitter smile turned the corners of Martin's mouth for a second, but he made his expression blank again, and continued watching the police down the block.

"I know how you feel—since you FBI fellows did exactly that to us at State last year," Martin observed, watching Sloan from the corner of his eye.

Sloan frowned, but then chuckled and nodded, leaning back and crossing his arms. "Touché."

Before coming to Argentina last fall—spring, actually, here—Martin had worked for the Office of the Chief Special Agent at the Department of State. He and his colleagues had nabbed more than a few *Abwehr* agents in the U.S. illegally, using fake passports or immigration visas. But then in June of last year, President Roosevelt ordered the consolidation of all domestic counter-espionage activity under the FBI.

Martin still hadn't entirely forgiven Sloan and the FBI for that. After working with him for almost six months here in Argentina, Sloan had earned his grudging respect. But that didn't mean Martin had to like him.

"Harriet wants to invite you for dinner on Saturday," Sloan said. "Eight o'clock, at our place. Just a small gathering, to celebrate the end of summer. Will you come?"

Martin shrugged. He didn't have plans, of course. And he also knew Mrs. Sloan's little dinner parties annoyed her husband. "Thanks, I'll be there." He got up, laid a few pesos on the table, and nodded to Ricardo Messini inside the café.

"You going back to the embassy?" Sloan asked. At Martin's nod, he stood. "I'll go with you."

Martin would have preferred some solitude, but he couldn't say no. They walked in silence to the subway station a block down the avenue. Line D ran southeast toward central Buenos Aires, and the inbound train was almost empty at this time of day; the few *Porteños* who weren't already on siesta were taking the outbound train home.

"I'll call the police chief this afternoon, see if they found the code book at Kortbein's apartment," Sloan said, quiet even though no one was around to hear.

Martin nodded, but said nothing. He doubted it. Any code book Kortbein might have in his possession would look like a regular book.

And besides, breaking Nazi codes was technically outside of their mandate.

"We've both got our reports to write," Sloan continued. "You'll get me a copy of yours before you submit it, let me review for any changes?"

"I always do."

Sloan watched him for a second, a strange look on his face. Then he looked away and crossed his arms. "I'll see yours, and you'll see mine; as usual. It's a good system we have."

"It works."

It did work well, actually—though Martin was loath to appear too enthusiastic about that.

They got off at the Plaza Italia, the end of the line, and walked the remaining blocks to the American embassy. The streets were practically deserted at this time of day, only a few foreigners and a handful of stray dogs to be seen moving around.

One of the dogs approached Martin, but stopped about five feet from him, his soft brown eyes both wary and hopeful. He was tan and white, short-haired, lean, with a long thin tail.

Martin reached into his suit pocket and removed the small hunk of empanada he had saved from lunch, and held it out. The dog sniffed the air for a second, then lunged out and took the bite from Martin's hand and scampered away.

"You feed that stray mutt every day?" Sloan asked, sounding judgmental.

"None of your business."

"It'll never go away if you keep feeding it."

Martin ignored him. Where else was it going to go, anyway?

The Argentine receptionist smiled at them when they entered the American embassy. "Good afternoon, Mr. Schuller; Mr. Sloan."

"*Buenas tardes, señora,*" Martin replied. His Spanish was still not much better than rudimentary, but he could manage that much without thinking.

It was a small courtesy that he never saw Sloan extend to the local hires at the embassy, though he knew Sloan spoke Spanish at least as well as he did; Martin had heard Sloan speaking with the local police on several occasions.

He and Sloan parted, heading to their respective offices. Martin sat at his desk and began composing his report for First Secretary Davis, his official boss. Once finalized, copies would also be sent to the Ambassador, the Assistant Secretary of State for Intelligence, as well as to Martin's old boss at the Office of the Chief Special Agent.

When he'd finished the draft, he stepped from his office into the open space occupied by four typists who jointly served the First

Secretary, as well as the multiple Second Secretaries and Third Secretaries.

"I have a preliminary report that needs typed for review," he said to the quartet. "Who's available?"

Rosa Linda Bianchi stood and held out her hand. "I can do it, Mr. Schuller. I am not too busy."

Her accent was good, but with a charming Latin lilt. She was tall, and with her three-inch heels her golden brown eyes were level with his as she looked him directly in the eye, smiling.

"*Gracias*," he said with a nod and backed away.

"You're welcome, Mr. Schuller," she replied in English

"I'll need two copies—one for me, and one for Mr. Sloan downstairs."

"Yes, I remember," she said, her smile never fading. She watched him walk back to his office.

From the corner of his eye, Martin saw the other three girls give Rosa Linda side-eye while their fingers still clicked the keys of their typewriters.

Yes, she was a flirt. Yes, she was beautiful. And young. And unmarried. And she seemed to like him...

Martin sat and forced himself to concentrate on his work.

A young American consular officer knocked on his door a while later, and waited in the open doorway.

"Come in, Bob," Martin said, motioning with his hand.

"A packet came from Washington today on the clipper," the young man said, handing three envelopes to Martin. He was about twenty-three or twenty-four, slender, and wore the basic uniform of the low-level consular officers in the Foreign Service—black slacks, white dress-shirt, black necktie. No jacket indoors.

"Thanks." Martin had heard the roar of the Pan Am clipper this morning, but had forgotten about it in the excitement of the midday activity.

For the last three years, the Pan Am clipper had brought air mail from New York to Brazil and Argentina; the State Department used their service to carry diplomatic packets to and from the embassies. It had reduced the transit time from seventeen days to less than forty-eight hours.

Martin flipped through the envelopes and saw that one of them was from his old coworker—and friend—Joe Hansen, from the Office of the Chief Special Agent. It was particularly thick, and he tore into it first.

At the top of the stack of paper was a note typed on official State Department letterhead, dated March 12, 1940:

> *Confidential*
> Dear Mr. Schuller,
>
> I have enclosed herein several Photostat copies of memoranda received in recent weeks from our diplomatic missions in Germany, which I have determined to be of interest to your office. Viewed together, these documents point to an operation of some size, whose mission is to smuggle raw materials out of Argentina, for use by the German armed forces.
>
> You will no doubt find this information useful in your work. Per standard operating procedure, copies of these documents have already been provided to the Federal Bureau of Investigation.
>
> If additional relevant intelligence comes to light, I will be certain to forward copies to you post haste.

I am, very cordially yours,

Joseph P. Hansen
Office of the Chief Special Agent

Martin perused the documents; the Germans were somehow obtaining war materiel from Argentine mines, in violation of the country's neutrality under the Declaration of Panama. He and Sloan would have to look into that.

At the bottom of the stack, he found a second letter from Joe, hand-written on personal stationery.

Hi there, Martin! How are you? It's not often that I find something relevant to you, so I'm taking the opportunity to send you a note.

I am well. Our work never ends, as you know. Busier than ever, actually, even with the "phony" war in Europe. I can't share details, of course. You understand.

I confess that I miss having you around the office to work with. Sam is good for consultation, you know, but he's an old fellow. Compared to you and me, anyhow. In the six months since you left, I've wondered if I should transfer to Foreign Service work.

I hope you're enjoying life down there in Argentina. A charming fellow like you, I imagine you dancing the tango with a

*beautiful woman every night. At least, that's
what I would do in your shoes! Ha!*
    Write me back when you get a chance.
    Your friend,

    Joe

Martin almost laughed out loud at the reference to tango. Joe knew better, of course; Martin had never been "charming." That was part of the teasing.

"...that's what I would do..." Of course, Joe didn't know that Martin knew better. That it was an act. A carefully orchestrated act.

Several letters awaited Martin in his mailbox when he got home that evening. He might have guessed, since the clipper had arrived that day with mail from the States.

There was a letter from his mother, as well as one from his sister Helen, and one from his youngest brother, Ed. But the envelope he opened first was a thick one addressed to him in his ex-wife's handwriting. The envelope contained four letters—one each from his three children and their mother.

He read the kids' letters first. Their childish phrasing and super-short anecdotes about school made him smile.

He set Becky's note aside and read the other letters from family. The news from home was nice, even if he hardly cared about any of the nearly-forgotten neighbors and acquaintances they talked about. He did appreciate hearing what his nieces and nephews were doing.

One of his mother's letters in January had told him of his grandmother's passing. The death of his last living grandparent had come as a blow, but today's letter was full of innocuous news about people he once knew while growing up in Reading, Pennsylvania.

When he couldn't put it off any longer, he went back to Becky's letter.

It was short, a single page of her monogrammed stationery, written in her flowing hand with the fine point of an expensive fountain pen.

March 10, 1940

Dear Martin,

You'll be glad to know I have made arrangements for the children to visit you in Argentina for their summer vacation. Your attorney gave me no choice, as I am sure you are aware. I will take advantage of the inconvenience by taking a shipboard vacation of my own. The children and I will travel together on the SS Argentina in June, but I shall make a round trip while they stay with you.

We shall arrive in Buenos Aires on June 17th. Then I will return to meet them on August 15th. I will have them back home in time for school, which begins September 3rd.

I trust you are prepared to look after them for two months.

Becky

He took a deep breath and set the letter aside. It could have been worse than one passive-aggressive comment about his lawyer. He jotted the dates on his calendar in the kitchen.

The thought of seeing his kids for two months gave him a big grin that didn't fade for several minutes. He went back and re-read their letters, and chuckled all over again at their words.

Now he just needed to figure out what they were going to do while he had them.

Hutson

2

Saturday, March 16, 1940

Eight guests arrived at the Sloans' apartment in the *Barrio Colegiales* as dusk faded to a soft twilight. A cool breeze came in off the Rio de la Plata, easing the sultry heat of a late-summer evening.

Harriett Sloan had all of the windows open, and her white lace curtains billowed in the breeze. The sound of soft jazz music wafted through the air from a bar a few blocks away, accompanied by laughter and the din of conversations as crowds of *Porteños* enjoyed the last weekend of the season.

The guests included three mid-level Foreign Service staffers from the embassy, plus their wives—all of them in their thirties—as well as Martin, and one woman he had never met.

At thirty-two, Martin might have been the youngest one there, other than the unknown woman, who appeared no more than twenty-five. Reginald Sloan, forty-three, was clearly the oldest in attendance—a fact that may have contributed to his not-well-concealed discomfort.

"Martin, I'd like to introduce Ann Corley," Harriet said, with the type of smile that told him she was up to something. "Her parents are former neighbors of ours when we lived in Poughkeepsie. She used to babysit our girls when they were little, before we moved to New York. Ann, this is Martin Schuller. He works at the embassy. He'll be your dinner partner this evening."

"I'm pleased to meet you, Mr. Schuller." Ann Corley extended her hand to Martin palm in, rather than palm down in the usual manner.

Martin shook it as if they were meeting for business. "How do you do, Miss Corley?"

"Ann's touring Latin America to build up her resume," Harriet said. "She hopes to join the diplomatic corps someday. Isn't that right, Ann? Her mother wrote to me that she planned to be in Argentina for a few weeks, and asked us to help introduce her."

"Have you applied for the Foreign Service, Miss Corley?" Martin asked.

A brief frown crossed Ann's lips. "I wasn't allowed to take the exam. I was told I didn't meet the qualifications. I graduated *Suma Cum Laude* from Smith College, with political science as my major field of study. Clearly the reason I didn't qualify to take the exam was my sex."

She stated it so directly, it took Martin aback.

Harriet Sloan recovered faster than Martin did. "I'm sure that wasn't the only reason, dear. The government is probably reluctant to send *unmarried* women into foreign lands, for their safety." Her expression, and her tone, brightened as she added, "Perhaps it would help your chances if you married a man in the Foreign Service."

Martin could almost feel Ann stifling a sigh as she fixed Harriet with a polite smile.

"Political science was my major as well." He couldn't think of anything else to say. His own first reaction to her blunt statement was *surely that wasn't the reason*, but as he reflected, he realized he had never known any female Foreign Service officers.

"Oh, really?" Ann only sounded slightly interested. "At what university, if I may ask?"

"University of Pennsylvania."

"Oh! So you're an Ivy Leaguer. That surprises me, if you don't mind me saying so. You don't seem the type. But the University of Pennsylvania is different from other Ivy League schools, I suppose—they admit women, for one thing."

"Yes, I met my ex-wife there, actually." Martin felt awkward admitting that, for some reason.

Harriet Sloan jumped in and saved him. "Mr. Schuller has been to several countries. I'm sure he could tell you many stories about his adventures, and perhaps give you some tips that will help you."

Ann's smile grew, but Martin could see that it was still more for social politeness than genuine. "That would be lovely."

Harriet beamed and touched Ann on the shoulder. "Now if you'll please excuse me, dears, I'll let you get acquainted while I go look after my other guests."

Ann watched her go for a moment before turning back to Martin.

"You needn't feel any obligation to entertain me, Mr. Schuller. The truth is, I'd rather be at home with a book than have to make small talk with strangers—and I surmise you feel similarly."

Martin's half-smile was his only acknowledgement. The truth was, he felt relief.

"I will say, however—I also have a Master's degree in international studies from Boston College. I know I could pass that Foreign Service exam, if they'd let me sit for it. I wrote a letter to Eleanor Roosevelt, after they denied me. She wrote back, a lovely letter, urging me to travel abroad to bolster my credentials, and then reapply with my initials instead of my name. She was the one who suggested Latin America, to be honest; she mentioned the president's 'Good Neighbor' policy as a good reason, and I agreed. So, here I am."

"Has it been helpful?" He hated small talk.

"We'll see, won't we?"

An awkward silence fell over them.

Martin saw Ann watching the three female guests, who stood near the table with Harriet Sloan. The men were all gathered in the living room, at the threshold of the open French doors that led to the small balcony, two of them with cigarettes.

He took the opportunity.

15

"I'll let you join the ladies, and I'll see you at dinner."

The look she gave him was hard to read—enigmatic, but with perhaps a touch of irritation behind her eyes. He couldn't be sure. He nodded and turned toward the living room.

"I can't fathom why the Brits are so damned irritated," Mike Mattingly was saying when Martin came over. "Their own press calls it 'the Phony War.'"

"The French press, too," Roger Dean agreed, flicking some cigarette ash over the side of the balcony rail. He had a touch of southern accent. "They call it the '*Drôle de Guerre*'—strange war. Oh, hi there, Martin."

"Hi, fellas. I see you're discussing Mike's call from his British counterpart yesterday," Martin said, a hint of smile curling up one corner of his mouth.

"I'm not sure what they expect," Mike said, frowning. "It's a presidential election year, for crying out loud. They know that."

"Unlike you gents, I'm old enough to remember 1916," Sloan said, pulling a fresh cigarette from his inside jacket pocket. "Wilson campaigned on 'He kept us out of war.' Then not six weeks after his second inauguration, he asked Congress for a declaration of war. And he got it."

"I remember," Roger Dean said, a hint of scowl creasing his forehead. "I was eleven years old that election. I read the paper every day, after my father finished with it."

"I was ten, and I only read the funny pages," Mike Mattingly said, and laughed a little too hard. "Still, I remember my parents talking about it."

Martin kept silent. He'd been eight in 1916, and hadn't paid much attention to the presidential campaign. He was nine by the time the U.S. entered the Great War in April 1917. *That* he remembered.

And he remembered all too well the rash of anti-German feeling that had swept through Reading—a city that was forty percent German-

American. The rock through the window of his father's grocery store that spring still stood out, along with the crimson spray-paint spelling "HUNS" on the storefront.

"But Germany gave us reasons to go to war in 1917," Chuck Brady chimed in. "The U-boat attacks, and the Zimmerman telegram—Wilson was right to lead us to war. It's different now."

"And frankly, aside from a few naval skirmishes, *nothing is happening*," Mike Mattingly said, exasperated. "Is it too much to demand that they keep those outside of the Americas' security zone?"

"Of course not," Sloan said, scowling. "They've got the whole damn ocean to spar in, they don't have to do it fifteen miles off our shores."

A chorus of agreement rose from the group.

"Besides, there's no reason to think that both sides won't want to negotiate a settlement soon, since their mutual blockades are disrupting trade," Mattingly said.

Martin shook his head. "Hitler will never negotiate."

"That is the popular opinion," Mike Mattingly said, nodding toward Martin. "But I disagree. Hitler will want to negotiate a settlement with the British because it's in his best interest to do so. The German economy needs raw materials that are being blockaded by the Royal Navy."

Martin couldn't mention the classified intelligence he'd received from Washington yesterday, about a sizeable operation to smuggle raw materials out of Argentina aboard neutral ships—mica, platinum, and industrial diamonds for use by the German military. No doubt Hitler had similar operations in other countries, to smuggle other materials.

"Chamberlain would jump at a negotiated settlement," Sloan said, shaking his head. "That fella's got no backbone."

Mattingly looked pained. "I wouldn't go that far. He was chagrined after the last appeasement backfired. But sooner or later the British will negotiate to spare their shipping from German U-boats. Eventually, everyone acts in his own best interests."

17

"Not Hitler," Martin said.

"Even Hitler."

Martin shook his head. "The Czechs would disagree with you. On second thought, their Nazi overlords wouldn't allow them to disagree with you."

Sloan chuckled. "Good point, Schuller. I think that's checkmate, Mr. Mattingly."

Mattingly frowned. "No, it's still not the same. After Czechoslovakia, the British and French did nothing. After Poland, they declared war. It hasn't been much of a war, it's true—but the Royal Air Force did drop some bombs on German warships at Wilhelmshaven, and there were some dog fights with the Luftwaffe over the Rhineland. It was a warning, really—a message to Herr Hitler."

"And don't forget the French army's sortie into the Saarland," Roger Dean said. "That was a warning, too."

Normally Martin enjoyed geo-political discussions. But Mike Mattingly—who had spent his entire Foreign Service career in Latin America—didn't know what he was talking about in regards to Hitler, or Germany. Martin had a lot of expertise on both, and Mike's overconfidence in his own opinion grated.

"Hitler didn't call off the invasion of Poland, though, did he?" Martin asked.

"No—but it's been quiet ever since," Mattingly said. "Just naval skirmishes here and there."

Chuck Brady returned from the nearby liquor cabinet with a fresh glass of scotch on the rocks and a smile full of Texas charm. "Mike, if you're so convinced both sides are going to negotiate an end to the 'phony war,' how do you explain that rant you got from Cunningham today?"

Mike Mattingly worked in Economic Affairs; he'd taken a phone call at home from his counterpart at the British embassy, who gave him an earful about the joint protest sent to the King of England that morning from twenty-one American republics over the Royal Navy's engagement of the German ship *Wakama* in February, only thirteen miles off the coast of Brazil. Martin heard about the call when Mattingly phoned him afterward to vent, under the excuse that Martin worked in Political Affairs. Cunningham threatened that if the British received another protest over the more recent incident with the German ship *Hannover* off the Dominican coast, they might start buying beef elsewhere than the U.S. and Argentina.

"Well, they're not in that mindset yet," Mattingly said, a touch defensive. "Right now our neutrality irritates them. By the end of the year, it won't matter—and that's why they're so infuriating right now."

"I'm with Martin on this one," Chuck Brady said. He took a sip of scotch and then swirled it, making the ice clink the glass. "Hitler's biding his time, building up his munitions. He knows what his equipment can do—he proved it in Spain, and then Poland—he just wants more of it before he goes on the offensive again. I guarantee you, German factories are churning out tanks and planes as fast as they can put the parts together."

"Until they run out of raw material for those parts," Mattingly said.

Martin again held his tongue. Hitler would find his materiel.

"Empanadas?" asked a short, dark woman of about fifty, holding out a tray of the fried appetizers. As the men took some, she looked at Sloan and said, "Dinner be ready in thirty minutes, Mr. Sloan."

"Thank you, *Señora*," he said.

"*Gracias, Señora*," Martin said as she walked back toward the kitchen.

"Señora DelRio is frying steaks for dinner," Sloan said. "She's our neighbor's cook, on loan to Harriet for the evening. We've used her a few times before."

"She reminds me of our cook in San Marcos when I was a boy," Chuck Brady said. "Chicana gal, and a great cook."

"What do you think of the Yankees' chances this year?" Mike Mattingly asked Sloan.

"Ruth Bryan Owen," Martin said to Ann Corley when they sat down to dinner.

"I beg your pardon?"

"You said earlier there were no women in the Foreign Service. Ruth Bryan Owen was appointed Envoy Extraordinary and Minister Plenipotentiary to Denmark in 1933. She served in Copenhagen for three years, I believe. So not only serving in the Foreign Service, but a head of mission."

Ann regarded him with an arched eyebrow. "Yes, and her father was the venerable William Jennings Bryan, so hardly a representative example. Perhaps I should convince Al Smith to adopt me so I can have the same opportunities. But, that would mean I'd have to become Catholic, so perhaps not."

Martin frowned. He wasn't sure if she was mocking him, or Ruth Owen. Probably both. He looked around the table, but everyone else was engaged in their own conversations, oblivious to the little drama at his corner of the table.

"By all accounts, Mrs. Owen was a remarkable representative of our country," he said, testy. "I believe she was also a congresswoman for four years before President Roosevelt sent her to Denmark. I find your attitude toward her disrespectful."

"Oh, I mean no disrespect to Mrs. Owen," Ann said. "I apologize if what I said conveyed that impression. I meant only to point out the absurdity of holding her up as an example of female equality, when her own rise was aided in no small part by her parentage. The truth is, there is a dearth of women in the Foreign Service, and one or two examples to the contrary does not negate my point."

Martin felt his cheeks flush hot. He had been pleased to think of Ruth Bryan Owen before dinner, and was sorry he hadn't thought of her earlier, when Ann first brought up sexism. Now he felt like he'd made a fool of himself.

He disliked pushy people. And he was already irritated by Mike Mattingly's uninformed assessment. This could be a long dinner.

"For the record, I'm only going to be in Argentina for a few weeks, so you needn't feel obligated to entertain me," Ann Corley said, as if she'd read Martin's mind.

Her bluntness startled him, and he glanced around again. The others were still engaged in conversation, so no one appeared to overhear her declaration.

"Where are you going from here?" he asked, concentrating on being polite. "Uruguay? Brazil?"

"Paraguay, actually. And from there to Bolivia. I've already been to both Brazil and Uruguay."

"Did you enjoy them?" An awkward smile pasted on Martin's mouth.

"Very much," Ann replied, ignoring his discomfort. "I hated to leave both. Brazil is incredible—so vibrant and colorful. The people have such a spirit about them, it's impossible not to get swept up in their enthusiasm for life. The people in Uruguay are quieter, but nice to a fault."

"Have you just arrived in Argentina?"

"A few days ago. I'm staying in Buenos Aires for the week, and then I plan to tour the rest of the country for a week or two." She gave him a curious look. "Where do you recommend a person go to see the 'real Argentina,' Mr. Schuller? I'm open to suggestions."

Martin hated to admit that he had been few places outside of Buenos Aires since he arrived six months ago—and most of those had been within a hundred miles of the capital.

"I suppose it depends upon what you want to see," he said, buying some time.

"I'm open."

That's no help. "There are big cattle ranches all across the Pampas," he said, citing something he hoped wasn't too obvious. "Our steaks probably came from one of those provinces. The Pampas fans out around Buenos Aires, stretching all the way to the Andes. In the west they have some vineyards, around Mendoza and San Juan."

"I could learn that in the travel guide."

He looked down at his soup and ate a few bites in silence.

Harriet Sloan filled the silence a moment later.

"Martin, did Ann tell you about all the colorful people she's met on her trip so far?"

Martin saw Mrs. Sloan's eager expression, and didn't say no. "A little."

"She kept us entertained last night with anecdotes. You should *hear* them! She's encountered some real characters. Ann, tell him some of your stories. On second thought, why don't you tell the whole table, dear. Such amusing anecdotes."

Ann smiled at her hostess and launched into a series of tales that were indeed amusing. Everyone at the table listened attentively, and laughed at the appropriate times.

Martin was just glad the pressure was off him to maintain conversation.

Dinner ended a couple of hours later, but it seemed far later to Martin than eleven. He accepted his hat from Sloan and shook hands all around.

"Martin, would you be good enough to walk Ann back to her hotel?" Harriet Sloan asked him just as he was about to walk out the door.

He wasn't thrilled at the idea, but he nodded and said, "Of course. Where are you staying, Miss Corley?"

"At the *Conventillo Abasto*; it's an immigrant hostel in the *Barrio Almagro.*"

"Harriet, I told her I'd hire her a cab," Sloan said, gruff and scowling.

A frosty look crossed Harriet Sloan's eyes for the barest of seconds, and then she looked back to Ann Corley. "Ann, dear, if you'd rather walk and enjoy the evening air, I'm sure Mr. Schuller wouldn't mind escorting you."

Ann gave her a genuinely warm smile. "Thank you for the kind offer, but it's been a long day, and I'm very tired. I think I'll take the cab ride, if Mr. Sloan is still offering."

"You can share our cab," Roger Dean said. "We're headed your direction. Maryann and I live in Villa Crespo, so we have to go toward the city center. Almagro is just a little farther. Everyone else lives south."

"That's settled, then," Sloan announced. "Good night, everyone."

The look on Harriet's face was less than settled, but she smiled and bid her guests goodnight.

Martin was relieved, for multiple reasons. Beyond the fact that Miss Corley irritated him with her pushiness, he preferred to walk alone anyway.

It was a beautiful evening, and the warm air stirred in the breeze—the famous "fair winds" for which the city was named—and caressed his face like a tender lover. Latin music wafted on the breeze. As he approached the corner of Avenida Federico Lacroze, the live music grew louder, accompanied by the laughter and shouts of hundreds of people.

He stood at the corner for several minutes, leaned against the brick of a darkened building, and watched across the street. People streamed in and out of the *milonga*—tango club—in pairs and small groups, dressed to the nines, and all acting as if they were having the time of their lives.

He was envious, if he were being honest. Part of him desperately wanted to join the fun, but most of him dreaded the thought. He couldn't tango, for one thing. He wasn't a particularly good dancer in any case, though he could do a modest waltz, and a passable fox trot.

That much had been Becky's influence. She loved to dance, and for her sake he had taken classes to learn some steps while they were dating. After they were married, they rarely went dancing.

The exterior of the club was lit in blue and red neon. But, the interior looked warm and inviting, lit softly by candles on the tables and old gas lamps on the walls. It seemed to beckon one in, and Martin almost crossed the street.

A group of young women stumbled out the door, squealing with laughter and chattering in rapid Spanish. He couldn't understand a word.

They crossed the street at an angle, facing away from his corner, but passing near. As they stepped onto the sidewalk a few yards from him, he recognized one of the young women in profile.

"*Buenas noches, Señorita Bianchi*," he heard himself saying, as if it were someone else using his voice.

"*Buenas noches*," she replied as she turned her head. "Oh! Mr. Schuller, I did not recognize you," she exclaimed, switching to English.

"Having a good time?"

"Yes, thank you." She said something in a low voice to her four companions, in Spanish, and then turned back to him with a dazzling smile. "Are you going into the club? We are just leaving, my friends and I, but we could go back inside if you—"

"No, no—thank you," Martin said, holding up his hands. "I can't tango. *No puedo bailar el tango*."

She laughed softly at his halting Spanish, then lowered her eyelids as she slowly turned away. "Then someone should teach you. Good night, Mr. Schuller."

"Good night. *Buenas noches*."

He watched her walk away, and couldn't help that his eyes drifted to the sway of her hips. She turned her head back before the group reached the next block, and caught his eye. He blushed, embarrassed, but her lips curled up in an amused—perhaps satisfied?—smile.

He shook his head as he turned away and resumed walking toward home. *She is far too young for you, Martin. Don't be pathetic.*

Or desperate.

Hutson

3

Sunday, March 17

Church bells woke Martin the next morning. Buenos Aires was a very Catholic city, if not particularly strict or conservative about it. He'd gotten used to church bells ringing from every conceivable direction on Sunday mornings, making it impossible to sleep past eight-thirty.

It was just as well. It gave him the chance to get out in the neighborhood and enjoy the peace and quiet while most of the inhabitants were ensconced in the pews.

He dressed in his blue suit and headed out. His apartment was on the third floor of a five-story building with an elevator, but he took the stairs.

It was just a block to the Avenida Cabildo, where he bought a copy of the Herald, the city's English-language newspaper. His favorite little café stood across the avenue, at the entrance to the *Barrio Belgrano*. Belgrano was a bit more upscale than Colegiales, the middle-class neighborhood where he lived, and the streets there were shaded by big, leafy trees.

There were a few people inside the café that morning—a middle-aged man in tweed with black-framed glasses sipped espresso while poring over three volumes spread out on top of one another on the little table he occupied in the corner; a young couple by the window held hands across the table, smiling and whispering.

Martin took his usual table—he came here three or four times a week—and a young waiter, about twenty, tall and thin with thick wavy brown hair, approached him.

"Good morning, Mr. Schuller. The usual?" he asked in Spanish.

"Good morning, Javier. Yes, thank you," Martin replied, also in Spanish. He'd learned quickly how to order food in his new language.

He perused the paper, and Javier brought him a steaming cup of black coffee. A few moments later, Javier brought a plate with a *media luna manteca*, a popular Argentine breakfast roll similar to a croissant, but a touch sweeter and not as flaky.

"*Guten Tag, Herr Schuller,*" he heard a familiar voice say, and looked up to see Miguel Cohen and his wife Eva.

"*Guten Tag, Herr Rabbi,*" Martin replied. "*Und guten tag, Frau Cohen.*"

Martin had met Miguel Cohen about a week after arriving in Buenos Aires almost six months ago. They frequented the same cafés and bakeries, and soon became friends. Miguel was one of the few people in Buenos Aires with whom Martin was on a first-name basis; though when Eva Cohen was around, as today, they tended to greet each other more formally. With Martin's limited knowledge of Spanish, and the Cohens' complete lack of English, they always conversed in German, which all three spoke fluently.

"Still not a religious man, I see," Miguel teased as he and Eva took the table next to Martin's.

"Not from a lack of your influence, Rabbi."

Javier stopped by, and the Cohens ordered bagels and coffee in Spanish—Miguel's black, Eva's with cream.

"What do you have planned for your day of rest, Martin?" Miguel asked with a mischievous gleam in his dark eyes, switching back to German.

"As little as possible," Martin replied. "And I assume that since your day of rest is over, you plan to work today, Rabbi?"

Miguel chuckled. "A little, perhaps a little."

"Our son starts his first year at university next week," Eva said. "We have shopping to do in the city."

"Jorge is going to the National University in Córdoba," Miguel said, beaming.

"You must be very proud." That was evident from Miguel's face, but Martin said so anyway.

"Oh yes, we're both very proud of our 'Gito," Eva said.

Miguel's smile turned wry. "We're both proud, but Eva's a little sad, too. She cries sometimes when she thinks no one's looking."

"Miguel!" Eva whacked his hand, a momentary shocked expression on her face. Then the shock cracked into a sheepish smile, and they shared a laugh.

Javier brought their bagels and coffee, and they stopped laughing to thank him in Spanish.

"My sister's coming to dinner tonight with her family," Miguel said, turning rueful. "Her four children, plus our four children—you see why Eva and I are here now, *alone*."

Martin chuckled. "You have my sympathy, both of you."

"Thank you," Miguel said. He put the fingers of his left hand together and shook them at the ceiling, glancing up as he did so. "This is likely the only peace and quiet the Almighty is going to give us today."

Martin always got a kick out of the irreverent way Rabbi Miguel Cohen had of scolding God sometimes. No Christian minister he'd known would ever do that.

"Any news from your children?" Eva asked, stirring her coffee.

"As a matter of fact, I received letters from them yesterday. They will be here for two months this winter—that will be summer in the Northern Hemisphere, so they'll be off school."

"That's wonderful news," Miguel said, looking genuinely pleased. "You must be excited to see them."

Martin nodded, surprised at how choked up he felt. "I am," he managed to say without his voice cracking.

"We know you've missed them," Eva said, giving his forearm a sympathetic pat with her gloved hand.

Martin nodded again, but said nothing, certain that his voice would crack this time.

"How old did you say they are?" Miguel asked.

Martin cleared his throat. "Marty's eight years old, but he'll turn nine while they're here. Jackie turned six in the fall—I mean, spring, it was October—and Stevie turned five shortly after that."

Eva beamed. "Ah, those are wonderful ages. They must be excited to see you, and excited for a new adventure, yeah?"

Miguel nodded in agreement. "Those are good ages—old enough to do things for themselves, but not old enough to have a smart mouth yet." He chuckled. "You are in a good place for the next two years, Martin. Maybe three, if you are lucky."

But I'll be here for most of the next two years, and they'll be in Philadelphia, Martin thought with a touch of bitterness. He kept his expression passive and thanked the Cohens for their kind words.

He finished his breakfast a few minutes later, collected his newspaper, bid them good day, and good luck with the family dinner.

"Oy, vey," Miguel muttered.

Monday, March 18

"Good morning, Mr. Schuller," Rosa Linda Bianchi said with a bright smile as Martin walked to his office. She was already tapping the keys on her typewriter, while the other three girls uncovered their machines. They echoed "Good morning, Mr. Schuller," somewhat less enthusiastically.

Martin felt the same way on Monday mornings.

Especially when it was hot and muggy, and the building already felt stuffy. He put his hat on the rack by the door inside his office, and placed his jacket on the back of his chair. He fanned himself with a manila folder and flipped on the switch to the little air conditioning unit in his window. With any luck, his office would be cool in thirty minutes.

He looked over news reports from around the country, and read through the ticker on his desk as it occasionally spit out blurbs from the wire services.

As the embassy's Information Officer, part of his duties included serving as press liaison. He usually spent the first hour of his day going over the previous day's news, and deciding what comment, if any, he should make. Later in the morning, he'd meet with his boss, the embassy's First Secretary, to vet those comments; and then he'd hold an audience with ten or a dozen reporters around noon.

It wasn't his favorite part of the job, standing in front of those reporters and answering their questions as vaguely as possible, but he had become good at it over the summer.

And sometimes they gave him good tips.

He was expected to lunch at least once a week with one of his counterparts at the British or German embassies. The purpose of these lunches was to share information in a mutually beneficial way, that wouldn't compromise the United States—and Martin hated them. He enjoyed the diplomacy, and didn't mind being secretive when he needed to be; but, deep down he hated behaving in a way that felt fake.

His calendar said he had no lunch appointment today, so he breathed a little easier.

His phone buzzed around ten o'clock.

"Mr. Schuller, I have a call for you from Mr. Thomas Mayweather, British Embassy," Rosa Linda's lilting voice said over the intercom.

Martin sighed and pressed the intercom button. "You can put that call through, Miss Bianchi."

The call rang through a few seconds later, and Martin took a deep breath before answering. "Martin Schuller, Third Secretary."

"Good morning, Mr. Schuller. Thomas Mayweather speaking. Is this a good time?"

Is it ever? "Yes, what can I do for you?"

"I heard an interesting bit of news this morning. Something that wasn't in the papers." Mayweather's accent was crisp and polite, and BBC-precise in its Received Pronunciation.

"Oh?" Martin knew where this was going, but waited for Mayweather to say it.

"Yes. A reliable source informed me that a certain Helmut Kortbein, a German national with long-time permanent residency here, was arrested Friday afternoon in Belgrano for possession of an illegal radio transmitter."

Mayweather paused, clearly awaiting some sort of response.

"You don't say?"

"My source tells me the police were notified by an outside informant that Kortbein regularly made illegal broadcasts."

"That's very interesting. Did they happen to find the transmitter?"

"I think you know that they did." Mayweather sounded annoyed.

"What makes you think that?"

"The informant wasn't one of ours, that's what."

It was a remarkably candid statement for the Brits. Mayweather must really be annoyed.

The line was silent for a moment. Martin waited.

"I've said before that I'd appreciate being included in that sort of thing," Mayweather said, now clearly testy. "We're the ones at war with the bloody Nazis, not you Yanks."

Martin resisted the urge to say something along the lines of *"This is our hemisphere;"* citing the Monroe Doctrine right now wouldn't be helpful. Especially since the British had been involved in Argentina since its independence.

"You know I can't comment."

"I thought that likely," Mayweather said. "I'd like to state for the record that we can be very cooperative. I believe our interests align here."

Martin knew better than to agree. "The United States is officially neutral."

"As is Argentina, but that doesn't mean we don't all have shared interests. I'm sure you'd agree with that."

Martin seized the opportunity to deflect. "Our three countries share many economic interests. If you'd like to discuss economic cooperation, I'll refer you to Mr. Michael Mattingly, Third Secretary for economic matters. But I believe he routinely works with a Mr. Cunningham at your embassy."

The line was silent for several seconds, and Martin imagined Thomas Mayweather fuming on the other end.

When Mayweather replied, though, his voice was steady and even. "The United Kingdom and the United States were allies in the last war, Mr. Schuller, if belatedly so. It seems natural that we should be allies again in the current struggle. I assume your President Wilson's words about keeping the world safe for democracy still ring true. And there has been no greater threat to democracy in our lifetimes than Herr Hitler's maniacal regime."

Martin could think of quite a few American politicians who would argue that Stalin's regime was the greater threat to democracy, but mentioning that would only sidetrack the conversation into irrelevant territory, since the Soviet Union was also neutral in the current "Phony War."

And while it was common knowledge that several thousand U.S. troops had been sent to Russia in 1920 and '21 to fight the Bolsheviks alongside the struggling White Russian forces, it was official government policy not to comment on that.

"As I said a moment ago, Mr. Mayweather—the United States is neutral. Thank you for your call, and I've noted your objection to our neutrality. Is there anything else I can help you with?"

"No. Thank you for your time, Mr. Schuller," Mayweather said, his words clipped. "Good day, sir."

The line clicked off.

After his noon press briefing, Martin handed his notes to one of the secretaries, Maria Elena Ferrer, to type up for his file. There had been no significant new information from the reporters, but one never knew when one of the seemingly insignificant tidbits might someday connect with others to form something more meaningful.

He put on his hat and went out for lunch, holding his breath as he passed Sloan's office on the ground floor. He saw from the corner of his eye that the Special Agent was on the phone and didn't have his jacket on, so he breathed easier as he headed for the exit.

It was hot, but a good breeze mitigated the humidity, so he chose an outside table at a nearby restaurant. He ordered a chicken *milanesa*—a breaded filet in the Italian style that also reminded him of a German schnitzel—with fried potatoes and salad, and a half-liter glass of the local pale lager.

"Oh! Hello, Mr. Schuller."

Rosa Linda Bianchi stood next to his table, between him and the restaurant's front door. Her wide-brimmed red hat was tipped upward in the latest style, and matched her dress. Something about her tone didn't sound as surprised as it was meant to.

"*Buenas tardes, Señorita Bianchi*," he said, rising from his chair. He paused for a second, uncertain. "Would you care to join me?" His mouth had gone inexplicably dry.

"Thank you very much," she said, and allowed him to pull out her chair.

"I thought you usually ate lunch with the other girls from the office," Martin said as he retook his seat.

She made a strange face. "Yes, usually—but they can be petty and jealous sometimes. This morning they were all insufferable, so I left by myself."

"I'm sorry to hear that," he heard himself mutter, feeling almost outside of himself, but still aware of the nervous flutter of his stomach. He told himself he was just hungry.

The waiter returned and rescued him from his awkwardness, handing Rosa Linda a menu.

"I was so surprised to see you outside of that *milonga* on Saturday night," she said as she perused the menu, or pretended to. "I didn't see anyone with you. I would expect a man like you to have a woman on his arm to go dancing."

"I wasn't out dancing," Martin said. "I was coming home from a dinner party. Special Agent Sloan and his wife had eight people over for dinner, and I was walking home from his place."

"That sounds very nice," she said, closing the menu. "Do you live in the *Barrio Colegiales*?"

"Yes." Martin felt his mouth going dry again. He took a longer drink of the beer than was necessary.

"That's wonderful. I live with my family in the Colegiales. I am surprised I have not seen you there before."

"I don't go to the *milongas*," he said, feeling surprisingly bashful about that. "I don't dance much."

"Perhaps you haven't found the right dance partner," she said, and then smiled at the waiter when he came to take her order. She ordered the *Choripán* with iced tea.

"Iced tea is very American, isn't it?" she asked when the waiter had departed.

"It's popular in the States," he agreed. "I believe it was invented there."

35

"I'm embarrassed. I must be so careful not to make a mess with my *Choripán*. But it is very good here."

Martin thought her profession of embarrassment seemed a touch affected. And yet he still sympathized. "I'll have the waiter bring you an extra napkin."

They chatted about work until their food arrived.

"Oh, *pollo milanesa!*" she exclaimed, sounding genuinely delighted. "My parents were born in Pavia, in Lombardy—not far from *Milano*. My grandmothers make many varieties of *milanesa*. My favorite is the *Pollo Milanese Picatta*," she said, giving it the Italian rather than Spanish pronunciation that time. "But a plain *milanesa* like yours is good, too."

Martin couldn't help but feel that last was added to make him feel better. "It reminds me a bit of the schnitzel my mother and grandmothers used to make."

"Lombardy was ruled by Austria for a long time, I think, no?" She arched an eyebrow as she looked at him.

Martin suspected she knew perfectly well that Austria had ruled Lombardy for almost two hundred years. But she was allowing him to be the expert. "Yes, that's true. Do you speak Italian, Miss Bianchi?"

"Yes, of course," she said, then leaned far over her plate to carefully take a bite of her *Choripán*; and some of the meat fell onto her plate. "My parents were quite young when their families came to Argentina, but their homes spoke only Italian. They say they learned Spanish in school."

"Did you speak Italian at home when you grew up?" Martin asked, intrigued.

"A little, but mostly Spanish."

"My family spoke German and English at home when I was a child."

"Oh, that is interesting," she said, and carefully navigated another bite. "Did your parents come from Germany? Or Austria?"

He chuckled. "Neither. My parents were born in Pennsylvania. That's a state in the northeastern part of my country. So were my grandparents, and my great-grandparents, too." Seeing her questioning look, he explained, "There are parts of Pennsylvania where families have spoken German for two hundred years."

"That is amazing!" She looked genuinely amazed, and not just for show.

"It's starting to go away, though. My children only speak English."

"You have children, Mr. Schuller?" A guarded look came to her golden brown eyes.

"Yes, my ex-wife and I have three children. We've been divorced for six months."

The guarded look faded, mostly, but there was still a hint of a veil over her eyes. "I have heard of people getting divorced, but I don't think I know anyone."

And that's that. "I suppose you do, now."

Her expression brightened. "Yes! I suppose I do, now." A pleased sort of half-smile crept across her mouth, and she took another bite of her sandwich.

He wondered if she felt more modern or sophisticated now that she knew a divorced man.

They got back to the embassy at two o'clock. A few feet behind the security guard stood a slightly-built man in his late thirties, with his arms crossed and the toe of one of his shiny black shoes tapping on the floor. His wavy brown hair was styled perfectly, nothing out of place, and he wore an expensive pin-striped double-breasted suit with a silk handkerchief folded neatly in the pocket.

He frowned at them. *"Usted es treinta minutos tarde, Señorita Bianchi. Cuál es la razón?"*

"Lo siento mucho, Señor De la Tour," she said, lowering her eyes and hurrying toward the stairs.

Martin understood most of what Rosa Linda and her supervisor said. "It was my fault, Señor De la Tour," he said in English. "Señorita

Bianchi and I were having lunch, and I wasn't paying attention to the time. I didn't realize I had made her late. Please accept my apologies on her behalf."

De la Tour appeared caught off guard by this. "Yes, of course, Mr. Schuller. My apologies."

Martin nodded his thanks and continued upstairs to his office.

There was a knock at his door ten minutes later.

"It's open."

"Mr. Schuller, if I may have a *word* with you, please?" the diminutive man said in English. Juan-Carlos Alberto Maria De la Tour-Calvo was the supervisor over many of the local staff at the American embassy, including Rosa Linda and the three other girls sitting outside of Martin's office.

"Yes, of course. Have a seat."

"Thank you, but I think I shall stand," De la Tour replied, and closed the door. He was short—only five-foot-seven—so Martin supposed he often remained standing to maintain a sense of authority.

"What's on your mind?"

De la Tour clasped his hands in front of his chest, and gave Martin an indulgent smile. "My *dear* Mr. Schuller, it seems I need to broach a rather *delicate* subject. I hate to make you *uncomfortable*, but I'm afraid I *must* speak."

Martin suppressed a laugh at De la Tour's overly-elaborate English diction. "This is about me bringing Miss Bianchi back late, I presume?"

De la Tour gave him a look of exaggerated concern. "Yes, that is *part* of it—but I'm *afraid* I have more to discuss."

"Go ahead." Martin leaned back in his seat and folded his hands across his belly. As a Third Secretary, he technically out-ranked De la Tour, but he found that taking on a posture of faint indifference tipped the balance in his favor regardless.

De la Tour cleared his throat, and dabbed nervously at the thin little mustache that he waxed as if it were thicker. Recovering his composure a second later, he smiled at Martin in an indulgent way.

"Yes, of course. You see, Mr. Schuller, as *supervisor* of the local girls at this embassy, it is my *obligation* to maintain *propriety* at all *costs*. I don't know what were the rules at your *last* embassy, but at *this* one I must *insist* upon no—shall we say—*fraternization* outside of work between the members of *my* staff, and American *Foreign Service* officers. I'm *sure* you agree, we *must* not give off the appearance of impropriety, no *matter* how innocent an encounter may be."

Martin was always amused at the effusive way that De la Tour talked with his hands, which served to draw additional attention to the overly expressive way in which he spoke.

"I understand, señor," Martin said, sitting up and leaning forward on his desk. "It will not happen again."

De la Tour bowed his head and swept his hand with a flourish in front of him. "*Thank* you, Mr. Schuller. I will leave you to your work. Good afternoon."

The short little man hurried out the door with tiny, almost mincing steps, which seemed comical in their rapidity.

Martin laughed, and got back to work.

Hutson

4

Wednesday, March 20 - Bahía Blanca, Buenos Aires Province,
Argentina

Six-hundred-fifty kilometers south of the capital city, a white-
haired man named Juan José Sauermann stood on the sandy beach and
cast his line far out into the gentle rolling waves of the estuary, the
"white bay" for which his city was named. Sea breezes blew his hair
back from his face as he slowly turned his reel. A short distance away, a
young boy in short pants and striped tee-shirt crouched in the sand,
examining shells. A forgotten fishing pole lay between them.

The summer tourists were gone, and the man and his grandson had
this stretch of beach largely to themselves. A trio of old men, about his
age, fished about fifty meters away, but otherwise things were quiet.

The evening sun behind him, sixty-five-year-old Sauermann stared
directly at a two-mast steamship moored to a wharf less than three
hundred meters to the east, glowing golden in the sunlight. It was a
Cameron-class steamship. The miniature Union Jack in the upper left
corner of the otherwise solid red flag on its rear mast showed it to be
operating in the British Merchant Navy—what in other countries might
be called the Merchant Marine.

Sauermann had been watching the loading of the ship for two
hours, while fishing on the nearest beach. He had noted the name—the
SS Clan Ross—and now counted the crates being transferred on-board
by crane.

When he'd walked by the port that afternoon on his way to the beach with his grandson and their fishing poles, he noted the crates stacked on pallets, marked with the name of the slaughterhouse on the other side of the city. Sides of beef, he could tell by the faint scent of fresh meat that wafted on the breeze.

After forty-six years working at that slaughterhouse, Sauermann knew exactly how many sides of beef fit into a three-cubic-meter crate, and how many crates fit on a pallet, so it was easy to do the math now while he fished and counted what the cranes moved.

"Are we going home soon, abuelito?" the boy asked, shuffling over to Sauermann.

"Just a little longer, my boy," the old man answered, his Spanish still carrying a German accent after all these years here.

Juan José Sauermann—born Jan Josef Sauermann in Bavaria in 1874—had come to Argentina at the age of nineteen in January 1894. He'd heard there were jobs to be found there, and though he knew no one in the country, plenty of his fellow emigrants aboard the ship to Buenos Aires told him they were heading south to Bahía Blanca, where they had relations. He arrived by train to find the small city on the southern edge of the Pampas did indeed have a large and thriving German community.

Shortly after he retired a few months ago, a man approached him while he fished alone on a beach a few kilometers west of here, closer to his home. The man greeted him by name in German, and asked if he were willing to help the Fatherland in its struggle against England.

After a lifetime here, Sauermann was Argentine through and through—but he had never lost his love of Germany and its people, and he still wrote to his brothers and sisters there. After forty-six years he'd absorbed the innate Argentine resentment toward the British, which arose in spite of the fact that Britain was Argentina's most important foreign trade partner. British rule over the *Islas Malvinas*, which they called the Falkland Islands, was considered an insult.

He agreed to the proposition without reservation.

So now, whenever he heard that a British merchant ship had docked at Bahía, he made a point of fishing at the sandy point beside the port. It was not far from his daughter's house, so it was easy to bring his grandson, Oscar Sauermann-López. That eliminated any suspicion.

The loading finished, he watched the crew of the SS Clan Ross begin securing the hold. He reeled in his line, and told Oscar to collect his pole. "It is time to go home."

After dropping his grandson at his daughter's house near Plaza Adrián Morado Verez, Sauermann walked a mile to the quiet neighborhood where his little cottage stood. When he reached the gate to his front yard, he heard the deep blasts of the horn on the SS Clan Ross, signaling departure. He smiled to himself.

He kissed his wife, Maria, on the cheek while she cooked, and they greeted one another in Spanish. She had also been born in Bavaria, but was only three years of age when her family came to Bahía Blanca in 1879, so she did not have his German accent. He told her he had work to do in his shed, and walked through the back door.

He sat at the work bench. On a slip of paper, he wrote out a short message in pencil. Today was the fourth day of the week, so he rewrote it, adjusting every letter in the original message to the fourth letter after it.

Then he opened a cabinet and removed the battered old valise. He opened it, put on the headphones that were connected to the shortwave radio inside, and began adjusting the dial until he found the signal he wanted.

He opened the book he kept in the cabinet—Goethe's *Faust*, in German. Today was the 20th, so he turned to page twenty. This told him the greeting to use, and he carefully adjusted the letters of the first line by four.

He tapped out a quick test message, and waited a few seconds until the expected reply came. Then he transmitted his encoded message:

For Firefox.
SS Clan Ross departing Bahia Blanca 16:24.
Loaded with 90000 sides of beef.
The Piper.

There was silence for almost thirty seconds, before the acknowledgment message came over the air. He switched off the radio. He struck a match and burned the paper with the message, letting it fall to the dirt floor as ash that he stomped into oblivion.

German Embassy, Buenos Aires

A young army lieutenant manning the radio room that evening took the message transmitted by the agent known as The Piper. He hurried down the corridor to Commander Fiedler's office.

"Message for you, from The Piper," the lieutenant said.

"A British shipment?"

"Beef," the lieutenant replied. "Left port this afternoon."

"Put it on my desk. I will take care of it."

Shortly before eleven o'clock that night, Commander Gustav Fiedler of the Kriegsmarine—the German navy—entered the darkened German embassy by a back door, and went upstairs to his office using only a tiny flashlight for illumination. He unlocked his office, and found the decoded message on his desk.

He switched on the shortwave radio in the corner, allowing it to warm up for a couple of minutes. Meanwhile, he re-checked the log to verify the call signal for the U-boat that was scheduled to be surfacing about twenty nautical miles off the coast of Uruguay.

At precisely eleven o'clock, he tapped out the U-boat's call signal, paused, and then tapped out his own code name—Firefox. He paused again, and then tapped out the first line of page twenty in Goethe's *Faust*, adjusted by four letters.

It took about thirty seconds before the U-boat's signaler replied, in code: *Verified, go ahead.*

Fiedler transmitted the name and cargo of the target ship, its departure time of 16:24 from Bahía Blanca, expected speed and direction. It would still be off the coast of Argentina, Fiedler knew, but would soon be in international waters. The U-boat could trail it until it left the 300-mile security zone of the Americas.

A moment later, the U-boat replied: *Acknowledged, target received.*

It would be a shame for all of that beef to end up at the bottom of the Atlantic. Beef was becoming scarce in Germany these days, thanks to the British blockade.

But it was far preferable that those 90,000 sides of beef feed the fish in the ocean, than feed the people of Great Britain.

Thursday, March 21

Fiedler's phone rang shortly after eleven o'clock that night. "Yes?"

"Message received for you, Commander," the army signaler reported.

"Affirmative, or negative?"

"Affirmative, sir."

"Thank you, Lieutenant."

Fiedler smiled as he set the phone receiver back on its cradle. The SS Clan Ross, along with its crew and cargo, now slept forever at the bottom of the Atlantic.

Hutson

5

Friday, March 22

Sloan caught Martin as he was heading out for lunch.

"Hold up, there, Schuller," he said, hurrying out of his office to catch up to Martin at the front door. "I was hoping to get a chance to chat with you this morning, but my workload kept me tied to my desk."

"You have intelligence to share?" Martin asked. "We can go back to your office to talk in private."

"Yes, I do, but it's brief, and we can talk here."

Martin understood. The hall, usually busy, was empty right now. The Argentine staff all had the day off for Good Friday, so the only people around were American Foreign Service staff, and half of them were out to lunch.

"I got a notification this morning in the pouch from Washington that might interest you," Sloan said. "The Bureau is going to send additional agents to Argentina in the next two or three months. I've been instructed to facilitate the establishment of a larger operation here. The Ambassador was notified as well, so I'm sure you'll hear about it through your own channels, but I wanted you to hear from me first."

"I appreciate that."

"I don't know many specifics—how many agents, for what duration—but I got the impression this isn't short-term." Sloan lowered his voice and leaned closer. "And it isn't just Argentina. The Bureau plans to send agents to several Latin American countries. That part wasn't in the communiqué to the Ambassador, so keep that to yourself, understand?"

Martin nodded. "Understood. And thanks." He started to turn toward the door. "Was there anything else?"

"Nothing that can't wait until later this afternoon," Sloan said. "I'll walk you out."

Martin cringed, hoping Sloan wouldn't ask him to lunch.

"Harriet asked me to invite you to Easter dinner on Sunday," Sloan said, putting on his hat as they stepped into the bright sunshine. "Just a small gathering, nothing too formal. Better than being by yourself on the holiday, right?"

"That's very kind of her. Tell her thank you," Martin said, noncommittal.

"She said to come over around one o'clock. We'll eat at one-thirty."

Martin considered for a second, and decided Sloan was right—it was better than being alone on the holiday, thinking about his kids hunting Easter eggs far away in Philadelphia.

"I'll be there."

The bells of the church across the Plaza began to chime, a low, slow, forlorn sound. Soon bells from other churches across the city answered.

"Sounds like mass is over," Sloan said, sounding cynical, almost a mutter. "I'll never understand why they want to celebrate the gruesome death of the man they follow. Makes no sense at all." He glanced at Martin. "You're not a religious man, are you, Schuller?"

"Not particularly." Martin didn't elaborate. He never discussed the reasons why he wasn't. "I take it you aren't, either?"

"No, I'm a third-generation atheist."

This caught Martin off-guard, and he raised his eyebrows. "Really?" He wasn't sure he'd ever met an atheist before. He'd heard of them, of course, but he was positive he'd never met anyone who claimed to be one.

"Don't act so shocked. I'm a rational man, Schuller, and I don't buy into superstition of any kind." Sloan shook his head.

"You said 'third-generation?'"

"That's right. My grandfather was shunned by his family when he became an atheist. Of course, that was seventy years ago, and it went against Victorian sensibilities. He was an early proponent of Darwin's theories, and that didn't win him many friends. He joined the Free Thinkers Society, and he met my grandmother there; she and her whole family were members, and they were more or less agnostic. They raised my father to be rational, and when he was old enough he decided to be atheist. Same with me."

Martin found that fascinating, but wasn't exactly sure why.

"But you'll still celebrate Easter?"

Sloan shrugged. "Sure, why not? We hid Easter eggs for the girls when they were young. As they grew up we taught them it was a festival to welcome spring fertility. Seems strange to be in the fall here, don't it?" He chuckled and turned away. "I've got an appointment to get to. I'll come to your office later to fill you in on some shortwave radio broadcasts out of Bahía."

Saturday, March 23

The pull of the Latin music was almost hypnotic.

Martin had been reading in his arm chair, as he often did in the evenings. The breeze blowing through his open window carried the faint sounds of music and laughter from distant *milongas*—tango clubs—and he found it hard to concentrate on the book in his hands. Finally, he set it aside and put on his jacket and hat to take a stroll.

It was a pleasant evening—warm, but mild with a steady breeze. The full moon cast a bright glow over the neighborhood, and the few scattered clouds in the sky seemed to shine like molten silver.

His feet carried him to the Avenida Federico Lacroze, a few blocks from his building. A streetcar went by as he strolled up the sidewalk, and the driver rang his bell. The music was louder here, and the smell of beef grilling over charcoal filled the air.

There were two *milongas* on the avenue as it passed down the middle of the *Barrio Colegiales*. Martin paused when he approached the one he had passed last weekend, where he'd seen Rosa Linda Bianchi with her girlfriends.

He wondered if she were inside the club at that moment, laughing and drinking with her friends. Dancing the tango with young men.

He could picture her in an evening gown, with a low back and a slit high up one leg. A handsome and rakish young man in a stylish black suit, with dark hair slicked with brilliantine, held her tight against him with one arm on her back. His thumb caressed the valley of her spine above the seam of her dress, and the other hand held hers at a right angle. Their legs encircled one another as their feet moved in time to the music.

With every step of the dance, her bare leg appeared and disappeared through the slit of her dress—

"Are you ill, sir?" a man asked him in Spanish, jolting him back to reality. He realized with a start that he was sweating.

"No, I am well, thank you," he replied in Spanish, tipping his hat to the gentleman and the lady on his arm.

"Very well," the man said, touching the rim of his hat. "Good evening."

The lady gave Martin a brief look of concern as she passed, but then turned toward the club as they hurried across the street, her high heels clicking on the pavement.

Martin removed his hat and wiped his brow with his handkerchief. He fanned himself with his hat a few times before returning it to his head.

He turned to walk back home, and his cheeks felt hot in spite of the cool breeze. It had been far too long since he'd been with a woman.

6

Sunday, April 7 - Salta Province, Argentina

The boat's engine was a low rumble as it made its way slowly up the dark river. It was a moonless night, but Gustav Fiedler was wary of watching eyes. The occasional cries of a troop of monkeys in the trees made him jumpy.

The total darkness here in the *Yungas*—the subtropical broadleaf jungle in the far north of Argentina, near the headwaters of the Bermejo River—allowed for a dazzling array of stars overhead as they glided up the cut through the canopy formed by the river. These provided just enough light to see the shimmer of ripples contrasted against the blackness of the water, and the shadow of the trees overhead on either side of them, so Fiedler had ordered all unnecessary electrical lights shut off.

The air was heavy and still, warm even in the dead of night, in contrast to the cooler fall temperatures that had recently graced the nighttime at Buenos Aires, some six hundred miles to the south-southeast as the crow flies.

It had been much farther than that by water, traveling up the Paraná River into the *Gran Chaco*, and then up the smaller Bermejo into the *Yungas*. Fiedler had been forced to spend the days below deck and out of sight, only emerging at night to breathe fresh air, free from the stench of coal fire, sweat, and pungent cigars.

The captain approached Fiedler at the bow. He was a swarthy man with sharp, angular features—probably of Andalusian descent, Fiedler assumed, which meant traces of Arab and Moorish blood deep in his roots. But he had come highly recommended.

"Commander, the landing is just ahead, over there on the left." The captain spoke slowly, so Fiedler could understand his Spanish.

Commander Fiedler looked in the direction the captain pointed, and he could see the shadow of the tree line fall away from the water. "Signal them."

The captain made a "Whist! Whist!" sound to one of the crew, who flashed a blue light three times.

A few seconds later, a triple flash of blue light answered from the shore.

The boat's engine slowed further, and they glided up to a dock that was only visible because men with flashlights waited there. They caught ropes cast from the boat's crew as the engine died, and quickly tied her up.

"After you, Commander," the captain said, motioning toward the gang plank one of his men lowered to the dock.

"Where is the man who speaks German?" Fiedler asked the men on the dock, in Spanish.

"I speak German, sir," a deep voice replied in that language, and a burly man in a dirty white tank top and tattered khaki pants stepped forward. "I am Peña, the one you spoke with on the telephone."

Fiedler regarded the big man in front of him. He didn't look like the educated man Fiedler had pictured from their brief conversations in German over the last several weeks. Peña was dark, like the captain, but also like the captain he at least appeared to be white, of more or less pure Spanish extraction—unlike the majority of the men surrounding them, who were clearly of the hybrid variety known as *mestizos*, people of mixed Spanish and indigenous ancestry.

That was one of the unfortunate downsides of conducting an operation in the far north of Argentina, which was much less European than the rest of the country.

"You are in charge here, Mr. Peña?" Fiedler asked in German, the haughty tone and posture coming naturally.

"I am, sir," Peña said. "Let me show you what we have delivered for you. Follow me."

Peña motioned with his flashlight, and Fiedler hurried to fall into step beside him, rather than trail behind. They strode to a collection of several trucks, the backs covered in canvas awning to hide the contents. Peña opened the tailgate of one, and ordered one of the men standing there to help him haul a heavy wooden crate onto the ground.

It landed with a hard thud, inches from Fiedler's polished boots.

Fiedler sniffed in distaste, but kept his complaint to himself. He watched Peña take a crowbar to the lid, prying the nails away until the crate opened. He pulled away handfuls of straw, and then the contents of the crate reflected the glow of the flashlights back to Fiedler's eyes.

A pile of black diamonds sat before him, of irregular shapes and sizes.

"As you can see, sir, all of these have deep flaws," Peña said, picking up several diamonds in rapid succession, and turning them in the light to show the internal flaws. "Industrial grade diamonds—no good for the jewelers, but perfect for your machines."

Fiedler crouched down and ran his fingers through the pile inside the crate. If these had only borne smaller flaws, this collection would be worth more than the economies of some small countries.

"Very good, Peña. How many?"

"Seventy kilos of industrial diamonds," Peña replied. "Three weeks' of full production. The rest of the shipment is mica—all of these trucks."

"We shall inspect those next," Fiedler said, rising. He strode to the next truck. "That box, back there. Bring that one and open it for me."

They repeated the process at each of the trucks, with Fiedler picking a random box instead of allowing Peña to choose one. Fiedler didn't trust these men not to have a predetermined crate of the promised goods, while the others were stuffed with something worthless.

Once he'd satisfied himself that the shipments were genuine, he turned back to Peña. "Have them loaded onboard at once."

Peña gave the order, and two dozen men sprang to action, hauling crates from the backs of the trucks, lugging them onto the boat, and then below deck to the freight room.

The job was finished in less than half an hour. Fiedler descended to his tiny room, opened the safe he'd brought with him, and counted out two million pesos.

He marched to Peña with intense pride, trying not to allow a smug smile to ruin the severe look. He handed over the stack of bills, to mutters of amazement from the workers around him.

Peña counted the stacks, and then frowned. "This is a half-million short."

"I will pay you another half-million pesos after the shipment has been weighed and verified, and loaded onto the barge at Buenos Aires, undetected."

Peña's face contorted. His hands fisted at his sides. "That was not the arrangement."

"I have altered the arrangement. If that is not agreeable to you, the Reich can find another willing supplier."

Peña glanced to his right, made a tiny nod, and Fiedler heard the click of a gun cocking on either side of his head.

After a brief second of panic, Fiedler's haughtiness returned. He was from a proud Prussian military family; he would not be intimidated by these jungle outlaws.

"I have done my research on you, Mr. Peña," he said, raising his chin in defiance. "Raúl Ernesto Peña-Camacho, residing at number two thirty-five on Calle de San Martín in the city of Salta. We have agents who will pay a visit to your family, should anything happen to me."

Peña stared at him for several seconds, dark eyes narrowed.

"It would be a shame if something *unfortunate* were to happen to your little daughter, Anna-Maria, on her way home from the San Felipe Neri school," Fiedler added.

Peña blanched. Then he waved his hand, and his men lowered their guns.

"That is much better. As long as you have not cheated us, and as long as your men in Buenos Aires get these crates loaded onto the freighter under the noses of the customs inspectors, then this is the first transaction in what will be a very lucrative deal for you, Mr. Peña. Good evening."

Fiedler clicked his heels and gave Peña a crisp nod, then spun around and marched back to the boat without looking back. Once on board, he motioned for the captain to cast off, and went below deck without a word.

7

Tuesday, April 9

Martin's telephone rang at one-thirty in the morning, rousing him from a deep sleep. It took his brain several seconds to grasp what was happening, and by the time he got up from bed and walked into his living room to answer the line, it had rung at least fifteen times.

"Hello?" he asked, too sleepy to remember to say it in Spanish.

"Is this Mr. Schuller?"

"Yes, who is this?"

"Jack Townsend, Associated Press. I'm sorry to wake you, but I thought you'd like to know what's going on."

Martin knew Jack Townsend from his press briefings. His brain was starting to catch up, enough to hear the excitement in Townsend's voice. "What is it, Mr. Townsend?"

"The Germans invaded Denmark this morning," Townsend said. "They crossed the border at four-fifteen local time—so quarter past midnight here. The night crew called me when they saw the report come across the wire, and I rushed to the office. More reports started coming over the wire. This is really happening."

Martin rubbed his face. *Damn it!* His mind was racing now. "Any chance this is just a ruse, something to distract the British blockade ships?"

"Not likely," Townsend said. "The invasion is being supported by naval and air bombardments. There are also reports of German landings on the coast of Norway, and heavy fighting there. Details are scant, though. Wanted to let you know I filed a story, so it will be in the morning papers."

"Thanks," Martin said. He wondered if this escalation would mean more violations of the Americas Security Zone by the belligerents. "Who else have you called?"

"I called Thomas Mayweather from the British embassy first, asked him for a statement. He declined to comment." Townsend's tone said he wasn't surprised. "I don't speak French, so I didn't bother calling any of their men. I was coming up on deadline, so I had to get the story written PDQ, or I would have called you sooner."

Martin wasn't exactly pleased that Mayweather got the news before he did, but he couldn't fault Townsend for first seeking a statement from one of the warring parties.

And Mayweather might have already heard the news from other sources anyway—in fact, Martin realized it was likely the intelligence agencies in London had sent out secret high alerts to their embassy contacts the moment they had the news.

"I appreciate the call, Mr. Townsend. Get some rest."

"Any time, Mr. Schuller. Maybe remember this the next time you've got something, and let me have it first?"

"We'll see."

Martin got to the embassy a half-hour early that morning, and found it buzzing with activity. Several American reporters from the various wire services crowded the foyer and shouted questions to him as he entered.

"I have no comment at this time, but I'll have a statement for you as soon as possible," Martin said

He'd called his boss, First Secretary Davis, as soon as he hung up the call from Townsend. As expected, Davis was none too pleased to be roused at that hour, but quickly came around to the importance of the news. He promised to relay it to the ambassador right away.

So at least Martin didn't have to worry about either of them being blindsided by reporters' questions. *Thank God for small blessings.*

And thanks to Jack Townsend for the heads-up; he would have to throw him a bone sometime soon.

He checked the news ticker the moment he sat at his desk. Denmark had surrendered after just six hours of fighting; casualties were reported, but no definite numbers.

By contrast, heavy fighting was being reported at several Norwegian ports. Casualties were said to be high, but specifics were fleeting.

Mike Mattingly stopped by his office a few minutes later. Like everyone else this morning, he seemed hurried.

"Morning, Martin," he said, almost breathless. He nodded toward the news ticker. "What's the latest?"

"The King of Denmark announced their surrender about an hour ago," Martin said, grim. "In Norway, the government and the royal family have fled Oslo, destination not revealed."

Mattingly blew a low whistle. "That was fast. What do you think the German objective is? Breaking the British blockade?"

"That's probably part of it. If they take the coast, they'll use the Norwegian fjords to launch naval attacks on the British. And Danish airfields get the Luftwaffe several hundred miles closer to manufacturing targets in northern England. But the biggest gain Hitler would get from Norway is iron ore for his war machine."

Martin couldn't help thinking that he'd pointed out at Sloan's dinner party a couple weeks before that Hitler would find a way to get the raw materials he needed.

"Any response from the British? Or the French?" Mattingly looked about as excited as concerned.

"Nothing official, at least that I've heard," Martin said. "But there are unconfirmed reports that British forces are crossing the North Sea, headed for Norway."

"Sounds like the 'Phony War' won't be so phony anymore."

"No. You still think the Brits and Germans are going to negotiate a settlement?" Martin couldn't help the dig.

Mattingly scowled briefly, but then nodded in resignation. "I suppose I deserve that."

"Don't worry about it," Martin said, and glanced again at the ticker as it kept scrolling. It was going to be a busy day.

The typing pool arrived at eight o'clock. As soon as they were seated, Martin asked them to open a line for him to the German embassy.

"Right away, Mr. Schuller," Rosa Linda hastened to say, drawing side glances from the other three.

"I need to be connected to Georg Umbach."

"Yes, sir."

She buzzed his intercom a few minutes later. "I have the German embassy on the line for you, Mr. Schuller. It is the secretary for Mr. Umbach."

Martin picked up the line. "This is Martin Schuller, Third Secretary at the United States Embassy," he said in German. "I am holding for Propaganda Officer Georg Umbach."

"I am sorry, sir. Mr. Umbach is not available right now," the secretary replied.

Ha! I bet he's not. Martin noted with some surprise that her accent wasn't Spanish, though he couldn't place it. Not a local hire, then? That would be unusual—but leave it to the Germans to bring over clerical labor from the Fatherland because they didn't trust local secretaries.

"Could you please tell me when Mr. Umbach will be available to speak with me?" Martin asked.

"I couldn't say, sir. He is in a meeting with the ambassador and other top staff."

I just bet he is. Martin was only a little surprised by the candid response—the German Foreign Ministry had always been more forthcoming with the American Foreign Service than they had ever been with the British or French, even before the declaration of war.

"Will you please leave a message for him to call me as soon as he is able?"

"Yes, I will, Mr. Schuller. Good day."

Martin gathered with the rest of the American staff in the ballroom after lunch for the commemoration Ambassador Armour had scheduled to mark today's 75th anniversary of Lee's surrender at Appomattox.

"I know there's been some excitement today, with the events in Europe," the ambassador began. "Our government has made no official statement yet. Secretary Hull was called in the middle of the night, and he came back from vacation early. I'm sure we'll hear more from Washington soon. In the meantime, I'm meeting with the Argentine Foreign Minister on Friday, and I expect his government will have a proposal for a united statement from the American republics."

The ambassador cleared his throat and looked at the notes in his hand. "Seventy-five years ago today…"

The ambassador's speech touched on "freedom from bondage," and ended with "One nation, indivisible." Martin couldn't help thinking of the millions of people in Czechoslovakia, Poland, and now Denmark, living in bondage to Nazi oppression.

Martin still sat at his desk at five o'clock, working on reports and continuing to monitor the scrolling news ticker. He was barely aware that the rest of the embassy was closing down. He was exhausted from the barrage of bad news coming from Norway, where one port after another fell to the Germans. The capital Oslo had been the one bright spot for most of the day, holding out and even sinking German ships—until news arrived of its fall.

He looked up at the sound of a tentative knock on the door frame. Rosa Linda stood in the door, watching him.

"Yes, Miss Bianchi?"

"Will you still work much longer, Mr. Schuller? I can stay late if you need me to type something, or to fetch something for you."

"Thank you, but there's no need. You can go home."

"Would you like for me to make you some coffee before I leave?"

That would actually be nice, since Martin wasn't sure how long he was going to stay. "Yes, thank you."

She returned a few minutes later with a steaming cup on a saucer, plus a glass of water. He thanked her and blew across the top of the cup. As she walked away, she paused in the doorway and turned her head back toward him.

"If there is nothing else you need from me, Mr. Schuller, I will go home now."

"No, have a nice evening. *Buenas tardes.*"

He meant only to glance up at her as he said it, but his eyes were caught by the provocative way she stood with her back to him and her hip cocked.

Her faint smile told him she'd noticed where his eyes landed. "*Buenas tardes,*" she echoed, sultry.

He watched her glide out, and his cheeks flushed.

Thursday, April 11

For three days Martin's working hours had been filled with war news from Norway, as British naval and air forces targeted German ships in the fjords. The Luftwaffe retaliated, and both navies had now lost ships, costing thousands of lives.

The war news from Norway, and the constant requests from reporters concerning those events, had completely distracted Martin from his usual tasks.

In a conversation that afternoon with his Foreign Ministry contact, Raúl José Andrews-Barrington, Martin learned that the Foreign Minister planned to discuss a formal protest from the American republics in his meeting with Ambassador Armour tomorrow. Martin drafted a quick memo to the ambassador and First Secretary Davis, so they would be prepared for Dr. Cantillo's proposal.

By the time he left the embassy late for the third night in a row, he was utterly exhausted. Still, he knew his mind wouldn't let the day's events go after he went home.

A thought had been playing inside his mind for several days. Now, as he walked to the subway stop to catch a train back to the *Barrio Colegiales*, he paused and gave the idea some consideration.

It was silly, really, he told himself; still, it would be a distraction, and it might be enjoyable.

He changed direction, and caught a streetcar going toward the *Barrio Recoleta*.

An affluent and up-scale neighborhood of large mid-nineteenth century Beaux-Arts mansions and townhouses just to the northwest of the city center, Recoleta was the main reason Buenos Aires was often called the "Paris of South America." Martin felt a tad out of place walking the sidewalks in his respectable but common navy blue work suit, amongst the elegantly-dressed residents of the barrio.

He stood and stared at the door for several seconds, unsure. *Last chance to back out...*

He stared at the gold letters etched on the frosted glass door— Señora Duarte School of Tango—then screwed up his courage and walked inside.

Hutson

8

Monday, April 15

Martin was on his way upstairs to his office when one of the Argentine young men working on the clerical staff hurried after him and called his name.

"Mr. Schuller, could I speak with you privately, please, sir?" the young man in glasses asked, in accented English. He was about twenty years old, and well put together. He wore a gray sweater vest over a white shirt and black necktie. His dark brown hair was thick, but cut short and neatly combed, and his eyebrows were thick and dark, but—unusually—trimmed short.

"Of course," Martin said, a little surprised. He wasn't sure anyone on the clerical staff had ever asked to meet with him before. "Mr.?"

"Antonio Rivera," the young man replied.

"How do you do?" Martin extended his hand, which the young man regarded with shock, and then smiled as he shook it. "Let's talk in my office."

The four secretarial girls were already busy pounding away at their typewriters when Martin and Antonio walked past them, and they all watched surreptitiously through lowered eyelashes. Martin wondered what the speculation would be after he closed his door.

"What brings you up here, Mr. Rivera?" Martin asked, motioning for Antonio to take a seat in front of his desk.

Antonio looked hesitant, which Martin found odd, since the young man had requested the meeting.

"It is safe in here? No one listening?"

Martin wondered how sensitive Antonio's news might be. Often, amateur sleuths made mountains out of mole hills. He decided to indulge the young man and played along. "Yes, we check these offices for bugs periodically. We're unmonitored." That wasn't untrue, though the likelihood of anyone wanting to bug the American embassy was small.

A nervous smile passed across Antonio's face, but he seemed to relax into his seat. "I know someone to whom you should talk, who saw something this weekend you might want to know about."

That piqued Martin's interest. "A friend of yours?"

Antonio made an uncertain sort of half-shrug. "Someone I know. We share friends."

"OK, tell me about him, and why I want to talk to him."

"His name is Roberto, and he works the nights at the freight docks in the *Ante Puerto*. He saw crates loaded onto a ship, that weren't on the log book, lots of crates. He said it wasn't a forget."

"Wasn't an *oversight*," Martin gently corrected. "Something that is just forgotten is called an 'oversight.'"

"O-ver-sight," Antonio repeated, slowly, weighing the syllables. "It was not an oversight."

Martin thought of the intelligence Joe Hansen provided a few weeks ago, about smuggling war materiel to Germany on neutral ships. "What ship was it?"

Antonio shook his head. "I do not know, but Roberto can say."

"Was it an Argentine ship?"

"I do not know. Roberto can tell you that thing."

Martin nodded. "He knows you work at the American embassy?"

"Yes, I told him." Antonio looked sheepish all of a sudden. "He thinks my job is more important than a clerk."

Martin chuckled. No harm in that, he supposed. "What does he think you do?"

Antonio shrugged. "I never say definite things. I just—how do you say?" he waved his hand in a circle, searching for the word.

"You *implied* it was something bigger."

"Yes, that is it—I imply. I let him make assumptions, that is all."

"And so he told you about this thing he saw, because he assumed you would be interested in news like that." *Or impressed by it.*

"Yes, sir."

"That's good for us," Martin said, giving Antonio a reassuring smile. "What did you tell him about me?"

Antonio looked sheepish again. "I...implied...that I work with you. I said 'A man I work with, an American, will want to know that.' I said I could arrange for him to speak to you."

Martin couldn't help an amused smile. "Did you say my name?"

"No, sir," Antonio replied, raising his chin in obvious pride.

The kid's enjoying playing at being a spy. Martin decided to let him. "When can I meet with him?"

Antonio thought for a moment. "I think he works tonight. I can take you to see him."

"Let him know I'm coming," Martin said. "I don't want to surprise him. But don't tell him my name. Find out what time we should meet, and let me know before we leave work this evening. Understand?"

"Yes, sir."

"Can you get ahold of him before he goes to work tonight?"

Antonio looked confused. "What does it mean, 'get ahold?'"

Martin forgot sometimes that the local hires, though they all spoke English fluently, did not speak idiomatic English. "I'm sorry—it means will you be able to speak to him before he goes to work?"

"Yes, Mr. Schuller, I can speak with him this afternoon."

"Good, then come back here and let me know what time he says, and where. You're available to go with me to meet him tonight?"

"Yes, of course, sir."

"Thank you."

"Is there anything more?" Antonio asked, starting to get up, hesitantly. "I must go back to work, or Mr. De la Tour will be angry."

"No, nothing more. If Mr. De la Tour gives you a hard time, just tell him to come see me."

Antonio looked a little confused, but he nodded—if he'd never heard the expression 'a hard time,' he at least figured out the gist of it. "Yes, I will. Thank you, Mr. Schuller."

Not unexpectedly, Juan-Carlos Alberto Maria De la Tour-Calvo knocked on Martin's door ten minutes later.

"Mr. Schuller, may I have a word with you in *private*, please?" he asked in his accented English.

"Of course, have a seat," Martin said, motioning to the chair in front of his desk as De la Tour closed the door. But as usual, the diminutive Argentine remained standing.

He wore a look of exaggerated concern, and he clasped his hands in front of his chest. "Mr. Schuller, I was told that you met with one of my *employees* a short time ago—Antonio Miguel Rivera-Ferrari. He did *not tell* me why, however, so I grew *concerned* that he was hiding some *transgression* from me. Is anything wrong? Has there been a *problem* with his performance that I should address?"

Martin gave De la Tour his most reassuring smile. "No, thank you, señor. There is no problem."

De la Tour did not look convinced. He took a step toward the corner of Martin's desk, and then paused. He gave Martin an elaborate hand gesture. "If I may *approach*, Mr. Schuller?"

Martin suppressed an amused smile, and nodded. "Of course."

"Thank you." De la Tour stepped around to the side of Martin's desk so that he stood only a few feet away. "Please be *assured* that it is no trouble to involve me in matters that require *correction*. It is *always* my desire to keep you *most* happy with the performance of my staff in support of your *very important* work. If there is *any* matter that I can improve, no *matter* how small it may be, please make use of me."

Martin knew De la Tour was dying to know what they had discussed. His flamboyant way of speaking, always entertaining, was dialed up a notch or two.

"I appreciate that, Mr. De la Tour. But really, there is nothing that needs improvement. Mr. Rivera did not disclose the nature of our conversation because I asked him not to speak of it. It was a confidential matter. Thank you for confirming his trustworthiness."

The look that crossed De la Tour's hazel eyes was a combination of surprise and hurt—probably at being left out—and for a moment Martin felt sorry for the supervisor.

"Of course, Mr. Schuller," De la Tour said, recovering his composure, and giving Martin a bow. "I am *most* pleased that a member of my staff has been of *service* to you. Thank you for the *trust* you have placed in him."

"I appreciate the follow-up from you." Martin reached for a file on his desk. "Now if you'll excuse me?"

"Yes, yes! Of course, Mr. Schuller." De la Tour gave him another bow, this time with an elaborate flourish with his right hand, and exited.

Martin allowed himself a chuckle after the flamboyant supervisor departed.

He actually liked the earnest little man. He was a few years older than Martin—probably late thirties—and a "confirmed bachelor," as it was said around the office. He did a good job in his role supervising some of the local staff, and he was always impeccably polite and deferential.

Martin remembered the Thanksgiving reception at the Ambassador's Residence last November. It was late spring—which he was still not used to at that time—and so the sun stayed out late, and several of the mid-level Foreign Service Officers had gathered on the portico after dinner, talking shop over cocktails while the evening sky turned red.

The liquor had been flowing all afternoon and evening, and tongues were loosened. Martin was careful to remain sober, as was Sloan, but most of the rest were in one stage of inebriation or another. As the topic of conversation moved to office gossip, some of those present aped De la Tour's flamboyant gestures and diction, in an exaggerated and mocking fashion.

Sloan had laughed along with them, but then he suddenly scowled over his tumbler of bourbon. "If he's such a raging homo, why not fire him?"

Several of those present looked embarrassed. "Well...there's no proof," Chuck Brady said in his slow Texas drawl, sheepish. "Can't really fire the man without proof, can you?"

"Why the hell not?" Sloan replied, frowning.

Brady looked taken aback—whether by Sloan's directness, or his swear word, Martin wasn't sure. "Well...I don't know...not my area, actually."

Something about the way Brady passed it off like that irritated Martin. "Proof or not, what does it matter?" He thought of Joe Hansen back in Washington. "If he's kept it to himself, what do you care? As long as he does good work, let him keep doing it."

Sloan regarded him with a strange expression. "Anyone who engages in illegal and obscene behavior—regardless if he 'keeps it to himself,' as you say—opens himself to bribery and blackmail, and endangers the work of this embassy."

"It's not illegal, actually," Mike Mattingly said, gesturing toward Sloan and accidently sloshing a bit of liquor onto the stone floor. "Argentina's fairly unique in that; unlike most countries, they don't outlaw sodomy."

"It's true," Roger Dean said. "And De la Tour can hardly think we don't *know*, can he? How could he be at risk of blackmail?"

Sloan didn't look satisfied, but he shrugged and lit another cigarette.

That information had surprised Martin, and for some reason the news pleased him. Now, four and a half months later, Martin was glad De la Tour—and others who were like Joe Hansen—didn't have to worry about arrest and imprisonment.

It was a cool, clear night, and Martin enjoyed the long walk from the back door of the embassy, north through narrow streets of the *Barrio Retiro*, past grimy brick buildings to the sprawling dockyard known as *Ante Puerto*, where smaller ships docked. Antonio Rivera walked beside him, fidgeting with his hands.

"Relax," Martin told him.

Martin glanced around often without letting it show, and was convinced that no one was watching or following them. He knew how to take precautions, from years of undercover work back in the States, when he worked for the Office of the Chief Special Agent. There was a quarter moon tonight, already high in the northern sky, which provided some illumination on the dark streets. But Martin was confident they were unobserved.

They were to meet Antonio's acquaintance Roberto outside of the dockyard at nine o'clock, beside a large brick warehouse that was closed up for the night. Sailors' bars occupied the next block down the street, closer to the main gate of the dockyard, but this block was deserted. Martin hesitated at the corner when they first arrived, observing the men coming and going from the taverns for a moment, before motioning for Antonio to lead them on.

A muscular young man in dark trousers and an open-collared light blue working-man's shirt leaned against the corner of the warehouse as they approached. Antonio called his first name, and extended his hand.

After shaking Antonio's hand, the young man looked at Martin.

Antonio also looked at Martin. "This is Roberto Calderon, the man I told you about."

"*Usted es el norteamericano?*" Roberto asked. "*Señor Smith?*"

Martin was pleased that Antonio had not used his name, as instructed. He wasn't surprised that Roberto didn't speak English, which was another reason to be glad Antonio had come along.

"*Sí,*" he answered. "*Hablo un poco de español, pero no mucho.*" He looked at Antonio, and said in English, "Tell him you'll translate for us."

Antonio did as instructed.

"Now ask him to tell me what he saw, in detail. And tell him not to leave anything out."

"Yes, sir, Mr. Sch—Smith." Antonio's lips tightened into a thin line at the near flub, but he took a breath and translated Martin's words.

Roberto Calderon began to speak at length, and after several seconds Antonio started translating. "He says it was early on Sunday morning, between one and two o'clock. There was a boat that tied to the end of a wharf, not beside. It was a river boat, not an ocean ship. There were freight ships tied to both sides of that wharf, so the boat was not easy to see from the yard. The men on the boat, plus some men from the dockyard, unloaded many crates from the boat, and men from the freight ship next to the boat came out to take the crates onboard."

Martin interrupted. "How many men were on the river boat?"

"He says ten or twelve."

"Were they Argentine?"

"He says he thinks so." Antonio said something more to Roberto in Spanish, and then translated Roberto's reply. "He says everyone spoke Spanish, and they didn't sound foreign."

"What about the men from the freighter? Were they Argentine?"

Roberto shrugged, and Martin didn't need a translation of his answer. "*No lo sé.*"

"Was the freighter an Argentine ship?"

"*Sí, Argentino.*"

Martin didn't wait for a translation. "What ship was it? And where was it going?"

"The *San Miguel*, sailing to Santos, Lisbon, and Bremen."

Two neutral ports, and then on to Germany. Martin nodded. "Tell him to continue. What happened?"

"He says no inspector came, and no one took a report for the Customs Officer."

"He's sure of that?"

"Yes, he's sure."

"What was he doing when this all happened?"

"He says he was driving a forklift down the wharf, but he had finished his job early and took a break to smoke a cigarette. That's when he saw the boat getting tied to the end of the dock."

Good timing, Martin thought. "Did anyone see him watching?"

"*No, señor.*" Another answer that Martin didn't need translated.

"Are you certain?"

Roberto and Antonio spoke back and forth for a moment, and Martin watched them, comprehending only a little, before Antonio provided a translation.

"He says he was in the shadow of the freight ship he had loaded with his forklift. Where he stood, no one could see him, he is certain."

Martin nodded, almost satisfied. "Had he already lit his cigarette?"

A look of concern crossed Antonio's eyes before he translated. *He didn't think of that, and he's scared of the answer.*

"He says he lit it when he got out of the forklift, but he stubbed it out when he saw the boat. He got closer because he was curious what it was, it was not usual—" Antonio paused while Roberto added something. "And he says he was in the shadow the whole time. He is certain no one saw him, or they would have called to him."

That was reasonable, Martin agreed. "Has the San Miguel left port?"

"Yes, it sailed today."

Damn! He reached into his pants pocket and removed a fifty peso note—roughly eleven U.S. dollars—and handed it to Roberto. *"Muchas gracias, señor."*

The note disappeared into Roberto's pocket. It was probably more than he made in a day. He locked eyes with Martin and held them for a second before nodding and turning away.

Martin watched him walk toward the gate of the dockyard and disappear inside. He turned to Antonio and nodded for them to leave.

They walked in silence for a couple of blocks before Martin spoke. "How long have you known Mr. Calderon?"

Antonio shrugged. "I don't know—a few weeks, I think. Not long."

"How did you meet?"

Antonio's expression turned to stone, and his posture stiffened a bit as he walked. He stared straight ahead. "We have a friend we share. I met Roberto through my friend, Javier."

There was more to the story, Martin could tell, but he left it alone for the moment. "So then, you wouldn't say that you know Mr. Calderon well?"

"Not well." Antonio cast a quick glance sideways at Martin. "But I believe him to be truthful, Mr. Schuller."

"Would your friend Javier vouch for him?"

"I don't understand—vouch?"

Martin tried simpler wording. "Would your friend Javier tell me that Mr. Calderon is a truthful person, one who can be trusted?"

"Yes, I think Javier would say that."

Martin glanced around to make sure no one stood nearby before asking in a lower voice, "Does your friend Javier know what you do for work?"

"He knows I work at the embassy, for the Americans," Antonio said. "I don't tell him exactly what my work is."

"But you call him your friend, someone you know well?"

Antonio looked at him, one eyebrow arched in curiosity. "Yes, I know Javier a long time. I don't know how long he knows Roberto Calderon, but a while, I think."

That's good enough, Martin decided. "Can I meet your friend Javier?"

Antonio shrugged. "Yes, I can take you to his place of work. We can go there at lunch time, if you want to."

"He works at a restaurant?"

"Yes, he is a waiter. I will find out when he next works, and I will take you there. It is in Belgrano, if that is not too far from work?"

Martin shook his head. "No, it's not too far. But I'd rather meet him when he's not working, when he has plenty of time to talk. Can you arrange that?"

"Yes, sir. I will ask him."

"Thank you, Antonio." Martin hadn't asked permission to use his first name, and he waited to see if there were any objection. He didn't really expect one, but one never knew. "Come to my office tomorrow, after you've talked to Javier."

Tuesday, April 16

Martin made extensive notes the next morning of the meeting with Roberto Calderon, and put them in the file he'd created with Joe Hansen's note about the Germans' smuggling operation. He considered for a moment whether he should pass this along to Sloan now, or wait until he'd talked with Antonio Rivera's friend Javier.

He'd gotten in trouble before for not being cooperative enough with the FBI—but that was in his old role back in Washington, when he had defied an order from the Chief Special Agent to turn something over to Sloan.

"Once bitten, twice shy," Martin mumbled to himself. He slipped his jacket on and took the folder downstairs to Sloan's office.

"Morning, Schuller." Sloan motioned Martin in with his hand, but didn't rise from his chair. "What can I do for you?"

"I thought you might want to see this," Martin said, and tossed the folder onto Sloan's desk. "Evidence of a clandestine operation to smuggle war materiel out of the country, on neutral ships bound for Germany."

Sloan's eyes narrowed. He picked up the folder and started reading.

"Why didn't you tell me about this yesterday?" Sloan demanded when he finished reading, and slapped the folder onto his desk.

"I wanted to wait until I knew what Mr. Rivera's contact had seen," Martin said. "I was told the FBI was already informed of State's intelligence that this was happening. Didn't you know about it?"

Sloan's lips pursed. "I received a notice to be on the lookout for signs that this was happening, yes. But until I read this, about your little meeting last night, I had no idea anyone had seen signs of it."

"I'm trying to verify the reliability of my source, but I believed him." Martin looked at Sloan a moment, trying to gauge his mood. "We could go to the local police with this, but it wouldn't do any good since the ship has already left. I think we should wait."

Sloan nodded and stood. "I agree. We need to know much more about this operation—for starters, what it is they're smuggling, where it comes from, and how often they ship it. Then we can engage the local authorities to find out how extensive the operation is, and who's involved."

"Once I find out if Roberto Calderon is trustworthy, I'll have him call me the next time that boat arrives with unreported cargo. Or another boat like it."

Sloan shook his head. "No, have him call Mr. Rivera. He's an embassy employee, so he's already passed a background check. Rivera can call you." He pointed his finger like a scolding boss. "Don't ever give your phone number to a new informant. Always arrange a more secure form of communication. Got it?"

Martin felt the anger rising in his cheeks, but he fought it down. Sloan was right, of course; and he was the expert from years of law enforcement work with informants.

"Got it," he replied, not fully able to keep the resentment from his tone.

On his way out of Sloan's office, Martin saw Antonio Rivera and two other young Argentine men from the clerical staff listening to Juan-Carlos De la Tour relaying some instruction with elaborate gestures.

One of the young men, a tall blond with a wavy swoop of hair over his forehead, stood with his hip cocked, in a slightly effeminate posture. Martin was surprised he'd never noticed it before. *Just like the clerical boys back at State headquarters*. He thought of all the so-called "faerie boys" who worked in the file rooms and mail rooms of the Old Executive Office Building.

He hadn't expected that in Latin America, though, with the *machismo* that was so common here. But then again, he supposed he shouldn't be surprised that De la Tour might hire boys of that nature.

His eye caught Antonio Rivera's for a second as he passed, and he nodded at the young man.

Antonio knocked on Martin's door that afternoon.

"Mr. Schuller? May I come in?"

Martin motioned him in. "Close the door."

"My friend Javier can meet with you tonight after ten o'clock," Antonio said. "I did not tell him your name, only that an American who works with me at the embassy wanted to talk to him, about Roberto."

"Where?"

"He said he would meet us at a tavern you choose, and you can buy him a drink. He works in Belgrano, but he lives in Almagro." Antonio hesitated a second, then added, "I also live in Almagro, so I can recommend a place, unless you already have a place to that you want to go."

Martin shook his head. "No, there is no particular place to *which* I would want to go. I don't know that part of the city well." But he knew Almagro was a relatively inexpensive barrio, quite the opposite of Belgrano. "You choose."

Antonio hesitated again, looking unsure of himself. Then he seemed to force a smile. "Meet me at ten-thirty at the corner of the street José Antonio Cabrera, and the street Gascón. There is a stop there for the streetcar. There is a tavern on the next block where Javier and I go often."

Martin agreed, and got back to work. He had information to send back to Washington in the week's diplomatic pouch.

9

The inside of the tavern called *Quartier Latin* was like nothing Martin had seen. The walls were bare brick, no plaster, and the lighting was dim. A well-worn wooden stage to his left stood one step up from the equally worn hardwood floor, but it was empty at the moment. The room was filled with plain tables surrounded by wooden chairs; about half of the chairs and most of the barstools were occupied.

Martin ascertained in two seconds that he was likely the oldest person there, other than the bartender. About three quarters of the patrons were young men in woolen trousers and thick button-down shirts with open collars and no necktie. Some wore flat newsboy-style hats, the others were bare-headed. The rest of those in attendance were young women in housedresses.

Not a fancy crowd, by any means. Or even middle-class respectable. It was the sort of place where people drank red wine from water glasses, or occasionally beer from bottles.

Most of the patrons were engaged in conversation, though it was not loud, and some sat alone reading from small and well-worn hardback volumes.

He turned to Antonio. "The name of this tavern, it's not Spanish, is it?"

"No, it's French," Antonio replied. "The Latin Quarter is the neighborhood in Paris where the university is. It is where many of the artists and writers live."

So they fashion themselves after Parisian bohemians. Martin decided to reserve judgement.

Antonio raised his hand and waved at someone in the back corner, and a tall, dark-haired figure stood.

Martin immediately recognized one of the waiters from his favorite café on the Avenida Cabildo.

Javier looked equally surprised to see him.

"Mr. Schuller? I did not know..." Javier began in accented English, but trailed off, looking to Antonio.

Martin cringed at his name being said out loud, but decided in this venue it didn't matter—if asked, any one of these patrons would say they remembered seeing an American in a nice blue suit and hat. He stood out like a sore thumb.

Antonio looked between the two of them a few times, mouth open in surprise. "You know each other?" he said in Spanish.

"Your friend works in a café not far from where I live. One that I visit often," Martin said, in English.

"I did not realize..." Antonio said, but his voice also trailed off, sounding unsure and awkward. He fidgeted with his glasses.

Martin took charge and pushed them through the awkwardness of the surprise. "Shall we sit?"

"Yes, please," Javier said, looking embarrassed, and motioned to the three empty chairs surrounding the small table. Once they sat, he seemed to get over his discomfort. "I am Javier Velasco. I have known Antonio Rivera for a few years, yes?"

Antonio nodded.

That wasn't what Martin was here to learn. "How do you know Roberto Calderon?"

Javier cast a sideways glance at Antonio, who looked toward the bar. He raised his arm for the waitress.

"I met Roberto through people we both know," Javier said, vague.

The waitress came to their table, and asked in Spanish if they wanted drinks. Javier ordered a glass of house wine for each of them. Then he pointed toward Martin. "He will pay the bill."

Martin understood enough Spanish to realize he was probably buying more than Javier's first drink.

Once the waitress had departed, Martin brought them back to the subject. "How well do you know Mr. Calderon?"

Javier shrugged. "Difficult to say. What is well? He does not come to places like the *Quartier Latin*, so we have not had long conversation. I do not know if he likes to read Manuel Gálvez, for example. Probably not, but I do not know it."

Martin agreed that Roberto didn't seem like much of a reader. But that didn't answer the main question. "How often do you see Mr. Calderon, and speak with him?"

Javier shrugged again. "I don't know—from time to time, no? It is not regular, not predictable."

Martin was beginning to wonder if this were a waste of time. The waitress arrived and set three small glasses of red wine in front of them, giving him a moment to consider his next move.

"Can you tell me if he's an honest man?"

"I think so."

"Would you trust what he told you?"

"Yes. Why wouldn't I?"

Martin decided that was the best he was going to get on that, and tried a different tack. "Does Mr. Calderon work anywhere else, besides the dockyard?"

A veil seemed to fall over Javier's eyes, which were a rich amber color. "Why would you think he would?"

Something about Javier's guarded tone raised Martin's suspicions. "Is he involved in illegal activity?"

Javier brightened suddenly, a huge grin making him appear affable—but Martin thought it seemed put on somehow.

"Why would I think such a thing? That is a strange thing for you to ask me, Mr. Schuller. You are not with the police, so it is strange, no?"

Martin couldn't argue with that, but he also couldn't explain why the question was relevant to what he needed to know. Perhaps it was a moot point anyway—Javier had said that he would trust what Roberto told him, and wasn't that the crux of what Martin wanted to know?

Antonio looked uncomfortable. Javier was looking across the table at Martin, waiting, so he nodded in agreement.

"You're right, I put that badly. I've been given some information from Mr. Calderon, and I just want to verify that he is reliable and honest, and that I can believe what he told me." That in and of itself danced on the knife's edge of what could be revealed without compromising the integrity of the information itself, but there was no way around that.

Javier smiled again, another broad grin that was striking considering how infrequently Argentines smiled at strangers. "Do not think it more," he said, bungling the English idiom. "If you don't mind me saying it, Mr. Schuller—this seems like a strange place for you. Do you like to go places to hear poets read?"

"I like to try new places," Martin said, noncommittal.

Javier shook his head, still smiling. "You do not seem like the type of man who will read or listen to poetry, Mr. Schuller."

In truth, Martin didn't read much poetry. But he had read poetry in school, and he could still appreciate it. And he disliked being typed so easily. "What makes you think I don't like poetry?"

Javier gave him a scrutinizing look. "You are a—how do you say it? A man who likes the things that are common, things that most men like. But not *common*, no. There is a different word…"

"Conventional?" Martin asked, feeling defensive. He did *not* think of himself that way. He was divorced, for heaven's sake.

"Yes, that is the word, thank you. You are a conventional man, who reads the newspaper at breakfast and drinks coffee only in the morning.

You dress like a conventional man in a suit, and you converse with other conventional men about business."

None of those specific things were untrue in and of themselves—except, perhaps, about coffee only in the morning—but Martin bristled at being called "conventional." That was almost as bad as "common." And not true in any case.

"You don't know me very well, Javier," Martin said, deliberately using the young man's first name, as if he were sitting in the café being served by him. "I'm not exactly as I appear."

"Ah, good!" Javier said, looking pleased. "Then you will stay and listen to the readings? I will read some of my own work later."

Martin glanced at his watch. It was approaching eleven o'clock. On a weeknight.

"I'm afraid I can't stay long, I have to work in the morning." He was painfully aware of how conventional that made him sound.

"Yes, I do also," Antonio agreed, nodding.

Javier shrugged in a careless sort of manner. "What a shame, but it is understandable. Perhaps some afternoon you will join us at *Las Violetas*—a coffee house, not far from here, where writers and poets gather, and sometimes we have unplanned readings."

"Yes, perhaps," Martin said. He finished his wine, then stood and dropped a few coins on the table. "I should be going. I'm sure I will see you again soon, Javier." He looked at Antonio. "Mr. Rivera, a word please?"

"Yes, sir," Antonio said, and rose. He muttered in Spanish to Javier that he would be back in a few minutes, and followed Martin to the door.

There was a chill in the air when they got outside, and Antonio shoved his hands into his pockets. Martin put on his hat.

"I trust you're able to communicate with Mr. Calderon without having to go through Javier Velasco?"

"Yes, I can reach him without assistance."

"Then let's keep the nature of our communication between the three of us," Martin said. "There's no need to involve Mr. Velasco further. He provided the confirmation I needed."

Antonio's eyes looked momentarily surprised, but the reaction was fleeting, and he nodded in agreement. "What should I tell Javier?"

That was the tricky part. "There's not much you can tell him. Can I assume you haven't told him my role at the embassy?"

"No, sir, I said nothing about what you do—only that I work with you there."

"Good. If he asks, just say I work with the press, and Roberto Calderon provided information about something a reporter friend of mine is writing about. Can you do that?"

Antonio gave him a firm nod. "Absolutely, Mr. Schuller. You can count on me."

"Good, thank you." Martin shook his hand and they parted. Antonio walked back inside, and Martin started walking down the sidewalk.

At the corner, he crossed the street, and stopped. Concealed behind the edge of a neighboring building, he could see inside the bohemian bar. The lighting had seemed dim while he was inside, but from out here it was sufficient for him to get a good view of the interior.

Occupied bar stools blocked his view of the table where he'd sat with Antonio and Javier, however. Poor luck, but he waited patiently.

More than twenty minutes passed before he saw the two young men stand, and walk around the bar toward the front door. He could see their lips moving, but of course he was unable to read lips in Spanish.

They lingered by the door for several seconds, and then they leaned toward each other to touch cheeks and kiss the air—the typical way Argentines greeted and parted from friends and family.

But Martin was sure he saw Javier's lips graze Antonio's cheek as they separated. That was not done. Of course, traditional standards meant nothing to a bohemian crowd.

At least, they wanted everyone to think they meant nothing.

Martin slipped back into the shadow as Antonio exited the tavern and walked away, hands shoved into the pockets of his jacket. Inside, Javier leaned across the bar, laughing with the bartender for a moment, and then returned to his corner table in the back.

Hutson

10

Saturday, April 20

The jacaranda and tipa trees that lined so many streets and plazas in Buenos Aires had turned golden in recent days, and on this day in particular they seemed burnished in the bright sunlight as Martin exited Señora Duarte's School of Tango in upscale Recoleta. The air had taken on the smell of fall almost overnight, and Martin took a deep, satisfying breath of it before walking west toward home.

The steps of the dance were coming along slowly but surely, and today he had experienced a breakthrough—thanks to Señora Duarte's lack of shame.

It was his fourth lesson, and he was every bit as stiff and wooden in his movements as he had been that first day a week and a half ago. The young Argentine women who danced with him, also students, seemed more natural at it. Finally, midway through today's two-hour lesson, Señora Duarte had stopped them with furious clapping of her hands, and told the girl partnered with Martin that day to step aside.

"Mr. Schuller, you are like a statue!" she scolded, switching to English for his benefit. Her words brought an embarrassed flush to his cheeks, even though more than half of the class couldn't understand English. They understood her tone. He glanced around at the rest of the class staring at him, and looked off to the side of the instructor's face.

"Tut! Tut!" she said, tapping his chin. "Look into my eyes. You will dance with me for the rest of the lesson." She was short, perhaps five foot one or five foot two at most, about fifty years old. Age had brought a plump softness to her middle, but she still had a dancer's legs. And she still had the carriage of a *prima donna* dancer.

"Now, take me in your arms. No, no, closer, like this. If you are going to embrace the tango, you must embrace your partner like you *want* her desperately. Even when you do not dance with a woman that you want desperately, you must *imagine* that you do." A wry half-grin pulled the corner of her lip. "It is not difficult for me to look at a man who looks like you and pretend—for you, maybe not so easy to pretend with me; but I know you can picture a woman that you want to embrace, perhaps one that you cannot have, but you want her still. Yes?"

With the way Señora Duarte was staring into his eyes, he knew he couldn't hide the truth. He nodded without a word, feeling his cheeks flush hot.

A satisfied look came to her face, and she shouted to the room in Spanish, "*De nuevo, una vez más!*" She nodded to the young man who served as her assistant, and he set the needle on the record and restarted the music. As the students began to move, Señora Duarte counted out sets of four in a sign-song rhythm in Spanish, her voice and pitch rising on the first syllable of "*cuatro.*"

"A little better," she said in English as they finished one run and turned to go back. "Still too stiff. You must be fluid, like the music—and like sex, no? You must imagine that I am her, the one you thought of, and *seduce* me with the tango."

He felt his cheeks flush hot again, but his imagination worked overtime, and he pictured Rosa Linda Bianchi in his arms. He could see the long shape of her arm, the thick dark brown waves of her hair, the warmth of her golden brown eyes.

And his steps clicked, became natural. His body moved differently. It was like magic.

"Much better!" Señora Duarte beamed as he spun her around.

When it was finished, he felt exhilarated. Also a little embarrassed, but mostly exhilarated.

It was a beautiful clear day, with a pleasant temperature, and the sidewalks were full of strolling window shoppers, mothers pushing baby carriages, and people walking dogs. Martin wasn't able to move with his usual long, fast strides, but on a day like today he didn't mind so much.

And he enjoyed the people-watching opportunities.

His stomach growled as he walked west along the Avenida Cabildo, and he decided to grab some lunch out rather than going all the way home and having to fix himself a sandwich. He passed from the *Barrio Palermo* into *Barrio Belgrano*, and his favorite café was a few blocks ahead.

When he stepped inside, the café was full with the lunch-time crowd, and he saw no empty table. Three waiters rushed from table to table—Javier, Teodoro, and Angel were working today—and the manager caught Martin's eye as he came through the door. He raised his hand in greeting and hurried forward.

"Good afternoon, Mr. Schuller," Ricardo Messini said in Spanish. "I am sorry we do not have a place for you this moment, but please wait five or ten minutes."

Martin was able to understand the majority of Messini's words, thanks in part to the careful diction the manager always used when speaking to him. It was a little courtesy that Martin always appreciated, and one of the reasons he had come to love this spot.

"Yes, thank you," Martin said, nodding to show he understood.

It was an additional opportunity for people watching, so Martin didn't object. Some of the patrons today were regulars, but perhaps half were people he had never seen before. It was a decidedly upper-middle-class clientele, as befitted the Belgrano location, but otherwise it was an interesting mix of young and old, couples and groups of friends.

He heard at least two tables conversing in Italian—not uncommon anywhere in Buenos Aires—and one group of four at a table near the window conversed in *Belgrano Deutsch*, the local German dialect common among the Argentine-born children of German immigrants.

German Argentines were the fourth largest ethnic group in the country, after Italian, Spanish, and French Argentines, respectively. Here in Buenos Aires, they had largely congregated in Belgrano; and in much the same way as had transpired in southeastern Pennsylvania over generations, a distinctive dialect of German had developed among the second and third generations in this neighborhood.

When he first arrived here at the end of September, Martin had to concentrate to understand overheard conversations in *Belgrano Deutsch*, just as other German speakers had to struggle to understand Pennsylvania Dutch—but now he rarely had difficulty eavesdropping.

This group—two men and two women about his age—were discussing one of the couples' recent weekend trip south to Patagonia to see the autumn foliage there.

He watched as a couple near the back paid their bill, but as Javier took the check and the money on the table, the woman rose alone and excused herself. Martin found it odd that Javier seemed to be clearing their table rather slowly, given how busy they were, so he watched the woman go into the ladies' room. He looked back at the table just in time to see the man slip more money into Javier's hand as he went to shake it. It was a quick move, and Martin would never have noticed it if he hadn't already been paying attention.

The man was in his late thirties, in a stylish navy blue suit not very different from Martin's, with brown hair slicked back with brilliantine. He thanked Javier for the excellent service with a touch too much enthusiasm.

Martin wondered what that was about.

As the man turned toward the front of the café, he spotted Martin watching, and looked down quickly. He met his wife with what seemed exaggerated pleasure when she emerged from the ladies' room, and when they exited together he stared straight ahead and did not look at Martin.

Ricardo Messini motioned Martin over as Javier finished clearing the table.

"Thank you for waiting, Mr. Schuller," the manager said in Spanish. "Javier will come back in a moment."

It was less time than that. The manager had barely started to walk away when Javier came to the table with a hint of smile. "Good afternoon, Mr. Schuller," he said, in English for a change. "Very nice to see you again."

"Hello, Javier," Martin said, also in English. He ordered beef empanadas and a glass of the pale lager.

Javier brought him the beer a moment later. "You should come back to visit the *Quartier Latin* tonight," he said, again with a hint of smile. "It is Saturday, so you can stay late this time, yes? You do not have to work tomorrow. I will be reading tonight at midnight. Antonio will be there, and some of our other friends. Some of them are very good."

Martin tried to think of an excuse why he couldn't.

"I'm meeting someone at a *milonga* near my apartment tonight. Perhaps another time?" *Not bad for making it up on the spot*, he congratulated himself.

A wry half-smile tugged the corner of Javier's lips, and he gave Martin a curious expression. "A *milonga*? That is, how to say, unexpected, Mr. Schuller."

"Not conventional?"

Javier shrugged. "Not for a North American. I hope you have a good time."

The crowd began to dissipate as the prime lunch hour passed, and Martin's food arrived quickly now that the kitchen wasn't busy. With the people-watching and eavesdropping opportunities fading, he ate fairly quickly, and Javier brought him the bill soon after the manager put the "Closed" sign in the window.

Martin knew he was now intruding on siesta time, so he paid and left a few minutes later. The manager thanked him, and Martin heard the door lock behind him.

Martin crossed the avenue to the Colegiales side. He saw the older man who ran the newsstand across the avenue pulling down the shutters, and he called out to him. *"Señor Guzmán, uno momento, por favor?"*

Martin had made a point early on of becoming friendly with all of the local shop owners within a few blocks of his home. That was second nature to him, coming from a smaller city like Reading, and it sometimes paid off in little ways—like now, when Guzmán stopped pulling down the shutters and waited a moment for Martin to hurry over.

Martin apologized in Spanish and bought the first magazine his eyes fell on that wasn't intended for a female readership. He'd never before been interested in Polo, but Guzmán wouldn't know that. He paid for the magazine, and walked back to the corner.

He stood on the corner for several minutes, leafing through the pages. He couldn't understand much of the Spanish, but some of the photographs were in color. It amused him to see photo captions with Spanish first names paired with English last names—Jorge Luis Hareford, Enrique Watson and others, photographed at the Hurlingham Club in the nearby town of the same name.

Guzmán finished closing up, and departed. Several minutes later, the waiters Teodoro and Angel exited the café together; Javier emerged alone a moment after.

Martin watched him walk west along the Belgrano side of Avenida Cabildo—the opposite direction than *Barrio Almagro*, where he lived—and Martin began following on the opposite side, keeping a distance. Javier was not looking around, so it was easy to observe him undetected.

There was a subway station two blocks up the avenue, and Martin realized this might be how Javier got home every day—taking the subway downtown, and then a streetcar south to Almagro. Martin was about to turn around when he spotted a well-dressed figure emerge from the shadows of a doorway, and he recognized the man from the café who had slipped Javier some money.

They met at the top of the stairs to the subway, exchanged a few words, but then instead of descending to the station, the man opened the passenger door of a Vauxhall sedan and put his hand on Javier's back as he got in. Martin watched the man get into the driver's seat and pull away from the curb. Traffic was light at this time of day, and Martin saw the car turn left at the next intersection and go south.

Something about this didn't feel right. Martin wondered if their destination was in Colegiales, or if they would loop back east toward Villa Crespo or Almagro.

As he turned toward home, Martin chastised himself for being nosy. It was none of his business what Javier did during siesta time. But he also had a near constant sense of curiosity about things he saw— which had served him well in his work—and it was especially keen regarding people he knew.

Plus, he couldn't get rid of the nagging sense that something wasn't right.

He walked into the *milonga* on Avenida Federico Lacroze around ten o'clock, and found the place only a little more than half full. Sizing him up as a newcomer to the scene, a raven-haired young hostess led him to a table near the back. He ordered a glass of their house wine and settled in to observe.

The interior lighting was dim but warm. Martin could barely remember homes with gas lighting when he was a child, before electrical lights became ubiquitous. The red velvet wallpaper and plush seating had a turn-of-the-century feel, and he supposed the club's owner had simply never bothered to replace the gas lights.

The floor was mostly empty. The orchestra sat in a raised box on the other side of the wooden dance floor. Martin counted two violins, a string bass, a guitar, one flute, one clarinet, and a piano, as well as two men playing an accordion-like instrument.

The club slowly filled as people began streaming through the door. Waiters and waitresses brought out plates of steaming steak or chicken *asado*, and the din of conversation increased as the wine and cocktails flowed.

The waitress came by and asked if he wanted another glass of wine. Martin was surprised that he had finished his first glass so quickly, in less than thirty minutes. That wasn't like him. Something about the atmosphere here had coaxed him into more frequent sips; or perhaps it was because he sat alone, with no one to talk to. He ordered another glass, resolving to drink it at a more normal pace.

Martin saw Rosa Linda Bianchi enter the club around ten forty-five, with a mixed group of young men and women. They were given the last large table in the joint, about twenty feet from where Martin sat. The three young men were noticeably gregarious in the way they held out seats for the four young women, and they each ordered a full bottle of wine. Martin had to chuckle; they were so clearly showing off for the ladies.

He remembered what it was like to be that young and that eager, and part of him envied them. They were on the edge of possibility at that age, when life seemed wide open.

If he were honest with himself, the happiest years of his life had been the two that he and Becky had spent in Europe, when he was twenty-three to twenty-five and Marty was little. Part of it had been the adventure of being abroad, of course, but much of it was the sense of possibility that came with being young.

Before real-life responsibilities became burdens. Before he and Becky had both changed.

He took a long sip of his wine, and put *that* out of his mind.

He concentrated on watching the activity on the dance floor, as it gradually filled with more couples dancing the tango. He watched their steps—some were more expert than others, but he found himself following the steps that most of the couples made, thinking *I could do that, with enough practice.*

"Mr. Schuller?" he heard a surprised voice say in English, and turned to see Rosa Linda standing a few feet away. He stood.

"Oh, hello," he said, trying to sound surprised as well, and not sure he succeeded.

"I have not seen you here before," she said, not looking displeased.

"This is my first time here."

"Alone?" She seemed surprised, and he was suddenly embarrassed.

"Yes, I am here alone." He wished he sounded more confident.

A teasing look came to her eyes. "I thought you said you don't dance the tango."

He felt his cheeks flush, and was grateful for the dim lighting. "I've been taking lessons. I came here tonight to see what it's like."

She gave him a sly sort of smile. "Perhaps you will dance later, then."

He bobbed his head. *Too enthusiastic,* he scolded himself. "Yes, perhaps so."

She flashed him a dazzling grin, and turned back toward her table and sauntered away.

He realized he was sweating as he sat down, and he slipped his handkerchief out of his coat pocket and surreptitiously dabbed at his forehead and upper lip. *Get a damn grip, Martin.*

A while later, the group that Rosa Linda was in got up and went toward the dance floor. One of the girls was left sitting with the other girls' purses, but Martin couldn't keep his eyes off of Rosa Linda, walking arm-in-arm with a blue-eyed young man with an Errol Flynn mustache.

They began to dance, and Martin watched their legs as they intertwined with each complicated step; watched as their hips pressed together and moved in time.

He looked at his hands, and then downed the last of his wine in one gulp. Taking a deep breath, he stood and marched to the table where they had left one of her friends.

She was a fair-skinned girl with auburn hair and big brown eyes, and she looked up at him in surprise when he appeared beside her chair.

"Good evening, Miss," he said in Spanish, nodding to her. "My name is Martin Schuller, and I am a friend of Rosa Linda Bianchi. You are?"

If his slow, rudimentary Spanish amused her, she didn't show it; or perhaps she was still stunned by his sudden appearance. Either way, she simply answered, "I am Andrea Mejía."

"Would you like to dance with me, Miss Mejía?" he asked, holding out his arm.

She took his arm with a muttered "Thank you, sir." He led her to the floor.

With her left hand in his right, and his left arm around her waist, he took a set of beats to breathe and remember the dance with Señora Duarte that afternoon. Then he began to move.

Andrea Mejía was a better dancer than he was, that became apparent after just a few bars—but she didn't utter any complaint that he kept their steps relatively simple.

They danced for the remainder of the number, and as the orchestra reset he asked if she would like to do another. She agreed, and they started dancing again as soon as the music resumed.

In the few seconds of silence in between the songs, he caught Rosa Linda's eye, and she looked surprised to see him on the floor.

During the next number, he made the mistake of glancing her way, and he missed a step and landed on Andrea Mejía's toe. She grimaced, but did not complain. He muttered an apology in Spanish, and concentrated on his partner—one of Señora Duarte's laws.

A moment later, there was a tap on his shoulder, and he turned around to see a well-dressed young man with wavy blond hair who asked him something in rapid Spanish that he didn't understand, but assumed to be along the lines of "May I cut in?"

He nodded, and stepped aside. The young man took Miss Mejía and moved her expertly across the floor.

Martin returned to his table, caught the waitress's eye, and ordered another glass of wine.

His stung ego was salved a moment later when he saw an older man cut in with Rosa Linda, sending her dance partner back to the table. Her new partner was dressed in a stylish gray suit with black pin-stripes, a red rose in his lapel, and appeared to be about forty with thinning black hair.

Martin noticed them talking while they danced, which was unusual. Concentration was essential.

The waitress brought his third glass of wine, and he took a long sip, no longer concerned about getting a little bit inebriated.

Rosa Linda danced with the middle-aged man for the next five minutes, and Martin watched them the entire time. They continued to exchange some conversation, and he wasn't able to read her expression.

After a couple of numbers, the man led her off the dance floor, but he didn't take her back to her table; nor did he take her back to his own. They stood in a corner near the bar, away from the crowd, not far from the lavatories, and spoke with their heads leaned close together.

Martin decided he needed to relieve himself now, and he strode toward the men's room. He slowed his stride as he passed Rosa Linda and her companion, and he overheard them conversing in words that didn't sound Spanish. *Italian*, he realized as he passed her. Their eyes met for a second before she was out of sight behind him, and he pushed through the door.

When he emerged from the men's room a couple of minutes later, they had moved toward the exit, and were still talking with their heads close together.

He sat for a few minutes, and drank his wine a little too quickly. Deciding this whole evening had been a waste of time, he got up without finishing the last of the glass, and bolted toward the door.

The man who had been talking to Rosa Linda was exiting at that moment, and Rosa Linda passed Martin on her way back toward her friends' table. He paused to nod to her on the way out.

"Good night, Miss Bianchi," he said to her in Spanish. "I will see you at work on Monday."

"You are leaving?" She looked and sounded both surprised and disappointed.

"Yes, I am sorry."

She switched to English. "I thought you were coming over to ask me to dance." The pout she gave him seemed a touch put on, but he let himself fall for it.

"Oh, um, yes—would you like to dance, Miss Bianchi?"

"Call me Rosa Linda—and yes, I would like to dance with you, Mr. Schuller."

"Martin."

"Martin." The way her lilting accent lingered over his name was intoxicating.

A few seconds later, her amused smile told him he'd been standing immobile, staring at her, when he should have given her his arm. "Shall we?"

The club took on a dream-like quality as he wrapped his arm around her, and they began to move. Everything in his periphery became blurred, clouded, and all he could focus on was her face, the warmth of her hand in his, the feel of her lower back as it flexed beneath his palm in time with their steps.

How was it that the real thing could feel more surreal than his imagination that afternoon with Señora Duarte?

Midway through their second dance, a young man came up to tap on Martin's shoulder, but Rosa Linda shooed him away with a wave of her arm and a deep scowl. Martin felt like he was dancing on a cloud after that.

They stopped to rest after four numbers. Thankfully, the hostess hadn't given away Martin's table after his aborted attempt to depart, so they sat and he ordered drinks.

"You said you didn't know how to dance the tango," she scolded him, play slapping his arm. "You dance the tango better than any American I have seen try."

"I've taken some lessons," Martin admitted, but kept to himself that the thought of dancing with her had been the motivation.

"Before long, you will become a true Argentine," she said.

Martin shrugged, not sure what to make of that. "I'll be here long enough to take advantage, I suppose."

Their drinks arrived, and Rosa Linda took an eager sip of the cool beverage, and fanned herself with her hand once she'd set down the glass.

"You come to this club a lot, don't you?" he asked. "Do you live nearby?"

"Yes, I live a few blocks away. But I also come here because my cousin plays in the orchestra. He plays one of the *bandoneones*." She pointed toward one of the young men with the accordion-like concertina on his lap.

"I live nearby myself," Martin said. "A few blocks."

She placed her hand on his arm, and it felt warm even through the layers of his jacket and his shirt. "Wouldn't it be peculiar if we lived close to one another? Maybe on the same block?"

"Maybe so. Which direction do you live?" he asked, putting his elbow on the table and leaning his chin into his hand. He felt a little goofy, but didn't care.

She looked around to get her bearings, and then pointed toward the corner of the bar. "That way."

He laughed, not expecting the visual explanation. He hoped she wouldn't think he was laughing *at* her, and was relieved when she laughed, too.

"I'll walk you home later, if you'll permit me," he said.

The look in her eyes said she'd permit more than walking her home, but he looked away and took a drink of his cocktail.

They danced a few more times, and Martin had a few more beverages than he would have liked. Even with sweating out a lot of it, he was still inebriated when they left the club at one thirty in the morning.

He had just apologized for keeping her out too late, when she said she needed to say goodbye to the friends that she had come with, and Martin realized they showed no sign of slowing down yet. As they stepped out into the chilly night, and she tugged her wrap tighter around her shoulders, he asked her if she would have preferred to stay with her friends.

"No, I prefer to leave with you," she said, slipping her arm through his and leaning against him.

She directed him around a couple of turns, and then had him stop in front of a five-story apartment building. It was less than two blocks from his own building, as the crow flies, but farther on foot, and facing the opposite direction.

"You were right," he said, facing her. "We don't live that far away from one another."

"Then it will be easy to see one another again," she said, meaningfully. "And not just at work." She leaned close to him, and turned her face up, and he realized she was inviting him to kiss her.

He felt a thrill of excitement sweep through him, followed almost immediately by a rush of panic. The last time he had kissed a woman other than Becky was in 1925, when he was seventeen years old. There was a lot of pressure on a first kiss, even without a gap of almost fifteen years since the last one.

He was thinking too much, and he knew it. He remembered Señora Duarte's technique from that morning's class, and he relaxed into her, placing his lips softly on hers and letting her determine the rest.

She leaned into him, and opened her lips slightly. He did likewise, and soon they had their arms around one another, holding each other tightly, mouths exploring.

A full minute passed before she pulled her face away, and he relaxed his hold on her. "I should go upstairs, before my father looks out the window and sees us doing this."

He nodded, surprised to learn she lived at home, and reluctantly let her go. She sauntered to the glass door and let herself into the building.

"Good night, Rosa Linda," he said as she stepped through the doorway.

She turned in the door and smiled at him. "Good night, Martin." She blew him a kiss, and then turned away and hurried toward the stairs.

A big stupid grin spread across his mouth so far it made his cheeks hurt. He turned toward home, and as he rounded the corner he had to resist the urge to jump up and kick his heels together.

11

Monday, April 22

Martin arrived early to the Richmond Café on Calle Florida for his afternoon tea appointment with his main contact at the Argentine Ministry of Foreign Affairs, only to find him already at the table. As usual.

"Ah, good afternoon, Mr. Schuller. Always a pleasure to see you. Please, have a seat." Raúl José Andrews-Barrington spoke impeccable English, with an accent almost perfect enough for the BBC, in spite of the fact that his ancestors had come to Argentina more than a century before.

"Always a pleasure to see you, as well, Mr. Barrington," Martin said, consciously careful with his own diction.

Given his lack of Spanish language skills when he arrived, Martin was grateful to have been paired with a Foreign Ministry diplomat who spoke perfect English, but he was soon a touch self-conscious about his own dialect in relation to Barrington's speech.

"I took the liberty of ordering you the ham sandwiches before you arrived," Barrington said, brushing a miniscule spec of lint from the arm of his silk suit. "I noticed you ordered them the last two times we met here, so I made the bold decision to save some time and order in advance. I hope you don't object."

"Not at all." Martin wondered what Barrington's rush was. "I saw your photograph in a magazine last week," Martin said, pouring some milk into the cup of tea that a tuxedo-clad waiter set in front of him. "You were dressed for polo, and sitting astride a black horse."

Barrington laughed spontaneously, and he sounded genuinely pleased. "Yes indeed! It was out at Hurlington Downs, about a month ago. My team had just won the match, and I scored the final point. They kept hounding me for a photograph, and I finally relented." He finished stirring the milk and sugar into his tea, and took a sip. "I had no idea you carried an interest in polo, Mr. Schuller."

"Newfound," Martin said, not elaborating.

At thirty years old, Raúl José Andrews-Barrington was a scion of one of the oldest Anglo-Argentine families in the country, which had arrived from England in 1818 to establish a bank in the newly-independent country. With a generations-long banking tradition to their name, the head of the family still ran one of Buenos Aires' largest private banks.

After graduating from one of the prestigious English academies in the suburban town of Hurlington, and then with honors from the National University in Córdoba, Raúl had stunned his family by deciding to go into government service instead of banking. It was the height of the global Depression, so he'd met less resistance than expected. His father's connections had gotten him a plum assignment in the Ministry of Foreign Affairs, where at least he got to hobnob with British and American diplomats.

"What did you ask me here to discuss?" Martin asked after the waiter delivered a tray of finger sandwiches—ham and mustard for Martin, cucumber and dill for Barrington.

"I have some information at my disposal that I believe will interest you," Barrington said, taking a little cucumber sandwich from the tray.

"I'm all ears," Martin said.

"So are the walls," Barrington said, quieter, countering Martin's idiom with another without missing a beat.

Martin regarded Barrington with an arched eyebrow, wondering then why they were meeting in a crowded English café at tea time if the discussion were that confidential.

Barrington looked back with a thin smile. "We'll have a nice civilized tea, and then we can accompany one another across the Plaza on the way back to our offices."

Martin nodded in agreement, wondering what information Barrington might have that would be so sensitive.

They chatted about Argentine politics, and the ongoing battle in central Norway between the British and the Germans. Barrington was, unsurprisingly, sympathetic to the British cause. The moment their sandwiches were eaten and the tea pot empty, Barrington waved over the waiter to pay the bill. A slight breach of etiquette, Martin noticed.

They continued to chat about local matters as they made their way north along Calle San Martín, past the crowds entering and exiting Harrods Department Store—the only branch outside of London—and finally reached the wide open space of the Plaza General San Martín.

"I know you have been involved in identifying several German secret agents in our country, who have been spreading Nazi propaganda and using illegal radios to broadcast sensitive information about Argentina to U-boats in the Atlantic."

Martin didn't ask how Barrington had come to know this. He was only mildly surprised, to be honest. He supposed officials in the police cooperated regularly with officials in the Ministry of Justice; and it wouldn't be a stretch for the Ministry of Justice to inform the Ministry of Foreign Affairs that aid had come from a member of the foreign diplomat corps.

Barrington paused, as if waiting to see if Martin would confirm. Martin stayed silent.

"We appreciate your assistance in these matters. And your discretion."

I have considerable experience with that, Martin thought. He nodded in acknowledgment of the appreciation, but waited for Barrington to continue.

Barrington hesitated, as if trying to find the right words. "I don't know what the prevailing feeling is in the halls of your government in Washington, D.C.," he ventured, choosing his words slowly and deliberately. "I know that your country, like ours, is officially neutral— but I also know that your country, like ours, is a mix of many nations, with many competing interests."

Martin wondered where Barrington was going with this. "The various ethnic groups in the United States are united in their love of our country and its democracy."

Barrington gave him an indulgent smile. "As are the various ethnic groups in Argentina. I meant only that during your country's years of neutrality in the last war, there was considerable difference between national groups within the United States in regards to which side had their sympathy."

"That's true," Martin said, unable to deny it. "The current situation is not a perfect parallel, however."

"That is what is unclear. Would you care to elaborate?"

Martin considered for a second. "It's true that there is a small movement among recent arrivals from Germany who favor Nazi symbolism and ideals, and they hold rallies and parades from time to time—but they are far from an influential political movement, and are mocked in the press. After a handful of arrests for espionage last year, the group has fallen into decline. There is nothing at all close to the level of sympathy that German-Americans felt for the Kaiser's Germany a quarter century ago."

Barrington nodded, thoughtful.

Martin wondered if Barrington's inquiry was for the benefit of the Argentine Ministry of Foreign Affairs, or for friendly contacts at the

British embassy. *Or both.* And wouldn't their ambassador in Washington have already provided that context?

They passed under the shade of the plaza's famous ombú tree, whose umbrella-like canopy spread more than thirty feet. This was a popular place for people to stop and take photographs, so they remained silent until they had passed clear of it.

"If I may speak confidentially?" Barrington asked.

"Of course."

"We are concerned with the recent increase in U-boat activity in the South Atlantic Ocean. Presumably, they are hunting British shipping—but we know that some have slipped close to the coast and deposited secret agents onto our beaches."

Martin considered that. The Germans had begun using the same tactic to land agents onto Long Island last year, to avoid sending them through immigration and customs at the port of New York. But he wondered why that would be necessary here. "Are you certain?"

"Reasonably so."

Which means you got the intelligence courtesy of the Brits—but they can't help you beyond that. "And you'd like our cooperation in identifying those agents," Martin ventured.

Barrington waggled his head back and forth, equivocating. "Yes," he said, slowly. "But not for the reasons you might think."

Martin was intrigued. "Oh?"

"It seems that most of the new German agents have not gravitated to German ethnic enclaves in Buenos Aires, or south to Patagonia, as previous agents did. Most of the German agents that infiltrated the country illegally this year have boarded trains or boats bound for the north—and then disappeared. Our government is not sure what to make of that pattern."

Martin's mind went immediately to the intelligence Joe Hansen had sent him, about German plans to smuggle war materiel out of Argentina on neutral shipping.

He wasn't about to reveal anything about that, however. Not without explicit direction from Washington to do so.

"That is very interesting," he said.

"I won't ask you to share your sources with us," Barrington said. "But if you could see clear to sharing any information you have as soon as you have it, it would be most helpful to us."

Martin knew what Barrington was asking. He also knew he couldn't comply, no matter how much he wanted to encourage the contact. "We'll cooperate with law enforcement whenever we can," he said, noncommittal.

"Of course." The look of disappointment on Barrington's face told Martin he knew exactly what he meant.

They neared the looming French Beaux-Arts façade of the *Palacio de San Martín*, the home of the Ministry of Foreign Affairs.

"This is where I leave you, Mr. Schuller," Barrington said, stopping to extend his hand, which Martin shook. "I'll be in touch again soon. Good afternoon."

Martin knocked on Sloan's closed door a few minutes before five o'clock.

"It's open!" Sloan called, and Martin let himself in. "Ah, Schuller, what brings you by?"

"I got some interesting information from my contact at the Argentine Foreign Affairs ministry today," Martin said, and proceeded to tell Sloan what Raúl Barrington had told him.

"Hmmm..." Sloan said, leaning back in his chair and tenting his fingers in front of his chin. "Gone north, he said? That is unexpected. Toward Paraguay, maybe? Or Bolivia? What do you make of it?"

"The northwest of Argentina is where many of the large mining operations are, in the foothills of the Andes," Martin said. "You remember the intelligence we got about smuggling war materiel? That would be a good place to start."

"Yes, it would," Sloan agreed, sitting back up. "That makes our next question, how far along is this smuggling operation?"

"We know it's already started shipping out," Martin said. "You'll remember I have an informant at the docks who's witnessed a couple of river boats slip into the dockyards after dark, tie up where they can't be seen easily—and unload a bunch of unmarked crates that were immediately put on board a freighter without inspection, or getting logged."

Sloan's eyes narrowed. "Sure, but for how long?"

"I don't think long. The first time Mr. Calderon noticed it was nine days ago. Then it happened again on Friday. If that pattern holds, it's about once per week."

Sloan's scowl deepened. "But we can't say the time nine days ago was the first, can we?" Sloan's voice had an edge. "Have you looked for other sources?"

Martin resisted the urge to respond in-kind. He controlled his anger and kept his voice steady. "I didn't think there's enough need to involve others yet. I think we need to keep this as quiet as possible. There's evidence to connect it to the intelligence we got from Washington, and another source wouldn't tell us anything more."

"Except perhaps whether this has been going on long," Sloan exhaled hard, shaking his head in frustration. "This new information seems connected, doesn't it?"

"Which is why I'm here."

"Yeah, I guess so." Sloan stared at him for several seconds before taking a deep breath and leaning back in his seat again. "You believe your informants are reliable?"

"They're reliable," Martin said. "Mr. Calderon hasn't been part of moving the mystery crates, but he's watched it from the shadows, and he says the same fellows have been involved both times."

"You believe him?"

"I do," Martin said with a firm nod.

"Alright, we'll believe him until we have a reason not to," Sloan said. "And your other source is one of our local hires at the embassy, right?" Sloan asked, eyes narrowing again.

"Yes. Antonio Rivera, one of the clerks here."

Sloan let out a snort, which took Martin aback.

"One of De la Tour's boys?"

Martin nodded. "That's right. He reports to Juan-Carlos De la Tour."

Sloan shook his head. "You know De la Tour only hires sissy boys, don't you? No, I don't have proof, so don't ask me. I just know. It ain't that hard to figure out, if you pay attention. De la Tour—well, he's the way he is. You know, a bit 'funny.' What they call, 'temperamental.'"

Sloan waved a limp wrist in a circle before continuing. "There's no sense denying it on his behalf, everybody knows anyways. If you pay attention, you'll see that De la Tour is *very* touchy-feely with the boy clerks under his supervision. I don't mean a little. I figure, if they haven't complained about it, or walked out, they must be ok with it. If you know what I mean."

He leaned forward and jabbed a finger toward Martin. "And have you ever noticed the boys he hires are all young and good-looking? And I don't mean 'handsome,' either—they're *pretty* boys. Pretty little sissy boys for the chief sissy to look at all day."

Martin felt his ire rising at Sloan's hostility, thinking about his pal Joe Hansen in Washington; but he kept himself from saying anything he would regret. "I think as long as they do their jobs well, we should keep the speculation about their personal lives to ourselves."

Sloan chuckled. "If your man at the dockyards is a friend of one of De la Tour's clerks, there's a mighty fine chance he's a little funny, too."

Martin stiffened. "So what if he is? That doesn't make him an unreliable source of information."

"If you say so."

"I do."

A tense silence hung between them for several seconds.

"You don't seem to have much problem with homosexuals, Mr. Schuller," Sloan said, scowling.

"If I had a problem with homosexuals, I wouldn't work at the State Department."

His light-hearted attempt at humor didn't soften Sloan's expression. "I'm concerned about blackmail—and you should be, too."

Martin frowned. "It's not illegal here, remember? I think that substantially lowers the prospect of blackmail. Don't you?"

"No, I don't," Sloan said, crossing his arms. "Fear of arrest is only one reason to want to hide their proclivities. This is still a conservative society, very Catholic and religious. These homos probably wouldn't want their families to find out how they spend their evenings, or who with. That makes them targets for blackmailers."

Martin had to admit that he knew nothing of Antonio Rivera's family life or background; let alone Roberto Calderon, who worked a blue-collar job. But he hated that Sloan had a point.

And he wasn't going to concede without a fight.

"So then, Mr. Sloan, are you suggesting that we disregard the information these men have given us? That we cast them aside and not accept any more tips from them? Do you have alternative sources lined up, at your disposal—and equally well-placed?"

Sloan scowled so hard his brows bunched together like fabric in a misfed Singer sewing machine. "No, that is not what I'm suggesting. Until we have alternative sources, we'll be forced to use the imperfect ones we've got."

"All informants are imperfect, you know that."

Sloan shook his head. "It's gonna have to be a calculated risk with these boys—until we can replace them with others who aren't so compromised."

Martin took a beat to disengage. There was no rule that he and Sloan had to share sources. He'd groomed these men on his own, and Sloan could use them or not as he saw fit.

"It's getting late," he said. "Let's meet again tomorrow morning, and make a plan. Good night, Sloan."

Martin was only half-surprised to see Rosa Linda lingering around her desk when he got back upstairs, slowly closing up. There were office doors open, and he could hear some of his colleagues still working; but no one was in the hall, so he winked at her as he passed.

"Oh, Mr. Schuller!" she called after him as he opened his office door. "I have that letter ready for your signature." She hurried after him, a blank piece of paper in her hand.

He closed the door the moment she passed through, and a second later had her pressed against the wall, his hands rubbing her lower back, their lips locked. As their tongues explored, her arms moved around his back, drawing him against her.

They broke the kiss a moment later, and his lips moved down to her neck. He breathed in deeply as he kissed the soft skin of her throat, and worked his way to the divot at the base. Her breathing came short and shallow as his hands slid up her sides to rest just below her arms.

Her hand slid down his back to his belt, and pushed his hips forward into her own.

He broke away from her a moment later, embarrassed that she'd feel his growing arousal. Besides, they had to be careful about appearances, with his office door closed.

He straightened his necktie before opening the door. She straightened her dress and smiled lasciviously at him. He winked as she walked out.

"I'll have that letter out in the morning's post," she said, sauntering back to her desk.

12

Thursday, April 25

The cobblestone streets south of the Plaza Dorrego were narrow, lined with shabby-looking buildings that dated to the colonial era. The *Barrio San Telmo*, near the dockyards of the *Puerto Madero*, was one of the oldest neighborhoods in Buenos Aires, Martin knew. It was also one of the poorest, particularly in the eastern portions, where it sloped down toward the river.

At midday, the streets were not too crowded, and almost all of the pedestrians moving about were women, of all ages, but most of them black.

Buenos Aires reminded Martin of Washington, D.C. in one regard, besides the presence of the national government—that the black minority was segregated into a specific part of the city, which seemed to suffer from the same careless neglect. He briefly questioned if he was in the right place, since the man he sought wasn't black.

He found the street he was looking for, and wandered east along the downward sloping narrow lane—moving toward the river. The air was heavy with the smell of brackish water and diesel fuel.

All of the streets leading to San Telmo from the central part of the city sloped downward, and Martin had noticed the sour smell of the estuary as soon as he got off the streetcar. As he wound deeper into the district, the unmistakable smell of sewage also wafted up from somewhere beneath the cobbled stones.

He found the house he was looking for, and hesitated in front of the door. The plaster on the exterior wall needed patching in several places, the thick wooden planks of the door seemed ancient and splintering, and the iron clasps bore signs of rust. He took a breath and pounded his fist on the door.

An elderly black woman answered his knock, probably in her mid-sixties, and he saw the initial look of surprise that fleeted across her dark eyes when she regarded him.

"Yes, sir?" she asked him in Spanish.

"I am looking for Roberto Calderon," Martin said, unsure. "Is this his home?"

"Yes. Who is looking for him?" the woman said, with a touch of suspicion.

"It's good, Mamá," a younger woman said, appearing from the shadows behind the old woman, wiping her hands on a ragged towel. She was significantly younger and lighter-skinned than the older woman, being probably mid or late twenties, and obviously mixed-race. She looked at Martin with a calculating expression. "Do you need for Roberto to go to work tonight?"

Martin had watched the evening shift change at the *Ante Puerto* dockyards for more than a week, and had determined that Roberto Calderon did not work on Wednesday or Thursday nights. Which was why he was here now.

"No, I am not from Roberto's job," he said in slow but steady Spanish. "I need to speak with him. This is his house?"

The young woman continued to stare at him with a calculating look, trying to figure out what his business might be. "Yes, this is his house," she said, a little slower for his benefit. "I am his wife. He is sleeping at this moment."

"I can come back," Martin offered. "When is a good time to come back?"

114

The young woman continued to regard him with the same calculating look in her rich brown eyes. "I always wake him at noon. It is almost noon now—I can wake him a little early."

Martin glanced at his wrist watch—it was just past eleven thirty-five. One of the reasons he had not come earlier in the morning was his suspicion that Roberto slept late on his days off. He had assumed—wrongly, it seemed—that he might get up earlier on the second day than on the first.

"It is no problem to come back," Martin began, but the woman cut him off with a stern flick of her wrist. "Roberto!" she called over her shoulder. "Come in," she ordered Martin, and he obliged.

Then she looked at the children who stood behind her, whom Martin noticed for the first time—a little girl of about six and a little boy of about four. "Go tell Papá that an important man is here to see him." As the children scampered off to another room, their mother called down the corridor, even louder than before, "Roberto!"

"Do you want coffee, sir?" she asked Martin over her shoulder.

"No, thank you," he said, and she disappeared into the back of the house.

"Papá is coming! Papá is coming!" the children sang as they skipped back into the room and followed where their mother had gone.

Seeing their carefree play made Martin's heart ache to see his own kids again. It had been almost eight months now. *Far too long.*

Roberto Calderon emerged from the corridor, yawning and pulling on a white tank. His arms and shoulders bulged with muscles from manual labor, and he wore the same dark trousers Martin had seen him wear at the dockyards.

His eyes widened when he saw Martin. "Mr. Smith."

"Good morning, Roberto," Martin said. "I am sorry to come to your home without invitation, but I need to speak with you about something important."

Martin was using just about the full extent of his Spanish vocabulary in this conversation, and he wasn't sure how successfully he would be able to convey the more complex portions of his plan. But it would not have been possible to get Antonio Rivera out of the embassy with him this morning, and unfortunately Martin had other things that needed done this afternoon that depended first upon Roberto's agreement.

Roberto's wife came back into the room, carrying a steaming cup of coffee that she handed to her husband. The two children trailed after her, the little girl now holding an infant on her hip. The baby was probably five or six months old, Martin supposed—old enough to hold its head up and look around while being held in one arm.

Roberto mumbled thanks to his wife, blew across the top of the cup, and took a sip. He touched the tops of his children's heads in turn, and then motioned for Martin to take a seat in a wooden chair. He took the chair opposite Martin, and the little boy and girl stood on either side of him, staring at the stranger in their home.

Seeing the four of them all in a row like that, Martin was struck at how unmistakably like their father all three children looked; they were a shade darker than he, and they had soft curls that he lacked, but the family resemblance was striking.

Roberto took another sip of his coffee, and then looked Martin squarely in the eyes. "What do you wish to discuss that is so important, Mr. Smith?"

Martin eyed the children. "Can we speak in private, Mr. Calderon?"

Roberto considered this for a few seconds, and then told the children to go to their mother and let Papá speak with the man alone.

Martin still wasn't sure how he was going to explain everything he wanted him to do. He had considered asking the young man to accompany him back to the embassy so that he could use Antonio as translator, but he dismissed that idea immediately. He didn't want to involve Antonio any deeper than he already was, and the last thing he wanted was for someone to tie Roberto to the embassy in any way.

"You work tomorrow night, yes?" Martin began. He could at least cement that in place before getting into anything else.

"Yes," Roberto answered, and took a longer drink of his coffee.

Martin looked up in thought, concentrating on the words he knew in Spanish that might convey what he wanted.

"Thank you for the information you provided the last two weekends," he began. Roberto nodded in acknowledgement, so Martin proceeded as best he could with his limited vocabulary. "I can pay more money than those times—much more money—for something special that you can do for me. With permission, it is a little bit dangerous, but only a little."

A strange look came to Roberto Calderon's hazel eyes, and he glanced quickly toward the back of the house. "We should not talk about it here," he said, quietly. "We will go to the tavern down the street."

Martin was leery of discussing this in a tavern, not sure how crowded it would be. "We need to talk someplace private."

"Of course," Roberto whispered. He downed the last of the coffee in his cup, got up from the chair, and disappeared into the back of the house. Martin heard a few words exchanged between Roberto and his wife, but couldn't understand what they were saying.

Roberto returned a few minutes later, buttoning up the front of a coarse blue shirt with a narrow band collar. He did not button it all the way, but left the top open. He motioned Martin out the front door.

It was a mild fall day, and the sun was shining, so Martin didn't question that Roberto had not grabbed a jacket.

Seeing no one within ear shot on the street, Martin resumed explaining what he needed. "The men who work with the boats, the ones that you saw with the boat that had the things that weren't written…" He was putting this badly, he knew, but he really couldn't do much better.

An amused smile spread across Roberto's lips. "Yes, I understand."

Martin considered his words carefully. "I think another boat will come soon. I need to know the ships there this weekend, I need to know the names. Can you do something for me?"

Roberto's cheeks flushed, and he looked around. "Yes, of course. What do you want for me to do?"

Martin wasn't sure how to describe it in Spanish. "I think I should make a picture for you." He didn't know how to say to destroy it after, so he mimed the motions of tearing up a piece of paper.

After a fleeting flicker of amusement, Roberto's expression grew serious again, and he nodded gravely. "Show me what I need to do."

13

Friday, April 26

It was nearly dark when Martin left the embassy by the back door at the end of the work day. With the advancing season, it was almost dark if you left any later than five-thirty. Tonight, however, that worked to his advantage.

It was a chilly night, but he had purposely left his overcoat behind, since it was a lighter color than his dark blue suit. He didn't want to be followed from the embassy.

For several blocks, he stuck to side streets with few pedestrians and even fewer street lamps, taking a winding route, and he stuck to the shadows along the edge of the buildings. His gaze darted around non-stop, alert for any curious eyes watching.

He reached the *Ante Puerto* in less than twenty minutes, and stood in a darkened doorway to put on a pair of false eyeglasses. Then he took a fake mustache from his pocket and stuck it to his upper lip. It wasn't a total disguise, but different enough that a stranger couldn't pick him out of a lineup.

The street along the edge of the dockyards was still busy with warehouse workers, but he emerged from the shadows and marched across the street with a deliberately purposeful stride.

If you act like you belong somewhere, he knew, usually everyone assumes that you do.

He found the office, a squat grimy brick building with a steel door and a single window. The lights were on, and he saw several people inside. He pounded his fist against the door, and a man inside shouted in Spanish for him to enter.

A middle-aged woman in a navy blue dress with white polka dots sat behind a typewriter just inside the door, and she greeted him in Spanish. *"Buenas tardes, señor."*

"Buenas tardes, señora. Tienen alguien que habla Inglés?"

"I speak English, sir," a man's voice said behind the secretary, and Martin saw a middle aged man with thinning black hair rise from his chair. He wore a white shirt and black necktie, but no jacket. "How may I help you?"

Martin pulled a heavy stock envelope from inside his jacket pocket. It was unsealed, and he removed a folded letter, typed on thick stock paper with official-looking letterhead, and handed it to the man. "My name is Hiram Jones, and I'm an agent for the Ajax Shipping Company out of Philadelphia. That is my authorization from the Customs Authority to inspect the SS Lehigh while it's loaded tonight."

Martin stood with rigidly straight posture, taking full advantage of his height and broad shoulders as he stood in front of the man, who looked sufficiently impressed at the letter. It was a brilliant forgery, and Martin was pleased at the man's reaction.

"You said the SS Lehigh?" the man asked, handing the letter back to Martin.

"That's right. It's all there in the authorization."

The man gave him an apologetic look. "I am sorry, sir, but I am not familiar with that ship. I don't recall the name."

"It docked earlier today," Martin lied. "In fact, your men should be well along with loading the cargo by now. It's set to depart in a few hours."

The man looked embarrassed. "My apologies, sir. I usually have a good memory for ships. I will check the log book. One moment, please. You may sit, if you like."

"Thank you, but I prefer to stand," Martin said, not willing to give up the advantage.

"Very good, sir. Just one moment, please."

The man crossed the office, muttering something in Spanish to a younger man at a desk that he passed. That man shook his head, replying "*No, no lo conozco.*"

Martin understood the reply, and resisted the urge to chuckle, keeping a straight face. *Of course you don't know it.*

The first man grabbed a large open log book from on top of a shelf in the back of the room, and ran his finger down the pages. He flipped the page twice, repeating the motion. He mumbled something to himself, shaking his head, and flipped back and forth, rescanning the pages.

At last he walked back to where Martin stood, still shaking his head. "I am sorry, sir, that ship has not docked here today, or yesterday. I thought perhaps it has been delayed, but I do not see it listed for tomorrow or the next day, either."

Martin gave him a withering scowl. "What sloppy record-keeping you have," he snapped, with just the right amount of indignation. "That ship arrived at one-forty-eight this afternoon. I have confirmation right here. See for yourself." He reached into his jacket again and removed a thinner piece of paper, folded into quadrants. He unfolded the fake telegram and thrust it at the man in front of him.

He watched the color drain from the man's face as he read the message—a single sentence in Spanish first, then repeated in English:

```
SS LEHIGH ARRIVED ANTE PORT OF BUENOS
AIRES TODAY 13:48
```

The purported "telegram" showed the sender as the Customs Office at the *Ante Puerto.* That had been Sloan's idea. Martin reluctantly agreed that it was brilliant.

"Well? Where is my ship?" Martin demanded, and the man looked up from the telegram, ashen, and he visibly swallowed.

"I—I don't know, Mr. Jones. I have no explanation—I don't—"

"Can you find my ship, or can't you?" Martin's voice raised loud enough that everyone in the office stopped what they were doing and watched.

The man stiffened, and his lips tightened into a thin line. "Of course, sir. We will locate it immediately." He motioned to the younger man he had addressed earlier, and instructed him in Spanish to go out and locate the SS Lehigh.

"I'll go with him," Martin said as the young man slipped into a jacket.

"I am sorry, sir," the first man said, looking and sounding apologetic. "Only authorized persons may enter the docks. Please wait here."

Martin waved the fake letter in the man's face. "I have authorization right here."

The man looked like he was trying desperately to stay patient, and barely succeeding. "Yes, you have authorization to inspect that ship—once we locate it."

Martin crossed his arms, stretched to his fullest height, and glared down at the man. "Do I need to file a complaint with your superiors? First you lose my ship, and then you won't allow me to come along when it's located. This is outrageous!"

The man's cheeks flushed red. "I cannot apologize enough, Mr. Jones. If you will please allow us to find your ship—"

"I don't trust your people to find it. How do I know he's not the one who lost it in the first place?"

"Sir, please—"

Martin pointed his finger at the man's face, and prayed he wasn't overplaying it. "Either you let me go along to find my missing ship, or I'll cable my corporate headquarters in Philadelphia to deduct twenty-five percent from the payment as compensation for your incompetence."

The young man waiting by the door with his jacket said something to the other man in Spanish, sounding exasperated.

Martin understood few of the young man's words, but he imagined he'd said something along the lines of "Just let him come along already, or he'll never shut up."

The man in charge looked about ready to throw his hands in the air. He nodded to the young man at the door.

"Very well, sir, you may go with him." His tone as well as the hard look on his face said that he had reached his limit.

Martin put his hat on, gave the man a crisp nod and a curt "Thank you," and followed the younger man out the door.

The clerk carried a piece of paper and a pencil, and as they passed each wharf he wrote down the name and identification number of the ships moored on either side of the dock. *"Para verificación,"* he explained.

Martin nodded in silence. It stood to reason he would do that. With any luck, Martin would be long gone by the time the young man returned to the office to compare his notes to their master log.

And while they walked Martin noted the names of the ships in his own memory. He silently repeated them, in order, before each new ship.

A steam whistle blew three long blasts, signaling the shift change, and hundreds of men stopped working and headed *en masse* toward the exit. The young man from the office stopped and held up his hand, saying something to Martin in Spanish, of which he only understood the word for "Stop."

They waited as groups of men passed by, covered in dirt and grease. Martin watched as outgoing foremen handed clipboards to the incoming foremen. He scanned the crowd of night-shift workers preparing to enter, but didn't immediately see Roberto Calderon.

After the commotion of the departing day-shift ebbed, Martin and the young man from the office moved on to the next wharf while the new shift workers clocked in and headed to their respective work stations. They continued the process from before—the young man writing down the ship names and identification numbers, and Martin silently memorizing them in order.

A couple of docks later, Martin spied Roberto climbing into a forklift. They nodded to each other in silence, and Martin glanced at the office worker to make sure he hadn't seen.

Roberto fired up the forklift and drove it at full speed several blocks beyond Martin and the office clerk.

"Slow down!" the clerk shouted after Roberto, in Spanish. "Limit five kilometers per hour in work areas!" Martin guessed Roberto was moving at nearly three times that rate.

A moment later—just after the irritated clerk went back to looking at moored ships—a loud crash of metal on metal rang through the area.

Martin saw the collision out of the corner of his eye, having watched for it. Roberto swung the wheel of his forklift, steering it into the rear left side of an idling truck; he jumped out at the last minute and hit the ground in a controlled roll.

"Ay, Dios Mio!" the clerk said, and muttered an angry stream of rapid Spanish, of which Martin understood nothing. As the young man marched toward the incident and the shouting men that now surrounded it, he glanced back at Martin and added in slower, more enunciated Spanish, "Please wait here, Mr. Jones."

Martin counted to sixty in his head while he watched the clerk hurry toward the accident; then he scampered toward the next wharf, darting into the shadows of the Brazilian freighter moored there. He stood half-concealed behind an unmanned crane, and waited.

He had to be patient. He knew Roberto was arguing that the driver of the truck pulled out in front of him, an assertion that the driver was certain to dispute. As Martin had wanted, Roberto had arranged the incident in an area that was filled with workers. There would be plenty of potential witnesses, though Martin was sure most had been too busy with work to have actually seen it. Still, the clerk would have to call security, and take names and statements.

It was at least fifteen minutes before he saw the clerk moving back toward where he had left Martin. Roberto appeared a moment later, looking around before dashing down the deserted wharf toward where Martin waited.

"We do not have much time," Roberto whispered out of the side of his mouth to Martin, standing in front of the crane as if he were inspecting the gear shift in the cab.

"The men you saw with the river boat? You got their names?"

"Yes."

"They are working tonight, all of them?"

"All that I saw that night are here tonight," Roberto said with a slight shrug. "I do not know if others are involved."

"I understand," Martin said, removing a notepad and pencil from his pocket. "What are the names?"

Roberto gave seven names. Martin read them back, and Roberto nodded.

"I must get back to work," he said, and hurried away.

Martin slipped the pad and pencil back into his pocket and followed at a more leisurely pace, allowing distance to open between them. He was nearing the end of the dock when the clerk from the office appeared to his right, looking cross.

"Ah, there you are, Mr. Jones," the clerk said, his eyes narrowing in suspicion.

"*Buscando mi barco*," Martin said, more slowly than necessary, exaggerating his accent. As soon as the words were out of his mouth, he scolded himself for not inserting an erroneous *"por"* after the verb, to solidify the effect.

The clerk gave him a doubtful look, but said nothing as he motioned them forward once again.

Martin had hoped to be gone before the clerk returned; he'd supposed the clerk would have returned to the office after the incident, and at least momentarily have forgotten about Martin. Now he would have to improvise.

It was strangely quiet now, with no one around. That seemed odd. He heard a man whistle above them, to his left, and he glanced up to see a bearded sailor in a blue and white striped shirt on the deck of the Brazilian freighter, on the starboard side of the stern, looking down toward the ground somewhere in front of Martin and the clerk, waving his arm in a wide arc over his head.

It took Martin a second to register that the arc originated at their position, and ended in the direction they were headed.

Too late, he saw the figures of two large men emerge from the shadow of a small shack less than twenty yards in front of them. The floodlight on the corner of the shack illuminated the area, but it was behind them, casting their faces in shadows. Flat caps further obscured the tops of their faces, and he saw them raise their neckerchiefs over their chins and mouths.

Martin had only a second to take on a defensive stance, but the clerk to his right seemed oblivious. When the young man opened his mouth to say something, one of the men punched him in the jaw and sent him sprawling.

Martin faced off with the other one, and raised his arm to block a punch. He lowered his shoulders and plowed forward into his attacker's midsection, sending them both to the ground. Martin used the momentum to land on top, but before he could land a blow his opponent's legs clamped around his waist so tightly he thought he might break in half, and the next thing he knew he was being swung sideways.

He kept his head enough to lean away from the direction of the fall. Still, the left side of his face scraped the pavement.

But his head had not landed hard enough to concuss him and knock him out. He managed to land an elbow in his attacker's crotch, and the leg clamp immediately released.

He jumped to his feet too fast, and the blood rush made him woozy for a second. As he regained his equilibrium, he felt the tickle of blood flowing into his eyebrow.

He saw the clerk staggering away, holding his side and limping toward the office without looking back. The thug who had beaten up the clerk was now striding toward Martin. He stepped over his companion, who still writhed on the ground, clutching his crotch.

Martin started to raise his fists when he was grabbed from behind. Unseen men held his arms back, while the oncoming thug slammed his fist into Martin's right side—once, twice, three times. Martin felt lightning behind his eyes as the pain radiated up from his ribs.

"You should not have snooped here," a voice hissed into his right ear as he crumpled against the arms holding him. "This area is forbidden. Remember that. Leave, while you are still able."

They released him, and he felt someone shove him in the back, sending him careening forward. He was able to stop his fall. He scraped his palms on the rough pavement, but the pain in his right ribs and his left temple were all he could feel.

He took half a second to note that his fake glasses had disappeared, lost in the scuffle, but his fake mustache was still glued in place. He noticed his hat lying on the pavement a short distance in front of him, and he pushed himself forward, rising and getting a running start, scooping up the hat as he passed.

"Don't come back," he heard in Spanish as he hurried away, suddenly aware of the eerie absence of any dock workers milling about in the area.

Martin didn't look backward as he ran toward the exit and into the dark streets. He didn't pause until he reached the far corner of a quiet warehouse, where he took a moment to catch his breath and reach inside his jacket to make sure his notepad was still in the pocket.

He was relieved to find it still there.

A trickle of moisture ran out of his eyebrow and stung the corner of his eye. He wiped it away, and noticed blood on the back of his hand. He took his handkerchief and pressed it against his brow while he caught his breath.

At least he had the list of names. He'd lock it in his office tonight, give it to Sloan tomorrow, and they'd start looking into each of them.

That meant the night had been a success.

14

Martin's ribs ached as he climbed the stairs from the subway station and walked gingerly toward home.

Two blocks from his building, he rounded a corner and saw Rosa Linda on the opposite side of the street with a group of three other young women, dressed for going out. She spotted him, and called his name, waving.

He waved back, trying not to raise his arm too much, and winced at the pain that shot through his side.

Rosa Linda spoke to her friends, and then hurried across the street. As she neared, he saw a concerned look in her eyes.

"Are you alright, Mr. Schuller? Did you hurt yourself?" she asked. Then her eyes widened when she saw the cut above his eye, and the discoloration he had no doubt was there as well. "*Ay, Dios mío!*" she exclaimed. Then in English, "Martin, what happened?"

"It's not important," he said, trying to sound unconcerned.

"*No es importante? Ay caramba, mi amor*—how can you say it is not important? You are hurt. How did this happen?"

He felt a flutter in his stomach at the words *mi amor*. "I was just in the wrong place at the wrong time." It wasn't untrue. Seeing her anxiety clearly unassuaged, he added, "A couple of thugs mugged me."

"'Thugs mugged?' What is that?"

He had to smile at her confusion. "A thug is a big bad fellow. Mugged means robbed on the street."

"Did you call the police?"

He put his hand on her arm, spoke soothingly. "It's alright. It's taken care of, don't worry."

"Mmmm." Her lips drew into a thin line. "Come, let me help you. Take me to your home, I will take care of your cut."

"It's not necessary," he said. "You should go have fun with your friends, I'll be fine. I can clean my own cut."

She muttered a rapid string of Spanish that sounded blistering in its incomprehensible brutality. The only word he picked out was *"estúpido"* amid a long string of other sounds. He started to protest, but she cut him off. "Go! Take me with you, and let me take care of you."

"Yes, ma'am," he muttered, and took her arm.

Once inside his apartment, Martin gingerly took off his jacket and hung it on the coat rack under his hat. He fingered a small rip in the side seam, judging that it could be fixed easily enough by a good tailor. Then he showed her the first aid kit in the bathroom.

"Come along, Mr. Stubborn Man," Rosa Linda said, grabbing the knot of his necktie and tugging it loose. "You can't let me nurse you if I cannot see where you are hurt." She began unbuttoning the front of his white dress shirt.

He helped by untucking it, and when she'd finished with the buttons he tugged it off and laid it across the back of the commode. He saw that she noticed him wince as he took off his shirt, but he was relieved she didn't point it out.

He wore a sleeveless white tank under the dress shirt, and she inspected the bruise on his right shoulder.

"Bath cloth?" she asked.

"Washcloth." He grabbed the one that he draped over the faucet of his bathtub. She ran it under cold water in the sink, and placed it against his right cheek and eye. The coolness of it relieved the soreness.

"Hold it there," she instructed, and then soaked a cotton ball with rubbing alcohol. The alcohol stung as she dabbed at the cut above his eyebrow, and an involuntary grunt escaped him.

"If it stings, you know it is working," she said. "My mother always said that to me and to my brothers when we were little children."

"Was that supposed to make it easier?" he asked, allowing a wry half-smile.

She swatted at his hand. "Don't be rude." But he saw amusement tugging at the corners of her mouth.

She took the washcloth back and rewet it, then put it against the bruise on his shoulder. Then her fingers trailed slowly down his side, as if feeling each bruised rib. Her eyes rested on the faint pinkish stain on the fabric.

"You hurt here?" she asked.

He shrugged, and she gave him a crooked frown, the type that said she knew what he was not saying. So she tugged his undershirt up and took a look herself.

"*Ay, caramba.*" Then she looked up at his face. "Off," she ordered.

He reluctantly removed his undershirt, not a comfortable task, and his ribs screamed at him for it.

In the mirror behind her, he saw a patch of raw-looking abrasion on his right ribs. Rosa Linda dug around in his first aid kit, removing more cotton balls, and soaked them in rubbing alcohol. He gritted his teeth against the sting, and noticed that the cotton balls came away pink. She continued cleaning the wound for several minutes, and the sting of the alcohol eventually became so chronic as to seem tolerable.

When she finished cleaning the abrasion, she taped a bandage over the wound. Then she rewet the wash cloth and cooled the surrounding bruise, careful not to wet the bandage.

"Thank you," he said, quiet.

"You're welcome, Martin." She held his gaze for a moment, and then her eyes traced down his bare torso.

While her left hand held the cool damp washcloth against his ribs, her right hand moved up to his chest, circling the pectoral muscles. Then she ran her fingernails over the dusting of short blond hairs.

He put his hand on top of hers at the center of his chest, right over his pounding heart, and looked into her warm brown eyes. She stared back, unblinking, and he thought he saw want in her expression. It had been a long time, but he was pretty sure he still recognized that look.

He kissed her. The wash cloth dropped from her hand, and she put her arms around him and rubbed his back. He pulled her to him, not too tightly, due to his bruised ribs, but enough that the smooth fabric of her dress pressed against his bare stomach.

They kissed for a long moment, and he moved his hand up to the middle of her back and unfastened the back of her dress. It went loose around her shoulders.

She slid her hands between them and frantically tugged at the buckle of his belt, never breaking their kiss, and then worked her fingers on the buttons at the fly of his pants.

He pulled her dress up over her hips, and let his hands rest on the soft skin above the waist of her panties for a moment, before pulling the dress higher, breaking their kiss so he could get it off over her head.

"Ay, Dios mío," she muttered, wrapping her arms around herself—for warmth or for modesty, he wasn't sure. He held back for a moment, and admired the beauty of her shape as she stood there in her underwear and brassiere.

Then she rushed forward, throwing her arms around his neck, pressing her body against his, and kissing him again. He winced and grunted at the pressure on his ribs, and she relaxed her embrace without pulling away or stopping her kiss.

She was panting when she pulled her lips away a moment later. "Do you have—ay—do you have one of those things—what is the word?"

She means a rubber, he realized, and suddenly his stomach was jumping with butterflies. "No," he said. He hadn't owned a condom in years. Becky had preferred a diaphragm after Stevie was born, and since the divorce—well, there just hadn't been a need.

And he had no idea where to buy them in any case. *Damn it!*

"*Ayyyyyy...*" she groaned, visibly deflating in front of him.

He released a long, slow breath. Maybe this was for the best. She was ten or eleven years younger than him. And they worked together. This was probably saving them from making a big mistake.

But Rosa Linda had a different take on the situation. She recovered, and sauntered back to him. "Then tonight we can only do this," she whispered. She slid her hand down the front of his boxer shorts and wrapped her fingers around him. With her other hand, she took his hand and guided it down the front of her panties.

His breath came short and fast. It had been almost a year since the last time he had been intimate with anyone. *What the hell*, he thought, and kissed her until they were both spent.

Four miles to the southeast, in a tiny apartment in the *Barrio Almagro*, Javier Velasco got up from the narrow bed and slipped into a pair of underwear—the fashionable new imported style known as "briefs" or "jockey shorts"—and stepped over to the stove on the far side of the room. He struck a match, lit the burner, and put a kettle on.

The husky forty to forty-five year old man lounging naked on Javier's bed was in no hurry to get up and get dressed. "I checked the time, we still have twenty-five minutes," he said.

It was true, Javier knew. The man had paid for a full hour, rather than ala carte services, though most didn't insist on taking every single minute of their hour. This one—Javier only knew him as Paco—always did. Javier slipped his fingers into the waist of his jockey shorts, and slowly and seductively slipped them down over his hips, finally letting them fall to the floor.

"Ay, you are a beautiful one," Paco said with obvious appreciation, his eyes roaming over Javier's form while his hand slid down to his own groin.

If the middle-aged fellow could arouse himself enough to perform again, Javier would eat his own shorts. But an hour had been paid for, so Javier would oblige and at least give Paco something to sear into his memory for when he had to go home to his wife. He closed his eyes and rubbed his hands across his chest and stomach.

The kettle began to whistle. Javier opened his eyes and bent down to pull up his underwear, but Paco stopped him.

"No, boy—do it naked."

Javier relented. He didn't like to go near the stove uncovered, but he could use caution if needed. He stood a few inches farther away than usual while he turned off the gas burner, and had to lean over the counter to pour the tea into two cups.

He carried the cups across the small room, and set one of them on the bedside table next to Paco.

"Go back to what you started before," Paco said, and Javier obliged. He closed his eyes, and ran his hands over his body. He leaned his head back as his hands slid down toward his penis, to give Paco a better show.

And he let his mind browse the collection of fantasies he kept stored for these occasions. He had several favorites that always did the trick—Roberto Calderon and a forklift was one—but tonight he settled on one of the newest additions.

The blond American wasn't Javier's usual type, but he was ruggedly handsome, very masculine, and Javier was certain that underneath his fancy business suit he had a sexy body. At least, in his imagination he did, and that was what mattered right now.

Mr. Schuller had large hands, and Javier imagined that his own hands were Mr. Schuller's. That did the trick.

"Oh, that is so hot," he heard Paco say from nearby, but he repeated the line in his own head in Mr. Schuller's voice, complete with the sexy North American accent. Paco's rough hand cupped Javier's right buttock, but he let that be part of the fantasy with Mr. Schuller.

This was no different from what he provided the men who paid him for his time and services. He gave them something to fantasize about when they closed their eyes while making love to their wives, so that they could see it through. He had enough experience now that he could substitute any man's face, any man's body, into any sexual situation that excited him at the moment.

This one proved to be one of his best fantasies, and it carried him through the rest of Paco's time.

"That was amazing," Paco said after he had gotten dressed, and placed one hundred pesos on the table. He put his hands on Javier's shoulders, and kissed him on the cheek. "I will see you again soon, you little devil."

He left Javier's apartment with a smile on his face. That was nearly as satisfying to Javier as the one hundred pesos. Nearly.

Javier knew he would never support himself writing poetry, but he needed the time to be able to write it or he would go mad. That was why he worked as a waiter at a café in upscale Belgrano instead of in an office, but it didn't pay quite enough to afford his own apartment without having to share the rent.

So he took on customers. It was a means to an end, and it worked.

It had started by accident. He had been lounging in the grass of the Paseo de la Victoria off Avenida Rivadavia one hot afternoon after school in November 1936, when he was seventeen. He had taken his shirt off and lain back in the grass with his eyes closed, and after a while a shadow passed over him. He looked up to see a man standing over him, and he recognized him as someone who had been sitting alone on a park bench when Javier got there.

"You are a pretty one," the man said. He was fairly young and pretty himself, Javier considered, with wavy black hair and piercing blue eyes. "How much?"

"Pardon?"

"Twenty pesos?" the young man asked, glancing around before taking the money from his pocket and showing it to Javier—along with what he pulled through his open fly.

Young Javier was stunned into silence, a strange sensation gripping his belly—both repulsed and aroused at the same time.

"Thirty pesos?" the man said, taking another bill from his pocket.

So Javier had gone with him, and had sex with the man in the back seat of a Hispano-Argentina H6, parked at the back of a nearby alley.

Intense shame washed over him afterward, and when he got home he ran straight to his bedroom, shoved the thirty pesos in the back of a drawer, flopped on his bed and cried.

And yet, when he slept that night, he dreamt of the encounter in the back seat of the car, and his arousal was undeniable.

He fantasized about it often after that, and on many afternoons that summer he returned to the park to seek out the man. Eventually he encountered him again. Luis—he eventually learned the man's name—became his first regular customer, meeting weekly in the park and ending up naked in the back seat of the H6.

Javier would have done it for free. It felt good, it was exciting, and Luis was handsome and so mature—twenty-five years old, he learned, with a job in an office. The thirty pesos Javier got after each encounter seemed like manna from heaven.

But then he fell in love. He started going to the Paseo de la Victoria every afternoon in hopes of seeing Luis there, but he was usually disappointed. What shocked him was how intensely that disappointment hurt. He would mope around his parents' apartment at night, and his father assumed he was in love with a girl who had another boy. Javier let his parents believe that.

But those days when Luis was there, waiting for him in the park, he felt such joy he thought his heart would soar into the sky and take him with it. And when they joined together in the back seat of Luis's car, Javier felt his feelings overflow, filling him with warmth and passion.

And then one afternoon in early March 1937, as the new school year was about to begin—Javier's final year in school—he allowed himself to say "I love you" while Luis was inside him.

That created an awkward moment, when they both held very still. Then Luis had closed his eyes and forged through, almost frantic, afterward saying nothing while they got dressed. Javier felt intense fear gnawing at his belly.

Then, after giving Javier his thirty pesos, Luis took the opportunity to put his hand on the boy's cheek for a few seconds. "You sweet, stupid boy," he said, and then opened Javier's door.

That was the last Javier ever saw of him.

The biggest lesson he took from it was to never, *ever* fall in love. That final year of school in 1937, he found he could easily identify the boys whose eyes lingered just a second too long on his when they passed in the hall, or who looked surreptitiously at places they shouldn't; and he used that to maneuver them into situations that led to exploration. He became very experienced.

That was also how he and Antonio Rivera came to be friends.

But Javier had learned more than one lesson from that summer, and after graduating from school the following December, he knew how to get money if there was no better way.

And so for the last two and half years, it had been one of his most reliable streams of income.

Antonio knew about Javier's side business—it was an open secret in the bohemian circle they fell into after leaving school—though they never talked about it. For that, Javier was grateful. It was rare to find a friend who would not judge you for something like that. Javier knew he was lucky to have a friend like Antonio.

He had suspected at one time that Antonio might be in love with him, but Javier frequently mentioned his aversion to love as a matter of course, so he felt no guilt about leading Antonio on, no matter how many times they ended up in the same bed after a late night at the *Quartier Latin*.

Besides, it was good to have a real friend who could also provide additional benefits from time to time. They both benefited.

But that Mr. Schuller—Javier had known him from the café in Belgrano for several months now, and he never once got the feeling that Mr. Schuller was the type of man who held any interest in men. So when Antonio brought him into the *Quartier Latin* the other night, it had been a surprise in more than one way.

An intriguing surprise.

Javier wondered if Antonio were having an affair with the handsome American. Surely he would say so to his good friend. Wouldn't he?

Javier slipped off his jockey shorts and lay back on his bed. The smell of male sex still hung in the air, and he closed his eyes and imagined himself with Antonio and Mr. Schuller, the three of them in the same big bed at some fancy downtown hotel.

This would be his new favorite fantasy.

15

Monday, April 29

"I'm getting nowhere," Sloan declared as he marched into Martin's office unannounced that afternoon.

"The missing *Abwehr* agents up north? Or the illegal shipments?"

"Both," Sloan said with a frown. "But I meant the missing German agents, specifically."

"The trail went cold?"

"Yep. They seem to have disappeared without a trace. Local police claim no sightings of any foreign newcomers. The Argentine Federal police say they haven't received any tips from citizens up there, either."

Martin wasn't exactly shocked. A tad disappointed, but not shocked. "Maybe that river boat I identified will lead them to the hidden agents."

Sloan snorted. "Unless someone's covering it up."

Martin had wondered that himself. Local officials could be bribed to keep silent, which would eliminate the most obvious and reliable sources of information. Argentine Federal law enforcement might not have the resources—or the drive—to go up there beating the bushes to see what might fly out.

"If so, there's not much we can do about it."

"Unless we head up there ourselves, and do some old-fashioned detective work," Sloan said.

Martin cringed a little on the inside. His job here in Argentina was more complex and broad than just investigating German agents doing illegal acts in the name of their Third Reich; unlike his previous position at the Office of the Chief Special Agent in Washington, he wasn't able to set aside time to do much investigative work outside of the capital.

"I'm afraid you'll be on your own up there," he said. "I can't spare the time away from the embassy."

Sloan looked at him with a curious and mildly surprised expression. "I thought you'd jump at the chance to get out of the office."

Ordinarily, I might. But those days are over. "It's just not feasible, with everything I have to do here."

Sloan shrugged. "It's possible the Argentines will get the job done on their own, I suppose. We might not have to trouble ourselves."

Martin wasn't fooled. He knew Sloan was disappointed. He wanted to get up there and catch the bad guys. Martin supposed he should be flattered that Sloan wanted to include him in the first place.

"We have sources here in Buenos Aires that could net us more leads," Martin reminded him. "How are you coming along with grooming new informants?"

Sloan's eyes narrowed. "You know that takes time."

Martin chuckled. Of course he knew that. He just enjoyed the opportunity to needle Sloan about it, since he disapproved of Martin's informants. "Keep me posted."

"Uh huh," Sloan said, and left Martin's office.

**

Rosa Linda knocked on his open office door shortly after five o'clock.

He smiled when he saw her standing in his doorway. "I was hoping you'd stop by," he said, rising from his chair and walking over to meet her. "I'm sorry we never got much chance to talk after Friday night," he whispered when he reached her. He touched her arm briefly, after making sure no one was watching from the hall.

"You were very busy today," she replied. "You came and left many times."

"That's true," he said. "It was a busy day. And it would have been difficult for us to discuss it here, even if I had the time to. Maybe we can go to a café in a little bit, and talk about things over a cup of coffee."

"That is a good idea. But before that, will you come to the supply closet and help me get something off of the top shelf? The other girls have already left, so I can't have one of them hold a stool for me, and I'm afraid to do it by myself."

"Of course," he said, and followed her toward a supply closet around the corner.

She pulled a cord to turn on the bare overhead light bulb, illuminating the small room filled with folders, pens, pencils, steno pads, typewriter paper, and other supplies. She stepped onto a stool and stretched to reach a box of paper on the top shelf.

Martin's hands instinctively went to her waist.

She stepped down from the stool, but then placed the box of paper on a lower shelf and pulled the closet door shut.

"Let's have more to talk about with coffee than only Friday night," she murmured, and kissed him while unbuckling his belt with one hand, and unbuttoning the fly of his pants with the other hand.

After a moment of panic that they might get caught, Martin reasoned that none of the men still working in the offices would come to the supply closet themselves, and the girls had all left for the day. He allowed himself to get caught up in the moment.

Thirty minutes later, they were seated at a café along Avenida Santa Fe not far from the American embassy, two steaming cups of coffee on the table in between them. The Argentine work day would be ending soon, but for now the café was not full.

"I hope that you aren't uncomfortable with what happened Friday," Martin began, knowing instantly how stupid that sounded in light of what transpired in the supply closet a short time before.

She looked amused, but waited for him to continue.

"I guess what I mean is—I hope that you aren't uncomfortable working together after the way we have behaved behind closed doors recently."

"I am not uncomfortable, Martin."

He felt relieved. "Good," he breathed. *One down.* The next question was trickier. "How do you feel about what we've done? I mean—what are your intentions for us?" He felt his cheeks flush.

"I feel good about what we have done, Martin," she said, reaching across the table to take his hand. She stared into his eyes. "I have wanted to for many months. You could tell, yes?"

Martin didn't admit that he hadn't really, until recently; in retrospect, the signs had been there. "I thought so, but I wasn't completely certain."

"You were afraid to be wrong," she guessed. She exhaled in frustration. "Young women are not supposed to tell men how we feel about them. We are supposed to give them little signs so that they pursue us. With some men, it is easy. You are the frustrating kind of man who does not react immediately. So I had to be bold."

He smiled at the memory from Friday night.

She reached her other hand across the table and placed it over their clasped hands. "You do not think me *too* bold, do you? It is a big danger for a young woman to be bold like that. A man might think we are too—what is the word?"

"Too forward?" he offered.

"Too forward," she repeated, slowly, testing out the words. She seemed unsatisfied.

"Too loose?" he suggested, immediately blushing at the fact that he said that word out loud to a female. When he was younger his father would have knocked him up the side of the head for saying that to a woman.

"What does it mean, 'too loose?'"

He blushed harder, and her eyes narrowed as she stared at him, bemused by his reaction. "Well, it's what is said about a woman who—well—who does what we did Friday night a *lot*."

A flash of anger crossed her golden brown eyes, and she stiffened, pulling her hands away from his. She let out a blistering string of angry Spanish words that flew by far too rapidly for him to comprehend any of it.

He held his hands up for her to stop. "Whoa, whoa, whoa—that is not what I think at all. I just—I thought that was the phrase you were looking for. You were asking me if I thought that about you after Friday, and the answer is no, I don't think that."

For starters, it was far too outdated of a concept.

And with that, his mind flooded with angry memories of boys in his high school saying that about Susan after she disappeared, sent away to wherever it was that they sent girls in trouble. He'd punched another boy in the mouth after school one day for saying that, which had shut them up—but it only meant they waited to say it after he was out of earshot.

He cleared his head of the past and concentrated on the beautiful young woman sitting across from him now. "You never answered my question," he said.

"What question?"

The bigger question, he thought, and took a breath. "What do you want to happen between us? Are we just having some laughs? Or is this something more than that?"

She looked a little confused. "Having some laughs? Like what they say in American movies?"

"It means being casual, not serious."

"Oh," she said, comprehension dawning. "You want me to be the bold girl and say what you should say to me as a man."

That stung for a moment, but he chalked it up to cultural differences—one of the warning bells that had been going off in his brain for weeks now. There were bound to be more misunderstandings from their different backgrounds, he knew.

"I like women who can articulate what they want."

She leaned back and crossed her arms. "I like men who say what they want."

Impasse. Against his better judgement, he heard himself saying, "I don't want to be casual. I want you to be mine, and I'll be yours."

A sly grin spread across her face, and then she beamed at him, and reached across and took both of his hands in hers. "I am glad."

Martin felt relieved that she felt the same way. He'd been confident she did, mostly, but it was still good to hear from her mouth.

Now I've got to figure out where the hell to buy rubbers in this damned country, he thought. That was a surmountable obstacle. The bigger issue was to figure out how to manage this when his kids came in June.

He had no idea how to handle that.

16

Wednesday, May 8

Numbers. Always numbers. Commander Gustav Fiedler was an efficient man, in the best Prussian military tradition, but he was not a numbers man. Military efficiency and effectiveness were rarely synonymous with numerical precision. These meetings to discuss numbers bored him immensely.

And he grew easily frustrated at the waste of time.

Captain Nieburh, on the other hand, seemed to relish going over columns of numbers in excruciating detail. Today, however, he was unexpectedly eager to rush through them, and after an hour he announced the reason.

"I have orders from the High Command in Berlin," he said, swelling with pride. "Top secret—no one is to repeat any of this outside of this room. Violations will be dealt with severely."

Fiedler sat up even straighter than usual, alert.

Satisfied that he had everyone's undivided attention now, Captain Dietrich Nieburh—German Naval Attaché to Argentina—revealed the latest war plans, involving tight cooperation between the Wehrmacht, the Luftwaffe, and the Kriegsmarine.

Murmurs of excitement rippled through the room, occupied by German military staff attached to the embassy, and a small contingent of the highest-ranking civilian members of the embassy staff—limited to the ambassador himself, and his inner circle. All had high security clearance.

145

Finally! Fiedler thought with glee. *The Fatherland will have vengeance for the last war.*

He thought of his own father, killed at the Somme in 1916, leaving young Gustav to care for his mother and sisters at the age of fifteen. He thought of the family fortune squandered in less than five years by his mother's greedy brother, who took advantage of young Gustav's inexperience.

But the French were also to blame. Their crippling reparations after 1919 had prompted the Socialist fools in charge of the new republic to print money nonstop, sending inflation through the roof. Even with faulty management, his father's legacy could have lasted twice as long if not for that unbelievable inflation. And for that, the Socialists and the French were to blame.

The Reich had already suppressed the SPD—*Sozialdemokratische Partei* –at home, thanks to their great Leader.

And now they would finally take care of the French.

"These actions will increase the High Command's need for Argentina's mica, platinum, and industrial-grade diamonds," Nieburh said, looking toward Fiedler and those sitting beside him. "I expect the orders to triple at least. You men will lean on your suppliers to increase their deliveries. If necessary, we must broaden our base of suppliers. Questions?"

"Our suppliers will demand higher compensation," Fiedler said. "Additional suppliers will mitigate this, but not eliminate the increase entirely."

"Excellent point, Commander," the Naval Attaché replied, and Fiedler felt himself swell with pride. "This has been anticipated, and some increase in price will be tolerated to satisfy the need. We have been asked to hold this to as little as possible. Any increase of more than ten percent should be approved by my office. We are not to risk bankrupting the Reichsbank, yes?"

"Are we to risk unfulfilled orders because a bunch of Latin American mine operators refuse to cooperate with our price requirements?" one of the old Army men asked. He was a white-haired major in his early fifties, soft around the middle, who'd had his commission reactivated the previous September after twenty years of civilian life. Fiedler found him inefficient.

But what else would Fiedler expect from someone with tainted blood? Rumor had it that Josef Weinzapfel's paternal great-grandfather had been born a Jew in Darmstadt, and converted to Lutheranism in the 1830s in order to marry an Aryan girl. Being one eighth Jewish was not sufficient admixture to categorize the major as a *Mischling*, which would have rendered him ineligible for military service—one quarter was the threshold for that—but it did disqualify him for a prestigious Certificate of Aryan Blood. Fiedler was proud to carry his.

"I would suggest, Major Weinzapfel, that we should not allow ourselves any squeamishness in our methods of persuasion," he said, barely concealing his disdain.

"Well put, Fiedler," Captain Nieburh agreed with a nod. "All of you will do what you must. The Fatherland is depending on us."

Friday, May 10

Martin's telephone woke him at two-thirty in the morning, and he lugged himself out of his warm bed and threw on a robe as he trudged to the telephone in his living room.

"Hello?" he asked, and almost forgot to repeat it in Spanish.

"Mr. Schuller? This is Jack Townsend, Associated Press. I'm sorry to wake you again, but I know you want to hear the news."

Martin rubbed his face. "Did the Germans launch another invasion?" he asked. "Which country this time?"

"Four countries—Luxembourg, Belgium, the Netherlands, and France—all simultaneously. The reports coming over the wire are that it's a massive operation, launched at dawn—which was about an hour ago. Tanks, bombers, paratroopers, the whole shebang. If these reports are confirmed, it will shock the world."

Martin took a second to digest this information. "Any word on how many divisions are involved?"

"Yeah," Townsend said, a strange tone in his voice. "You're not going to believe it."

"Try me."

"There are some conflicting reports, of course, but the majority are putting it around a hundred and forty divisions."

Martin let out a low whistle.

"My thoughts exactly," Townsend said.

"I assume you've already called the French and British embassies?"

"You bet I did," Townsend said. "The French confirmed the invasion, but that was it. They have no official comment at this time. The British were even more tight-lipped, as you can imagine."

"They always are," Martin muttered.

"You can say that again," Townsend agreed. "I don't suppose you have a statement for me?"

Martin almost laughed out loud. "That's pretty bold, even for you, Mr. Townsend."

"I have to try. Deadline's coming up real quick."

"Yeah, I bet. Listen, if you give me some time to figure out what's going on, I'll see if they'll let me give you a scoop before everyone else at the briefing later."

"I'll take it. Gotta run now, the story's not going to write itself."

The line clicked dead, and Martin set down the receiver. "Damn it!"

**

If Martin thought the American embassy was a zoo the day of the invasions of Denmark and Norway—was that really only a month ago?—it was nothing compared to the buzz of activity there at seven o'clock this morning. It was still dark outside, a full hour before the start of business, and all American personnel had already arrived.

What perhaps surprised him the most was the presence of Juan-Carlos De la Tour, hurrying around to fulfill any requests that would normally fall to his staff.

"Ah, Mr. Schuller," he said when Martin passed him in the hall. He clasped his hands in front of his chest and spoke earnestly. "As I told Mr. *Davis* already, the secretaries and clerks have all been called in *early*, and they should begin arriving very *soon*. They are *all* prepared to work *late* tonight if that is *needed*. In the *mean*time, *please* let me know if there is *anything* I can do for you."

"Thank you, Mr. De la Tour, I will."

The day passed in a blur of phone calls and news reports. His contacts at the British Embassy, the French Embassy, and the German Embassy were all eager to speak with him and justify their positions, but also terribly short on time. It made for frantic conversations, trying to cram as much information into one moment as possible.

And all the while, reports over the wire services continued to fly out of the ticker on his desk:

French reserves called up.

British expeditionary forces dispatched to France and the Low Countries.

German tanks crunching their way through the "impenetrable" Ardennes Forest as if it were made of match sticks.

French and British forces engaging the Germans head-on in Belgium.

France preparing to issue conscription notices.

German forces in control of Luxembourg.

Before he knew it, it was six o'clock.

"Mr. Schuller?" Rosa Linda's voice caught him off guard and jolted him up from his immersion in the reports on his desk. His startled heart raced for a moment.

"Oh, I'm sorry, I didn't notice you there," he said, attempting a weak smile.

"You look exhausted, Martin," she said, quieter, stepping into the office.

He hated to admit that he was, but he just nodded without a word. He knew it was obvious.

"You should go home," she said.

He shook his head. "I've got too much to address yet this evening," he said. Seeing the concerned look on her face, he hastened to add, "But I won't stay too late, I promise. Why don't we meet for dinner tonight? Nine o'clock?"

"Yes, dinner," she said, and turned away, but looked back with the same concern clouding her golden brown eyes. "You need some rest before you eat. Don't work too late."

He attempted another weak smile, but with a touch more success this time. "I won't, I promise."

"All of the girls have been released to go home," she said. "Do you need me to do anything for you before I leave?"

He shook his head again. "No, thank you, dear."

She looked sad as she nodded and walked out the door.

"Wait!" he said, a little too loudly, stopping her in her tracks. He had half-stood when he called to her, and held that position awkwardly for a second before deciding to just stand up.

"Yes?" She looked at him, confused.

"There is something you can do for me before you leave," he said, tugging loose the knot of his neck tie. "Close the door."

Once the door was closed, she hurried to his side of the desk, and their lips met. His fingers flew as they opened the buttons of his shirt, and then he tugged the ends up from the waist of his pants. She unbuckled his belt and unbuttoned his fly while he pulled her dress up to her waist and then lifted her up to sit on his desk. He fished a condom out of his pocket without looking.

They never broke the kiss.

He barely got the condom in place in time, so hurried were they both. It was awkward and frantic, but also exciting, and incredibly cathartic.

It was over in two minutes, but they were both sweating and panting for breath.

"*Ay, Dios mío,*" she breathed, smoothing her hair with one hand and her dress with the other. "You were like a bull."

He chuckled and nodded, but looked down and concentrated on refastening his pants.

He walked her to the door. "I'll pick you up at nine o'clock," he said, and kissed her before opening the door for her to leave.

As luck would have it, Juan-Carlos De la Tour happened to be walking by at precisely that moment. He saw them, and his eyes narrowed. Rosa Linda blushed and looked at the ground, mumbling "Good night" and hurrying away.

De la Tour looked at Martin with an expression that bordered somewhere between scandalized, admiring, and outraged. "Mr. Schuller!" he began, flustered.

Martin looked De la Tour in the eye, held his finger in front of his pursed lips, and released a barely audible "Shh."

"But—"

Martin shook his head, never breaking eye contact, and after a few seconds De la Tour looked away. He pretended to be concerned with an invisible piece of lint on the arm of his suit jacket. He sniffed loudly as he again faced the direction he had been walking.

"We will discuss it on Monday," he said quietly as he walked past. "Good evening, Mr. Schuller."

Shit! Martin was furious with himself for being incautious. And why was he suddenly acting like a horny teenager again? He was thirty-two years old, he should be able to control himself better than this.

Now, their relationship was known—by Rosa Linda's boss.

Martin had no doubt they would indeed discuss it on Monday. He knew De la Tour's position, but he was not about to give in to it. Or allow the little man to report him.

17

Monday, May 13

"It is *unseemly!*" De la Tour sputtered after Martin told him that he was not about to stop seeing Rosa Linda.

"It is *private*," Martin said. "It is between Miss Bianchi and me. No one else need be concerned."

"Miss Bianchi is an *employee* of this *legation*," De la Tour said. He held his hands out in a pleading gesture. "You *must* consider my *position*, Mr. Schuller. I am *responsible* for the young men and *women* under my *management*. We *must* maintain at all *times* the appearance of *decorum* and *respectability*. If *anyone* were to find *out—*"

"No one will find out," Martin said.

De la Tour puffed up like a blowfish, and a deep frown furrowed his brow and turned his lips in an upside down U-shape. He struck the palm of his hand hard against his chest. "*I* found out. And if I did, then *others* may as well."

Martin knew the little man had a point. "That won't happen again. Friday was an unusual day, as you know. It was very trying, and we lost our heads. That will not be repeated, I assure you."

De la Tour looked barely placated. "I must speak with Mr. Davis about this." He sniffed. "I will get his decision about how I should proceed."

Martin banged his fist on the desk, and it echoed around his closed office, making the little man jump.

"I will not allow you to do that, Mr. De la Tour." Martin hadn't been this angry in months. "What Miss Bianchi and I do in our private time is none of your concern, and none of Mr. Davis's concern, either. I will not have you dragging our names through the mud."

De la Tour puffed up again. "It is my *duty*," he said.

Martin felt something snap inside him. There was nothing he hated more than a self-righteous attitude. He balled his right hand into a fist, and held it tightly in front of him, just above his desk. "If you ruin Miss Bianchi's reputation, or get her fired from her job, I won't be able to stop myself from knocking your block off."

De la Tour blanched and took a step back. "Mr. Schuller, let us remain *civilized* about this—"

"Shut up!" Martin snapped, and De la Tour fell silent. "If you drag our names through the mud, I'll drag yours there, too."

De la Tour swallowed hard. "What do you mean?"

"I don't think I'm the only one who has been 'inappropriate' with one of your employees, sir. If you tell Mr. Davis about my relationship with Miss Bianchi, I'll tell them about your relationships."

De la Tour feigned confidence, but it was as transparent as the lace doilies that decorated his desk. "My *dear* Mr. Schuller, it will surprise *no one* at this embassy that I prefer *men* to *women*. That is *hardly* unnoticed, I think."

"But perhaps it hasn't been noticed that you've carried on with some of the boys under your management." Martin watched De la Tour blanch again. "Pablo," he added, for emphasis.

"You cannot prove that."

"And you cannot prove that anything is going on between me and Miss Bianchi. You didn't actually see anything, did you?"

De la Tour cocked his head to the side and considered Martin for a moment. "You are a *most* fascinating man, Mr. Schuller. Do you play *chess*?"

Martin shook his head, silently waiting.

De la Tour forced a smile, and clasped his hands together. "I think we should call a *détente*, Mr. Schuller. We shall go back to the way things were *before* Friday evening."

"That's a wise decision, Mr. De la Tour," Martin said. "Good day, now."

After the little manager left, looking crushed at the brusque dismissal, Martin felt remorse for resorting to blackmail to get his way.

But it had worked.

Tuesday, May 14
Martin read the news report the next afternoon and put his forehead in his hand. The commander of the Dutch army had surrendered the Netherlands to the invading German army. After just four days of fighting. It was incredible.

The remnants of the Royal Dutch Navy had evacuated to England just prior to the surrender, taking with them most of the Dutch royal family.

There were reports that small groups of Dutch soldiers in the southwestern province of Zeeland were continuing to fight the Wehrmacht in small-scale actions. But with no hope of rescue by British naval forces, that was doomed from the start.

He thought of the minerals from Argentine mines, diverted by unknown operators, smuggled to Germany, and now powering the Wehrmacht's production as they blasted across Europe.

This was not good.

Saturday, May 25
"Thank you for agreeing to see me," Thomas Mayweather of the British Embassy said, rising from the park bench to shake Martin's hand.

"My pleasure," Martin said, his breath crystallizing in the air. It was a chilly morning, and he kept his hands in the pockets of his tan overcoat.

The sky was partly cloudy, but bits of sunshine came down from patches of blue sky. Mayweather wore a dark gray overcoat and brown leather gloves. This early on a Saturday—nine o'clock—the Plaza General San Martín was nearly deserted, just a few people walking dogs, widely scattered.

"I assume we're here to discuss the situation in Europe," Martin said.

"The deteriorating situation in Europe, Mr. Schuller," Mayweather said. "But yes, among other things. Come, let's stroll a while."

They walked toward the edge of the square, and strolled the perimeter. Martin waited for Mayweather to speak.

"The situation in France and Belgium has become dire," Mayweather said at last. "The Germans' drive to the channel was extraordinary, and it has cut off hundreds of thousands of British, French, and Belgian troops from the main French force stretched along the south bank of the Somme. The Germans are in control of more than eighty percent of Belgium, and are continuing to push the Allied forces back. To the sea. "

Martin was vaguely familiar with the geography. The Wehrmacht, determined not to fall again into a quagmire in northern France, as in the last war, had for the last two weeks sent armored divisions hurtling to the west in a rapid drive to the sea. And it had worked brilliantly. After occupying The Netherlands, and being now in control of most of Belgium, the Wehrmacht had created a shrinking circle of territory held by Allied forces—surrounded by the Germans on three sides, with the English Channel behind them.

"I've read the reports over the wires."

"The situation on the ground is worse than what is being reported," Mayweather said. "I am not permitted to share specifics with you, but His Majesty's Government has determined that an evacuation is needed, to commence at the earliest possible moment."

"That will be a dangerous operation," Martin said, knowing that the Luftwaffe had established air superiority over the Low Countries almost as soon as the invasions began.

"Indeed." Mayweather looked and sounded glum, but determined.

Martin wondered what Mayweather wanted by giving him this information. In light of the events in Europe, Martin highly doubted there was any information he could provide to Mayweather in return that the Englishman would find useful. And this wouldn't be about American neutrality—the British Foreign Ministry would have addressed that directly with Ambassador Kennedy in London, or through their own ambassador in Washington.

After a moment of silence between them, Mayweather supplied the answer.

"As you might well imagine, Mr. Schuller, British Intelligence is quite busy in other theaters, battling Nazi spies in Allied territory. They have no resources to expend in neutral territory at the moment, even if we are aware of a possible need."

So that was it. "I see," Martin said.

"I'm sure you are already aware of the need of which I speak."

Martin was pretty sure Mayweather meant the smuggling operation—or operations—that Martin was already working on. It was impossible to know for certain without showing his own cards, and he wasn't authorized to do that.

"It's possible," he said, staying vague.

"By that, I believe you mean that you are aware of the need, but you are uncertain if I speak of the same need as the one of which you are aware. Am I correct?"

Martin allowed a faint smile. "That's it in a nutshell."

"Very good," Mayweather said. "Then I shall lay my cards on the table, as you Americans say. We are aware that the Nazis have sent agents into several Latin American countries—to spread their propaganda, and to secure natural resources which are needed by their military forces. As I am sure you are aware, Argentina is one of those countries."

Martin neither confirmed nor denied.

"We also know that your FBI has sent special agents into these Latin American countries to track down these Nazi agents, and arrange for their apprehension by local authorities. I know this is not news to you, Mr. Schuller—we both know you have been cooperating with an FBI special agent assigned to your embassy here. And you have been successful in arranging for the local police to arrest a few German agents."

Mayweather stopped walking, and turned to look Martin in the eye. "There, I have laid it out for you. Now can you confirm for me that what I have said is true?"

Martin found himself in a difficult position, not authorized to confirm anything, but also not comfortable taking without giving anything in return.

"I'm not permitted to confirm anything, as I'm sure you can imagine. However—"

"Yes?" Mayweather raised an eyebrow.

Martin glanced around, confirming again that no one was nearby. Still, he lowered his voice and stepped closer to Mayweather. "Strictly off the record, agreed?"

Mayweather considered a moment, and then nodded. "Agreed."

"Off the record, I would say that your sources of information are reliable."

Mayweather nodded. "That is the conclusion on which we had planned to operate in any case, confirmed or not, if that makes you feel better about it, Mr. Schuller."

It did a bit, but Martin didn't address that. "Is that all you came to find out?"

"No. Well, strictly speaking, yes—that is all I came to learn from you. But that is not the only reason I asked you to meet me. As I said, we were prepared to proceed with the assumption that our information was correct, so your confirmation was not of critical importance. And yes, I will keep it strictly off the record, as you request."

"Thank you," Martin said, not sure if Mayweather had intended that to be as backhanded as it came across.

"As I said before, British Intelligence lacks the resources to devote to neutral countries, which of course includes those Latin American countries that have been infiltrated by Nazi agents. But since your FBI has already taken steps to address the issue on your own—without consulting the Allied powers, I might add—we are prepared to cede this theater of operations to American intelligence."

It's our hemisphere, not yours, Martin reflexively thought. But upon a moment's reflection he could concede that as the main combatants against Hitler's Germany, the British and French still had an interest in German infiltration of the Western Hemisphere.

"That is good to know, Mr. Mayweather," Martin said. "May I quote you on the record in my report to Washington?"

"I would prefer you use a code name for me, rather than my actual name—but yes, you may quote me."

"Done. Do you have a preferred code name?"

"You can call me Swordfish."

"You got it," Martin said. He assumed Mayweather had a different code name at his own service. "In my report I will describe you as 'a senior staff member at the British embassy in Buenos Aires.' I won't disclose your identity to anyone, not even those in the chain above me, unless you agree. You are my source, so I can protect your identity."

"That is most agreeable of you, Mr. Schuller," Mayweather said. "Which brings us to my next point of discussion." He paused while a middle-aged woman walking a Maltese Terrier passed them going the other direction.

"Yes?" Martin prompted after she had passed.

"Beyond merely allowing you sole hegemony over the counterintelligence operations in Latin America, we are prepared to assist you as we are able, whenever salient and credible information comes into our possession which could lead to the apprehension of a Nazi agent here."

Martin had wondered if that might be part of the deal, but he had hardly dared to hope it. "We would appreciate your assistance very much, Mr. Mayweather."

"It is in our interests to cooperate with one another."

Martin wondered if there were a subtle rebuke buried in that sentiment. He concluded that there probably was, but he didn't take the bait.

Mayweather stopped walking again and turned to face Martin. He extended his hand, and Martin shook it.

"Thank you again for meeting with me on short notice, Mr. Schuller. I look forward to our alliance. Together we'll get those Nazi bastards. Good day." He touched the rim of his hat and turned away.

Martin got the message loud and clear—*together*. But for now, he was excited by the prospect of having some access to British intelligence. They were renowned across the world for a reason.

And if the information that nabbed a Nazi agent, or busted up an entire Nazi smuggling ring, happened to come from his source—whose identity only he knew—Martin would officially be credited with the bust.

The excitement felt like electricity running through him as he hurried back to the embassy to write up a quick draft of the conversation before his memory could grow imprecise.

Monday, May 27

"This is unbelievable," Sloan said as he read the copy of the report that Martin handed him.

Martin took satisfaction in Sloan's reaction. First Secretary Davis had been equally excited when Martin handed him the official report a short time ago, but somehow it was the knowledge that Sloan was impressed that really satisfied him.

"Who is this Swordfish, anyway?"

"Confidential. Sorry."

Sloan frowned. "You know we're supposed to cooperate down here."

Martin shook his head. "And you know that doesn't include disclosing the identities of confidential sources."

Sloan leaned back and crossed his arms. "You disclosed the identities of Rivera and Calderon."

"That's because they didn't ask me to keep their identities only to myself," Martin said, crossing his own arms and staring down at Sloan. "Swordfish did, and I have to honor that. You'd do the same, and you know it."

"Yeah, yeah," Sloan said, relaxing a little. "When are you meeting with him again?"

"That hasn't been determined yet."

"You think soon?"

Martin resisted the urge to tell Sloan to mind his own business. "Probably. I can't really say for certain."

"Hmmm," Sloan said, and put his elbows on his desk. "Remember, we've got several Special Agents from the Bureau who are set to arrive here in a couple of weeks, on permanent assignment. If you happened to have some good tip from this Swordfish when they got here, it would do us both a lot of good. We only get one chance to impress the newcomers with what we've accomplished, and with the state of our investigations."

Like I don't already know that? Martin didn't let his irritation show. "I know how to reach Swordfish if I don't hear from him first. We'll have something."

"I suppose you heard the British started evacuating troops last night from Dunkirk, France."

Martin nodded. "Yes, I heard that. I'm afraid it's going to be impossible for them to get everyone out before the Luftwaffe destroys the harbor. But it's better than nothing."

"I suppose so," Sloan said, not sounding all that interested. "I wonder what your new source has to say about it. Maybe call him up tomorrow morning." Sloan started looking at the papers on his desk.

I don't need you to tell me how to do my job, but Martin resisted the urge to say that. "I'll fill you in—if there's anything you need to know."

He turned and walked out of Sloan's office, satisfied with that little dig.

Tuesday, May 28

The King of Belgium announced his country's surrender to Germany. The news clicked across the ticker on Martin's desk mid-morning. He waited a moment until he saw it reported from a second wire service, and then he picked up the phone and asked one of the secretaries to connect him with Thomas Mayweather at the British Embassy.

It was almost five minutes before a secretary rang him back, announcing that she had Thomas Mayweather on the line.

"I saw the news about Belgium," Martin said after picking up. "That has to make matters worse for your Expeditionary Force at Dunkirk."

"It bloody well does!" Mayweather snapped. "Sorry, Schuller— nasty business, got everyone on edge. The word is that Mr. Churchill is furious, thinks the Belgians should fight to the end. Even if that's only a few days."

"And the evacuation from Dunkirk?"

"It's being accelerated," Mayweather said. "Can't give you specifics, of course, but suffice to say His Majesty's government is doing everything in its power to rescue as many British and allied troops from northern France as is humanly possible to do. Anything more than that, I'm not at liberty to say."

"I understand," Martin said. He paused a second, slightly uncomfortable, but then added, "And Godspeed to all of them."

The line was silent for a second, and then Mayweather replied, sounding a bit taken aback. "Thank you, Mr. Schuller. I appreciate your good wishes, and I will share them with my colleagues here. Good day."

Rosa Linda knocked on his open door a few moments later.

"Come in," he motioned, and smiled at her after she came close.

"I saw you finished your telephone call," she said. Then she lowered her voice and added, "I want to remind you about dinner with my parents this evening, eight o'clock."

"How could I forget?" Martin said, smiling at her, but feeling apprehensive on the inside. It had been more than a decade since he'd met a girlfriend's parents for the first time, and he'd forgotten how nerve-racking the experience could be.

"They are most eager to meet you," she said, but her smile seemed nervous as well.

"And I them," Martin said. He rose from his chair and escorted her to the door. "I'll let you know if I need any revisions to those letters. Thank you, Miss Bianchi."

"Yes, sir," Rosa Linda said with a head bob, and hurried back to her desk.

Hutson

18

Rosa Linda met him at the front door of her building a couple of minutes before eight o'clock. He had a bouquet of Gerbera Daisies in his hand that he'd picked up at the florist shop on the corner.

"Those are lovely, Martin!" Rosa Linda gushed when she saw them. "Are they for me, or for my mother?"

"For your mother," he said, kissing her on the cheek. "I'm trying to make a good impression."

"She'll love them," Rosa Linda replied, hiding any disappointment she might have felt.

They walked up to the third floor, and she took him to the last door on the left. "Relax, they will love you."

How could he relax, when he knew none of them except Rosa Linda spoke English with any fluency? His Spanish was still lacking, and he was anxious about it showing.

She opened the door and he took a deep breath before following her inside.

His breath caught in his throat when he saw the crowd of people.

"Papá, this is Martin Schuller," Rosa Linda said to the man sitting in the arm chair in the corner.

He stood and looked at Martin. He was forty-nine years old, Rosa Linda had said. His wavy hair was mostly gray at the temples, but still black everywhere else. He had deep laugh lines around his mouth and deep crinkles at the corners of his dark eyes, which now stared at

Martin. He wore a gray cardigan sweater over a slate-blue button-down shirt with a gray neck tie.

"It is a pleasure to meet you, Mr. Bianchi," Martin said in Spanish, extending his hand.

Leonardo Bianchi continued to stare at Martin for a second before shaking his hand. "You work with my daughter?"

"Yes, sir," Martin said. "We work together at the American embassy." He enunciated his words carefully, anxious about making any mistakes.

"Welcome to our home," Leonardo Bianchi said, still staring into Martin's eyes. Then he motioned to the crowd of people who had gathered in the living room at the sound of Martin's voice. "This is my son Carlos, and his wife Margarita, and their two children. Over here is my son Francisco, with his wife Juliana, and their two children. This is my daughter Juana Maria, and her husband Ramón Amici-García; the little baby is theirs."

As he shook hands all around, Martin thought he'd never remember all of these names.

Leonardo Bianchi grabbed an eighteen-year-old youth by the back of the neck, and patted him squarely in the middle of the chest. "And this here is my youngest son, Alessandro, who lives with us, just like Rosa Linda."

"I call myself Alejandro," the youth said, shaking Martin's hand.

"We named you Alessandro after my father, who died the week before you were born," Leonardo Bianchi said, gruff.

Martin made a note to quietly ask Rosa Linda at the earliest opportunity what she called her younger brother.

"Maria!" Leonardo yelled. "Come, meet Rosa Linda's guest."

"In a minute! I am cooking—unless you want cold veal for dinner," a voice called back from behind the kitchen door.

Leonardo looked at his older daughter, and nodded his head toward the kitchen. "Juanita, go in there and take over so your mother can come and meet Mr. Schuller."

Juanita did as she was instructed, but looked back over her shoulder as she went and said, "You know she won't until she's ready." Then she disappeared behind the kitchen door. Her two sisters-in-law followed right behind her.

Martin heard rapid chatter behind the kitchen door, but couldn't make out a word of it.

"A glass of wine, Mr. Schuller?" one of Rosa Linda's older brothers—Carlos, wasn't it?—asked Martin, holding up a decanter.

"Yes, thank you." It might help calm his nerves.

Rosa Linda appeared at her brother's side with two glasses.

"What do you and my daughter do together?" Leonardo Bianchi interrupted Martin's attention, tapping his arm.

"She is one of the secretaries who works with me and my colleagues," Martin said. Then in a bid to win some favor, he added, "Of the four secretaries, she is the best one."

Leonardo Bianchi's lips pursed. "I meant, what do you and my daughter do together when you take her out? You are older than she by many years, so what interests both of you?"

Martin felt his cheeks flush in embarrassment. "I take her to dinner, or we go out for coffee. A few times, we have gone to a *milonga* to dance the tango." And that was all he was going to say.

A wry hint of smile came to one corner of Leonardo Bianchi's mouth. "The tango, eh? Not many foreigners can dance the tango as well as an Argentine. Do you enjoy the tango, Mr. Schuller?"

"Yes, I enjoy it much," Martin said. It was only a slight exaggeration.

"My daughter is a good dancer," Leonardo said, smiling at Rosa Linda as she handed Martin a wine glass.

"Martin is a good dancer, too, Papá," she said, and took a sip from her own glass. "We have a good time together."

"That's nice," he said, smiling at this daughter. Then he looked back at Martin and the smile was gone. "What work do you do at the American embassy, Mr. Schuller?"

"I'm one of the Third Secretaries," he said, knowing immediately that the title would mean nothing to anyone in the room. Except for Rosa Linda, who already knew. "I am the embassy's Information Officer. I work with diplomats from the Argentine Ministry of Foreign Affairs, and diplomats from other embassies, and we share information. I also work with journalists, to give them information for their newspapers and radio programs."

Mr. Bianchi's eyes narrowed a little. "What kind of information?"

Martin shrugged, trying to buy a few extra seconds to think of a way to explain it in Spanish. "It is different every day," he began, still searching for a good explanation. "Right now, there is a lot of war news from Europe, but there is also news about the election for President of the United States later this year."

Leonardo Bianchi gave Martin a scrutinizing sort of look for a few seconds. "Your President of the United States is a leftist, no?"

"He is center-left more than leftist," Martin answered, having perfected this answer to numerous Argentine conservatives who asked the same thing Bianchi just had.

"Hmmm," Bianchi grunted with a nod. "That is what we have here in Argentina, too. President Ortiz is from the Radical Civic Union. I have read that your president's policies have been much like our president's policies."

Martin had heard this many times. It was an oversimplification, to be sure, but not entirely inaccurate. "They are similar sometimes, but not always. Different countries need different things."

"Ah, that may be true, but neither has ended the Depression, correct?"

Martin nodded. "That is correct. The Depression has not ended in the United States, either—but it is much better than it was seven or eight years ago. It is similar to here in Argentina."

Leonardo Bianchi gave him an appraising nod. "You talk like a diplomat. You must be good at your job."

Martin wondered if Mr. Bianchi intended that as a backhanded compliment. He just smiled and nodded to his host. "Thank you."

"Papá has strong opinions about business and the Depression," Rosa Linda said, slipping an arm through Martin's in an almost protective gesture.

"I am a manager at the Hispano-Argentina automotive factory, I'm sure Rosa Linda told you this," Mr. Bianchi said, motioning toward his daughter.

Martin was certain she hadn't, but he didn't contradict his host.

"Papá would prefer that Vice President Castillo replace Ortiz as President of Argentina," her brother Carlos said.

"Ramón Castillo would bring policies that would actually help Argentine business, and end the Depression," their father said.

That fits, Martin thought. Vice President Ramón Castillo was from the National Democratic Party—commonly called "the Conservative Party"—and many of his supporters regretted the coalition with the center-left Radical Civic Union that had won the 1938 elections. Castillo was also sixty-six years old, a remnant of a bygone social era when conservative landowners had dominated Argentina.

"Even Papá has to admit that business has gotten better," Francisco said, teasing his father. "Their lines have expanded. You should hear him complain about the 'Little Black Heads' he has to hire these days."

"Francisco! Shame on you," Rosa Linda hissed, but Francisco laughed.

Leonardo Bianchi looked up at the ceiling. "Mama Mia!" he said in Italian.

"Little Black Heads?" Martin asked. He was unfamiliar with the term.

"Peasants from the northern provinces," Francisco said, a little dismissive. "They come to the capital in droves, looking for work, and they clog up the slums on the outskirts of the city."

"Ay, politics and business!" a new voice said behind them, and Martin turned to see a short, plump, graying woman in a filthy apron standing behind them, wiping her hands on a dish towel.

"Mamá, this is Martin Schuller," Rosa Linda said.

"Good evening, Mrs. Bianchi," Martin said, rising, and handed her the bouquet of Gerbera Daisies. "Thank you for the invitation to your home."

"Thank you, Mr. Schuller, they are beautiful," Maria Sofia Bianchi said to him. "Juanita, daughter, put these in water. Hurry, hurry!"

She motioned her older daughter away, and Juanita hurried back into the kitchen with the flowers.

"I hope you like Italian food, Mr. Schuller," Mrs. Bianchi said, beaming. "Italian mamás, we cook. You do not look Italian, so I have to tell you. My son-in-law Ramón, Juanita's husband, his papá is Italian, but his mamá is not, so I had to explain to him also the first time he came to dinner."

"It is like at my Italian grandmother's house," Ramón Amici-García said, a little timid, and Maria Sofia Bianchi whacked him on the arm.

"You were so skinny when Juanita first brought you here. But you look much better now." She pinched his cheek and then patted it affectionately.

Martin was glad he wasn't skinny.

"The food is ready," Mrs. Bianchi announced to the room. "Come and eat, everyone."

Martin held back with Rosa Linda while everyone else mobbed the door to the dining room.

170

"Don't worry," she said in English. "Papá gave the same scrutiny to Ramón the first time he came here. I think he likes you."

"What makes you think so?"

"He has not thrown you out the door."

From the look on her face, he wasn't sure if she was teasing him or not.

"I was surprised at all the people here when I first came," he said. "I thought it was just going to be dinner with your parents."

"Alejandro lives here, and Mamá always invites the rest of the family to dinner for every opportunity. She likes to cook a big dinner, and she likes to have everyone together."

That answered the question about what Rosa Linda called her younger brother.

"Come, come!" Maria Sofia Bianchi said in Spanish from the open doorway to the dining room. "You must eat while the food is still hot. Mr. Schuller, you will sit next to me, and Rosa Linda, you sit on my opposite side."

Martin's jaw about fell off when he saw the amount of food heaped on the long dining room table. Even with fifteen people, not counting the baby, Martin wasn't sure they would make a dent in those dishes. There were two pans of lasagna Bolognese, and two big platters of veal scaloppini, plus bowls of carrots and roasted potatoes.

"Come, sit, sit!" Mrs. Bianchi said, patting the chair beside hers. She sat at the end of the long table closest to the kitchen, opposite her husband.

Martin thanked her, waiting to sit until after Rosa Linda sat down across from him. Martin took some of everything, but with every dish that passed by, Mrs. Bianchi encouraged him to take more than what he had. "You are a big man, you need more than that."

He just smiled and obliged. When he was finished he looked at his heaping plate and wondered how he would ever get through it.

"You like Italian food, Mr. Schuller?" she asked between bites of lasagna.

"Yes, very much. This is all wonderful, thank you."

"Schuller—that is a German name, I believe yes?"

"Yes, it is."

"Is all of your family German? Or are you a mix, like my son-in-law Ramón?"

Martin finished chewing a bite of veal, and dabbed at his mouth with his napkin. "My family is all German, but we have been in America, in the same city, for almost two hundred years."

"Do they have Italians in your city?"

Martin nodded. "Some, yes. And there are many Italian-Americans in Philadelphia, which is not far."

She looked at him, thoughtful. "Germans are sometimes Catholic, and sometimes Protestant, I believe yes? Are you Catholic, Mr. Schuller? Or Protestant?"

Martin took a breath before answering. "I'm neither, but my family is Protestant."

"Neither?" Maria Sofia Bianchi looked confused for a second, and then she smacked both of her hands on the table before raising them toward the ceiling and looking upward. "Mama mia!" she shouted, bringing a hush to the table. She turned to Rosa Linda and let loose with a rapid string of forceful Italian.

Rosa Linda answered briefly in Italian a few times, but her mother's blistering string of words wouldn't be interrupted for more than a few seconds.

It occurred to Martin that he was likely the only person at the table who didn't understand Italian.

At last, she finished. She crossed her arms and nodded firmly, looking back and forth between Rosa Linda and Martin.

"Mamá says I am to bring you to Mass on Sunday with the family," Rosa Linda told him in English. "She insists."

Martin wondered what the consequences of refusal might be. He weighed his options for a couple of seconds—finding them all bad—and finally replied in English, "We'll talk about it after dinner."

Rosa Linda said something quietly to her mother in Italian, and she replied something before turning back to Martin with a somewhat warmer expression, though not quite back to her previous joviality.

"We will get you fixed up right with God, Mr. Schuller," she said in Spanish, patting his hand. "It is no *wonder* you are not yet married!"

Martin didn't dare bring up that he had been married once, and was now divorced. God only knew how that news would go over.

After dinner, followed by dessert of bread pudding topped with *dulce de leche*, Martin could barely move without discomfort. He was sure he hadn't been this full since his last Thanksgiving with his family, a year and a half prior.

"Did you get enough to eat?" Mrs. Bianchi asked as he grabbed his hat and overcoat to leave.

"Yes, it was all wonderful, thank you."

"I will send a piece of lasagna home with you, for later," she said, and hurried into the kitchen.

"Best not to say no to her food," Rosa Linda said to him with a wink.

Maria Sofia Bianchi returned a moment later with a large piece of lasagna wrapped in wax paper. "Put it in the oven for ten minutes at one hundred degrees, and it will be as good as it was at dinner," she said with a twinkle.

Then she patted his cheek—a surprisingly affectionate gesture, he thought, a little taken aback—and said, "We will see you Sunday morning for Mass. I will ask the priest to talk with you. Don't worry, we will look after you, yes?" And she patted his check again before wishing him good night.

173

Martin felt his gut clench, but the look in Rosa Linda's eyes warned him to say nothing about the subject. He thanked her mother again and wished her good night.

Rosa Linda told her family that she was walking Martin out, and she closed the apartment door behind them, to a chorus of "Good night" in both Spanish and Italian.

"Mamá likes you," she said in English. "She would not make such a fuss about Mass if she didn't care for you."

Thanks, but no thanks. But how could he explain?

"Rosa Linda..." his voice trailed off while he considered what he could say.

"I know you don't want to go, Martin, but you must. No one says 'no' to Mamá once she has made up her mind."

"No."

She looked at him as if stung. "What do you mean, 'no?' Just 'No' and nothing else?"

"Listen to me—I have my reasons for why I don't want to go to church, but they are my reasons, and none of anyone else's business."

She stopped at the stairs and looked at him, searching for something behind his eyes.

"Did the priest do bad things to you when you were young?" she asked, whispering.

"What? Oh, no—nothing like that."

"I am not naïve," she said. "I have heard things that priests have done sometimes to school girls—or to altar boys. But most priests are good."

"That's not what I'm talking about," Martin said, face starting to flush with anger. He reminded himself that his anger was not really directed at her, but it didn't change the fact that she was the one in the line of fire. "Let's just say that I've seen how nasty and judgmental church people can get, and I want no part of it."

174

Especially now that we've been intimate. They were careful, but it had crossed his mind that history could repeat itself.

He never talked about what happened with Susan, or what happened after the news of her pregnancy spread. He only ever spoke in the vaguest of terms about how the church community had treated him.

And he wasn't about to open up about it now.

Rosa Linda touched his arm. "You don't have to tell the priest about your divorce. It will be our secret."

"Let's just leave it that I'm a grown man, and I have my reasons, and I don't have to justify myself to anyone."

She crossed her arms and glared at him. "I see."

He could see the anger burning behind her golden brown eyes, and he scowled, growing defensive. "What does that mean?"

"I am not good enough for you to listen to, or good enough for you to argue with. You just say, 'this is how it is for me,' and I am supposed to accept it without question."

"That's not it at all."

"No? Then why won't you discuss it?"

"It's just—damn it! I have my reasons, ok?"

Her scowl deepened, and her eyes flashed. "Then you don't need to worry about being asked back here. We will mind our own business. Goodnight, Mr. Schuller." She spun on her heels and marched back to her family's apartment.

He watched her disappear inside without so much as a backward glance.

19

Friday, May 31

Rosa Linda barely spoke to him the rest of the week.

The American embassy was officially closed on Thursday for Memorial Day, and instead hosted a reception in the afternoon for embassy staff and certain members of the diplomatic community in Buenos Aires. Rosa Linda didn't attend.

Finally, on Friday afternoon when she came into his office to deliver a letter for him to sign, he saw a crack in her professional façade. Something in her eyes when he handed the letter back to her, and the second that she lingered after taking the letter, told him there was an opening.

"I wonder if you might like to go dancing tonight," he said, a touch too loudly, and she glanced back at the open door before returning her gaze to him.

"I am going with my friends to a *milonga* in the Palermo tonight," she said, her voice flat.

"Oh, well then, perhaps we could have dinner together tomorrow night."

She hesitated, unsure, so he plunged ahead. "And after dinner we could go see an American movie; or perhaps go to a poetry reading instead at a coffee house in Almagro. Whatever you'd like."

She turned back to face him head-on. "I should not stay out late on Saturday night, since I am going to Mass with my family on Sunday."

He cringed at the words, spoken with a direct stare. "You're not going to convince me to go," he said, quietly. He hesitated, part of him wondering if he should tell her why—but he never spoke of Susan, and the thought of digging it up now made his stomach turn. He stayed in the present. "But that doesn't mean I don't want to see you."

She looked down. "I want to see you, too," she said, just above a whisper.

He got up from his desk, ignoring the open door altogether, and reached for her hand. He stood close to her and said to her ear. "Good. Tomorrow night?"

She nodded, and held his hand for a couple of seconds before pulling away and walking to the door. "I will have this letter posted right away, Mr. Schuller."

Saturday, June 1

After a late dinner at a small Armenian restaurant in Almagro, Martin walked with Rosa Linda a few blocks to the *Quartier Latin* coffee house. It was a cool evening, but not cold, and Martin had opted for no overcoat. Rosa Linda wore a short-sleeved green dress with a matching wrap.

It was after eleven o'clock when they walked through the door of the *Quartier Latin*, and Martin was not surprised to see it full.

"I don't think we'll get a table," he said to Rosa Linda in English. "We can still catch the late show at the movie palace, if you want."

"No, we can stay here," she said. "I don't mind standing, if the poetry is good."

Martin knew he couldn't actually vouch for that, only from hearsay. And that was not from impartial sources.

"I'll get us something to drink." He ordered them two glasses of red wine.

While he was waiting for the bartender to fill two glasses, he felt a hand on his left arm, and looked over to see Javier Velasco standing beside him.

"Mr. Schuller, what a nice surprise!" he said in Spanish. "Did you come to hear me read tonight? Antonio must have told you I'm the first one at midnight."

Antonio Rivera hadn't said anything at all about Javier since their meeting. "No, he never mentioned that. Is that a good thing, to read first?"

"It is a *very* good thing!" Javier said with a broad grin. "I get to fire up the audience. I'm glad you are here for it."

The bartender handed Martin two glasses of wine, and Martin slid a few pesos across the bar. He turned to Rosa Linda and handed her a glass. "Javier, this is my girlfriend, Miss Bianchi. This is Javier Velasco, who works at a café I like on Avenida Cabildo, in Belgrano."

Rosa Linda gave Javier her hand, and Martin noticed he barely touched her fingers when he shook it, giving her a cool stare. "Pleasure to meet you, miss," he said with no enthusiasm.

"Mr. Velasco has told me that he is the first poet to read tonight," Martin told Rosa Linda, in Spanish for Javier's benefit, and she gave Javier an interested look.

"Ah? That is an honor to read first, yes? What do you call the piece you will read for us?"

"It is an original work," Javier said. His tone was a little frosty, Martin thought. "If I say the title now, it will ruin the surprise."

"I look forward to hearing it," Rosa Linda said, and took a sip of her wine. Then she slipped her arm through Martin's and leaned against him.

Javier nodded his head to them. "I hope you enjoy the show." Then looking at Martin, he added, "I will find you after I have finished. I am eager to hear your reaction to my poem."

"We'll be right here," Martin said. Javier nodded without a word, and held his gaze for a moment before turning away and striding back to his table in the far corner. The same table where Martin and Antonio had met with him a few weeks ago.

"He's a nice fellow," Martin told Rosa Linda in English. "I'm looking forward to hearing his poem. I just hope I can understand what he says." He laughed in a self-deprecating way, and she smiled and put her hand on his chest.

"I will translate for you if you need me to," she said. "You can whisper in my ear that you need help."

Javier sat in his usual chair in the corner, from which he could survey the entire establishment, and crossed his arms. It was warm in the club tonight, but he felt cold inside.

"What's the matter?" Antonio asked. "You are not usually nervous before a reading."

"Nothing is wrong," Javier said, too sharply, and kept his arms crossed.

"Was that Mr. Schuller I saw at the bar?" Antonio craned his neck to see over the crowd.

"Yes. He has a woman with him, and he introduced her as his girlfriend."

Antonio looked at him with one eyebrow arched.

Javier knew Antonio could see through his petulance. He forced a smile and patted his friend's arm. "I am offended for you, I suppose," he said, feigning jocularity. "I assumed you and Mr. Schuller are..." he let his voice trail off, and made a motion with his hand below the table.

Antonio's eyes widened. "No! My God. Did I say something to give you that impression?"

Javier shrugged in an exaggerated sort of way. "No, nothing you *said*..." he let his voice trail off again, suggestive. Then he grinned salaciously, and leaned close to Antonio's face, clasping the back of his neck in an affectionate way. "He is very handsome, though, is he not? You would like to, I think."

Antonio looked back at him with a strange expression. Then he looked over toward where Mr. Schuller was partially visible behind a crowd of people. "Yes, he is handsome—but you know he is not my type. I prefer men closer to our age. *You* are the one who likes men older than thirty."

Javier saw Antonio give him a side glance.

"Well, then, if you aren't interested in him, you wouldn't mind if I..." he let his voice trail off again, suggestively.

Antonio laughed and shook his head. "No, it would not offend me—but it might offend him. I haven't seen any sign that he is like us."

"Ha! You know as well as I do that many men hide it well." Javier patted him on the back of the head. "I have been surprised many times by the men who come to me. Haven't you?"

Antonio started to shrug, but then nodded. "Yes, it's true. But listen to me—consider my position, and that Mr. Schuller is an important man where I work. Don't come on too strong, or you will risk my job. Understand?"

Dear, sweet Antonio—you of all people should know I never *come on strong*. No, whenever he wanted someone, Javier prided himself on being a master of seduction, making a man come to him.

He grabbed his friend's face in both hands and kissed his cheeks, one and then the other. Then he patted Antonio's cheek with deep affection.

"Don't worry, my friend. I will not jeopardize your position. Trust me."

Javier climbed onto the stage and took the microphone. His poem was new—he'd written it a few days before—but he knew every word by heart.

He introduced himself, for the few members of the audience who didn't already know him. Then he looked directly at Mr. Schuller, standing near the bar, and began.

> "Why is it, my handsome one,
> That you have come to live in my thoughts?
> Others come to visit,
> A moment or an hour,
> But you have laid claim.
>
> What is it, my handsome one,
> That makes me long so for your presence,
> When you never leave my mind?
> Others come to call,
> But you drive them out."

Across the room, Rosa Linda leaned against Martin and rested her chin on his shoulder, whispering the translation into his ear...

Until the "handsome one" described by the poem became a little too familiar. The rugged man with blond hair who carries himself with confidence bordering on swagger that is neither forced nor feigned, nor the acts of a bully—she found her throat constricting, and her eyes narrowed into a glare at the poet on stage.

> "I know from whence it comes, my handsome one,
> This command of being.
> The man who carries himself thus,
> Hides more than the usual surprise in his pants."

Rosa Linda didn't translate that stanza. She listened in tight-lipped silence.

Whether it was because she'd stopped translating, or because of the cries of genuine surprise from the audience—some gleefully surprised, others shocked—Martin turned his head toward her.

"What did he say?" he asked, his voice stony.

"He is going on and on about the man's clothes," she lied, assuming that Martin had at least understood the word *pantalones*. Then she waved a dismissive hand in front of them. "It is not a good poem."

The poet was quite animated now in his delivery, the words dripping with emotion. Half of the crowd inside the *Quartier Latin* leaned forward in rapt attention, while the other half sat stiff like statuary. His language was quite suggestive now, alluding to what he longed to do with the "surprise."

Rosa Linda wondered why the manager of this establishment didn't throw him off the stage.

The poet crescendoed to an ending loaded with longing, and was met with enthusiastic applause from half of the patrons. And silence from the other half.

Martin figured out the poem was about him before Rosa Linda stopped translating. That much was obvious. The attention alone made him uncomfortable; the fact that such praise of his looks and bearing came from a young man made him want to crawl away.

He wondered—not for the first time—if Joe Hansen had ever felt that way about him. If he had, Joe had the decency never to voice it. Javier Velasco had no such scruples, apparently.

Martin wished he could discern what the rest of the poem had said, which had so clearly excited or angered the audience members. And about which Rosa Linda had obviously lied. Badly. But part of him feared the answer.

While the second poet read his latest work from a notebook, Martin saw Javier making his way through the crowd toward them. The patrons he passed either clapped him on the back in unspoken congratulations, or glared at him and refused to budge out of his way.

Javier stood next to Martin, looked toward the stage and listened to the closing stanzas, and then during the applause he turned toward Martin with a grin that looked a bit nervous.

"What did you think of my poem?"

Martin thought of something positive to say. "I was impressed that you had it memorized. The next man didn't."

Javier's smile faltered, and his eyes grew guarded. "Is that all that impressed you?"

"You delivered it so well, with such feeling. You moved the crowd."

Rosa Linda inserted herself in the space between them, and slipped her arm into Martin's. She addressed herself to him, but kept her eyes on Javier.

"Martin, it is time to leave, I think."

Martin looked into her eyes and saw that it wasn't a request. He turned toward Javier, hesitated an awkward second, and then extended his hand to shake. "Congratulations, Javier. Best of luck with your poetry. Good night."

He nodded and put his hat on as he turned away and made for the door.

Javier watched Mr. Schuller and his girl walk out the door, his heart plunging into his gut. His face flushed hot with embarrassment, and he looked around to see if anyone had watched the interaction. The crowd was occupied with their own conversations, but he couldn't help feeling that everyone had seen his rejection. They were all laughing at him on the inside.

He slapped his hand on top of the bar, and when the bartender came over, he ordered wine. "Just give me the whole bottle."

Javier stumbled over the stoop on his way out of the *Quartier Latin* two hours later. Antonio put his arm around his shoulder to steady him.

"You had too much wine," Antonio admonished, but Javier waved it off.

"It's good for an artist to get roaring drunk from time to time," he slurred. But he also put his arm around Antonio's waist and leaned hard against his friend to steady himself as they walked down the street toward Javier's building.

"You should eat some bread before you go to sleep," Antonio said when Javier stumbled over a crack in the sidewalk. "And drink some water."

"Bread and water, how Spartan."

In truth, Javier rarely got drunk, and almost never this drunk. But Mr. Schuller's reaction had stung, and when he left moments later with that *girl* on his arm—well, Javier wanted to forget that. And wine led to forgetting.

Except it hadn't entirely.

At the corner a few meters ahead of them, a man and woman embraced, their mouths locked in a deep and passionate kiss. Javier's imagination called up Mr. Schuller and that girl doing the same. And more.

He turned his head to kiss Antonio's cheek, and let his lips linger there for several seconds. "Thank you for taking me home," he said, giving his friend's waist a squeeze.

Then he let his hand slip down to the seat of Antonio's pants, and gave that a little squeeze as well. "Want to stay tonight?" he whispered into Antonio's ear with a wolfish grin.

A whistle blast behind them made them stop in their tracks. Antonio spun around, but Javier was slower to react.

A police officer strode toward them, whistle in one hand and baton in the other. "You two, stop right there."

"But we aren't doing anything wrong, sir," Antonio said.

"I saw what you did," the police officer said through clenched teeth. "Indecency in public is against the law."

"Yes, it is," Javier agreed with an exaggerated nod. Then he pointed back at the man and woman on the corner, who still had their arms around each other, but had turned their heads to watch the little drama playing out so close-by. "You should definitely arrest them for it."

The cop shook his head, muttering an epithet.

"I am helping my friend home so that he does not hurt himself," Antonio said. "He has had a little too much wine, that is all. He will not bother anyone, I promise."

"You are under arrest," the officer growled, and put a hand on one shoulder apiece, gripping hard, and pushed them back the way he had come. When they rounded a corner, another police officer stood next to a police car.

"We won't get out of jail until Monday morning," Antonio hissed out the side of his mouth after they'd been shoved in the back seat, before the police could get into the front.

"We'll find a way out," Javier slurred, and fell silent as the police officers got into the car and sped off.

20

Sunday, June 2

Javier was awakened by the loud metallic clang of a hard wooden baton swinging against the iron bars of the jail cell. His head pounded, and he squinted his eyes at the bright lights.

"Velasco!" the guard shouted. "Javier Velasco!"

Javier glanced at the three other men in the cell—Antonio, who watched him with concern, plus two strangers—and then raised his hand.

The guard unlocked the cell door and swung it open with a loud creak of rusty metal. "Your brother is here to collect you." The man's tone said he wasn't at all sure that *brother* was accurate.

Javier knew it wasn't. He rarely spoke to his family, even though they all lived in Almagro, and he would have never called any of them to get him out of jail. There was no possibility anyone had contacted them without his permission, either; he had no prior arrests, and Velasco was a common surname, so there was no way the police could have identified his next of kin already.

He hid his bemusement and got up, glancing at Antonio as he passed. He gave his friend the tiniest of shrugs before passing through the open cell door.

A man of about thirty stood waiting in the public room when the guard led Javier out through the windowless door. The clock on the wall behind him said that it was four thirty-five. The man was tall and broad-shouldered, in a dark gray suit and narrow black tie, and he immediately crossed his arms and scowled at Javier.

"Mamá has been worried sick since you didn't come home last night," the man said in an accent that sounded vaguely familiar. "We called all of the hospitals, and finally found you here." He almost spat out the last word.

It was a brilliant performance, from someone that Javier had never laid eyes on in his life. Under better circumstances, he would have applauded. Instead, he lowered his eyes in fake contrition and muttered, "I'm sorry."

"Tell that to Mamá," the man said as he grabbed Javier by the arm and tugged him forward.

Javier allowed himself to be pulled along. The guard standing at the exit opened it without a word, and Javier thought the cold night air on his face was the best thing he'd experienced in a long time.

The man loosened his grip on Javier's arm once the door had closed behind them, but didn't let go. He led Javier across the street, not stopping until they had rounded the corner and stood in the shadows between street lamps.

"*Lehenik eta behin, euskaraz hitz egiten al duzu, Velasco jauna?*"

Javier shook his head. He hadn't understood a word, but he recognized the sound. His grandparents spoke Basque to each other when they didn't want the rest of the family to know what they were saying.

"I thought you might know our mother tongue," the man said, once again in Spanish. "It would mean we have less fear of being overheard, but it is not critical."

"Who are you?"

"My name is not important, but you may call me *Unai*, or Shepherd if you prefer. I know much about you, Javier Velasco. I am an associate of SIV—Basque Intelligence Service. We have watched you for some time."

Basque Intelligence? Watching him? Javier was stunned. "Why?"

"You are in a position to learn useful things," Shepherd said. "Also, your grandparents originated in Gipuzkoa, so we are hopeful that you will be inclined to help our cause."

"What cause?"

The man's hazel eyes held his for a long moment before he spoke. "I must ask for your discretion. Please keep this conversation only between us. Do you agree?"

"Yes." Javier was good at keeping secrets.

"Our homeland was given extensive autonomy under the Spanish Republic, but now that has all been taken away by the *caudillo*, Generalisimo Franco. He rules with an iron fist, and he is working to suppress our culture and our language.

"Under the Republic, our people had our own intelligence service, and when the Nationalist rebellion began four years ago, we lent our services to the Republican cause. When Franco won, we were forced to flee Spain. Many of us came to Argentina.

"Ever since the Luftwaffe bombed Guernica, we have been dedicated to destroying the Nazis. There are many Nazi spies working in Argentina, Mr. Velasco. We intend to root them out. In this effort, I think you can help us. Will you help us?"

Javier's imagination ran wild with images of cloak and dagger intrigue and danger. "I don't want to kill anyone."

A hint of smile cracked Shepherd's serious expression. "We need informants more than we need assassins, Mr. Velasco."

Javier weighed his options. "If you want my help, get my friend Antonio Rivera out of jail. He was arrested with me—but you probably already know that, don't you?"

Shepherd did not immediately respond, and Javier watched his face closely, but it gave no clues to his thinking.

"We are not prepared to entrust our mission to Mr. Rivera," Shepherd finally replied.

"Antonio is trustworthy," Javier said, raising his chin. "He can keep a secret as well as I can."

But Shepherd shook his head. "Your friend Mr. Rivera works at the American Embassy. While he may be trustworthy under normal circumstances, we cannot trust that he would not reveal us to his employers. They are a neutral country, and we do not know their intentions."

Javier scrambled for options. "We don't have to tell him anything," he suggested. Then his thoughts crystalized, and he added with more confidence, "You can leave as soon as you post his bail. I'll tell him I did it. But if you leave him in jail, I won't help you."

Tense silence hung between them for several seconds.

"Very well," Shepherd said. "I will take care of it. You should go home now. I will contact you soon. Good night, Mr. Velasco."

He touched the rim of his hat and crossed the street, back to the jail. Javier stood in the darkness and watched him until he had entered the building. He wondered what reason Shepherd would give for bailing out Antonio, since he couldn't use the brother excuse a second time. But that wasn't his problem.

He watched long enough to see Antonio come out of the station, whistled and waved to him, and then hurried toward home.

21

Tuesday, June 4

Martin looked up at the knock on his office door.

"Worked through lunch again today?" Mike Mattingly asked. Standing next to him, Chuck Brady wagged a finger at Martin in mock scolding.

"Sorry fellas, big news day," Martin said, nodding at the ticker on his desk.

"What's the latest?" Chuck Brady asked, taking a step inside Martin's office, looking eager.

"The Germans have launched a final assault on Dunkirk. I don't think they'll be stopped this time."

"That'll put an end to the Brits' evacuation," Mattingly said. "Gotta hand it to them—it was one helluva run."

Martin nodded. "Based on reports out of Dover this morning, they got most of their men out already, plus over a hundred thousand French. And it's still going."

"You met the new FBI boys yet, Martin?" Chuck Brady asked, and his crooked smile made Martin wonder if he wanted to.

"No, I've been holed up in here most of the morning." He'd almost forgotten that the new contingent of FBI agents arrived this morning on the SS Brazil.

Mattingly's lips tightened. "I wouldn't drop what you're doing to rush down there."

Martin arched an eyebrow. "Not impressed?"

191

Brady scoffed. "I haven't seen that many cold fish in one place since the fire went out at the Baptist fish fry."

Martin chuckled at the image. "I have to talk to Special Agent Sloan later, so I'm sure I'll be introduced then."

"Good luck with that meeting," Mattingly said, and Brady laughed and slapped him on the back as they turned and walked out.

Martin knocked on Sloan's closed door that afternoon. He heard Sloan's muffled shout "Come in!" over a low din of commotion.

Martin opened the door, and found the room crowded with seven men—the six new special agents, presumably. One was sitting next to Sloan behind the desk, looking over some papers in front of them. Another sat at the end of the desk, scribbling onto a notepad. The other four stood at filing cabinets along both walls, leafing through folders.

At least four of them were smoking cigarettes, judging by the number that sat smoldering at the edge of ashtrays scattered around the room, and Martin almost coughed when he first stepped in.

"Ah, Schuller, come in. These are the men the Bureau sent down to establish a permanent presence here."

Sloan introduced the six men, who all looked at Martin with varying degrees of indifference, barely pausing from whatever they were doing to nod his way as their names were said.

"Martin Schuller is one of the Third Secretaries, the Information Officer for the embassy," Sloan said. "He and I work closely together on any intel that State receives that's pertinent to Nazi criminal activity here."

The agent sitting next to Sloan—the one he'd introduced as Wilson—stood half-heartedly and extended his hand toward Martin. The handshake was firm but brief, and Wilson muttered that he looked forward to working with Martin. Then he went back to the papers in front of him without another look.

"Likewise," Martin muttered.

"What brings you down, Schuller?" Sloan asked, an edge of impatience to his voice that was new.

"That communique from our embassy in Rio de Janeiro that arrived late yesterday; you said it could wait until today."

Sloan nodded. "Oh, right, that—leave it here with us, we'll take care of it. Thanks." He held out his hand, but his eyes had returned to his desk.

Martin handed him the copy he'd made for the FBI, stifling his frustration at the lack of discussion.

"Anything else?" Sloan asked, barely glancing up.

"No," Martin said, and walked out.

Monday, June 10

Italy's declaration of war on Britain and France came as only a momentary surprise. Once Martin thought about it, the delayed entry of Italy into the war on the side of its purported ally was exactly what should be expected of Mussolini.

The French battle-lines had already collapsed. French forces were in full retreat across northern France. The road to Paris was wide open for the Wehrmacht. Italy was jumping into the fray just in time to help defeat an all-but-beaten foe, and probably gain some easy spoils.

It was an item he would have to address in a press briefing, given that Italians were the largest ethnic group in Argentina; but he didn't expect it to get much more than yawning attention. He wrote up a quick statement that he'd include with other items to go over with First Secretary Davis later that morning.

He perused some items that had come in the diplomatic pouch that weekend, aboard the Pan Am Clipper. He made a mental note of a couple of items.

At the bottom of the short stack there was a letter from Joe Hansen, typed on official State Department letterhead, dated June 5, 1940—last Wednesday.

Confidential
Dear Mr. Schuller,

I have enclosed herein several copies
of memoranda which I believe to be of
interest to your office. Viewed with
previous documents sent to you, these
suggest that German Military Intelligence
has built a network of supporters in
Argentina and Brazil who are prepared to
offer material support to the German war
effort, in violation of neutrality laws in
those countries.

Additionally, I have learned in
conversations with my confidential
contacts at the Office of Naval
Intelligence that ONI believes that
Dietrich Niebuhr, German Naval Attaché in
Argentina, is the organizer of multiple
smuggling rings which have moved thousands
of tons of war materiel illegally aboard
Spanish and Portuguese vessels.

My sources confirmed that ONI has
shared this information with the FBI as
per requirements, and with the American
Naval Attaché in Buenos Aires, so it is
possible that you have learned this
information through other sources locally.

As always, when additional relevant
intelligence comes to light, I will be
certain to forward it to you at the
earliest opportunity.

I am, as always, very cordially yours,

Joseph P. Hansen
Office of the Chief Special Agent

Martin leaned back in his chair and exhaled hard. He rubbed his hand across his face. This was a much larger operation than he'd anticipated. Not a backwater project for the Abwehr, but being run by the German Naval Attaché himself.

It was hardly surprising that Captain Brereton, the U.S. Naval Attaché to Argentina, hadn't shared Nieburhr's connection to the smuggling rings. He may or may not have shared it with Major Devine, the American Military Attaché. Either way, military and naval attachés at American embassies almost never shared such information with their State Department hosts.

It did irk Martin a bit that Sloan might have already had intelligence identifying Niebuhr as the mastermind of the smuggling operations, but hadn't shared it. But then, Sloan was busy with the newly arrived agents, and Martin wanted little to do with them. They'd been dismissive of him when they were introduced; that and subsequent snubs were too much for Martin to forget.

As a Naval Attaché, Dietrich Niebuhr himself was untouchable, with diplomatic immunity. But most members of his networks across South America would not be, and this is where Martin and the FBI needed to find leads. It would be a difficult egg to crack, but at least they could start with surveilling Niebuhr.

Martin sighed and looked at the calendar pinned to the wall beside his desk.

It was one week until his kids arrived, and he'd started counting the days. They had departed New York on June the first, aboard the SS Argentina, one of two steamships that regularly made the route between New York and Buenos Aires. The other was the SS Brazil, which had brought the new FBI Special Agents last week.

In his spare time, Martin had jotted down a list of things to do in Buenos Aires and the surrounding region. He had also arranged for some time off in July, around Marty's birthday, and during those weeks he hoped to take the kids north to see some of the tourist attractions up there, such as the Iguazú waterfalls—and particularly the section known provocatively as *Garganta del Diablo*, the Devil's Throat.

A trip north would also be a nice break from the cloudy and chilly winter weather in Buenos Aires, and a welcome change of scenery.

The big question was when and how to introduce them to Rosa Linda, and how much to include her in his plans. He'd avoided that issue so far, but the clock was ticking. He hadn't even broached the subject with Rosa Linda. He'd only said that his kids were coming to visit for two months.

He knew he needed to find out what interest she had in spending time with his children. For some reason, he was always reluctant to bring it up. There never seemed to be an opportune moment, for one thing. And he was a bit nervous about what she would say.

Whether he was more afraid of her being enthusiastic about spending time with his kids, or reticent of it, he wasn't sure.

Tuesday, June 11

"What do you want to talk about?" Rosa Linda asked as they took their empanadas and walked toward the nearby Plaza de Congreso.

Martin had asked her to lunch, and suggested empanadas from a street vendor precisely because they could eat them while walking. He thought the park-like atmosphere of the plaza was the best place to broach a potentially sensitive topic.

"You know that my children are coming here for their summer vacation," he said, aware of the irony that it was winter here, and barely fifty-five degrees Fahrenheit today. Rosa Linda was bundled up in an overcoat and scarf.

"Yes, I remember. When do they arrive?"

"On Monday." He watched her for a reaction, but saw none. "You know I'm going to spend most of my free time with them, since I haven't seen them in nine months. That means we won't be able to go out as often as we have, and probably no late nights dancing."

She slipped her arm through his as they crossed the street to the plaza. "I understand, Martin. Your children are important. You must spend time with them before others."

He had rehearsed the conversation in his mind countless times, but he was still hesitant. He flicked a stray speck of pepper from the edge of his half-eaten empanada, steeling himself. "I don't know if you'd like to meet them sometime? Or maybe spend some time with the four of us together?"

He held his breath.

Her face lit up. "Martin, I think that is a wonderful idea. I love children. I wondered when you were going to ask me—or if you would ask."

He breathed a little easier. "So maybe let's plan for you to meet them sometime late next week, after they've settled in a few days. You could come to my place for dinner."

"That would be nice," she said, but then she gave him a sideways glance. "Will you cook? Or will you hire someone to cook?"

He laughed. "I can cook for myself, and I guess I'd better learn to cook for the kids, too. But for all of us together, I'll pay my neighbor to make something."

"Do you need me to teach you to cook things your children will like?"

He was about to reflexively decline, but thought better of it at the last minute. "I would love some help, thank you."

"Then we should begin right away, since there is not much time. I will come to your apartment tonight, and every night until Monday." The firm way she nodded her head told him she would entertain no argument to the contrary.

197

"Yes, ma'am," he said with a smile.

He couldn't help it that his mind went to less wholesome things than just cooking.

Friday, June 14

Martin got to the embassy a half-hour early that morning, but his hopes of avoiding a throng of the press were dashed as soon as he rounded the corner and approached the entrance. They started shouting questions at him when he was still twenty yards away.

"Mr. Schuller! Any statement on the fall of Paris to the Nazis?"

"Not at this time."

"Mr. Schuller! Has Ambassador Armour made any changes to the embassy's security in light of the news from France?"

"I'm sure his office will answer that question as needed."

"Mr. Schuller! Any statement on President Roosevelt's promise to support Great Britain and France with material resources? How will that affect this embassy's relations with the British and French legations in Argentina?"

"Our embassy has always maintained cordial and cooperative relations with the British and French embassies, and I expect that to continue. Now if you'll excuse me, gentlemen, I'll have more for you at a briefing later this morning. One of our secretaries will let you know the time. Excuse me."

They continued to shout questions as he walked inside the building, but he ignored them. So, it was going to be that type of morning.

He wondered why such a big reaction, when none of this was a surprise after the French government declared Paris an open city on Monday afternoon. For three and a half days, it had been public knowledge that French forces would not defend their capital, in order to avoid its destruction. This morning's occupation by the Wehrmacht was expected.

Expected or not, Martin still wondered what had transpired in the City of Lights this morning, when the German military came marching in. He hurried upstairs to his office, and checked the wire service tickers before even removing his hat.

No disturbances were reported, but he knew the Nazi censors wouldn't allow bad news. The full truth would wait until reporters from neutral countries left Paris and returned to neutral ground to file complete reports. Some intrepid reporter was certain to find a way to cross the battle lines in the next few days, regardless of risk.

That would likely occur before classified reports from the American Embassy in Paris made their way through the diplomatic pouches by train to Lisbon, and from there aboard a Pan Am clipper to New York.

Roger Dean knocked on Martin's door a little while later.

"I got some news from my contact at the French Embassy," he said, sounding harried. The stress accentuated his Kentucky accent. "He said the French government has already withdrawn from Tours and is fleeing further south—perhaps all the way to Bordeaux."

Damn. "They're going to surrender, aren't they?" Martin said, leaning back in his chair.

Roger looked pained. "I don't see how they can't. They've lost the bulk of their fighting force to casualty or capture. Mostly capture. The remnants they've got left aren't enough to save them."

"I was afraid you'd say something like that." Martin thought of the war materiel the Germans were smuggling out of South America, and wondered how much advantage that might have given their forces. *If it was the straw that broke the camel's back…*

Roger took a step inside Martin's office. "It's unbelievable, isn't it? I mean, who could have foreseen this? The French had the largest and best equipped army in Europe. And yet, five weeks after the invasion, they're on the verge of surrender. I'm still struggling to believe it's all true."

And it boosts Hitler's popularity that much more, Martin thought, angry more than glum.

"Do you believe in miracles, Martin?" Roger Dean asked.

Martin took a deep breath. "I'd like to—but no, I don't."

"Do you know anyone at our embassy in Paris?"

Martin shook his head. "By reputation only."

"I have a couple of friends there," Roger said, sounding wistful and looking worried. "Fellas I worked with in Ottawa. I'm thinking of going to Ambassador Armour's office to ask if he's received any word about the status of our personnel there. All I've heard is the French government made Ambassador Bullitt the acting mayor of Paris for its last day of freedom. He would have been the one to officially turn over the city to the Germans."

"As diplomats, they can't be harmed, you know that," Martin said. "And as representatives of a neutral country, they wouldn't even be detained. As long as there was no fighting in the streets, they should be fine."

"Yes, I know you're right. I'd just like to know, when we get news."

Martin felt bad for him. "Maybe the ambassador's office can send a cable to Washington," he suggested. "These are extraordinary times, after all."

Roger nodded, but didn't immediately respond. After a few seconds, he said, "Well, sorry to keep you from your work. I'd best get back to mine. We'll talk again soon."

22

Monday, June 17

Martin spotted them coming down the First Class gangway before they saw him waiting on the shore. Marty walked in front, wearing a baseball cap and a navy blue jacket over a brown sweater; right behind him Martin could see the heads of Jackie and Stevie, walking side-by-side, probably holding hands.

And right behind them walked Becky, looking elegant in a red dress with white lace collar, white gloves, and a stylish red hat tilted upward from the back of her head.

He knew she'd be there, of course. She'd never let the children travel alone for seventeen days. He was a little surprised that she was disembarking with them, rather than waiting on board and watching from the railing. But only a little surprised.

Marty was almost to the bottom when he saw Martin waving, and his face broke into a big grin that made Martin's heart melt.

"Dad!" he shouted, and ran the last several yards to him. He threw his arms around Martin's waist, and Martin removed his ball cap and rumpled his blond hair.

"Look how big you've gotten," Martin said, and patted the back of his son's head.

"Daddy! Daddy!" Jackie and Stevie called from the bottom of the gang walk. Martin saw Becky's hands on their shoulders, preventing them from running off the way their older brother had.

"Come on, let's go meet them," Martin said to Marty, resting his hand on the boy's shoulder as they walked up to meet his two younger children. And his ex-wife.

He ignored her at first, picking up his daughter and his youngest son in turn, hugging them and kissing them on the cheek. He gave five-year-old Stevie a little tickle as he put him back on the ground, eliciting a squeal of giggles.

"Hello, Martin," Becky said as he straightened back up. "You look well."

"Hello, Becky. So do you. Did you have a good voyage?"

"Yes, thank you. We ran into rain a couple of days, going around Brazil, but it was smooth sailing. And it was warm until a couple of days ago, between Santos and Montevideo. The ship was enjoyable—which is good, since I have another sixteen days aboard her before we get back to the States."

He heard the subtle rebuke in her words, and ignored it.

"We've been to five countries now, Daddy," six-year-old Jackie said. She was dressed in a navy blue version of the dress her mother wore, which was fitting since she looked so much like Becky, right down to the curly brown hair. Her patent leather shoes were black and shiny, and she wore white gloves like her mother.

"Five? Wow, that's a lot for just six years," Martin said, crouching down in front of his daughter. "Can you name all of them for me?"

"Ummm," Jackie began, looking up in thought and putting a finger to her lips. "There was Uruguay, and Brazil, and Trin—Trin—"

"Trinidad," Becky prompted.

"Trinidad. And...what was the other one, Mommy?"

"St. Thomas, U.S. Virgin Islands," Becky said. "But that's not really a country, sweetie—it's a U.S. territory."

Jackie counted on her fingers. "And the United States makes four."

Martin patted her cheek. "I know a lot of grown-ups who haven't been to that many countries."

"I've been to lots more than that," Marty said, raising his chin with a boastful look.

"That's true, you have," Martin agreed. "You were pretty little, though."

"I've been to three continents now, Dad," Marty said.

"That's true, too."

"And *they've* only been to two," Marty added, nodding to his younger sister and brother.

"Don't be rude, Marty," Becky said, scowling. "What have we discussed about boasting?"

"It's behavior unbecoming a gentleman," Marty said, almost mumbling, clearly reciting something he'd heard more than a few times.

"That's right, and we are always to behave like gentlemen and ladies, aren't we?"

Martin resisted the urge to roll his eyes, and it took some effort. His children all nodded their heads earnestly, clearly knowing the drill.

"How about we go collect your luggage, and catch a cab home?" Martin said, clapping his hands together in an attempt to make it sound exciting.

"Why don't you children wait right here a few minutes, while your father and I look for your luggage," Becky said. "Don't go anywhere, and hold hands—*all* of you."

Marty made a face, but he took Jackie's hand and watched his parents walk a short distance away.

"Did you want to talk about something in particular?" Martin asked as they walked to the cordoned off area where the First Class luggage was assembled.

Becky handed a ticket to the middle-aged black porter, who bobbed his head and hurried off to collect their things.

"Two months is a long time to take care of the children all by yourself, Martin," she said. "Are you sure you're prepared?"

"Absolutely. I have lots of activities planned. They'll have a good time, I promise."

"And the rest of the time, when you're not doing your planned activities?"

He scowled, resenting the implication that he couldn't keep them entertained. "What do you mean?"

"Marty brought a stack of comic books with him, even though he's read them all multiple times. He has a couple of other books in the steamer trunk, but you know that won't keep him occupied the whole summer—or winter, I guess? That's the other thing—they're missing out on having a summer by coming down here."

"I've got a couple of trips planned to the north of the country, where it's warm," Martin said. "And don't worry about Marty and books—Buenos Aires is full of bookstores, including a couple that specialize in books in English. One of them is quite large, so even Marty won't make it through all of them."

His attempt at levity only earned him the barest of closed-lip smiles from Becky.

"Regular trips to a bookstore will be good for Marty—but I meant what I said about all three of the children missing out on summer by being here. Their friends will all be engaged in outdoor activities that they'll miss—swimming, boating, baseball."

"Winter isn't all that cold here," he said, motioning toward the partly-sunny sky. "It's like Georgia, or South Carolina."

"It's too cold for swimming or boating, though, isn't it? They'll still miss summer."

Martin scowled at her and crossed his arms. "Are you saying they'd be better off staying in Philadelphia with their friends rather than spending time with their father? And experiencing another country and culture?"

"What I'm saying is that you've been a bit selfish insisting that they give up their summer to come see you."

Martin felt his anger rising into his face, and his temples pulsed. He was about to lash out at her, to point out that she was the selfish one to want to keep them all to herself and not share them with him; but instead he said, "The judge doesn't agree with you, obviously."

Her expression turned frosty, but then the porter arrived, hauling a large steamer trunk in both hands, while a younger and skinnier black porter trailed behind him, carrying three suitcases.

"I'll get us a cab," Martin said, and turned away.

He motioned the kids into the back seat of a taxi a moment later, and the porters loaded the luggage into the trunk. Martin was irritated to see Becky climbing into the back of the cab after the kids.

She must have seen the look on his face. "I thought I'd tag along, and see where the children will be staying for the next two months."

And checking out my living arrangements, on the pretext of making sure they're "suitable" for the kids. But really, you just want to satisfy your own curiosity, so you can feel superior.

He got into the front seat so he wouldn't have to sit next to her, or crowd against the kids.

The cab took them from the port westward up Avenida Brasil, along the south edge of the *Barrio San Telmo*.

"Wow, look at that!" Marty said, pointing out the window. "What are those things?"

"That's the Russian Orthodox Cathedral," Martin said. "Those are called Onion Domes, and they're common in Russia. Argentina is a country of immigrants, like the United States is. A lot of Russian and Ukrainian immigrants came to Argentina in the last forty years."

They passed a few plazas on the twenty-minute drive to his apartment in Colegiales, and the kids kept pointing out the windows at things.

"Look at the palm trees!" Marty said.

Martin chuckled.

When they arrived at his building, he had Marty carry his own suitcase, while Martin took Jackie's and Stevie's, and he tipped the driver to carry the trunk.

They went upstairs, and Martin showed them the bedroom they'd share, across the hall from his own. He'd already had three little beds delivered and set up, and a book-shelf put up on one wall.

"Go ahead and start unpacking," he told them. "Then you can say goodbye to Mommy, and I'll show you around the neighborhood."

He led Becky back to the living room. "You want something to drink?" His tone was flat, formal. "I can make you a cup of coffee."

"No, thank you," she said. "The children won't like having to share a bedroom again. They each have their own bedroom at my parents' house."

"They shared a room all those years in Washington."

"Yes, but that was a year ago. They've grown since then."

Not that much. "You'd better not keep the taxi wanting, with the meter running. Kids! Come say goodbye to Mommy."

She flashed him a look before the kids came running out, and she smiled down at them. "Give me hugs," she said, and embraced them all in turn. "Be good for Daddy, and I'll see you in a couple of months. Write to me, I expect lots of letters."

"We will," Marty said.

Jackie started to cry. "I don't want you to go, Mommy."

Becky cast Martin a quick sideways glance, and then knelt down in front of her daughter. "I know, dear, but it won't be for so very long. August will be here before you know it, and we'll go home."

"And we'll have lots of fun while you're here," Martin said, rubbing the back of Jackie's head.

Now Stevie started to cry—probably because his big sister was—so Martin reached down and picked him up. "Oof, you're getting so big," he said to the boy, grinning at him, and rumpled his light brown hair. "Big boys don't cry, do they? Go on, wipe your tears. That's a good boy.

Now say goodbye to Mommy, and then Daddy will take you out for some ice cream. Does that sound good?"

Stevie nodded, sniffing. He held his arms out to Becky, but Martin didn't let him go, just stepped closer so that he could lean over and hug Becky again while Martin held onto him.

"Listen to Daddy, and be a big boy," she told Stevie, rubbing his cheek with a gloved thumb.

Becky left a moment later, and Martin stood in the middle of the living room, a sniffing Stevie in his arms, while Jackie hugged his leg.

"OK, let's go finish unpacking all your things," he said. "Then when we're finished, we can go get some ice cream, and I'll show you around our neighborhood."

They got to the ice cream shop a couple of blocks from the apartment as the workers were locking up for siesta, and Martin had to bribe them ten pesos to delay closing a few minutes. He also promised to bring his children regularly if they did him this favor, and they reluctantly agreed to delay their mid-afternoon rest to serve up some ice cream with *dulce de leche.*

"Dad, can you teach me how to say those words?" Marty asked as they sat at a table by the window, eating their ice cream.

"Sure, kiddo, I can teach you some Spanish," Martin said. "Or I could teach you German instead, if you want."

Marty shrugged. "Maybe. But I think Spanish would be better, since that's what everyone is using here."

Martin couldn't argue with that reasoning, and suppressed any disappointment that his son hadn't jumped at the chance to learn their ancestral tongue.

After they finished the ice cream, siesta was in full swing, and everything was closed. He took them to the subway, and they caught a train downtown.

The tan and white short-haired dog approached them as they walked from the Retiro subway station to the American embassy, and came close before sniffing the air nervously in front of the kids.

"Sorry, pal," Martin told the dog. "I don't have any food for you today."

"Can I pet him?" Marty asked, starting to hold his hand out.

"He probably won't let you," Martin said, and at that moment the dog scampered away. "He's a stray, and they're pretty shy. He only lets me touch him if I've given him food first."

"What's his name, Daddy?" Jackie asked.

"I haven't given him one. He's just a stray, he doesn't belong to anybody."

"Can we keep him?" Stevie asked, bouncing on his toes.

"I don't think so, squirt," Martin said, and patted his youngest son's head. "Come along now, we're almost to Daddy's workplace."

At the embassy, Martin took them straight toward the stairs. He had no intention of stopping by Sloan's office. He was probably with the new agents, anyway.

Juan-Carlos De la Tour came scurrying over as they passed, a delighted look on his face, and he clapped his hands together twice.

"Mr. Schuller, what an *unexpected* surprise!" he gushed. "These *darling* ones must be your children? Oh, my *goodness!* I must say, sir, *this* one looks *exactly* like you." He nodded at Marty, who looked back at him with a curious expression.

"Yes, this is my son Marty, my daughter Jacqueline, and my son Steven. Kids, this is Mr. De la Tour, who works here at the embassy."

"*How* do you do?" De la Tour said, shaking Marty's hand.

"Fine, thank you," Marty said, a funny look on his face.

"We're on our way upstairs, so I can show them my office," Martin said. "Say goodbye to Mr. De la Tour, kids."

"Goodbye!" Jackie and Stevie said in unison, waving.

De la Tour bowed with a theatrical flourish of his hand as they walked away.

"Dad?" Marty whispered as they walked up the stairs.

"Yes, kiddo?"

"What was wrong with that man?"

Martin suppressed a laugh. "Wrong?"

"Yeah. He acted kind of funny."

Martin allowed himself a smile, but didn't laugh. "Mr. De la Tour is just dramatic. That's just the way he talks."

"He's kind of weird," Marty said, face screwed up.

Martin shrugged. "Maybe a little *eccentric*—but the world is full of all sorts of different people. Mr. De la Tour is a nice man. I hope you kids won't be rude to anyone who's different."

"OK," Marty said, and left it at that.

They passed the four young women at their typewriters, and the clacking of keys slowed a bit as they passed. Martin saw Rosa Linda's eyes widen, and then they met his and held them a minute, looking excited and maybe a little flustered.

"Kids, these ladies do all of our typing and filing, for me and some of the other men who work on this floor," Martin said. "This is Miss Bianchi, Miss Alvarez, Miss Gallo, and Miss Ferrer. Ladies, these are my children. They're visiting from the States for a couple of months. "

"Hi!" Jackie said, waving. Stevie echoed her.

"Very pleased to meet you," Marty said.

Martin felt a touch of pride at Marty's manners, even if that was Becky's doing.

"Hello," the ladies said in turn.

"Are you excited to see your father, and to see Argentina?" Rosa Linda asked, rolling her chair to the corner of her desk and leaning her elbows on her knees so she could look at them on their level.

"Are you from Argentina?" Jackie asked, wide-eyed. "You talk kind of funny."

"Jackie! That's not polite," Martin scolded, tapping a finger on the top of her head.

Rosa Linda laughed. "Yes, I am from Argentina. Do I have a funny accent in English?"

"A little," Jackie said, suddenly bashful.

"Say something to us in Spanish," Marty said.

Rosa Linda's face lit up. She looked up at Martin, and her golden brown eyes seemed to dance. She said to him in Spanish, "Your children are absolutely darling, Martin! I mean, Mr. Schuller," she caught herself, glancing back at the other girls, who were still typing slower than usual. "This one looks exactly like you, it is amazing. And such a little gentleman." She nodded at Marty, and then winked at the boy.

"Thank you, Miss Bianchi," Martin replied in Spanish. Then in English to the children, "Come along, kids, I'll show you my office."

He unlocked the office door and flipped on the light. The radiator on the far wall popped and whined. "Here it is, this is where Daddy works every day."

"That's a picture of us," Marty said, sounding surprised, and picked up the framed photograph of the three children from Christmas, 1938. "We're kind of little."

"Well, that was about a year and a half ago," Martin said. "Maybe we should get a new one taken while you three are here, and I can keep it on my desk."

"That's a good idea," Marty agreed.

"Don't touch those papers," Martin scolded Stevie, and the five year old pulled his hand back. Seeing the stung look in the boy's big blue eyes, Martin took a lighter tone. "Those are important government business, and we've got policemen in the building who will come get you if you accidentally tear them. I'd have to protect you."

"You'd protect me from the *policemen*, Daddy?" Stevie asked, giggling.

"I don't know, should I?" Martin asked, kneeling down and tickling the boy, who collapsed in a squeal of laughter.

"Ho, there!" Mike Mattingly said from the open doorway. "If you don't keep that racket down, the ambassador will send Mr. Davis to reprimand you."

His smile at the kids said that he was teasing them; but Martin still caught the element of warning.

"These must be the children you took the day off for?" Mike asked. Without waiting for a reply, he stuck his hand out to Marty. "Hi there, I'm Mr. Mattingly. You are Master Martin Schuller, Jr., I presume?"

"That's right," Marty said, shaking Mattingly's hand.

"Mike, these are my other two, Jacqueline and Steven."

"How do you do?" Mike said, shaking each little hand in turn. "I know your father's been looking forward to your arrival for a long time. I bet you're excited to see a new country, aren't you?"

"I've been to ten countries now," Marty said.

Mike Mattingly's eyes widened. "You don't say? That's a lot for such a young man. How did you manage that?"

"We lived in Europe when I was little," Marty said. "For two years, right, Dad?"

"That's right. And we still count Austria as its own country, don't we? It was, then."

"I'd say it counts, then," Mattingly agreed with a decisive nod for the boy. "Do you remember all those countries?"

"No...but we have lots of pictures. I've looked at them a whole bunch of times. I took them to school a couple of times so my teacher could see them."

"Can you name all of those countries?" Mattingly asked.

"Sure," Marty said with a shrug. "There's Austria—we lived there—and Germany, Czechoslovakia, Hungary, and Switzerland. Plus now I've been to Trinidad, Brazil, Uruguay and Argentina."

"That's only nine," Mattingly teased.

"United States of America!" Stevie shouted, bouncing on his toes.

"Inside voice, Stevie," Martin said.

"That's impressive," Mattingly said, and stood back up. "Are you here long, Martin?"

Martin shook his head. "Just for a little bit. I wanted the kids to see the embassy, and meet some of the folks here. We'll be on our way shortly."

"Alright, then we'll talk more tomorrow."

"Anything I should know?"

"No, it can wait until you're back at work tomorrow. Goodbye, kids. It was very nice to meet you."

"Goodbye, Mr. Mattingly," the children all said.

"He works with you, Dad?" Marty asked.

"That's right."

"Does he have any kids here?"

"Yes, he and Mrs. Mattingly have two children, I believe. They're a little bit older than you, but maybe we can arrange to meet them at a park this weekend. Would you like that?"

"Yeah, maybe they can have fun with us."

Martin should have known his kids would want to play with other American kids. He should have made those plans before they got here. "Alright, then, I'll call Mrs. Mattingly tonight and set something up for Saturday. They live in the next *barrio* over from ours. That's the Spanish word for neighborhood, or district."

"*Barrio*," Marty repeated.

"That's right," Martin said, smiling down at his son and patting the back of his head. "We live in *Barrio Colegiales*. Can you say that?"

"*Barrio Colegi- Colegiales*," Marty repeated, stumbling over the pronunciation a little.

"You'll get the hang of it."

"Dad? Can we meet those kids tomorrow?"

Martin saw the hopeful look on his son's face, and his heart ached a little. "Sorry, sport—they've got school tomorrow. It's not summer vacation here. But we can do it on Saturday."

"What will we do tomorrow while you're at work?"

"Señora Rodriguez will watch you while I'm gone. She's the housekeeper who comes during the day. I've engaged her to stay with you children while I'm at work."

"Is she nice?"

This question surprised Martin. "Yes, she's very nice. And she speaks pretty good English, so she'll be able to take care of you while I'm away. She can take you to the park after she's finished her cleaning. Maybe she'll bring over her grandchildren one day, and you can play with them."

"Do they speak English, too?" Marty asked.

"I don't know," Martin said. "You can ask Señora Rodriguez tomorrow. And maybe she can help you learn some Spanish."

Marty nodded, looking pleased with that answer.

Martin turned to Jackie and Stevie, who were sitting on the floor, cross-legged, facing each other and playing some sort of game with their hands.

"Come on, kiddos—let's go meet some of Daddy's other colleagues. And then you'll meet my boss, Mr. Davis."

He knew he'd better not neglect that introduction.

Hutson

23

Saturday, June 22

It was a mild day, almost sixty degrees, and the sun in the cloudless sky made it feel warmer than it was. The park at the Plaza Juan José Paso was crowded with children running around and laughing. The sun's low winter angle in the northern sky cast Calle Moldes in shadow, but the park was bathed in sunlight.

Martin sat with Mike and Susan Mattingly on a park bench, watching their children and chatting. The Mattinglys had two boys, ages eleven and nine, and Marty ran after them, playing a game of tag. Jackie and Stevie played on a teeter-totter.

"Thank you for coming to our neighborhood," Martin told Mike and Susan after the children had gone off to play. "The kids have come here every day with Señora Rodriguez, so it's the most comfortable place for them to meet new people."

"Our pleasure," Susan Mattingly said. "Our boys don't get to play with many American kids, so this is a treat for them."

"They seem to be getting along," Mike said, nodding toward the boys' tag game.

Martin was glad of that. He didn't admit that it was more difficult than he'd imagined to keep his kids entertained in a foreign country, especially one where they didn't speak the language.

"How long did it take your boys to learn Spanish?" he asked.

"Oh, they were little when we first went to Peru—Freddie was three, and Scotty was just one—so they learned it alongside English,"

Mike said. "Since then, we've been in Mexico and Bolivia. Aside from a few brief visits with family in Connecticut, they don't really remember the States, not well."

Martin nodded. That was what he and Becky wanted to avoid when he first took the counter-intelligence job back in Washington in 1933, when Marty was two, and Becky was pregnant with Jackie. They knew it would be difficult, raising a family while bouncing from country to country every two years. He'd wanted to jump at the opportunity anyway, but he also knew Becky was eager to be closer to home, no matter how much they'd both loved their time in Austria.

"Maybe they can help each other, then," Martin suggested.

A steam whistle blew several loud blasts, and a freight train rumbled by on the tracks south of the plaza, coming into the city from the southwest. Dozens of cattle cars rolled by, bringing in beef from the surrounding Pampas.

Fiedler met the train when it pulled into the railyard. He walked next to the track as it slowed to a stop. It irritated him that it was seven minutes late. Trains in Germany were always punctual.

He'd arrived early, and had now been waiting for more than twenty minutes, hidden between two empty freight cars, standing behind the iron link that connected them. He had his diplomatic passport in his pocket, should a nosy railroad security officer come snooping around and ask his business, though he hoped to not be seen at all.

Now that the train had arrived, he stepped out to locate the car he needed.

He was about mid-train when he spotted his contacts approaching. Two of them pulled a large, flat cart behind them, with a heavy tarp bundled on one side.

"Greetings, Mr. Schmidt," the leader said to Fiedler, in Spanish. They didn't know his real name, and he aimed to keep it that way.

"Good afternoon," Fiedler replied. "Let's go see what they've sent us today, Mr. Giordano."

They found the box car with the serial number they'd been provided, and Giordano's two associates hauled the door open.

Several head of cattle looked out at them. Peeking through their legs, Fiedler saw the stacks of crates lining the back of the car. He nodded that direction, and Giordano's two associates—Napolitano and Campignini—climbed into the car and set up a chain through the cattle, passing crates down to Giordano, who set them on the cart.

All three were Italians who had immigrated to Argentina as youngsters, between twenty and thirty years prior. All had been referred to Fiedler by the Political Officer at the Italian Embassy, a staunch Fascist who was quite proud that his country had finally joined the war, and was all too eager to be of any assistance to clandestine German operations.

His eagerness worried Fiedler—it often led to careless mistakes—but he needed the assistance in working with someone at the rail yard; so after mentioning his concerns to Captain Nieburh, who had overruled him, Fiedler accepted the references that his Italian counterpart offered.

So far, so good.

The cart was loaded about as full as it could safely be, Fiedler noted. The three workers spread the tarp over the crates, obscuring them from view, and tied it down at the corners.

They hauled the cart down a boardwalk across multiple sets of tracks, huffing and struggling with the weight, while Fiedler walked ahead of them. At the end of the boardwalk, they hauled it along the gravel toward an alley behind a large warehouse.

Here a truck idled, and the driver got out to help them load the cargo into the back. This driver was the son of German immigrants, Fiedler had been told. He was a big-built man with light brown hair and gray-blue eyes, wearing the coarse cotton blue shirt and dark woolen pants of a working man.

"You are Weierbach?" Fiedler asked him in German before he reached the cart.

"Yes, I am Carlos Weierbach," the man replied in German, but Fiedler noticed he didn't translate his first name from Spanish. "You must be Mr. Schmidt."

"I am. From what part of the Fatherland did your parents originate?"

"My parents are Bavarian," Weierbach said.

Fiedler nodded. The question was as much to verify Weierbach's fluency in German as anything else. But Bavaria was also one of the states within Germany that had the highest rate of party membership, so the fact that Weierbach's parents were Bavarian also boded well for his allegiance to the mission.

"Very good, Mr. Weierbach. Get back to work," Fiedler ordered. Weierbach nodded and complied.

Fiedler watched as the four men moved the crates from the cart to the back of the truck. Then Weierbach closed the back while the three Italians hauled the empty cart away. Giordano looked to Fiedler and touched the rim of his hat as they left.

"You know where you are going?" Fiedler asked Weierbach in German. Of course he did, but Fiedler wanted the excuse to speak to him for a moment.

"Yes, I have the pier number, and the name of the ship," Weierbach said, and Fiedler was pleased that he didn't blurt out either.

"Have you done this sort of work before?"

Weierbach shrugged as his only answer.

Discretion. A hint of smile stretched Fiedler's lips. "Very good, Mr. Weierbach. If you complete this task without mishap, we will have more work for you in the near future. The Fatherland thanks you." Fiedler clicked his heels together and nodded in the old-fashioned German manner, which he still preferred to shaking hands.

Weierbach nodded in return, though he didn't click his heels. He climbed into the truck and backed it away.

Fiedler remained until the truck had disappeared down the road that led toward the *Ante Puerto*. Then he slipped back through the parked box cars and disappeared across the tracks.

Martin held Jackie's and Stevie's hands while they walked home, and Marty walked beside them.

"Did you have fun meeting the Mattingly boys?" Martin asked his eldest.

"Yeah, they were pretty swell," Marty said. "We're going to their park next time."

Next time. "When is that? Did you already work something out?"

"Yeah, next Saturday afternoon, I said you'd take us to meet them at their park in *Barrio Villa Crespo*. They said it's bigger."

"Oh, you said I'd take you, did you?" Martin teased, and poked his son's shoulder with his elbow, not letting go of Stevie's hand.

Marty had a sheepish smile. "Yeah. You don't mind, do you, Dad?"

Martin laughed. "No, I don't mind. I'll set it up with their parents."

They passed a school on the next block. "Señora Rodriguez said her grandchildren go to school there," Marty said. "They come to the park after school, and play with us for a little while, until we have to go home before it gets dark."

A Catholic church stood on the opposite side of the street from the school—Señor del Milagro—and Martin wondered if that were the church that Rosa Linda attended with her family. It was only a few blocks from their apartment building, so it stood to reason that it was.

He still hadn't worked out exactly how he was going to introduce Rosa Linda into the children's lives. They'd met her at the embassy that first day, of course, but somehow he'd have to introduce her as his girlfriend.

    That was a tough one. He had no idea how to go about it.

24

Martin called Rosa Linda that night after the kids went to bed. Her father answered.

"Good evening, Mr. Bianchi. This is Martin Schuller calling. May I speak with Rosa Linda, please?"

There was a second's hesitation before Leonardo Bianchi answered, his voice quieter than before. "Yes, she is here. You are lucky I was the one who answered the telephone, and not her mother. One moment."

Martin heard the clatter of the phone against the hard surface of a table, and then silence for a long moment.

"Hello? Martin?" Rosa Linda's voice whispered into the receiver, in English.

"Hi there," he said, immediately smiling at the sound of her voice. He realized he missed her. It was strange not going out with her on a Saturday night. Or any night this week.

"You could have been caught by Mamá," she whispered. "She would not have been kind."

Which is exactly the kind of judgmental attitude I expect from church people, he thought, but knew better than to give it voice. "I had to risk it. I wanted to talk with you, and couldn't wait until Monday morning at the embassy."

"I'm glad," she whispered, and he thought he could hear the smile in her voice.

"The children are asleep," he said, suddenly feeling giddy and excited. "You could come over for a few hours, and they'd never know."

"Martin..."

"I know, believe me—but it's worth the risk, don't you think?"

"What if one of them wakes up and comes out to ask you for a cup of water? They can't see us doing—you know."

"We'll just listen to the radio," Martin suggested. For a second, he believed that. "I just need to see you. I hate only seeing each other at work."

The line was silent for a second. "I understand, Martin—but your children are more important."

Martin felt his frustration rising. "We can't go on like this for two months," he said. Right now, that felt like forever. "We have to work out something, or I'll go crazy."

"We could go to lunch at the same café tomorrow, and pretend to run into each other accidentally," she suggested.

That wasn't the worst idea, Martin knew. Corny, yes—but not bad.

"Let's do it," he said. "Noon, tomorrow, at the Café Santi on Avenida Cabildo."

"I can be there at twelve-thirty," she replied. "After my family gets home from Mass."

"It's a deal," he said, and grinned from ear to ear. "See you tomorrow, darling."

Sunday, June 23

Martin and his children arrived at the Café Santi at quarter past noon. The café was not yet full with the usual lunch-time crowd—a testament to the country's church-going habits—and they were seated immediately.

The manager initially led them toward Javier's section along the side of the café, but Martin asked for a table closer to the front. In

Teodoro's section. He only wanted to deal with one thing at a time today.

"Can you translate this, Dad?" Marty asked, frowning at the menu.

"Of course," Martin said, and explained the sandwiches, chorizo sausages, and empanadas.

"We usually have dinner instead of lunch on Sundays," Marty said.

"Well, I prefer lunch like any other day, and we'll have dinner tonight as usual." Martin regretted his sharp tone.

Marty shrugged and looked out the window.

Javier hurried past, on his way to the kitchen, and his eyes caught Martin's for a second before shifting to the three children at his table. His eyes widened in surprise, and then a hint of frown crossed his mouth as he passed.

Teodoro came to their table, and Martin ordered a half-liter of the local pale lager for himself, and three Coca-colas for the kids.

"You can get Coke here?" Marty asked, excited.

"Of course," Martin replied, and nudged his son playfully with his elbow. "Did you think this was the wilds of Borneo?"

Miguel and Eva Cohen passed on the street, and Martin rapped his knuckles on the window to get their attention, then waved. "Come on, I want you to meet some friends of Daddy's," he said to his children, and then told Teodoro in Spanish that they would be right back.

"*Guten tag, Herr Schuller,*" the Cohens greeted him in German, and he returned their greetings.

"These are my children, here to visit me for their summer vacations," he said in German. "This is my eldest son Marty, my daughter Jacqueline, and my youngest son Steven." Then to the children in English, "Kids, this is Mr. and Mrs. Cohen, who live near here. I see them here often."

"Hello," Jackie said enthusiastically, waving. Stevie echoed her.

Marty just nodded and quietly said, "How do you do?"

"They don't speak German, unfortunately," Martin explained to the Cohens.

"It is understandable," Miguel Cohen said. "Our children only speak some, they are hardly fluent. It is the normal way of things, I think."

"Do they speak Spanish?" Eva Cohen asked in that language.

"A very little," Martin answered her, also in Spanish.

"That is a pity," she said, returning to German. "Miguel and I do not speak English, I'm afraid."

"Little bit English, not so good," Miguel Cohen said to the children in strongly-accented English, holding his fingers close together.

"We are going to Córdoba this afternoon to pick up our son Jorge from the National University," Miguel said to Martin, returning to German. "He has completed his first semester, and we will bring him home for the break. The next semester starts in July."

"Congratulations," Martin said. He saw Rosa Linda across the avenue, waiting for the light to change. He knew they needed to get back inside so the ruse would be convincing. "Enjoy the trip. We need to get back to our table. Good day." He touched the rim of his hat and ushered the children back into the café.

They had only been sitting for a moment when Rosa Linda came through the front door. She pretended to be surprised to see them, and came to their table.

"Mr. Schuller! I did not expect to see you here," she said in English, looking suitably excited at the "surprise" encounter.

My God, she could be an actress. Martin stood, and prompted Marty to stand also. "Good afternoon, Miss Bianchi. It's a pleasure to see you. You remember my children?"

"Yes, of course. How could I forget them?" she said, smiling down at them.

"Kids, say hello to Miss Bianchi."

"Hello, Miss Bianchi," they said in unison.

"Hello," she replied with a nod to each of them. "*Buenos días*, how we say it in Argentina."

"Would you like to join us for lunch?" Martin asked, and felt his stomach flutter with sudden nerves. "We haven't ordered yet, so I can have the manager bring over an extra chair."

"That would be lovely, thank you. You do not mind?"

"Not at all," Martin said, his excitement showing a bit too much, he thought. The kids didn't seem to notice, at least.

He caught the manager's attention and motioned him over. "Mr. Messini, would you bring another chair for the lady?" he asked in Spanish, to which the manager replied, "Of course, Mr. Schuller."

"That man knew your name, Dad," Marty said, tugging Martin's sleeve. "He called you *Señor* Schuller."

"I come here a lot. It's close to my subway stop, and I often get some breakfast here before work."

Once they were all seated, Teodoro came to take their orders. He was a stocky, square-faced fellow with a quiet demeanor—a stark contrast to the handsome and outgoing Javier. Martin ordered *carne asada* for himself and beef empanadas for his children, and Rosa Linda ordered the same as Martin.

After the waiter departed, Martin looked back at Rosa Linda and smiled. "I've been introducing the kids to Argentine food little by little. So far you've liked everything you've tried, right kids?"

Marty nodded. "It's good."

Jackie made a face. "I didn't like the spicy one, Daddy."

"Me neither!" Stevie half-shouted, grinning.

"Inside voice, Steven," Martin scolded. "I forgot about the chorizo night. Marty was the only one who liked the spicy sausage. Isn't that right, sport?"

"Yeah, I'm not a little kid like my brother and sister," Marty told Rosa Linda, who laughed.

"I don't think I liked chorizo until I was about your age." Martin saw her wink at his elder son, and then she patted Jackie's hand. "It's not bad to not like some things. You might when you get bigger."

"Hey kids, why don't you tell Miss Bianchi some of the things we've done since you came to Buenos Aires?" he suggested.

"Yes, I'm interested to hear everything," she said, putting her chin in her hand and leaning her elbow on the table so she could lean toward them.

"Dad took us to a big bookstore on Friday night," Marty said, lighting up. "They have lots of books in English. Dad bought me three."

"We went to the International bookstore on Avenida Rivadavia, in Almagro," Martin explained to Rosa Linda. "I got something for all of them. I confess it was my first time there."

"Oh, yes, I used to go there when I was learning English in school," Rosa Linda said.

"I want to go to the zoo," Jackie said. "Daddy said he'd take us next weekend."

"I haven't been to the zoo since I was a little girl," Rosa Linda said, smiling at Jackie. "You will like it." To Martin, she added, "It is not far from here, just over in *Barrio Palermo*."

"Maybe we should ask Miss Bianchi if she'd like to go to the zoo with us," Martin suggested to his daughter. "Would you like that?"

"Yes," Jackie said, nodding.

"Then why don't you ask her," Martin prompted.

"Would you like to go to the zoo with us, Miss Bianchi?"

"I would be delighted," Rosa Linda said to Jackie, reaching across the table to squeeze her forearm. "When are you going?"

"When are we going, Daddy?"

"How about next Saturday afternoon?"

"I think that would be wonderful," Rosa Linda said, and he saw in her eyes that she was thrilled to be included.

Maybe he didn't have to explain anything to the kids after all. Maybe he just included Rosa Linda in all of their weekend activities, and let them figure it out. He liked that idea. It would normalize her presence without pressure.

"We're open to suggestions," he said to her. "Any fun activities for kids in Buenos Aires we should check out?"

"*Ay*, let me think," she said, looking up in thought. "They are a little young for the theater or the ballet, and would probably be bored at the art museum."

"I'm afraid so. But maybe the symphony?"

"What a lovely idea!" Rosa Linda beamed.

"Mom goes to the symphony sometimes," Marty said, without irony. "I've never been, but my granddad plays records in his study, and it's always that kind of music."

"Do you like it?" Rosa Linda asked him. Her eager smile made Martin warm inside.

Marty shrugged. "Sometimes."

"Well, then maybe we'll do that one weekend while you're here," Martin said, and rumpled his son's hair. Even more than having another activity to do with the kids, the thought of taking them to their first symphony instead of Becky gave him intense satisfaction.

He could just imagine the look on her face when the kids told her.

25

Javier lay back against the pillow, half-listening as the young man next to him droned on, his arm bent behind his head. Thaddeus Acker was always a talker after sex, something Javier had come to expect whenever Thaddeus scheduled an entire Sunday afternoon.

Thaddeus was twenty-two—a year older than Javier—and a towhead blond with little body hair. His smooth body was thin but soft, with little overt musculature in spite of fairly broad shoulders. His blue eyes were too pale to be pretty, and his face might have been attractive were it not for the ridiculously small nose that bore a slight upward tilt at the end. And if Javier were in a critical mood, he'd notice that Thaddeus's cheekbones were rather small, sometimes giving his cheeks a sunken look.

The young man's best feature was his perfect skin, soft and creamy white without blemish. That, and, well, the really fat cock between his legs.

Thaddeus came to Javier a couple of times a month, for the last year or so, always on a Sunday afternoon, and always for three or four hours—the majority of which was spent in mostly one-sided pillow-talk, occasionally punctuated by some light caressing of Javier's body.

Javier suspected the young man was lonely.

He knew Thaddeus's entire life story by now. He was born in Baden-Baden, Germany, in 1918. His father was a soldier in the Great War, but had trouble finding work after. The family came to Argentina when Thaddeus was eight years old. After fourteen years in the country, he spoke Spanish without an accent. He was a dual citizen—a fact he mentioned frequently, for some reason—and a few years ago he'd been hired by the German Embassy.

He worked as a clerk, but a few months back he'd gotten a bit of a promotion—Javier wasn't clear on the details—so that his duties now included some courier work to Uruguay and Paraguay.

Thaddeus's droning voice became almost hypnotic, and as he stroked Javier's thigh, Javier slipped into his fantasy world, imagining Mr. Schuller beside him, stroking his thigh and talking about his life in North America.

He felt a stirring between his legs at the image.

"It's not as if we have any alternative, with the way the British navy is keeping German ships bottled up in their harbors," Thaddeus was saying. "So we have to use Spanish and Portuguese ships to move the freight, but without it being stopped by Customs on the way out. Last week I carried *forty thousand pesos* in an envelope for an inspector in Asunción who looks the other way."

Javier's ears perked up. He knew that men often said far more than they should after sex, but this still surprised him.

Mr. Schuller might want to know more about that, he thought. Perhaps this could get Javier back in Mr. Schuller's good graces. He needed to learn more. He needed to keep Thaddeus talking, and without changing the subject as he so often did, being a rambling conversationalist.

"That sounds dangerous," Javier murmured, trying to sound more impressed than he actually was. "You could be robbed by bandits and left for dead. You must be very brave." He put his hand in the middle of Thaddeus's chest and let it rest there.

Thaddeus looked over at him, a crooked grin tugging up half of his mouth. "It can be dangerous, yes," he said, a note of excitement coming to his voice. "But I don't worry about that. It's important work."

"I'm sure it is." Javier rubbed his hand in a circle on Thaddeus's chest.

"Well, I'd best be going home now," Thaddeus said, threw the covers back and swung his legs over the side of the bed.

Javier knew he needed to keep Thaddeus talking, get him to say more. He sat up behind him and put his hand on the young man's shoulder and tugged him back against his chest.

"Can't you stay a little longer?" He nibbled with his lips against Thaddeus's earlobe, and kissed down the side of his neck. Then Javier rubbed his hands down the pale white chest and played with the overly large pink nipples. They were as big as a peso coin, but the tips grew hard under Javier's finger tips.

He felt Thaddeus's breath coming short and fast; but then he pulled away, sitting up straight. "I wish I could, but it will be dark soon."

"Are you sure?" Javier whispered seductively, and slid his hand down Thaddeus's soft stomach to the mess of white-blond curls at his groin. Then he wrapped his fingers around the fat penis that had already grown half-erect. "Stay a little longer?"

He could feel the tension in Thaddeus's back muscles, and then suddenly Thaddeus swung around and grabbed Javier by the legs, pulling them up around his sides while he dropped forward on top, locking lips.

As Javier expected, the surprise second round of sex, quick and urgent, left Thaddeus in an exhilarated mood, and he spent the next half-hour lying beside Javier, talking.

Javier steered the conversation back to the clandestine missions.

"Are you always alone?"

"Usually," Thaddeus said, an unmistakably boastful tone matched by the grin on his face. "I know how to take precautions, and I can handle myself if I need to."

Javier doubted Thaddeus meant with his fists. He lacked the size to be a physical threat. "You carry a gun?"

"A nine millimeter Glock," Thaddeus said, his grin widening even more, if that were possible.

Javier aped at being thrilled. He propped himself up on his elbow, and leaned over Thaddeus's pale torso. "Have you ever shot anyone?" he asked, placing his right hand palm-down on Thaddues's chest.

"No, I've never had to," the young man admitted. Then, as if to reclaim the heroic upper-hand, he added, "But I could if I had to. And I would."

"Do you have the gun with you today?"

Thaddeus looked unsure before admitting, "No. I only carry it when I'm on a mission."

"How often do you do that?" Javier widened his eyes just so, hoping he looked and sounded thrilled.

Thaddeus shrugged in a cocky sort of way. "Pretty often, lately. Almost once per week."

"Then, you have a secret code name?" Javier asked, leaning forward eagerly and laying his other hand on Thaddeus's shoulder.

"Of course."

Javier knew he couldn't ask for it outright, so he just waited, letting his right hand make slow, seductive circles over Thaddeus's chest. The young man lay back in contented silence, arms raised and hands behind his head, a proud smile curving his lips. Javier leaned farther over him, now lying halfway across him.

"I didn't realize how important you are," he murmured between little kisses at Thaddeus's throat. "An unsung war hero."

He could feel Thaddeus's chest swell beneath him. Javier imagined his face glowing.

A moment later, Thaddeus repeated that he really did have to leave. Javier let him get up and dress quickly. Thaddeus laid a thick stack of bills on the nightstand, and turned back toward Javier with a grin.

"I don't want you to worry about me. I'll see you again next Sunday."

"I'll think of you often," Javier said. "I want to hear all about your adventures while you're away from me."

Thaddeus grinned from ear to ear as he put his hat on his head. "You will," he said with a wink, and let himself out.

Javier had no doubt that he would.

26

Tuesday, June 25

"I have that file you asked for, Mr. Schuller."

Martin looked up at the sound of Antonio Rivera's voice. The young man stood in his open door, several manila folders at his side. Martin hadn't ordered any file this morning.

"Come in." He motioned for Antonio to close the door. "Have you learned something?"

Antonio nodded, and the lenses of his glasses flashed the light of the desk lamp that illuminated Martin's work on this cloudy day. "Javier has identified a courier from the German embassy who takes bribes to customs officials at the northern border, and in Paraguay. Then those officials do not look at boxes coming from mines to Buenos Aires."

Martin's pulse quickened. This was just the sort of breakthrough he'd been hoping for.

"Is it someone Javier knows personally?" He hoped Antonio would note that it was a yes-no question, and answer accordingly.

"I think so, yes. I don't know certainly."

"You don't know *for certain*," Martin replied. "But that's OK, I can talk to Javier about that. Did he happen to tell you the name of the courier?"

Antonio shook his head. "No, sir."

Martin had figured as much. "That's probably best."

Antonio looked a little stung. "Why is that best, Mr. Schuller?"

"The fewer people who know the courier's identity, the safer it is for everyone." He didn't feel like elaborating, and left it at that. "Is there anything else?"

"No, Mr. Schuller."

"Thank you, Antonio. That was helpful. I'll follow up on it."

Martin waited behind his neighborhood newsstand on Avenida Cabildo, across the street from the Café Santi, pretending to read today's Herald—which he'd already read that morning. Ricardo Messini closed the café for siesta about quarter to two, and a few minutes later the waiters departed.

Javier walked south toward the subway station on Avenida Federico Lacroze, and Martin crossed the avenue a moment later and followed him.

He caught up to Javier just after the young man went through the turnstile, and walked toward the platform a few feet to the side of him. Martin cleared his throat to make sure Javier noticed him, but didn't look at him or say anything. There were still a decent number of people coming and going, and Martin was wary of watching eyes and listening ears.

From the corner of his eye, he saw Javier look his direction, but then face forward again immediately. *Good boy.*

They waited near each other on the platform for a moment until the Line B train arrived. Martin followed Javier through the sliding door, then toward the less crowded rear of the car. Javier took a seat in a deserted corner, and Martin sat a few seats away.

"I have something that interests you, sir?" Javier asked quietly in Spanish, a hint of coy smile curling the corners of his mouth.

Martin ignored the innuendo. "I heard you have information for me," he replied in English.

"I would have told you myself, but you have not been in the café for a few days. So I told Antonio to give you the message."

Martin glanced around to make sure there was still no one within ear shot. "You identified a German courier?"

Javier nodded, and slipped one seat closer to Martin. "A man I know a little bit, he works at the German embassy. His name is Thaddeus. He bragged to me that he does dangerous courier work. He said last week he carried a bribe to a customs official in Asunción."

That was an awfully bold thing to brag about, Martin thought, skeptical. "You believed him?"

Javier's amber eyes held Martin's gaze, unblinking, for several seconds. "Yes. You do not?"

Martin didn't answer that. "Did he say anything else?"

"The bribe for the Paraguayan official was forty thousand pesos."

Martin did the math. That equaled almost nine thousand U.S. dollars. That was far more than an average customs official made in a year. His skepticism grew.

"What do you think of that?" he asked, eyes narrowing.

Javier made a half-hearted shrug. "It's a lot of money," he said, as if that were the most obvious thing in the world, and he couldn't believe Martin was asking. "One could buy a lot of cooperation with such money."

One could indeed, Martin thought, not dismissing it out of hand, but still skeptical. He glanced around again to ensure no one had crept close, and then asked, "What else did he say about his courier work?"

"He said he travels to many places, bringing messages, and he works alone. He takes a gun."

Of course he does—if he's really telling the truth. And if he weren't, telling Javier that he carried a gun would be meant to impress...

Which meant this German was probably hoping to seduce Javier, Martin realized with a start. That made the whole thing unlikely—if not outright impossible. The Nazis murdered homosexuals in cold blood on the streets of Germany; they wouldn't hire one to do clandestine work.

"He works at the German embassy?"

237

Javier nodded.

That settled it, in Martin's mind. He would have gone through rigorous background checks in Germany before being sent abroad to one of their diplomatic missions. Unless he was a career diplomat, and a holdover from the Weimar days.

"How old is he?"

"He is twenty-two years," Javier said, surprising Martin with the precision.

"How do you know that?"

Javier shrugged. "He told me. It is a year older than I am."

Then definitely not a Weimar holdover. "Thank you, Javier," he said, getting up. Hitting dead ends was part of the job, but this one disappointed him. "If you learn anything more, send me a message."

He walked toward the center of the car as the train slowed, and exited at the next stop.

Javier watched Mr. Schuller walk away, his chest tightening. Mr. Schuller hadn't seemed interested in the news Javier brought, had even seemed a bit dismissive at the end. It stung his heart.

He wondered if he should have been more specific, or even provided Thaddeus Acker's name. Would that have made a difference?

His heart seemed to sink into his stomach as he pictured the look on Mr. Schuller's face, and he realized that it probably wouldn't have.

Then he crossed his arms, irritated. It was valuable information, he was certain of that. He'd been doing Mr. Schuller a favor by telling him first.

Now, he would tell *Unai* instead.

27

Friday, June 28

"Got time for a beer after work?" Sloan asked, knocking on Martin's door shortly before five o'clock.

"No, I have to get home to my kids. I'm a single father these days." He was glad to have the excuse.

Sloan frowned briefly, but then nodded in resignation. "I suppose you are. Who watches them during the day?"

"My cleaning lady, Señora Rodriguez. She'll want to go home to her husband as soon as I get there."

Sloan made a little scoffing sound. "If he's like most Argentines, he won't get home until eight o'clock, at least. Come on, have a beer with me. I've got news to share with you."

Martin didn't like being pushed. "I really shouldn't."

"It'll be quick, at that little place right around the corner. One beer, and then you can go catch your train. Just tell Señora Rodriguez you had a lot of work to do. That's not implausible, you know—there is a war going on in Europe, after all."

Martin acquiesced, nodding with a sigh and visible reluctance. "Since you've got news," he said as he reached for his hat. "Twenty minutes, no more." He'd slip Señora Rodriguez an extra five pesos tonight.

They chatted on the way about the French surrender on Monday, the twenty-fourth.

"I heard Churchill's furious," Sloan said.

Martin grunted. There had been a lot of talk around the embassy that week. "The allies agreed from the beginning not to negotiate a separate peace with Hitler. But Pétain broke that."

"They've got De Gaulle."

"That's true," Martin said. "The million-dollar question is, how many Frenchmen are going to leave France to join him in England?"

"I thought the million-dollar question was whether Hitler was going to get his hands on the French fleet," Sloan said, opening the door. "The Brits'll be done for if he does."

Martin didn't answer. Monday's armistice specified that the French government would keep their fleet, withdraw it from combat, and that neither Germany nor Italy would take any of the ships for themselves.

But Hitler had broken more agreements than Martin could count.

"What's the big news?" Martin asked a few minutes later, when the waiter departed from delivering their half-liter glasses of pale lager. The tavern had just reopened after siesta, and it wasn't crowded. The setting sun shone right through the front windows, making the entire space glow golden red for a few precious moments.

"I'm going back to New York. The Bureau's got a spot for me there. A new project." Sloan announced with a pleased look.

Martin was stunned, and it took him a second to remember to say, "Congratulations."

"Thanks, pal." Sloan raised his glass to Martin. "Schuller, I've enjoyed our time working together here, but I'm glad to be going home. Maybe we'll run into each other again someday, for some common purpose."

Martin took a few seconds to recover from the shock. "I thought you were stationed in Buenos Aires for the foreseeable future. Aren't you supposed to ease the new special agents into their role here?"

"That's done," Sloan said with a shrug. "They're set up, and they've gotten right to work. When I first heard they were coming, I wrote the Director asking for a transfer back to the States once they got going; New York, preferably. He obliged."

Martin wasn't entirely sure why this angered him. Sloan irritated him, and he'd never really liked the guy. He still carried some resentment of Sloan's role in taking undercover work away from him last year.

But this felt like being abandoned in exile.

"When do you leave?"

"Harriet and I sail in a couple of weeks, July fifteenth."

Martin took a long drink to gather his thoughts. "Do I have a particular liaison among the new fellas?"

"Wilson's the Special Agent in Charge, starting next week. Check with him." Sloan didn't seem to care.

"Will do," Martin said, and downed the rest of his lager. He laid a few pesos on the table and shoved his hat onto his head. "Tell Harriet I'll miss her dinner parties."

Sloan shrugged. "Tell her yourself at the Ambassador's reception on Thursday."

Martin replied with a curt nod. "Have a good weekend."

He stormed off in the direction of the subway station. He knew it was envy that made him so irritated by this news, but that didn't matter. He was stuck here for two whole years, and then to God only knew where next—while Sloan got to put in less than a year and then slip back home.

Next month, he'd be glad to have Sloan out of his business; but for tonight, he was mad as a hornet.

Javier found *Unai* sitting in a dark corner, dressed as a working man in a coarse blue shirt with band collar, and dark gray woolen trousers. A tumbler of whiskey on the rocks sat on the table in front of him. *Unai* nodded to him, but otherwise sat still.

Javier went to the bar and ordered a glass of red wine. Roberto Calderon entered a moment later, and joined him at the bar. He ordered a beer when the bartender brought Javier's wine.

"My contact is in the corner table in the back," Javier whispered out the side of his mouth to Roberto after the bartender walked away to pour Roberto's beer.

A moment later, the two young men joined the agent at the dark table.

"*Unai*, this is my friend—"

"You can call me Shepherd," the agent said to Roberto. "I will call you Owl. If you do not tell me your real name, I can never be forced to reveal it."

Roberto nodded, grave. "I understand, sir."

"Our mutual friend here tells me you are a dock worker, and that you have seen our enemies moving their cargo."

Javier understood that there were to be no names said aloud, even if known. *Unai* must be leery of being overheard.

Roberto answered. "Yes, I have seen things. I gave names to an American friend of my friend." He nodded toward Javier.

This caught Javier off-guard. He hadn't realized how deeply Roberto and Mr. Schuller had cooperated.

"When was that?" *Unai* asked, eyes narrowing.

Roberto shrugged. "About two months ago, I think."

Unai seemed to consider this for a moment. "Do these men still work at the Ante Puerto?"

"Yes, all of them."

Javier wondered what Mr. Schuller did with those names. He looked at *Unai*, who was sitting in silence for several seconds.

"Would you give the names to me also?" *Unai* asked finally. He laid two hundred pesos on the table.

Roberto eyed the money, but just shrugged. "What will it accomplish for me to give them to you also?"

A faint smile stretched *Unai*'s thin lips. "The Americans work with the police—but the police cannot always be depended upon to take action. We will take our own actions."

Javier and Roberto exchanged a look. They both knew the implication. Javier continued staring at Roberto even after he looked back to *Unai* and took a deep breath.

"Yes, I will give you the names."

Hutson

28

Thursday, July 4

The American-style grill sizzled in the yard behind the ambassador's residence, as specially-hired servants cooked hamburgers and hotdogs for the assembled embassy staff and their families.

The yard rang with the happy squeals of children running around with sparklers, chasing each other until one of the adults reprimanded them.

Martin stood in a huddle with Mike Mattingly, Roger Dean, and Chuck Brady, glasses of beer in hand, all keeping an occasional eye on their own children, but mostly content in the knowledge that they were safe in the enclosure. The afternoon festivities were not open to the public, generally speaking, though certain well-connected American ex-pat businessmen and their families had been invited.

"It's a topsy-turvy world, that's for damn sure," Chuck Brady said, shaking his head.

"You can say that again," Mike Mattingly replied.

"Has anyone heard if either one has backed out of tonight's ball?" Martin asked.

Roger Dean snorted. "I doubt it. I'm sure they'll both want to convince everyone in attendance that they were right."

The stunning news yesterday afternoon that the British had boarded without warning and captured French naval vessels anchored at Plymouth and Portsmouth; followed by the downright shocking news that the Royal Navy had attacked part of the French fleet anchored at

Mers-el-Kébir in Algeria, sinking a battleship and damaging five other vessels, had left them all speechless.

"They can save their breath," Martin said. He'd seen the news wire when he checked his office this morning prior to coming to the ambassador's residence. "The president told the French ambassador in Washington this morning that he would have done the same thing Churchill did."

Mattingly laughed. "You can bet Mayweather will corner you at some point tonight. If he doesn't, I'll eat my hat."

Martin kept to himself that he would welcome a private chat with Thomas Mayweather.

"So old Roosevelt's throwing his hat in with the Brits," Chuck Brady said. "Is anyone really surprised?"

"There's still the Neutrality Law to tie his hands, though," Mattingly replied.

Brady shrugged. "I bet that law won't last the year."

Mattingly shook his head. "It'll last until after the election. It's in place until at least next year, mark my words."

"Mark your words?" Roger Dean said with a nudge and a teasing smile. "Like how you said a few months ago they were all going to negotiate a quick end to the 'phony war'?"

Mattingly crossed his arms while the others laughed. "Alright, I deserve that. But you fellas know nothing big is going to change before the election."

Martin enjoyed seeing Mattingly get his comeuppance, good-natured as it was, but he decided to chime in and rescue him. "Barring any other big shifts in Europe, I think Mike's right."

"You mean, like Hitler invading England?" Brady said, arching an eyebrow.

Martin nodded. "Yeah, something like that."

"Whose job is it to keep the German ambassador away from the British ambassador tonight?" Roger Dean asked. "Not mine, I'll say that."

Chuck Brady groaned. "Probably mine and Martin's. Maybe you fellas could give us a hand once or twice, though? Like the good chums that you are."

"I suppose I could have a diversion or two ready to go," Mattingly said.

"Thanks, Mike," Martin said. "This isn't the first ball they've both been invited to since last September, is it?"

The others all shrugged. "No idea," Chuck Brady said.

"Don't look at me," Roger Dean said. "I haven't been invited to any embassy balls since Bastille Day last July. There was no war yet."

This won't be easy, Martin feared.

Reginald and Harriet Sloan arrived a few minutes later, and Harriet made a bee-line for Martin. After wishing him a happy Independence Day, she smiled slyly and added, "I got a letter from Ann Corley yesterday. She's taken a job in Brazil, working for a non-profit organization in Sao Paolo. She made some friends there on her first visit, and they helped her get the job. She's glad to be staying in Latin America, but still hopes to work for the American Foreign Service eventually. Do you know anyone in our consulate there who could help her?"

Martin shook his head. "I'm afraid I don't know any of our people there." He didn't know anyone at the embassy in Rio de Janeiro, let alone the consulate at Sao Paolo.

"Oh, that's too bad," Harriet said. "I'll give you her address, and perhaps you'd be good enough to write to her? I know she'd appreciate your help."

Martin knew it wasn't his professional help that Harriet hoped he'd give. He had no intention of writing to Miss Corley, but wouldn't disappoint Harriet. "If you give me her address, I'll be happy to write if I think of anything that might help her."

"Wonderful! I'll mention that to her when I write her back. I need to get a letter off to her before we leave next week."

"You're excited to return to New York?"

"Oh, very much! It's not that I don't like it here—it's a lovely city— but New York is home, and it'll be good to get our girls back there, too. I was excited to live abroad, I'd never been anywhere; but you don't realize how much you'll miss, do you?"

He agreed. Harriet excused herself and went over to a group of wives who were keeping close watch over the children with sparklers.

"You don't have to write to Ann, you know," Reginald Sloan said.

Martin suppressed the urge to reply that he didn't need permission. Instead he shrugged. "I'm not sure I'll be of much help to her, honestly."

Sloan guffawed. "You know that's not Harriet's aim, right?"

Martin ignored it. "You haven't said much about your new job in New York. Only that it's a new project. What are they going to have you doing there?"

Sloan waggled his head. "This and that."

Martin stared at him for a few seconds. "So something classified."

"You could say that."

"Back in counterintelligence? Catching Nazi and Soviet agents on U.S. soil again?"

"Not exactly."

Not exactly? Martin wondered what that meant, but knew better than to pry further. Still, he couldn't help a more general question. "A new challenge?"

Sloan shrugged. "It's a new initiative, yes. But it's not entirely new."

Martin decided to leave it at that. "I hope it goes well for you. It's been a pleasure working with you these last nine months." They both knew it wasn't really, but Martin said it anyway.

"Thanks, Schuller," Sloan said, and shook his hand. "We do work well together. You can count on Wilson, though. He's up to speed, and I think you'll be impressed with the operation he's got started. The Americas Security Zone is going to be much more than just words from now on."

"Good to hear," Martin said, and downed the last of his beer. More than he would have liked to take in one gulp, but it allowed him to shake his empty glass and excuse himself to get another.

"But *why* don't they have fireworks, Daddy?" Jackie said, rubbing her eyes while Martin tucked her into bed.

He pulled the covers up to her chin. "Because it's not a holiday here, remember? We talked about that this morning."

"But I want to see some," Jackie said, voice quivering.

Martin pictured Becky giving him an *I-told-you-so* scowl. "Now, now, no whining. Close your eyes and go to sleep."

He glanced over to see Stevie already asleep, mouth open. They'd run around a lot that afternoon at the Ambassador's picnic.

"Can I keep one light, Dad? So I can read?" Marty was sitting up in his bed, an open book in his lap.

Martin shook his head. "Time to put the book away, son."

"Al-right." Marty's tone and the way he elongated the word said that it wasn't, but Martin ignored it. From the doorway, he watched Marty switch off the last lamp, then wished them goodnight and closed the door.

Rosa Linda sat on the couch, and looked up from her knitting when Martin walked into the living room.

"They'll be asleep soon. They had a busy day." He sat next to her and kissed her cheek. "Thank you again for babysitting tonight."

"Martin, you'll wrinkle your tuxedo," she said, nudging him with her elbow.

"Yes, ma'am," he said with a crooked smile as he got up from the couch. She was right, of course. "What did you tell your parents?"

"I said I was going to the cinema with the girls from work. I told them it was…" she searched for a word, and then looked to him for help. "What is the word for two movies in one theater?"

"A double feature."

She nodded. "They won't expect me home early."

"Good." He leaned down and kissed her on the mouth. "I'll try to be home by midnight. If anything bad happens, call the embassy. The security guard answers the phone during these things, he'll find me."

"Nothing bad will happen. Now go, do your work." She shooed him away. He grabbed his hat, and wished her goodnight.

The embassy ballroom rang with laughter and conversation in multiple languages. A sextet orchestra played melodies by George Gershwin, Cole Porter, and Irving Berlin. The mantels and windowsills were decorated in red, white and blue bunting. Waiters circulated with trays of champagne and hors d'oeuvres, but Martin mostly waved off their offers. He stood in a group listening to the Japanese ambassador defending his country's war in China in unsteady English, and trying to find the words to address questions about the status of Shanghai.

"But there are still Japanese troops inside the International Settlement," the Brazilian ambassador pressed, in English.

"For protection of foreign residents, from Communist insurgents," the Japanese ambassador said, casting a glance at the Soviet ambassador on the other side of the room. "The International Settlement still governs itself."

"'Protection' my foot," Martin heard Thomas Mayweather mutter under his breath, and turned to see the British diplomat standing beside him. Martin took the opportunity to turn away from the conversation he'd grown bored with.

"I wondered when I'd see you tonight," he said to Mayweather. "I was beginning to wonder if you'd stayed home."

"Nonsense. I'm always thrilled to be invited to this celebration of your forebears' treason," Mayweather said, without a hint of irony.

It's been a hundred and sixty-four years, fella. "Our founding fathers put their very lives on the line for liberty."

"True, treason is a capital offense," Mayweather said, still without any sign of irony.

"They knew the risk they were taking. And that it was all worth the risk."

Mayweather looked at him with a strange expression. "Every English schoolboy knows that your 'founding fathers' didn't know what was best for them."

And you wonder why Americans don't want to jump in and help you every time you go to war with Germany. "I think clearly it all worked out pretty well for us." Martin didn't bother to keep the testiness from his tone.

"Well, you would think so, wouldn't you?" Mayweather said, feigning an affable smile and unconcerned tone. He glanced away, looking at the couples waltzing around the center of the room.

"Mers-el-Kébir," Martin said, and stopped for effect.

Mayweather snorted. "It seems your president is in agreement with Mr. Churchill that the action, though disagreeable, was necessary. Under the circumstances."

Martin wasn't surprised that Mayweather had heard about Roosevelt's conversation with France's ambassador to Washington. "Care to elaborate about the circumstances?"

Mayweather frowned. "You know the circumstances. The new French leadership, sitting in Vichy, is hardly trustworthy. We can't afford to take Pétain at his word. And the whole world realizes by now that Herr Hitler can't be trusted to keep his word about anything."

Martin nodded. "I've heard Marshall Pétain is quite a conservative."

Mayweather snorted again. "Mr. Churchill is a conservative. Monsieur De Gaulle is a conservative. Pétain and Laval are downright reactionary. In France, they and their lot are called 'counter-revolutionary.' The French Revolution was a hundred and fifty years ago, but the bloody Frogs speak as if it were still continuing to this day."

He faced Martin head-on, and his lips were a thin line. "There is every possibility that Pétain will throw in his lot with Hitler, Mussolini, and Franco. They're all cut from the same bloody cloth. Hitler may yet get his hands on the remainder of the French fleet, sitting at Toulon. If he does, they'll be more than capable of punching holes in the Royal Navy's blockade of the continent. Not to mention the increased strength in the Mediterranean could let the Germans overwhelm our garrisons at Gibraltar and Malta—" He stepped closer and lowered his voice. "—and allow him to deploy his own naval forces against the British Isles themselves."

Martin felt a tingle of fear run down his back and into his belly. He could find no words to respond to Mayweather's prediction.

"With the fall of France, Britain stands alone," Mayweather said, and the gravity in his voice weighed upon Martin's chest. "We are all that stands between Hitler and world domination. If Britain falls, the United States will stand alone—and Hitler won't give a damn about your neutrality. Think about that, Mr. Schuller. And see that your colleagues all think about it, too."

Martin got home a few minutes after midnight.

"I'm sorry I'm late," he told Rosa Linda.

She waved it off. "Don't be. I will tell my parents that my friends and I stopped for a glass of wine at the *milonga*. That will not seem so strange. I had a glass of wine here, so they will not be suspicious."

"Does that mean you have time to stay a little while?" He winked at her.

She swatted his arm. "Don't be rude. Your children are asleep in the next room. I will go home now like a good babysitter. I will see you at work tomorrow."

"We leave for our trip tomorrow, but I'll see you at work on Wednesday," he said, and wished her goodnight.

Martin tugged his bowtie loose and tossed it onto the top of his dresser. He hung the tuxedo jacket in the closet and unbuttoned his collar. He removed his cufflinks, and opened the drawer where he kept them—but something made him pause.

He stared at the contents of the drawer for several seconds. The stacks of boxer shorts and undershirts were even, and in the right places, but he was certain they had moved. It was tiny, almost imperceptible, but the distance between the stacks wasn't right. It was just off a little bit, not the way he generally packed them.

He checked the other drawers. They were the same—everything in its place, but not exactly right.

Frowning, he walked to the kids' bedroom door and cracked it open. He poked his head in, and saw them all three sound asleep. After a moment's hesitation, he looked in their dresser drawers, but found them undisturbed.

He went back to his room, huffing in irritation. When he was younger, he'd heard stories of women going through a man's drawers—and wallet—the first time she was left alone at his place, usually while he was in the shower. It was said that they were looking for evidence that he was married, or had another girl, or was deep in debt.

Martin didn't care how common it was, he was angry.

29

Saturday, July 6 – Bariloche, Argentina

It seemed strange to see snow piled high on the sides of the village square, when they'd just celebrated the Fourth of July at the ambassador's residence two days before.

It had been fifty-nine degrees Fahrenheit when they left Buenos Aires the previous afternoon, a typical partly-sunny winter day. The large thermometer on the wall beside the platform at the Bariloche train station a little while ago read minus two degrees Celsius—about twenty-eight or twenty-nine degrees Fahrenheit.

"The inn is over this way," Mike Mattingly said, motioning with his arm toward the far side of the cobblestone square. In his down-filled coat and matching woolen hat and scarf, he looked like he'd stepped out of an LL Bean winter catalogue. "Wait until you see this place, Martin. Old World charm in spades."

"Daddy, I'm cold," Jackie whined.

"Put your mittens on," Martin instructed his children. "I told you on the train that it would be cold here, didn't I?"

It had been a long train ride, almost twenty-four hours to traverse 1,537 kilometers—955 miles—southwest from Buenos Aires. For the last couple of hours, the views out the train window had been spectacular as they climbed into the Andes Mountains. The kids had enjoyed pointing out wildlife moving through the snow and rocky outcroppings, or waterfalls encased in ice.

The town of San Carlos de Bariloche—commonly called simply "Bariloche"—was built in the style of an Alpine village, complete with timbered buildings that would have looked at home in Austria or Switzerland. At an elevation of 893 meters—or 2,930 feet—Bariloche sat at the base of a giant mountain called *Cerro Tronador*. The mountain towered almost another 3,000 meters over them.

Martin scanned the mountainside for signs of the *Cerro Catedral* ski resort, but couldn't identify it. He supposed it was probably hidden behind the pine forests that surrounded the town. Twilight was settling over the area, though the reflection off of the snow kept it from being truly dark. The snow itself seemed to take on a bluish hue in the deep winter twilight.

There were few cars here, and their group walked directly across the square unimpeded.

The inside of the inn smelled of old pine wood, and the scent immediately took Martin back to his days in Austria almost a decade before. Behind the counter to their right stood a diminutive man of about fifty, bald with a white fringe of hair and wire-rimmed glasses. He greeted them in Spanish, though Martin thought he detected a hint of German accent in his speech. To their left the lobby was occupied by several couches and arm chairs, and a fire roared in an enormous stone hearth on the far side of the large room.

"Dad, look at the size of that fire," Marty whispered, tugging at the sleeve of Martin's overcoat. "Do you think they'd let us roast marshmallows?"

"I don't think they do that in Argentina, kiddo."

"Oh." Marty sounded disappointed.

"But they've got a great little chocolate shop around the corner," Mike Mattingly said to the collection of kids. "After we get settled, we'll go get some hot cocoa. What do you say, Martin?"

"Sounds good to me."

"I want hot chocolate!" Stevie yelled, bouncing.

"Inside voice," Martin scolded. He stood next to Mike at the counter as his friend—whose Spanish was far superior to his own—checked them in.

The room was small, with white plaster walls, but the same rough-hewn pine timbers for a ceiling and rafters that they'd seen in the lobby. There were two double beds covered in heavy quilts, and a small table between them with a lamp and a little clock.

A chest of drawers stood on the opposite wall, next to a small mirror. There were four drawers in the dresser, and no closet.

"Looks like we each get a drawer, kiddos," Martin said. "I'll take the top drawer, then Marty, then Jackie, and Stevie you get the bottom one. Let's get unpacked."

"Mommy doesn't let us unpack our own suitcases," Jackie said.

"Then I'll teach you how," Martin said, and opened Jackie's suitcase.

He showed Marty and Jackie how to organize a drawer, but then Stevie insisted on doing it by himself. Martin watched in pained silence as his youngest stuffed his clothes unevenly in a disorganized mess.

"Nice try, buddy," he said, touching the back of his youngest son's head as he shifted a few things so he could close the bottom drawer. "Let's go see if the Mattinglys are ready. Come on."

The Mattinglys were waiting for them by the fire in the lobby. "Isn't this the most charming place?" Susan said to Martin.

Martin agreed with a smile.

"I told you you'd love this place," Mike said, and took his wife by the arm. "Come on kids, let's go get some hot chocolate."

It was dark out, but the village square was illuminated at the corners by old-fashioned kerosene street lamps, and the warm glow from inside the store windows reflecting off the snow. The sky twinkled with countless stars, a sight that couldn't be seen in the brightness of Buenos Aires.

Freddie and Scotty Mattingly knew the way to the chocolatier, and hurried ahead of the others. Marty tagged along with them, listening in rapt attention as they described their skiing feats from last year.

Martin held Jackie's hand, and told her to take Stevie's. They walked alongside Mike and Susan Mattingly down Calle Mitre, as Mike told him about the ski lessons available to the kids. "And for you, too, since you've never skied before. But I bet you're a natural."

Martin shrugged in silence. *Just don't call me a 'skier,'* he thought, picturing the smiling face of *Der Skiläufer* from the newsreel last year.

They found the chocolatier on the far side of the square, and two older couples, probably mid-to-late fifties, stood outside the door conversing in German. Martin instantly caught the Austrian accent of the couple closest to the door, and smiled at the familiarity of it.

The inside of the chocolatier was crowded, and while they waited in line Martin amused himself guessing who was a tourist, and who was a local. Some of the customers wore ski apparel, making the guess easy; others required him to eavesdrop on their conversations in an attempt to confirm his initial guess.

Most of the conversations inside the store were in Spanish—and he thought he could detect the difference between a *porteño* accent and a local accent. But he could hear a few conversations in German, all of them between individuals who appeared at least fifty years old.

He'd read that Bariloche was originally settled by German immigrants some forty-five years previous, and that other German immigrants had followed once the railroad arrived, along with Argentines of other nationalities.

Once they'd gotten their hot chocolates and sat at a pair of tables near the drafty front window, he remarked on the German conversations to Mike.

"Yes, I noticed that last year," he said. "And there's a German restaurant about a block over from here. We took the boys there for dinner one night. Good wienerschnitzel. You want to try it tonight?"

"I'd love to," Martin said, having not had any good German food in quite a while. His stomach growled at the thought.

Next to them, Marty was regaling Freddie and Scotty Mattingly with tales from his comic books. "...and then The Batman swooped down in front of the robber, and he went 'Ka-POW,' right in the kisser." Marty mimed swinging a punch.

Martin wondered where Marty had heard the phrase "in the kisser." He imagined the look on Becky's face when their son used that kind of language, and he smiled to himself.

Marty continued his story. "The bad guy dropped the loot and ran away, but the police grabbed him. The Batman was gone before the cops saw him."

Mike laughed and looked back at Martin. "The things these kids read these days," he said, shaking his head. "Vigilante heroes punching bad guys. What's next?"

The Bozen Haus restaurant was built like a Tyrolean lodge, with soaring ceilings of rough pine rising in peaks with the roofline.

Martin noticed the reference to the former city of Bozen, Austria— now Bolzano, Italy—the capital of the South Tyrol. Owing to its geographical location south of the Alps, the German-speaking region had been transferred to Italy in 1919 after Austria-Hungary came out of The Great War on the losing side. North Tyrol, situated within the Alps, remained part of Austria.

Well, it used to be Austria, before the Anschluss, Martin thought with a touch of bitterness.

Former Austrian territory, with a majority German population— South Tyrol was like the Sudetenland in every respect, *except* that instead of democratic Czechoslovakia, it belonged to fascist Italy,

Hitler's ally; so the Fuhrer had made no demands on it. The hypocrisy was not lost on Martin.

The waitress who came to their table was a round-faced blonde woman in her early twenties, with a broad smile and a twinkle in her blue eyes. She greeted them in Spanish, and Martin asked if she spoke German.

"*Ja bitte,*" she replied, her smile broadening.

Martin ordered for himself and his kids in German—wienerwursts and apple sauce for Jackie and Stevie, wienerschnitzel with red cabbage and spaetzle for Marty, and sauerbraten with red cabbage and fried potatoes for himself. As he chatted with her, he noticed her accent sounded almost Austrian, but with a touch of Spanish lilt.

"Show off," Mike Mattingly said when Martin finished. He then proceeded to order for his family in Spanish.

"What did I get?" Marty asked. He made a face after Martin translated the order. "I don't like red cabbage."

"Sure you do," Martin said. "You used to eat it all the time at Grandma and Grandpa Schuller's house in Reading."

"No, I don't like cabbage."

"You like red cabbage," Martin insisted. "I remember. You're thinking of sauerkraut. You never did like Grandma's sauerkraut."

"I know what sauerkraut is, Dad," Marty said, his tone getting huffy. "I don't like *any* cabbage."

Martin considered scolding his son for his tone, but let it go. "Well, you used to like it."

"No, I didn't."

"I remember," Martin said, getting exasperated. He leaned close to his son's ear and lowered his voice. "And don't argue with me in front of people, young man."

"Do I have to eat it? I don't like it."

"Yes, you have to eat it."

Marty pouted, and crossed his arms. "Mom says you always have to have things *your* way," he muttered.

Martin seethed in silence. He wasn't angry at his son; not really, anyway—he was furious at his ex-wife for saying something like that in front of their children. He took a deep breath, and then a long drink of his beer.

If he were being fully honest with himself, though, he knew he was a little mad at himself, too. He had never exposed his children much to the food that he'd grown up with in a Pennsylvania Dutch home. Partly it was because Becky didn't know how to cook the way his mother did; but he knew Becky's Anglo-Saxon background wasn't the real culprit. For one thing, during their years in Austria, she had adored weinerschnitzel.

He remembered inviting friends from school to dinner when he was about Marty's age, and being embarrassed when they turned up their noses at the smell of his mother's sauerkraut, which always filled the house. Maybe he'd spared his kids the same embarrassment.

Then in his mind he heard his father remarking—in Pennsylvania Dutch, of course—at how "English" Martin's children were. That made it easy to refocus his anger at David Schuller. And that was always the most comfortable place to send it.

Martin excused himself to go to the men's room a few minutes later, and told Marty to watch Jackie and Stevie.

He found the restrooms in the back of the restaurant, in a small hallway. As he neared, he heard a couple of men speaking German in a booth, and he made inadvertent eye contact with one of them. The man was about forty, sitting across from a much younger man who didn't appear to be his son or brother; there was no resemblance. The older one had dark, wavy hair, with flecks of gray at the temples, hazel eyes, and a square jaw and cheekbones. The younger one was a towhead blond, pale, with a weak chin and a stub nose.

They stopped talking when Martin approached, and sat in tense silence as he passed them.

He thought that strange. He also noticed that they were the first people younger than fifty that he'd heard speaking German here.

After finishing in the bathroom, he slipped out the door quietly and lingered in the hallway, just behind a wall from the booth. The two men were conversing again, in German; their voices were low, but not whispers.

"What was the cargo?" the younger man said.

Martin immediately recognized his accent as being Alemannic—it was similar to the accent he'd grown up with in Pennsylvania Dutch country—so the young man was either Swiss or Alsatian, or perhaps Badener.

"Copper and lithium, aboard the Spanish freighter *Concepción*, from the port of Valparaiso," the older man said, in an accent that sounded vaguely northern German.

Not from the same region, Martin realized. He also noted that Valparaiso was a city in Chile, not Argentina. Bariloche sat near one of the old passes through the Andes from Argentina to Chile, so that was probably not a coincidence.

"I'll take that information back to Sargo," the younger man said. "I return to Buenos Aires in the morning. I'll relay this first thing Monday."

"And I am due back in Santiago by Monday," the older man said.

Martin's pulse quickened. The Germans were smuggling metals from Chilean mines aboard neutral Spanish ships. Given that the younger man said he'd take the information back to someone named "Sargo" in Buenos Aires—almost certainly a code name—that told Martin the mastermind behind the whole operation was located in the Argentine capital.

Martin made a note to research lithium when they returned to Buenos Aires. He remembered from the Periodic Table of Elements that it was a metal, but that was all he knew about it.

He suspected a military use.

In the distance, he saw a man rise from a table and make excuses to those seated with him, and Martin knew he couldn't remain in the bathroom hall listening to the German spies' conversation. He took a step back from the corner so that he could emerge normally rather than hugging the wall; and as he passed the spies' table he glanced at the young blond who would be returning to Buenos Aires in the morning, to remember his face.

Predictably, they stopped talking when Martin walked by. What Martin didn't expect was the eye contact from the young snub-nosed blond. Martin didn't see suspicion in the pale blue eyes, but he couldn't read what he did see there.

He nodded as he passed, in acknowledgment of the eye contact, and didn't look back.

Their food had arrived when Martin got back to the table.

"Ah, you're just in time," Mike Mattingly said.

"I might have guessed," Martin said, leaning over to breathe in deeply, savoring the aroma of the sauerbraten.

Beside him, Marty was digging into his wienerschnitzel and spaetzle with gusto, but pushing his red cabbage aside with his fork.

Martin took a deep breath and chose to ignore it. But Stevie and Jackie giggling across the table from him got his attention. "Steven Joseph, get your fingers out of your applesauce."

**

He saw the spies get up to leave a few minutes later and walk toward the door. He turned in his seat to watch them walk out, and saw them head in opposite directions.

"Excuse me," he muttered as he got up from the table.

"Where are you going?" Mike Mattingly asked, but Martin waved him off.

"Be right back." He hurried to the front door, glad to find no one standing around—the hostess was busy cleaning a table by the bar—and he slipped out and looked in both directions. The dark-haired middle-aged spy was just disappearing around a corner to the right; the pale young blond was walking away toward Martin's left, casually looking around.

Martin knew he couldn't follow either of them; for one thing, he had left his overcoat and gloves inside. Plus, he couldn't leave the kids at the table with the Mattinglys while he went off for an indeterminate amount of time.

He went back inside, rubbing his hands together against the cold.

"What was that all about?" Mike Mattingly asked him, eyes narrowing.

"Something for work," Martin muttered, giving Mike a look that said not to ask anything more. "How many hotels does this town have?"

Mike shrugged. "I'm not certain—probably four of five. Why? Thinking of changing to another?"

Too many to investigate. "No," Martin said, and didn't elaborate.

Sunday, July 7

Two hours spent trying to learn how to snow ski was plenty for Martin. He was freezing, bruised from countless falls, and his legs felt like they were made of rubber. By noon, he was sitting at the bar in the ski lodge, a hot pretzel with mustard on a plate in front of him, and a Brandy Alexander in a martini glass beside it.

He didn't usually drink hard liquor, but a day like today called for it.

He'd arrived at the bar before the lunchtime crowd—early enough to secure a seat close to the giant picture window looking up at the ski slopes, and not too far from the roaring fire in the enormous stone hearth. From here he could see Jackie and Stevie making lopsided snowmen with the other young children, supervised by a pair of smiling blondes in red ski suits and knit caps.

Marty was somewhere up on the mountain with the Mattingly boys. After an hour's lesson, he'd taken right to skis, far surpassing his father, and he took off after the older boys with barely a "See ya later, Dad."

Martin didn't mind, recalling the moment with a rueful half-smile. Marty was having the time of his life. At least the kids were having a good time, and he had this comfortable ski lodge in which to relax and stay warm. It was a pretty good deal, all in all.

"I thought I might find you in here," he heard Mike Mattingly's cheerful voice say behind him.

Martin turned away from the window and saw Mike and Susan Mattingly standing next to a pair of barstools, all rosy cheeks and grins.

Martin hurried to finish chewing a bite of pretzel, and shook Mike's hand in the interim. "Yeah, turns out I'm not a great skier," he finally managed to say.

"It takes lots of practice." Mike clapped Martin on the shoulder. "May we?" he indicated the empty seats.

"Of course."

"Don't worry, Martin, I'm not a very good skier, either," Susan said.

Martin gave her a grateful smile, though he knew it wasn't true—he'd seen her shushing down a slope after her husband, while Martin tipped over sideways into a snowdrift.

"That looks good," Mike said, nodding toward the frothy cocktail by Martin's plate. "Not sure it will help your skiing, though."

"I'm not sure I'm all that concerned," Martin said, and took a drink.

Mike laughed out loud, and clapped Martin on the shoulder again as he took the seat next to him. "I have an unfair advantage, I suppose," he began, and then looked at the bartender and said "*Una cerveza, por favor.*" He looked back at Martin. "When I was growing up in Connecticut, we went up to Vermont at least once each winter. I've been skiing since I was six years old. When we came to Buenos Aires from Bolivia two years ago, I was thrilled to learn that Argentina had a ski resort—brand new that year, in fact; but more than passable, wouldn't you say?" He motioned around the well-apportioned lodge.

Martin had to agree. "It's got lots of nice modern touches. I've been enjoying this big picture window—it lets me keep an eye on the kids while I stay nice and warm."

"You've got the right idea, Martin," Susan said.

"I'd forgotten your assignment is up soon," Martin said to Mike, in reference to the latter's statement about coming to Argentina two years before. "Next month, right?"

"That's right," Mike said, and thanked the bartender who set a tall glass of pale lager in front of him. "Just five more weeks."

Just when we were starting to become friends, of a sort, anyway. "Do you know where you're going next?"

"Not for certain," Mike said, and something in his tone told Martin there was more he wasn't saying.

"But you have an idea?"

Susan put her hands together in a prayer-like posture and looked up at the ceiling.

Mike shook his head at her. Turning back to Martin, he said, "Well, possibly—I've applied for a job back in Washington. A policy-making position in the Latin American division, so there's plenty of competition. Still, I think I've got a pretty good shot, with my experiences around the region."

"It'll be good to get the boys back in the States, and to be closer to family," Susan added.

Martin understood how she felt. Becky had felt that way after just two years in Austria—and by contrast, the Mattinglys had been in Latin America for eight years.

"I hope you get the job," Martin said, and raised his glass toward Mike. "Cheers."

"Thanks, pal." Mike raised his own glass and took a drink. "If I get the job, you'll probably still hear from me on a pretty regular basis, as we find ways to implement closer cooperation with our neighbors around the Americas."

Martin wondered if Mike's prospective new position would include access to classified information; and if so, how much. Perhaps none, if the focus was still economic cooperation—but he'd said "policy-making," so there was a possibility there would be more to it.

"Ah, here come the boys," Susan said, causing Martin and Mike to look toward the door, where Freddie and Scotty lumbered inside in their heavy ski boots, with Marty trailing behind.

"Good, let's get a table and order some lunch," Mike said, clapping his hands together.

Martin was more than reluctant to give up his prime location at the bar. But he could hardly stay there by himself while Marty joined the Mattinglys at a table.

He got up, consoling himself with the thought that although the seat would be snatched up by someone else right now, it would come empty again after the lunchtime rush. He popped the last of his pretzel in his mouth, and took his drink with him.

He met Marty at the table and patted the back of his head. The boy's cheeks and nose were bright red, and his eyes were tired, but with a decided twinkle.

"Having fun, sport?"

Marty nodded enthusiastically. "Uh huh!"

Martin put his hand on his son's shoulder. "I'm glad, kiddo."

Hutson

30

Wednesday, July 10 – Buenos Aires

Martin made eye contact with Antonio Rivera as he walked through the embassy the morning he returned to work. He nodded surreptitiously toward the stairs, and Antonio's tiny nod acknowledged the instruction.

Five minutes later he knocked on Martin's door.

Martin waved him in without a word, and motioned for him to close the door.

"When you got your job here at the American embassy, how did you hear about it?"

"There was an advertisement, and I came to apply." He regarded Martin with curiosity.

"How many applicants were there?"

Antonio shrugged. "Many. Perhaps ten. Mr. De la Tour said I was the best applicant."

I bet he did. "Do you remember the other applicants?"

Antonio frowned, and looked up in thought. "A little, I think. Why?"

"Do you remember a pale young man, about your age, with light blond hair—lighter than mine—very light blue eyes, and a small little nose that curved up like this?" Martin pushed the end of his nose up in demonstration.

Antonio shook his head. "I don't remember anyone like that, no."

Martin nodded. He'd assumed not, but he had to check. "It was just a curiosity, that's all."

Antonio turned to go, and on a whim Martin told him to wait. "By any chance have you ever seen advertisements for jobs at the other embassies?"

"I think so, yes."

"Which ones?"

Antonio shrugged. "I do not remember."

"Would you remember if I asked about the German embassy?"

Antonio considered a moment, and shook his head. "No, I don't remember any advertisement for a job at the German embassy. I am sorry, Mr. Schuller."

"Don't be. I was just curious. Thanks again."

First Secretary Davis had monitored the news reports while Martin was away, but not long after Martin was back at his desk, international news dropped a bomb on him.

Earlier that day, the French National Assembly, meeting in the resort town of Vichy—after purging all of the Communist delegates, and several of the Socialist ones—approved a new Constitutional Law, abolishing the French Republic, and granted all government authority to Marshal Phillippe Pétain.

Martin was stunned at how lopsided the vote was—569 to 80, with twenty abstentions. He hated to think what would happen to the eighty delegates who had voted "no," now that Marshall Pétain was legally a dictator with absolute power. *Brave bastards. Or foolish.*

He wondered what the State Department's official response would be, if any. He made a note to bring this up with First Secretary Davis when he met with him later.

Once Martin had gotten caught up with the work he missed during the extended weekend in Bariloche, he buzzed the intercom, and Maria Elena Ferrer was the one who answered.

"Yes, Mr. Schuller?"

"Would you have one of the clerks come up for an assignment, please?"

A few minutes later, a tall young man with a wavy swoop of blond hair over his forehead knocked on his door. "You have work for me, Mr. Schuller?" the young man said, his Spanish accent fairly strong.

"Yes, I do. What's your name, son?"

"Luciano Saenz-Brodeur," the clerk said.

"Mr. Saenz, I need for you to search for any books or journals that we have about mining operations in Chile," Martin said. "And also see if we have any resource books about metals and their industrial uses. If we do, please bring them to me."

"Yes, sir," the clerk said, and hurried off.

Martin didn't hold out much hope. The embassy had volumes of research material on Argentine mining—but Chilean mining would be a stretch. He had considered a midday trip to the library, but decided against it. For starters, he didn't have the time today; and secondly he was concerned that all of the resources there would be in Spanish, and he wouldn't understand what he was reading. He could probably find a librarian who could translate for him, but that would reduce security.

At least an Argentine clerk here at the embassy had passed a routine security clearance and signed a confidentiality agreement.

Luciano Saenz-Brodeur returned twenty minutes later with a large hardcover book, and set it heavily on the corner of Martin's desk. He gave Martin a weary smile.

"This book tells about metals and industry," the young man said. "I am sorry, Mr. Schuller, I found nothing about mines in Chile."

Martin wasn't surprised. "That's quite alright, Mr. Saenz. This one may give me what I need." He fished a five peso coin from his pocket and handed it to the clerk. "For your trouble."

The young man's face lit up like a Christmas tree. "Thank you, Mr. Schuller!" Five pesos would probably buy his lunch that day, with change to spare. He grinned as he pocketed the coin and departed.

The index showed a few entries for lithium. Martin thumbed through the pages and found a short entry—but what piqued his interest was a handwritten note in the margin:

> New lithium-based lubricating grease known to enhance performance of airplane parts. More shearing resistance, better performance at high temperature. U.S. manufacturers to import lithium carbonate, lithium stearate and hydroxystearate. –J.S. Dec 1938

Martin didn't recognize the initials. The specific mention of airplane use intrigued him, though. That was obviously what the Germans were after with Chilean lithium.

He drafted a detailed memo to the FBI liaison office, describing what he'd overheard in Bariloche, plus the uses of lithium for aircraft. He took it out to the girls in the secretarial pool. "I need this typed up right away, in triplicate."

"I can do it now, Mr. Schuller," Rosa Linda said, meeting his eye and smiling. He handed her the handwritten draft, and they exchanged more than a fleeting friendly glance.

Looking at Maria Elena Ferrer at the next desk, Martin asked her to call up a clerk.

Antonio Rivera came to his office five minutes later, and Martin gave him the book he'd used. "Please take this downstairs, I'm finished with it." Then he added in a lower voice, "Today is Javier's day off, I believe—if you see him tonight, please tell him to get in touch with me."

"Yes, Mr. Schuller," Antonio replied with a firm nod, and an unsuccessfully disguised look of excitement in his eyes.

He still thinks it's exciting to play spy. He hoped Antonio would never have to learn that it wasn't always exciting.

And could even be dangerous.

Hutson

31

It was growing dark when Martin climbed to Avenida Cabildo from the subway and began walking toward his neighborhood. He saw Rabbi Miguel Cohen walking toward him on the sidewalk, but he seemed distracted, looking at the ground rather than straight ahead. When Martin greeted him in German, he jumped and looked up, startled.

"Oh, good evening, Martin," he said, exhaling hard. "I did not see you, I am sorry to say."

Martin felt a touch of concern for his friend. "Is everything alright?"

"Yes, yes—it's fine now," Miguel said, waving a hand in an agitated circle.

"Did something happen?"

"Yes, yes—but it's not important. Don't trouble yourself, Martin."

"It's no trouble to me," Martin said. "If it has you this distracted, it must be something at least a little important. Anything I can do to help?"

Miguel gave him a weary smile, and his eyes spoke of grateful exhaustion. "Thank you, my friend—but it was my own foolishness. I should know better than to get into an argument with a crazy person. Especially a crazy person who already hates me before he even meets me."

Martin's eyes narrowed, and he felt his back stiffen. "Who?"

Miguel waved his hand dismissively, but Martin wouldn't be deterred, and repeated the question.

"*Ach*, it's nobody important. A couple of young men, probably university students—or university drop-outs, more likely. They were standing on Virrey Loreto, over by the *Universidad de Belgrano*, handing out propaganda leaflets and talking to people about the 'dangers of world Jewry.' I made the mistake of trying to engage one of them in intellectual debate. He was not interested in debate as much as shouting me down and making an example to the witnesses of 'how to treat a dirty Jew.' It was pointless."

Martin felt his face flush hot in spite of the evening chill. "Did they lay a hand on you?"

Miguel put up his hands and shook his head. "No, no—nothing like that. It was only words."

That barely made Martin feel better. "You should report them to the university administration."

Miguel shrugged. "I could, I suppose."

"I'll walk you home," Martin offered, but Miguel waved him off and shook his head.

"No need, Martin, thank you. It is a safe neighborhood, and our house is only a few blocks away. I will be fine."

Martin reluctantly agreed. "Alright, good night."

Still, he kept looking back at Miguel's retreating figure, and walked away slowly. When he finally reached the corner of Avenida Federico Lacroze, Martin paused and looked back one more time.

Miguel ambled along the sidewalk, not looking as distracted as he had before. Martin was glad for that—it was nearly dark, and at least his friend was paying attention to his surroundings. A moment later, Miguel rounded the corner onto the little side street where his townhouse was located, and Martin crossed into his own neighborhood and hurried home.

Friday, July 12

For the next two mornings, after he encountered Miguel at the café during breakfast before going to their respective jobs, Martin surreptitiously followed Miguel on his route north to the synagogue— which took him up Virrey Loreto, along the edge of the university.

Thursday morning was uneventful, and Martin hopped a streetcar back to Avenida Cabildo to catch the subway downtown. Friday was different.

At the southwest corner of the campus of the *Universidad de Belgrano* stood two tall young men shouting—one in Spanish, one in *Belgrano Deutsch*—about how banks were a conspiracy of world Jewry to steal from hard-working Christian families, and passing out leaflets to anyone who would take one.

Professors in tweed suits hurried past, ignoring them. Most of the students walking by ignored them, too, engrossed in conversations amongst themselves. But several gathered in a semi-circle around the one preaching in Spanish.

He stood out from the crowd, dressed in a mustard-yellow shirt and burgundy red necktie under a light gray checkered jacket, and his light brown hair was thick and wavy and brushed high atop his head in a foppish sort of way that made Martin think of spoiled rich boys who failed out of college and then blamed the professors. He did seem to have a certain magnetic way of drawing in the eight or nine people who stood around him.

The tall blond boy carrying on in the local German dialect had fewer hangers-on, and so he was continually shifting position to talk to passersby. When he turned around to face the street and those crossing it toward campus, his eyes locked on Miguel Cohen hurrying up the opposite sidewalk.

"There is one of the thieving Jews!" he shouted, pointing an accusing finger at Miguel.

Miguel appeared to hunch into himself, and he hurried faster, not looking at his accuser.

The blond boy shouted after him in *Belgrano Deutsch*. "That lying, thieving, filthy Jew tried to deny the facts a few days ago. When we wouldn't accept his lies, he scurried off like the rat that he is."

A larger crowd of students had stopped to listen to the blond boy's rant, and were now staring across the street at the retreating Miguel Cohen.

Martin had heard enough. Miguel might ignore the abuse and disappear around the next corner, but Martin couldn't ignore it. He stormed across Virrey Loreto and marched right up to the bigot.

"Just because you shout louder than everyone else doesn't make your hateful lies any more true," Martin said in standard German, pointing a finger at the young man's chest.

Now that he was close, Martin noticed as a sort of afterthought that the young fascist's hair was thinning on top, in spite of his obvious youth. Maybe that was part of the reason he was so angry.

A smug smile curled up the corners of the boy's lips, and he puffed up like a peacock, stretching his neck taller. He looked down at Martin, who was a tall man himself at six foot one.

"Traitors to the Volk are as dangerous as lying Jews."

Martin couldn't help himself; his anger snapped. He jabbed his finger at the young man. "*You* are the traitors to the Volk; you and your kind." He jabbed his finger again, staying just shy of touching the boy. "German culture was admired around the world before small-minded little men took charge over Germany and stamped out half of its culture—anything they didn't understand, or that made them uncomfortable."

The boy's face contorted, and even his ears turned dark red.

"Do not insult the Leader in front of me," he said through gritted teeth.

Martin squared his shoulders, unintimidated. "If by 'Leader' you mean the delusional megalomaniac who currently occupies the Chancellor's office in Berlin, I do not have words insulting enough for him, in any language. He has lied to Germany and stoked irrational fear in its people."

The boy shoved Martin backwards with both hands, almost knocking him into the street in front of an oncoming automobile that honked a warning.

Martin's right hand balled into a fist before he could think. But then the brown-haired boy was there, standing partially in front of his blond companion, turned toward him but looking back at Martin.

"Is everything under control, Fabiano?" he asked in Spanish.

The blond—Fabiano—replied in the same language, keeping his deep blue eyes locked on Martin. "I was trying to teach this German traitor not to insult the Leader."

"Do you need assistance teaching the lesson?"

Fabiano smirked. "Let's see if his big mouth still requires the lesson." He looked at Martin with a taunting smile, and beckoned him forward with a quick motion of his fingers. "What do you have to say now, traitor?" he asked in German.

Martin knew he should keep his mouth shut and walk away, but he couldn't. "I am not from Germany—but neither are you. You should know better than to believe the lies that the German chancellor tells the world."

Fabiano took a menacing step forward, and glared down at Martin's face from less than two feet away. "Stop calling the Leader's words lies."

Martin shook his head. "You live in Argentina, and there are people from all over the world living here. You should know better than to listen to narrow-minded nationalist propaganda. Spreading that propaganda to fellow Argentines is irresponsible. Do you know there is a synagogue just two blocks from here? Good, hard-working, peaceful

Argentines go to that synagogue, including two friends of mine, and your rhetoric puts them in danger."

Fabiano stared down at him with a taunting smile. "Your friends are criminals."

That was the last straw. Before he could think better of it, Martin's fist slammed into Fabiano's smug little Aryan chin, sending the tall blond hurtling backward into a lamp post before slumping down to the sidewalk, stunned and bleeding from the mouth.

The other one grabbed Martin by both arms and shouted in Spanish for others to help him subdue the criminal. Martin's knee came up swiftly and landed squarely in the preppy boy's unguarded crotch, causing him to crumple to the ground in a ball.

Others were grabbing at Martin now, and he struggled to twist out of their grasps.

Fabiano was standing now, his deep blue eyes cold with fury. As Martin evaded hands trying to grab his arms and shoulders, Fabiano came toward him and punched his fist hard into Martin's gut.

Martin doubled over, and unseen arms locked his own behind his back. Fabiano punched him in the gut again, and this time Martin kept his focus long enough to kick his leg up, and his leather-toed shoe collided hard with Fabiano's punching arm.

Fabiano shrieked and clutched at his broken forearm, and Martin took the opportunity to plant another hard kick against his exposed hip while he was distracted. He tumbled to the ground.

The unseen arms pulled Martin backward, and judging from the force pulling him he guessed it was two men. He heard countless voices shouting in Spanish. He couldn't understand a word in the cacophony.

In front of him, Fabiano was slowly and carefully pushing himself up from the sidewalk using his good arm. The preppy boy was also rising from the ground, where he'd spent the last minute curled in a ball clutching his wounded genitals with both hands. He glared at Martin with undisguised hate.

Then the sound of police whistles pierced through the shouting. Uniformed police officers seemed to materialize from nowhere, and at the direction of the crowd several of them took hold of Martin, Fabiano, and his preppy companion.

Two police officers hauled Martin out of the crowd and set him on the ground with a hard thump that rattled his brain. He couldn't make out the harsh words they were asking, so he said in slow, careful Spanish, "In my left breast pocket you will find my diplomatic passport." The police officers stared at him for a couple of seconds, so he repeated, "Diplomatic passport."

One officer shoved his hands inside Martin's jacket, and fished his passport out of the breast pocket. He opened it, stared at it for several seconds, and then stood quite straight and handed it back to Martin. "*Lo siento, señor.*"

He offered Martin his hand and helped him up from the ground. Then the officer raised his arm and waved someone over. A moment later, a man in a tweed suit and matching fedora came over with an open pad of paper. The uniformed officer said, "This man is a diplomat from the United States. Martin Schuller."

After verifying that the uniformed officer had checked Martin's passport, the man in the tweed suit gave him a deferential nod and addressed him in English. "I am very sorry to have troubled you, Mr. Schuller. I am Inspector Cardenas. You are free to leave, of course—but I request that you stay a little longer to answer a few questions I have."

"I'd be happy to."

"If it does not trouble you, would you tell me how the disturbance started?"

Martin explained that he'd crossed the street to confront the tall blond who was called Fabiano, because he'd shouted aggressive insults at his Jewish friend.

"What is your friend's name, if I may, Mr. Schuller?"

Martin hesitated a moment. "He was not part of this, he continued on his way, minding his own business. He ignored the insults. I did not."

"Thank you, Mr. Schuller. I only wish to corroborate that Fabiano Waldner was verbally aggressive to him. He is not of interest to me himself, but only as a witness."

Martin nodded. "His name is Miguel Cohen, and he is the rabbi at the synagogue near here."

"Thank you. Then what happened when you confronted Fabiano Waldner?"

Martin briefly described the exchange, and how Fabiano shoved him. "And then his compatriot stood in between us, preventing me from defending myself. He's the one in the yellow shirt and red tie."

"Yes, Marciano Robillard. Did he also attack you, Mr. Schuller?"

"Not at first. I tried reasoning with Mr. Waldner again, but he insulted me and my friend by calling us criminals. So I hit him. Then the other—Robillard?—tried to attack me, and I kneed him in the groin."

An amused half-smile had come to Inspector Cardenas's lips, but he held up his hands to stop Martin. "No need to say more, Mr. Schuller. You attest that they attacked you first, which is all I need to know. I only hope that you do not think this reflects badly on Argentina."

Martin shook his head. "Not at all, inspector."

Cardenas nodded in acknowledgement. "Thank you for your time. I will have one of my officers drive you to your embassy, or to your home if you prefer."

"Thank you, I would appreciate a lift to the embassy."

Cardenas looked confused. "Lift?"

Martin scolded himself for yet again thoughtlessly using idiomatic English with non-native speakers. "A ride to the embassy would be appreciated."

"Very good, I will arrange it. And I will also make sure that your name is not written in the newspapers."

Martin appreciated that most of all.

Fiedler sat perfectly still in the dark apartment. A little bit of light came through the window from the quarter moon, enough that he could see the outlines of furniture. He had chosen the center of the couch because it faced the front door.

The little clock on the mantle had chimed seven o'clock a short time ago, so it shouldn't be much longer, he knew. The stillness of his posture belied the rage that burned inside his brain while he waited.

He heard footsteps in the hall, and the hushed voices of two young men and a young woman, followed by the click of the lock. His exterior remained calm, but inside his muscles tensed.

The door opened, casting a bar of yellow light across the floor to Fiedler's left, and the silhouette of an arm pushed the light switch.

Fabiano Waldner gasped audibly when he saw Fiedler on the couch. Behind him, Marciano Robillard looked like he nearly jumped out of his skin. The girl beside Robillard watched him with concern.

"*Oh! Guten Abend, Herr Feuerfuchs,*" young Waldner said in German, using Fiedler's code name—Firefox.

Robillard whispered something to the girl, who disappeared. Fiedler heard her scurry down the hall.

Fiedler enjoyed the looks of discomfort on both of their faces. He regarded them with a cat-like smile. "Your task was to spread the teaching of our leader to those at the university who would be open to it. Your assignment was to bring people to our side—not to alienate them by behaving like street ruffians." He thought with distaste of the uncouth and violent behavior of the *Sturmabteilung* Brownshirts back home. "And not to spend a day in jail."

Marciano Robillard glanced back and forth between Waldner and Fiedler, trying to discern what was being said. "What's he saying?" he whispered to Waldner in Spanish.

Fiedler understood enough Spanish to comprehend that. He looked Robillard hard in the eyes. "Shall I repeat it in English, then?" he asked in that language. *"Ou peut-être en Français?"*

"In English, then," Waldner said, a touch of resentment creeping incautiously into his tone. "I don't speak French."

"I don't speak German, but that does not stop you from using it in front of me," Robillard hissed at Waldner in Spanish. Then he looked at Fiedler and said in halting French, "Perhaps we should cut *him* out by using only French from now on."

Fiedler exhaled loudly, letting his irritation show. Marciano Robillard might be many generations removed from his French immigrant ancestors—and God knew there were plenty of families in Germany similarly placed—but that didn't stop Fiedler from associating him with the worst characteristics of that hated nation. Robillard had been brought in because he was Waldner's best friend and flat mate, and was broadly open to the Leader's message.

"The function of propaganda is always to look positive," Fiedler said, in English. "You can show anger when you argue with opponents and expose their weakness to ridicule—judicious use of anger shows strength, which is a positive trait in those who would lead. But violence must always be carefully justified, or it appears to be madness."

Fabiano stiffened. "That traitor called the Leader mad. It demanded punishment."

Fiedler stood and took one long stride into the center of the room. Both boys were taller than he, but he stood with such rigid military posture that they both seemed to wilt in front of him. "Punishment will be dealt—but not in the public eye. Now, tell me about the man."

32

Monday, July 15

Martin's intercom buzzed. "Yes?"

Maria Elena's voice answered. "The front desk called for you, Mr. Schuller. There is a courier from the French Embassy downstairs. He told Mrs. Torres that he must deliver his message to you personally."

That piqued Martin's interest. He wasn't expecting any delivery, least of all from the French embassy, where he knew no one. "Tell Señora Torres that I'll be right down." He slipped on his jacket and hurried downstairs.

A tall, thin, black-haired young man stood in the hall behind the front desk, near the corner by Consular Services. Martin saw several of the young American consular officers casting curious glances at the Gallic stranger.

Señora Torres met Martin's gaze, and motioned her head backward at the young man. "I offered him to sit, but he say he prefer to stand."

Martin muttered "Gracias" as he walked past the desk, and extended his hand toward the young man. "I'm Martin Schuller."

The young man extended an envelope to Martin instead of shaking his offered hand. "*J'ai une message pour vous, de Monsieur Remy.*"

The young man waited in silence while Martin opened the envelope and read the one-line message in English on the slip of paper inside.

National Library, second floor, European History. Two o'clock. Destroy message.

"Cigarette, monsieur?" the young man asked, holding out a silver lighter. His expression was unreadable, but his dark eyes held Martin's.

Martin rolled the slip of paper like a cigarette, and held it out to the open flame of the courier's lighter. When the end lit, he dropped it on the stone floor to burn, then stamped on the ashes.

"Au revoir, monsieur," the young man said with a crisp nod, and strode across the foyer and out the door.

Martin arrived at the *Biblioteca Nacional* at quarter to two. He took the stairs rather than the elevator, scanning the faces as he went up two flights, and found the European History section on the second floor. He pretended to browse the titles, moving slowly down the aisle, glancing around constantly.

Several young men and women came and went while he waited, most removing a book and departing after a minute or two. University students, he supposed.

At precisely two o'clock, a dark-haired man in an expensive silk suit came down the aisle, and stopped midway to stare at the volumes on the Napoleonic Wars. He was in his mid-thirties, with hair slicked with brilliantine and a thin, well-groomed mustache.

Martin watched him for a moment, taking a hesitant step in his direction. The man glanced at him, met his eye, and then looked back at the book shelf.

"Mister Schuller?" he asked, just above a whisper, his French accent very thick.

Martin took another step toward him, standing now about five feet away. He looked at the bookshelf. "Yes, I'm Mr. Schuller."

"I am Mr. Remy." He paused while a trio of young women walked past the end of their aisle, and then glanced back at Martin. "You have an informant for the S-I-M inside your embassy."

SIM—Italian military intelligence. Martin couldn't remember the full Italian name, but everyone called them by the acronym anyway. He felt his chest tighten.

"Are you certain?" He knew better than to ask Remy how he knew.

"Absolutely certain. They know that you have informed of German agents to the police, and they know that you have brought many of your own agents to Buenos Aires recent. They have much knowledge more, but I cannot say the what."

Martin took a few seconds to ponder that. "Why are you telling me? France is now neutral."

Remy's mouth tightened. "I am Niçois." At Martin's confused look, he explained, "I am from Nice."

Martin nodded. That explained it—Italy had annexed Nice last month, after it invaded the south of France. Remy was no doubt displeased that his home city no longer belonged to his country.

"Do you know if the SIM has shared their information about us to the Abwehr?"

"I am without doubt of it," Remy said. He paused again while a young man came down their aisle, leaned down to remove an enormous volume from the shelf, and flipped through the pages.

Martin followed Remy's lead, and took a step away, crouching down and running his finger back and forth along the shelf as if he were looking for a specific number that was missing.

He considered every Argentine employee of the embassy, trying to guess a possible motive for betraying their employer. Money? Personal vendetta against a senior diplomat? Bribery? He heard that last in Sloan's voice.

Once the young man left with a book in his hand, Martin stood again and moved closer to Remy. "What do you know about the SIM's informant?"

"Only that it is a person who works at your embassy, one that can copy documents without question, only a little care."

The person whose face kept appearing in Martin's mind was De la Tour. He felt guilty about that, but he couldn't help the suspicion. Could Sloan have been right all along? He hated that possibility, but it would be irresponsible not to dig into that line of thinking.

"Is there anything else?"

"Be careful," Remy said, glancing around. "You are safest to imagine that everything is compromised, and do something different. But, it is also an opportunity, is it not?"

"An opportunity?"

"Yes. When you know that you have an informant in your midst, you can push him out by giving bad information. Tell a different something wrong to everyone who might be the informant, something that causes an action, and see what the action is. That will tell you what one bad information was used, and that will tell you the true informant. *Voila!*"

Martin had to agree that seemed simple enough. He'd have to think of nearly a dozen pieces of bad information—actionable bad information—but he was confident he could do that.

"Thank you, monsieur." He left while Remy stayed behind.

"That could be any one of them," First Secretary Davis grumbled after Martin relayed Remy's news.

Martin agreed. "I can begin planting bad intel as early as tomorrow."

Davis frowned. "We should probably consult the Bureau. At least make sure they're on board with us taking this sort of action."

Martin's lips tightened into a thin line, his only visible response to the resistance he felt to that idea. "They'll try to take over. It might be better just to inform them that we're treating this as an internal personnel matter. Make it a courtesy that we're keeping them in the loop, without leaving any opening for their involvement."

Davis sat back, silent for a moment, seeming to weigh the options. "I do want to keep this as quiet as possible. And you're right, Schuller—this is an internal personnel matter. But if we're going to put out bad information around the embassy, the FBI boys will need to know. The last thing we want is for the Bureau to take action based on hearsay they've picked up around the office, and then later find out it was misdirection all along. Hoover would be furious."

Martin agreed with that. "I'll draft a memo. I'll keep it brief, just a short summation of our plan; a warning to question the accuracy of anything they might hear around the embassy over the next few weeks. I'll omit specifics."

"Yes, do that. And let me know when you have the false intel ready to disseminate. Let's start with Mr. De la Tour."

It was harder than Martin imagined. Not only did he have to come up with more than a dozen pieces of misinformation that were both actionable and plausible, he had to think of ways to convey them to the various Argentine employees secretly and believably. That last part proved to be the most difficult.

This was outside of Martin's wheelhouse. He worked for hours after he put his kids to bed, and stayed up late to finish it. Even so, he made changes to several plans the next morning in his office while yawning over his third cup of coffee. When he was finally satisfied with the end result, he took it to First Secretary Davis.

He was proud of himself when Davis signed off on it after one read-through. *I might make a decent spook one day*, he mused on his way back to his office.

Tuesday, July 16

Martin typed the memo to the FBI liaison office while the embassy staff was away at lunch. He took it downstairs to the Bureau's office personally.

FBI Special Agent in Charge Wilson frowned when Martin handed the memo to him. As Martin turned to leave, Wilson called his name. "Wait just a moment, Mr. Schuller."

Martin turned back and waited.

"When did you find out about this leak?"

"Yesterday," Martin said, "As you can see, we're taking action right away."

"How did you find out?"

Martin wasn't about to give that up. "I'd prefer to keep my source confidential, if you don't mind."

Wilson's eyes narrowed. "You say this is a 'courtesy' in case we hear things that might be deliberate misinformation. Wouldn't that mean the integrity of your experiment had been compromised?"

Martin felt his heart sink into his gut. It would indeed. He salvaged the humiliation as best he could. "Yes, well, we would appreciate knowing if that happens."

"I'm sure you would. Perhaps this means State ought to beef up its background checks for local hires."

"One thing at a time," Martin said, his lips tightening. "We haven't had this issue in the past, so it's an isolated occurrence. We'll concentrate on finding the guilty party first, and then address any future steps."

"The Bureau should consult with the ambassador on changes to your hiring procedures for Argentine staff," Wilson said. "We can leverage our law enforcement experience and local contacts."

Martin nodded, crisp and formal. "I'm sure the ambassador will reach out to you when he needs to. Good day."

"You asked to *speak* with me, Mr. Schuller," De la Tour said after knocking on Martin's door that afternoon. "*How* may I be of *service* to you?"

"Can you type, señor?" Martin asked.

"Of *course*, sir," De la Tour replied with a wave of his right hand and a bow of his head. "Are you *dissatisfied* with the typing of the *girls* up here? Is there something I should *address*?"

"No, nothing like that. There is something of a highly sensitive nature that I need typed, and it should not be viewed by anyone on your staff. Can you help me?"

"Absolutely, sir," De la Tour said with a flourish and a bow. "I will take care of that immediately, Mr. Schuller."

"Just remember that no one else can see it," Martin said, handing De la Tour a plain manila envelope with a handwritten page inside. "Type this in triplicate, and have all three copies back to me by two o'clock."

Martin stayed late to present a summary to First Secretary Davis after all of the local staff had left at the end of the day. He included brief notes about his interactions.

"Is this everyone?" Davis asked, reviewing the paper Martin had handed him and running his finger over the list of names. "I think you've forgotten one of the girls—Miss Bianchi isn't listed. I'm surprised by the omission, since she sits right outside your office, Schuller."

Because it's not her, Martin thought, aware that he couldn't articulate for the First Secretary his reasons for coming to that conclusion. "I'll rectify that first thing in the morning, sir."

Hutson

33

Wednesday, July 17

Martin took an early lunch break the next day, and walked a few blocks to a bookstore. It was easy to locate the store's *Hispanidad* section, the popular movement of nationalist Argentine authors who culturally copied Spanish literature. And most prominently displayed in the middle of the *Hispanidad* section were the recent works of Manuel Gálvez.

It made Martin's stomach turn sour to pick up one of the volumes—Rabbi Miguel Cohen had told him at the café this morning that it was unabashedly anti-Semitic, and openly admiring of Italian fascism—but he swallowed his feelings and took it to the cash register.

The young woman who rang him up grew noticeably quiet when she saw the title he was purchasing. He could almost guess what she thought of him, and wished he could assure her that it wasn't true.

She asked him a question too rapidly for him to catch all of the words, and he had to ask her to repeat herself. She arched an eyebrow in surprise at his accent.

"I asked if you want this wrapped, if it is a gift," she repeated, in English.

"No, it's for me," he said in Spanish, cringing on the inside as he did.

A curious look crossed her dark eyes. She said in English, "This does not have a translation in English, sir." She seemed to be asking if he was sure he wanted to try reading it, with his obviously limited grasp of Spanish.

"*Está bien*," he said.

She became quiet again, and quoted the price in Spanish.

He hurried out of the store before anyone who might recognize him saw him with the Gálvez book. He kept the front cover turned toward his leg as he walked toward the center of the city to hide the title.

But then he took a seat on a park bench across the street from the Italian embassy, and opened the book to pretend to read it, boldly keeping the front cover facing toward the embassy's door. He pretended to read while he watched the comings and goings.

He wasn't sure exactly what he hoped to see, but trusted he'd recognize it when he saw it, whatever it was. He settled in for a long watch.

Friday, July 19

On his third day sitting on the bench around midday, in his second hour there he saw a tall man in an expensive gray silk suit, with brilliantined black hair—who looked familiar for some reason—strutting down the sidewalk toward the Italian embassy. The familiar-looking man strode through the front door, whipping his hat from his head as he crossed the threshold.

Martin tried to recall where he'd seen the man, but nothing came to mind. Still, he was certain he had seen him before.

The man reappeared some thirty minutes later, and strutted back up the sidewalk in the direction from whence he had come.

After waiting several seconds, Martin closed his book, got up from the bench as casually as he could, and started walking the same direction. He waited until he got to the corner to cross to the same side of the street as his quarry, to make it less obvious he was following. He hadn't noticed anyone watching, but he couldn't account for all of the windows.

The sidewalks were crowded at the height of the lunch hour before siesta, which made it trickier to keep the man in sight, but also gave Martin some cover from being noticed. If the man were even concerned about a tail.

They turned up the Avenida Corrientes, heading east, and crossed the Plaza de la República near the city's new quadricentennial obelisk. Martin slowed to increase the distance between them as they crossed the green space around the obelisk in the middle of the square.

On the other side of Avenida 9 de Julio, the man entered a nine-story office building.

Martin held back a minute before entering the building.

A security guard stood at a front desk—*unusual*, Martin thought—in the process of locking desk drawers. He looked up at the sound of Martin's shoes on the polished marble floor.

"The building is closing for siesta, sir."

"I have an appointment to meet with the man that just entered," Martin improvised. "I tried to catch up to him on the street, but he was too far away."

The security guard nodded. "Yes, Mr. Mariani has a fast stride."

"Are the elevators automatic?" Martin asked, thinking it probable in a new-looking building with an expensively-apportioned lobby such as this one. An elevator operator would have gone home for siesta by now, if it were manual.

"Yes, sir—but I cannot allow you to go up alone. Allow me to phone Mr. Mariani for you."

Martin could think of no reason to decline, so he thanked the guard and pretended to wander aimlessly around the lobby while the guard made the phone call. He read over the building directory posted between the elevator and the front door.

One company name caught his attention—Buon Italia, Importer of Fine Italian Goods. Intelligence agencies often used importers and exporters, either as a cover business, or as informants.

"Excuse me, sir?" the security guard called, and Martin turned around to see him holding his hand over the mouthpiece of the black telephone receiver. "Mr. Mariani says that he is not expecting anyone until after siesta. Perhaps you have the wrong time?"

Martin knew that he still carried the fake business card for Hiram Jones of the Ajax Shipping Company, since he had not needed it that night at the Ante Puerto. Because men collected other men's business cards all the time, he had seen no risk in holding onto it.

"Please tell Mr. Mariani that Hiram Jones of the Ajax Shipping Company is here to see him," Martin said in careful Spanish. "The appointment was made many weeks ago, and it may not have my personal name."

"One moment, sir." The security guard relayed the information into the phone, and there was a long pause that made Martin nervous. Finally, the guard said "Thank you, Mr. Mariani," and hung up. Then he told Martin to please wait.

A moment later, the elevator door opened, and the man that Martin had followed emerged. His dark brown eyes caught Martin's, and held a questioning expression as he approached, his right hand extended.

"You are Mr. Hiram Jones?" he asked in accented English.

Martin handed him the business card. He replied in English. "Yes, I'm Mr. Jones. Thank you for seeing me, Señor Mariani."

"I am afraid there was a mistake made with the appointment, and my secretary did not record it on our calendar," Mariani said, placing a hand on Martin's shoulder to guide him toward the elevator. "But it is fortunate that I do not have another appointment instead, so I have the time to meet."

"I'm glad that we didn't have to reschedule, since I'm only in Argentina for the week," Martin said, watching Mariani press the button for the seventh floor.

Mariani gave him an inquisitive look as the elevator door closed, his head cocked. "I am curious why a North American firm wishes to meet with me. I facilitate the importing of Italian products for the Argentine market only. I have no experience with your importation laws in the United States."

"I see it was not explained previously," Martin said, buying time to improvise.

"No—as I said, there was a mistake with the appointment, and it was not recorded." Mariani's tone was polite, but growing cool.

"I am not seeking assistance with importing Italian goods to the United States," Martin said, a touch slower than usual, and hoped that it seemed to be for the benefit of a foreigner, rather than his need to think on his feet. The elevator door opened on the seventh floor, buying him a few extra seconds while Mariani motioned for him to exit first. "Rather, my firm has an excess of items that we imported from Italy, and have not been able to sell, which are now taking up valuable space in a Philadelphia warehouse. We seek to resell them to the Brazilian and Argentine markets, to cut our loss."

"I see," Mariani said, opening the door with the name "Buon Italia" stenciled in gold letters across the glass. "We are a small firm, as you can see by the size of our office. How do you come to seek our help with your resell, Mr. Jones?"

A referral was the most logical explanation, but Martin didn't have a name at the ready; so his mind seized on the first Italian surname that sprang up. "I was given your name by Mr. Bianchi." It was a common enough surname, so Martin hoped that Mariani knew at least one Mr. Bianchi. There was a good chance.

He was not prepared for the response. Mariani's eyes widened in surprise. "My brother-in-law?"

It was then that Martin recognized Mariani, and realized where he had seen him before.

34

"You asked to see me, Commander?"

"Sit down, Acker." Gustav Fiedler was well-practiced at the intimidating stare, but even so he was pleased at the way it made the blond young man seated before him morph from eager to apprehensive in a matter of seconds.

Once Thaddeus Acker began to squirm, Fiedler broke his silence.

"I have reliable information that the American embassy has knowledge of our lithium operation out of Chile." He paused for effect, and saw beads of sweat begin to appear on Acker's pale upper lip. "You are the courier we sent to Bariloche on two occasions in as many months, to meet with our agent from Santiago. It was an assignment of great trust."

Thaddeus Acker swallowed hard, and bobbed his head overmuch. "Yes, sir. I am grateful for the trust you have placed in me."

Fiedler leaned back in his chair, and crossed his arms over his chest. "On at least one of your trips to Bariloche, you were overheard by an American agent."

Acker turned even more pale, if that were possible. His mouth hung open for a second, and then he shook his head emphatically. "That's not possible, sir. We took every precaution. We followed the protocols to the letter."

Fiedler pursed his lips. He would have to review the protocols again. "Be that as it may, you were overheard, and the Americans are now aware that we are shipping lithium out of Chile—in violation of Chilean neutrality. The Americans are quite rigid in their defense of this hemisphere's neutrality. As we've discussed."

Acker's forehead glistened with sweat, even though the room was quite cool. "My deepest apologies, Commander. Please know that I am loyal to the Fatherland, and I will do anything to correct my error."

Fiedler sat forward again with a curt nod. "I am glad to hear that." He opened a drawer and pulled out a folder. He removed a stack of photographs, and spread them out on the desk, facing Thaddeus Acker.

"Tell me if you recognize any of these men."

Martin went directly to De la Tour's office the moment he got back to the embassy. He found the supervisor at his desk.

De la Tour looked up in surprise at Martin's sudden appearance. "Mr. Schuller, what an *unexpected* visit. What *can* I do for you?" Then his expression grew serious when Martin closed the door.

"I need to see the personnel file of one of your staff. It's a matter of some urgency—and strictly confidential."

"Of *course*, Mr. Schuller. I am most *happy* to be of *assistance* to you. Which employee?"

The remainder of the meeting with Mariani at the Buon Italia office had been brief. Martin had made up a first name, which Mariani naturally said he did not recall; Martin speculated that "Mr. Bianchi" may have met Mariani at a cocktail party, some inconsequential introduction, which had nonetheless been memorable to this Bianchi fellow. There was an awkward discussion about the type of excess goods sitting in the Ajax warehouse, and then Mariani had expressed regret, but he was really not interested.

Now, in De la Tour's office, Martin's eyes fell on the full name typed on the tab of the personnel file the supervisor handed him, and he felt his heart sink into the pit of his stomach.

Rosa Linda Luisa Bianchi-Mariani

Martin had been in Argentina long enough to have learned that full, formal names in Spanish always hyphenated the individual's own surname with the mother's maiden name —even if this long form were not often used in casual interactions or routine business.

The man with whom Martin had seen Rosa Linda conversing with in Italian at the *milonga* all those weeks ago—Rosa Linda had said it was her uncle. At the time, Martin suspected that was a euphemism, but it appeared she had been telling the truth.

About that, at least.

The light inside the club had been dim, but Martin had no doubt that the man conversing in Italian with Rosa Linda that night was the same man who seemed so familiar when Martin saw him exiting the Italian Embassy this afternoon. Giancarlo Mariani, importer of fine Italian goods.

And probably an informant for the Italian military intelligence service, SIM.

"Mr. De la Tour, I need for you to do me a favor."

Martin ran into Chuck Brady as the latter was leaving the Consular Services area and heading for the stairs. He accompanied Chuck back up to their offices, using their small talk as reason not to even glance at Rosa Linda or the other typists when he passed them.

He stayed holed up in his office for the remainder of the day, catching up on the work he had set aside while he kept watch on the Italian embassy the last few afternoons.

Rosa Linda knocked on his door at five o'clock, and he forced himself to smile at her.

"I have a question about that report you asked for, Mr. Schuller," she said, slightly louder than necessary, for the other girls' benefit. Then after taking a few steps toward his desk, she added more quietly, "You have been away so much the last few days, and now it is almost the weekend. I did not want to leave work without seeing you."

He forced his smile wider, faking an excited grin, and motioned her closer. He stood and met her at the corner of his desk, placing both hands on her shoulders and staring into her soft brown eyes.

"Marty's birthday is next Friday, and I will be on vacation all of next week," he said, watching her reaction. She looked crestfallen, and lowered her eyes; he wondered what she was really feeling. "I'm taking the kids to a guest ranch for a few days, out on the Pampas. We can ride horses, and Marty can dress up like a *gaucho*." He put a finger on her chin and lifted her face. "This is last minute, I know—but I wonder if you'd like to go away for the weekend, and join us at the *estancia*? I could get you a room next to ours. What do you say?"

Her eyes lit up for a second, and then clouded. "My father would never allow it. An unmarried woman cannot travel alone."

"I already thought of that," Martin said, and reached for the letter sitting on his desk. "I got our friend Mr. De la Tour to write a letter that you can show your father, saying that you and several other girls are needed to accompany some of our diplomats to Córdoba for a trade summit. See? It's on embassy stationery, and signed by De la Tour himself, with his full title. Your father wouldn't forbid you from going if you showed him this, now would he?"

A delightfully surprised smile spread slowly across her lips as she read the letter. "No, of course he wouldn't. *Ay*, Martin—how did you arrange this?"

"Let's just say that Mr. De la Tour owes me a favor."

"That is wonderful! I'll go right home and pack a travel case. When do we leave?"

"Tonight. The train leaves at ten-fifteen—but before you go home, would you take this downstairs to Consular Services, and ask Robert Clark to put it in the diplomatic pouch for Washington? It needs to go on the Clipper tomorrow. You can catch him if you hurry."

He handed her an envelope that he had folded shut, but had not sealed.

"Yes, I will do it right away." She paused at the doorway and half-turned toward him, adding in a quiet voice, "I will meet you and your children at the station at nine-thirty." Then she rushed out.

He watched the door for a moment to make sure she didn't suddenly return, and then opened his desk drawer and removed a folder. He put it inside a small attaché case, grabbed his overcoat and hat, and left.

Hutson

35

Saturday, July 20 – Estancia Luján, Córdoba Province

The taxi stopped on the dirt drive in front of a sprawling single-story house, with large windows set inside earth-toned plaster walls, under a red-tile roof. Martin didn't wait for the driver to open his door for him, and got out to stretch his legs. The morning sun was still low in the northeastern sky, but there were few clouds, promising some welcome warmth later on.

After more than 30 minutes in the cab from the train station in Córdoba to the *estancia*—Spanish for cattle ranch—which followed a nine-hour overnight train ride, Martin was only too happy to see the wide-open grasslands, dotted with cattle and the occasional *gaucho* on horseback. He arched his back and stretched while the kids scrambled out of the cab and began pointing at the unfamiliar sights.

Martin gave his hand to Rosa Linda to help her out of the back seat, and an attendant in a black suit emerged from the front of the house. His face was tanned and deeply lined, but there was only a bit of gray scattered through his black hair. He bowed his head to Martin.

"Welcome to Estancia Luján, sir. Your name, please?" The man's tone was crisp and formal, but his Spanish sounded rougher than what Martin had become used to in Buenos Aires.

"Good morning. I am Martin Schuller, with my children; and this is Miss Rosa Linda Bianchi. I reserved an extra room for her yesterday."

"Yes, Mr. Schuller, we are expecting both of you. I will tell the housekeeper that you arrived." He picked up the handles of their suitcases where the cab driver had set them, and carried them all inside by himself—one in each hand, and one under each arm—with no apparent exertion.

"Are you a gaucho?" Marty asked the attendant in slow, hesitant Spanish, hurrying alongside him.

"I have been a gaucho since I was no bigger than you," the man said, more slowly than before. "But now, I only ride part of the day."

Martin wasn't sure how much his eldest son had understood, but Marty nodded as if he had.

Inside the spacious foyer, which opened onto a courtyard arranged around a fountain, the attendant set down their bags long enough to retrieve two brass keys, which he handed to Martin. Then he took their baggage and led them along a colonnaded corridor around the courtyard to neighboring rooms.

Martin unlocked Rosa Linda's room first, and then handed her the key. "Come to our room after you've gotten yourself settled," he said in English.

Martin leaned back against the pillows he'd propped up at the head of his bed, pretending to read through the file he'd brought along, while Marty sat crossed-legged on the floor with a comic book, and Jackie and Stevie played nearby.

"Come in," he said in response to the knock at the door.

"I have finished unpacking," Rosa Linda said, entering the room. Her eyes fell on the manila folder in his hands.

A couple of seconds passed before she frowned, and glanced up to look into his eyes.

"Did you bring work with you? Martin, you are supposed to be on vacation."

Martin tried to look contrite. "A report that Mr. Sloan wrote right before he left. I didn't have time to read through it yesterday, so I brought it along."

"Put it away, so that we can enjoy our time," she scolded.

"Yes, ma'am," he said, and closed the folder. "I'll need to send a cable back to the embassy later, but it can wait."

He got up and crossed the room, letting his fingers brush her hand on his way past. He opened his suitcase, closed the folder inside, and locked it. He put the key into his pocket.

He turned toward the kids, clapped his hands together, and grinned at them. "Let's go ride some horses."

Buenos Aires

Javier spotted *Unai*—he couldn't think of him as "Shepherd"— sitting near the back of the tram, reading a newspaper. The bench in front of him was one of the few empty seats, and Javier wondered if that was on purpose.

He took a seat on the empty bench, but right next to the aisle so that he could see *Unai* out of the corner of his left eye. Nervous butterflies filled his stomach.

The Basque intelligence officer didn't say a word, nor did Javier see him glance up from the newspaper. Javier had to force himself to sit still and wait.

Passengers came and went at each stop, but the two of them remained almost to the end of the line in Barrio Almagro. When it reached the stop near Javier's apartment, Javier hesitated a second before rising. He would have to assume the spy would follow him off the tram.

A few seconds after he started walking toward his building, he couldn't help but look back at the tram that was starting to pull away from the stop. *Unai*'s tall figure leapt off a couple of seconds after it started to move, tucking the folded newspaper under his arm as he began following Javier. He made brief eye contact with Javier, and then crossed the street and walked toward the park a block away.

Javier found him sitting on a park bench. He took a seat on the opposite end of the bench, so that several feet of empty space lay between them.

"Your appointment with Thaddeus Acker for tomorrow, it was cancelled?" *Unai* asked without preamble.

Javier nodded, wondering how *Unai* knew that. Or knew that Thaddeus was a client.

"There have been developments at the German embassy," *Unai* said. "They know that they have had a breach, and they are taking measures."

Javier felt his pulse quicken. It was exciting, this spy talk. Still, he wondered what this had to do with him. "Thaddeus is involved?"

"He has been sent north. Unexpectedly. It is outside of their pattern."

"What can I do?"

"Your friend at the American embassy, Mr. Rivera—can you arrange for him to meet me? Today."

"I think so."

"Mr. Rivera must not speak of this to anyone, until after I have given him instructions. Lives may depend upon his discretion. Do you understand?"

Javier felt his heart skip a beat, then flutter in his chest before starting to pound. He felt himself start to sweat, in spite of the coolness of the winter afternoon. "I understand."

Unai was silent for several seconds, and when he spoke again he sounded hesitant.

"We have started working with their Federal Bureau of Investigation...but my contact there is away from Buenos Aires, with no explanation. I need to warn them that one of the American diplomats has been mentioned in conversations the Abwehr has had with their agents here—" he paused and shrugged before adding, "one of whom is also our agent."

Javier felt his stomach drop. He knew which American without having to be told.

"You know the American," *Unai* said, as if he'd read Javier's mind. "I pray that Mr. Rivera will know where we can find him."

"Why?" Javier asked, his voice cracking as his throat went dry.

Unai looked Javier in the eye, and his expression was stony. "Martin Schuller is in danger."

Estancia Luján, Córdoba Province

Martin arranged his pants so that they appeared to be flung carelessly across the arm of a chair, making sure that the pocket with the suitcase key faced up. His suitcase stood next to the chair. The second he heard the knock on the door, he hurried to answer, bare feet padding on the cold tile floor. He opened the door only part-way.

"Oh!" Rosa Linda said, covering her mouth in surprise when she saw him wearing a bathrobe. When he closed the door, she looked around the room. "Where are your children?"

Martin forced a genial smile. "I paid Señor Molina a hundred pesos to entertain them for a half-hour."

Her brow furrowed, and she crossed her arms. "You said we were all going to dinner."

"And we will—in a half-hour." He took a step closer to her, put his hands on her arms, and kissed her. His stomach took a tumble. *Good lord, what if she doesn't say no?*

She kissed back ardently, and he forced the worry from his mind so he could act naturally. He put his arms around her and pulled her against him.

Just when he thought he'd have to go through with it, she pulled away, shaking her head. He suppressed his relief.

"Martin, we mustn't. Your children could return, and then what would you say?"

He'd gambled she would say that, but he hung his head and groaned in mock frustration. "It's been so long!"

She put her hand on his chest, between the folds of his bathrobe. It was warm, but a sharp chill ran down his spine.

"I know, darling, but it is not for much longer. Your children are only here for one more month."

He exhaled hard and rubbed his hand across his face. "I know you're right. I couldn't help myself. Forgive me?"

She smiled at him, but it didn't extend to her eyes. "Of course I will. Now get dressed for dinner."

"I need to clean up first. I'll just hop in the shower for a few minutes, it won't take long. Wait here?"

"If you like," she said, her smile warming.

He went into the bathroom and started the faucet, then turned on the showerhead. He waited a moment, listening for sounds from the other room, but heard nothing. He opened the shower curtain as noisily as he could, pleased at the metallic scrape. He slipped out of the bathrobe and tossed it onto the floor near the door, where she was certain to see it lying.

He stayed out of sight, wearing boxer shorts that had been hidden by the robe. He tugged the shower curtain closed, making maximum noise. He stuck his arm inside to disrupt the fall of water with his hand, to simulate the sounds of a man showering.

And he waited. His heart pounded.

A moment later, he heard the click of his suitcase lock. He counted to twenty.

He crept to the open door and peaked out to see Rosa Linda sitting on the bed, looking in confusion at the open manila folder in her hand. His suitcase lay open on the floor at her feet.

"You've been spying on me."

Her head snapped up at the sound of his voice, and her eyes widened. Her mouth opened as if to say something, but no sound came out.

He reached her in two strides, and jerked the folder out of her hands.

"That doesn't belong to you," he said through gritted teeth. The papers inside were gibberish, so there had been no risk; and even though he knew going in that she was the one, the confirmation still felt like a sharp punch in the gut.

"Martin, I—"

"Shut up!" He would never strike a woman for any reason, ever, but at that moment he knew what the temptation felt like.

Instead, he looked away from her, and marched to the door. He threw it open, and nodded at the FBI agents waiting a few feet away, at the edge of the courtyard.

Special Agents Wilson and Avery entered the room without removing their hats, and positioned themselves on either side of Rosa Linda, who had stood.

"Miss Bianchi, you'll come with us, please," Wilson said, grabbing her elbow and tugging her toward the door.

Her eyes were wide with terror, and barely focused on Martin as she was pulled past him.

"Martin, it is a mistake. You must believe me. I love you!"

He glared at her.

She tried to jerk her arm away from Wilson, but he didn't let go. She raised her chin in defiance. "You cannot arrest me. You have no authority in Argentina."

"You're not under arrest," Wilson said. "We're just escorting you back to Buenos Aires. Now move."

Martin watched in silence as Wilson pulled her out into the courtyard, his gun barely visible at the small of her back.

Agent Avery paused at the door, looked back at Martin, and touched the rim of his hat. "We'll take care of it from here. Thanks for the tip-off. Enjoy the rest of your vacation, Mr. Schuller."

His eye dropped to Martin's boxer shorts, and he smirked and shook his head on the way out.

Martin had no doubt his state of undress would be part of an amusing story among the G-men back at the embassy. He didn't care. It had worked.

And at least Sloan hadn't been here to see it.

After closing the door, Martin shoved the manila folder back into his suitcase and closed it. Then he stood very still for a moment before slamming his fist onto the top of the bedside table.

36

Tuesday, July 23

Martin was strapping his saddle onto the bay mare he'd been assigned for the week, and was about to put his foot in the stirrup when the sound of his name made him pause.

Molina, the front attendant, came hurrying into the stables with a piece of paper in his hand. His breath crystalized in the morning chill.

"A telegram arrived for you, Mr. Schuller," he said. "From Buenos Aires."

Martin thanked him, and fished a two-peso coin out of his pocket. He told his kids and their instructors to wait a moment, and he walked several steps away before tearing open the telegram. It was in English:

> SIMON WENT FISHING BUT DIDNT CATCH ANY FISH
> STOP

Martin exhaled hard, trying to release the frustration. Knowing this was coming didn't make it easier.

The paper in the unsealed envelope that he had given to Rosa Linda at the end of the workday on Friday, the one he'd told her to take to Robert Clark in Consular Services, had mentioned a secret shipment arriving on Monday aboard a bogus ship at a certain wharf. This telegram meant that SIM agents had been spotted watching that wharf on Monday.

Even though he'd caught Rosa Linda going through his folder on Saturday, it only proved that she was a snoop; this was the confirmation they needed that she was passing along information to the SIM.

He struck a match and burned the telegram. Once the ashes had scattered on the floor, he strode back toward his children and their horses.

He'd been foolish with Rosa Linda, but he was going to put that behind him.

Javier was surprised to see Antonio at his door that evening.

"My friend, I wasn't expecting to see you today," he said, and stepped aside to let him in. "What brings you by?"

"Strange things are happening," Antonio said, quietly, even though they were the only ones in the single-room apartment.

That piqued Javier's curiosity. "Oh? What sort of things?"

"Rosa Linda Bianchi, the typist for the American Foreign Service officers upstairs, has not shown up for work this week. And today, two of the FBI agents from downstairs cleaned out her desk. No one has said anything, but rumors are flying."

That did interest Javier—especially the part about the FBI agents.

Antonio continued. "The girls and the other clerks think she was fired for having an affair with Mr. Schuller. But I don't think so. Mr. Schuller isn't the kind of man who would let that happen, even while he is away."

Javier thought back to his most recent interaction with *Unai*, three days before. This couldn't be a coincidence.

He put his hands on Antonio's shoulders and stared into his face for a few seconds, to signal this was serious. "My friend, can you find out for me where Mr. Schuller has gone on his trip? It is very important. He is in danger."

Wednesday, July 24

Martin felt lighter today, and he and the kids enjoyed a brisk ride with a small group along a winding trail through the Pampas grass. It was a warm afternoon without a cloud in the sky—almost twenty degrees Celsius, according to the thermometer at the stables, which Martin translated to sixty-six or sixty-seven degrees Fahrenheit, about five degrees warmer than Buenos Aires.

His bay mare followed behind his kids, Marty on a chestnut mare, and Jackie and Stevie on roan ponies. They had all become decent riders this week, and today's trail was a touch more rugged than the previous days' trails, crossing creeks and climbing grassy swells dotted with grazing cattle.

The dapple gray mare behind him picked up its pace and trotted up beside Martin's. "They are cute together, no?"

The rider, Raúl Peña-Camacho, nodded forward, where his daughter Anna-Maria rode next to Marty. She was about a year younger than Marty, and at the moment she was chatting in rapid Spanish while Marty only half-looked her direction, his face a mask of confusion.

"I don't think my son understands much of what she says," Martin said, in careful Spanish.

Peña threw his head back and laughed. "That will never change, my friend."

Peña had arrived with his family from Salta on Sunday, and they had been given Rosa Linda's now-vacant room next to Martin's. He was a friendly sort, who always chatted with Martin whenever their families met in the stables, or shared a trail ride. Unlike his daughter, he spoke slowly so that Martin could understand.

"We live in a city, so this is the first time on horses for my children," Peña said.

"Mine also."

"They have enjoyed it, no?"

Martin nodded. "Very much."

"You as well, my friend?"

Martin smiled, and nodded again. He had enjoyed the time, more than he'd expected. "A friend in Buenos Aires suggested this would be a good place for our vacation, and he was right."

"You are staying the full week, like us?"

Martin shook his head. "No. We leave tomorrow afternoon." He thought he saw a look of disappointment on Peña's face, so he added, "Unfortunately."

"You could add an extra day or two to your stay," Peña said. "I am sure they do not have your room reserved again until the weekend. Stay, my friend. Enjoy this time with your children. Your work can wait until next week."

Martin chuckled. "We're not going back to Buenos Aires yet. My son's birthday is Friday, and we are going to see the Iguazú falls. There is a boat that will take us close. I think my children will like it." He hated that his Spanish was still basic; it felt like he couldn't really describe the anticipation of seeing the largest waterfalls in the western hemisphere.

Peña's face lit up. "Ah, Iguazú! You will love it. Very beautiful. Especially the Devil's Throat—you must make sure you see it, it is the most spectacular part."

Martin couldn't help but smile. He felt the same enthusiasm. "The boat will take us to that part."

Peña looked forward. "I know that Anna-Maria will be sorry to see your son leave." Then he laughed again, and spurred his horse forward to say something to his daughter that Martin couldn't hear.

Salta, Argentina

Eight hundred kilometers to the north, the telephone rang in Gustav Fiedler's hotel room. He answered on the first ring.

"Yes?" he said, in German.

"You were right, Commander," the voice on the other end said in accented German; quietly, as if he were afraid of being overheard. "They will be at Iguazú on Friday."

"Mmm," Fiedler grunted, frustrated and vindicated at the same time. "Then you know what must be done."

There was silence on the line for a couple of seconds, and Fiedler wondered if Peña was up to the task. But then the mining manager's voice returned, sounding resolute: "I will do it tonight, Commander."

"Good."

Fiedler hung up the phone and glanced at his wrist watch. Less than twenty seconds. It would take at least thirty seconds to trace a call, if anyone were trying to. The local police had been bribed, of course; but one couldn't be too cautious now that the Americans were aware of the operation. Fiedler did not know if they had paid more.

He looked out the open window at the plaza below, bathed in the soft red light of dusk. The twin spires of the colonial-era cathedral across the square glowed pink.

This had been a Paraguayan city prior to 1870; it would be easier for Fiedler now if it still were. Because it wasn't, he had to detour the shipment around the southern tip of Paraguay, via Corrientes, then back north to the crossing above Iguazú. They already had to bribe Brazilian customs officials for the current shipment—their largest to-date—and with the High Command's strict orders to control costs, he couldn't afford to have to cross Paraguay and bribe their customs officials as well.

Peña would call again only after he had killed the meddling American diplomat. If there were no call before Fiedler left in the morning for Corrientes, he would know to be extra watchful himself.

Martin relaxed on a bench in the courtyard, watching Jackie and Stevie walk around the lip of the fountain with their arms outstretched, playing circus tightrope walkers. Marty sat beside him, head leaned back on the top of the bench, staring up at the stars.

It was a cool, clear evening, and the sky was a canvas of stars. Martin didn't know any of the southern constellations except for the Southern Cross, but he still appreciated the beauty of the dark sky. An occasional breeze carried a chill, reminding him that it was still winter in this part of the world.

It was peaceful in the courtyard, which was softly lit by a dozen old-fashioned wrought-iron lanterns hung on the columns that delineated the encircling corridor. This house was over sixty years old, and Martin supposed the lanterns were original. He was glad they had never been electrified.

After a while, he clapped his hands together to get his children's attention. "I think it's time for three little gauchos I know to take their baths before bedtime." He stood amid a chorus of "Awww"s and shooed them all toward their room. "C'mon, let's wash off that trail dust."

As they passed through the colonnades in front of their door, he saw Raúl Peña leaning against the half-wall, bare-headed, facing the courtyard and smoking a cigarette. Martin bid him good evening, and unlocked his door.

"Good evening, friend," Peña said. "I wonder if I could have a word with you for a moment."

Martin hesitated in the open doorway while his kids filed inside. "Yes—but only for a moment. I have to clean my children." He hated how silly he sounded, but at that moment he couldn't remember how to conjugate the Spanish verb for "to bathe."

"Of course," Peña said, and waited a moment while Martin instructed his kids in English to go into the bathroom and get ready. When Martin came back into the corridor, Peña motioned with his arm. "Come, let us stroll for a moment."

A nervous tingle ran down Martin's spine and through his gut, but he couldn't explain why. Something about Peña's manner seemed a little off.

"My children are sad that you and your children are leaving tomorrow," Peña said. "Especially Anna-Maria. She has asked if your son Martín would write to her." He chuckled softly, and as they reached the narrow corridor at the back of the courtyard leading to a wrought-iron gate and the path to the stables, he motioned that direction.

Martin hesitated to enter a narrow corridor in the dark, but scolded himself for being silly. He and Peña strolled into it.

"Of course, I told her again that Spanish is Martín's second language, but she is full of hope that he will write letters to her." Peña lifted the latch on the gate and swung it outward.

"He can say words in Spanish, but he does not know how to write them," Martin said, forgetting the Spanish word for "to spell."

"He will learn that words in Spanish are spelled the way we say them," Peña said. "It is a shame that you will not be the one to teach him."

Martin saw the movement out of the corner of his eye, almost too late; Peña's arm came up, the dark silhouette of a horseshoe in his hand. Reacting instinctively, Martin just managed to lean back enough that Peña's knuckles grazed his forehead, and the horseshoe whooshed by harmlessly.

Martin bent his knees and lowered his head, then led with his shoulder as he threw himself forward, catching Peña in the midsection and knocking him to the ground. It was a move Martin had performed countless times in football when he was young, blocking a defender. It came back to him without thinking.

He landed on top of Peña, but the burly man flipped him over as if he were a rag doll. Martin landed hard on his back, and looked up to see Peña crouching over him, a knife glinting in the dim light of the stars.

Then a dark figure emerged from his right, grabbed Peña by the side of the head and twisted, hard.

Martin heard a loud crack. Then Peña slumped to the ground.

Martin scrambled backward like a crab, then shoved himself upright and backed away.

The mysterious man held out his hand, palm forward. "Mr. Schuller, wait, please," he said in slow, heavily-accented English. He took a step forward, and then explained in Spanish. "I have worked with Agent Sloan of your FBI, and now I work with your Agent Wilson. I could not reach him when I learned you were in danger, so I came here myself."

Martin peered through the darkness, unable to make out the man's face. "Who are you?"

"You can call me Shepherd. I was once an agent of the Basque Intelligence Service, now in exile in Argentina."

Basque Intelligence? Martin wondered what they were doing here, and what it had to do with him. "Who was Peña? And was that his real name?"

The man called Shepherd spat on the ground. "It is his real name. He is a director at the Andean Mineral Resources Corporation, which operates many mines in Argentina and Chile. He has been diverting some production for many months, and selling it on the black market to German military contacts." He motioned toward the house. "Come, let us get you back inside, and I will explain. The Germans learned that you know something about their operation—they don't know how much exactly, but they take no chances."

In the light of the lantern above the wrought-iron gate, Martin recognized his rescuer as one of the stable workers; the one called Bosco. Or, at least he'd thought he was an ordinary stable worker.

"We knew that they sent someone to eliminate you—so when I could not reach your Agent Wilson, I came here to warn you, and I recognized Raúl Peña from his photograph. I have been watching him."

Martin's mind raced. The Germans knew somehow that he was aware of their smuggling operation. *SIM told the Germans what Rosa Linda gave them.* His stomach turned sour.

He thought of his kids alone in their room, and he ran to their door.

Hutson

37

Thursday, July 25

Martin spent a sleepless night staring at the locked door of their hotel room. His pocket knife sat open on the bedside table. He was taking no chances.

He'd found his children entertaining themselves while they waited for him to come back, blissfully unaware that anything scary had happened. Martin tried to calm himself while the kids took their baths, but he wasn't successful.

In the morning, he packed their bags at first light, roused the kids, and checked out early. Since it was barely past dawn, the only transportation available was a beat-up Model A pickup truck, driven by a toothless old gaucho who took them to the nearest train station.

They stood in the chill on the platform, waiting nearly an hour for the train to Córdoba. The kids were quiet, sleepy-eyed, and occasionally yawned. No one else waited with them. It made Martin feel a little silly for leaving the estancia so early in the morning.

The eastbound train was short, only a few cars behind an old steam engine. Their car was nearly empty—an old woman with several chickens in wooden cages, a pair of young men in workmen's clothes and flat caps. The ride into Santa Fe took three hours, but Martin couldn't relax.

At the busy Santa Fe station, Martin found a phone booth, and instructed his kids to wait next to it, holding hands. He asked the operator for long-distance to Buenos Aires.

Once the Buenos Aires operator connected him to the American embassy, he asked Mrs. Torres to put him through to the FBI office.

"Legal Attaché's office." The words tumbled in a rush from a grizzled voice.

"Martin Schuller calling. I need to speak with Special Agent Wilson right away."

"Hold on," the agent who answered said. Martin heard the loud clank of the phone receiver hitting the desk.

"This is Wilson."

"Agent Wilson, Martin Schuller calling. There's been an incident."

"Frankly, I'm surprised Shepherd revealed himself to you," Wilson said after Martin finished filling him in on what happened the night before. "He's our source, and we swore to keep his identity secret."

That's the first thing you can think to say? Martin stifled his frustration. "He said he tried to speak to you before he came." He left unsaid that this was probably when Wilson was at the estancia apprehending Rosa Linda.

"The BIS has offered to help us in any way they can," Wilson said, but didn't elaborate.

"I wasn't aware that Basque Intelligence was still operating; let alone here in Argentina." Martin hoped Wilson caught the rebuke.

"Weren't you? One of Shepherd's local sources is also one of your sources, I understand. I assumed you knew. Don't know the man's real name, only the code name BIS gave him."

Martin noticed Wilson didn't share that code name. *Typical.* Which of his sources was also talking to Basque Intelligence?

"My children are with me, Agent Wilson. This is our vacation. I'd like to know if we're going to be safe at our next destination."

There was a brief hesitation. "If they knew you were at the estancia, they might know where you're going next."

"That was my thought exactly. What can you find out for me?"

"Who at the embassy knows your itinerary?" Wilson asked.

The question caught Martin off guard. "First Secretary Davis knows how to reach me. Aside from him, I've discussed our plans in general terms with several coworkers—Third Secretaries Mattingly, Dean, and Brady. I didn't think it needed to be secret, of course."

"No reason you should have," Wilson said, in a tone that he probably thought of as reassuring, though it came off gruff. "I'll talk with First Secretary Davis, and then we'll work our sources. You just go about your business, act normal, and we'll be in touch." The line clicked off.

Martin noticed Wilson hadn't asked him where he was going next. There was no reason to think their conversation wasn't private, given that this was a random public telephone booth. Martin could see no one lingering nearby, except his children.

He couldn't fault the FBI for being overly cautious, he supposed.

"Alright, kiddos, let's get our train tickets."

"I thought we were going to ride horses one more time before we left," Marty said.

"Don't whine," Martin said, irritated now that the kids were awake enough to question what they were doing. "Come along, now. Hold hands."

The express train to Corrientes took seven hours, and by the end Martin had almost convinced himself that no one had followed them north. They had to change trains here, and the evening air felt warm and sultry when they stepped down onto the platform. Martin led the children through the station, where the air was stuffy, and he looked forward to getting back outside when they found their platform.

He glanced around constantly as they hurried through the lobby, and then his eye caught a figure standing inside a telephone booth, and he couldn't help but stare for a couple of seconds.

The snub-nosed blond young man on the telephone noticed him staring. His pale blue eyes went wide, and he turned away in a hurry.

It was the young man he'd seen at the Bozen Haus restaurant in Bariloche earlier that month. One of the two who'd been talking about lithium shipments out of Chile, in German.

Martin checked his watch; the overnight train for Puerto Aguirre left in just twenty minutes. With three young children in tow, there was no way he could wait until the last minute to board.

But he had a few minutes to spare. First he needed a reason to linger. "Who's hungry? How about some empanadas for the road?"

There was an empanada vendor in the lobby, reminding him of a hot dog vendor at Grand Central, and he ushered the children there. He kept the public telephone bank in sight, and saw the snub-nosed young man scurry away a moment later, glancing back over his shoulder a couple of times.

Once they had their food in hand, he led them back toward the telephones, urging them to hurry. That had taken four precious minutes.

"Daddy has to make a quick phone call before we leave. Wait right here where I can see you, and hold hands."

He drummed his fingers on the shelf as he waited for what seemed like ages while the operator connected him to long-distance. He kept glancing at his watch. It was only two minutes before the Buenos Aires operator came on the line, but it felt much longer.

He grew agitated as the line at the embassy rang without answer. It was after seven o'clock, but he'd hoped the security guard would answer, and that the FBI agents worked late.

After the tenth ring, he asked the operator to connect him instead with the phone number of Richard Wilson. It took her almost fifteen seconds to find the listing, a reasonable amount of time, to be sure, but Martin trembled with impatience the entire time.

When there was no answer after ten rings, the operator told him to try again later, and clicked off.

"C'mon kids, we've got to hurry," he said, trying to make it sound exciting as he grabbed Marty's hand. "The train leaves soon, so let's see who can go the fastest without running."

"Commander!" the courier named Acker said a bit too loudly for Fiedler's taste, and he frowned at the young man who came to an abrupt stop in front of him, breathless.

"What is it?" Fiedler asked in German.

"I saw the American," Acker said, still catching his breath. "He walked through the lobby with three children."

Fiedler had to hand it to the man—pursuing an opposing agent with children in tow was a bold move, something he never expected an American to be sophisticated enough to do. "You are certain it was he?"

"Yes, sir," Acker said, his voice steadier now. "It was the man I saw in Bariloche, I am certain."

"Hmmm," Fiedler's hard exhale made it sound almost like a growl. "Find out if he boarded the train for Puerto Aguirre, and report back to me." Fiedler was all but certain that was where the American was heading, but he needed confirmation.

If so, Fiedler would have to deal with him personally, before he could interfere with the hired smugglers who would carry their cargo to Brazil tomorrow, crossing the river above the falls.

But first, he had other problems.

He spun on his heel and returned to the janitor's closet, opening the door with a key the local police had given him. Inside, bound and gagged and bloodied, sat the man they had caught watching them earlier today.

Two of his own men stood on either side of the chair where the man slumped against his bindings. Fiedler wouldn't entrust this interrogation to just anyone. He looked his men in the eye, and they both shook their heads.

He leaned down and lifted the bound man's chin with the silver eagle that adorned the tip of his black walking stick. He addressed him in Spanish. "You still won't talk? Tsk, tsk. You could save yourself so much pain. We already know that you work for Basque Intelligence, and that you are called Shepherd. You gain nothing by denying it." Fiedler slammed the bottom of his walking stick on the floor, sending a loud crack through the room. "You were waiting for us, before we arrived here. How did you know we would pass through here? Tell us, and you will suffer no further pain."

The man called Shepherd glared at him through swollen eyes.

"Was it the American?" Fiedler asked.

The man's eyes stayed steady, but his pupils dilated a little bit—enough to make Fiedler think that it was true.

He smacked him across the top of the head with his walking stick. The man grimaced and whimpered.

"Did they tell you what we're doing here? Did they send you to stop us? To do what they are not willing to do themselves?"

The man's eyes hardened, and he held Fiedler's gaze in obvious defiance.

"Such scruples, the Americans have," Fiedler said, shaking his head in disapproval. "They are too squeamish to do what must be done to stop us, so they send stateless Basque agents to do their dirty work for them. I am certain you were well-paid. It's a pity you'll never be able to enjoy those American dollars."

He stood and faced his men, addressing them in German. "Get him to talk, using any method you choose. Do not hold back. If he dies from it, he dies."

Fiedler spun on his heel and marched from the room. Regardless of what information they may or may not get from the Basque, he would deal with the American himself.

38

Friday, July 26, 1940

They could hear the roar of the falls before they got close enough to see them. Their first visual hint that they were getting close was the massive clouds of mist that rolled along the surface of the river.

Martin had planned their visit to the Iguazú Falls for the day of Marty's ninth birthday. They'd checked in this morning at an inn overlooking the central plaza in Puerto Aguirre, on the Argentine side of the river, and at noon had boarded a boat to take them upriver to the falls.

The jungle heat was oppressive, and the air was thick with humidity. Martin couldn't imagine what it must be like here after the end of winter. He was glad he was in shirtsleeves, and open-collared. A dark green bucket hat shielded his face from the hot rays of the sun. The other passengers on the boat were similarly casual.

The kids wore faded orange life jackets, tied up with well-worn laces that had once been white. Martin told Stevie for the umpteenth time to sit down and not let go of his sister's hand.

The boat, moving briskly upriver, began to rise up and down on the swells, and soon they rounded a bend and saw a wall of cliffs and waterfalls ahead of them in the distance. Mist rose like clouds from the base of the falls, punctuated by several rainbows from the bright sunlight.

Marty, who had been vocal in his disappointment at not staying at the estancia for his birthday, now lit up when he saw the falls. "Whoa," he said almost under his breath. A slow grin broke across his face.

"I knew you'd like it," Martin said, patting the top of his son's head, which was covered in a green bucket hat like his.

Jackie and Stevie began to squeal and giggle as the boat started rocking harder, moving ever closer to the falls. Many of their fellow passengers were laughing as well, holding onto the rails behind their seats. Martin leaned forward and grabbed his youngest, plopping Stevie onto his lap and putting an arm around him.

"So you don't fall into the water, buddy," Martin shouted over the increasing roar of the walls of water. Cool mist coated their faces, riding waves of tumbling air that rolled out from the towering falls that now loomed in front of them. Splashes of water rolled onto the floor of the boat, washing over everyone's feet. Jackie lifted her feet up with a surprised squeal, kicking them in the air and laughing.

The top of a wave landed on Martin's shoulder, catching him by surprise. Stevie covered his mouth and pointed, eyes squinting with glee. "Daddy got wet!" His rolling laughter was contagious, and Martin laughed with him. The next splash landed squarely on both of them, and Stevie's giggles rose.

Only one passenger didn't seem amused at the water that was starting to soak them all. Martin was still smiling from his amusement at Stevie, but he watched the man in curiosity for a few seconds.

He was tall and thin, with a sharp and narrow nose, brown hair that was combed back with brilliantine, and deep-set eyes that seemed to take in everything with disdain. Martin wondered what the man had expected instead of this.

The boat made a long arc in front of the falls, which seemed to stretch endlessly, and after a few minutes everyone on board was soaked. Then the boat made for the Brazilian side of the river, and hugged the shore for a quarter-mile before pulling up to a wooden dock located at the base of a deep fissure in the cliff.

Looking up, Martin saw a wooden staircase built into the fissure, leading up to a platform a couple hundred feet above them. To their right was a sandy spit of land that separated the main part of the river from a shallow pool crowded with giant rocks.

No Brazilian Customs official waited at the pier, only a couple of workers who caught ropes thrown by the boat pilot, plus a handful of passengers in life jackets waiting to board. Martin mused on the porous nature of the border here.

Most of the passengers on the boat got up to leave, and the boat pilot instructed them all—in both Spanish and Portuguese—to keep their ticket stubs to re-board later.

Martin nudged Marty's shoulder. "Let's go look around." He took Stevie's and Jackie's hands, and they stepped off onto the dock and walked toward the wooden stairs, joining a stream of people.

While they waited in line at the base of the stairs, Marty looked up, and then tugged the end of Martin's shirt. "Dad? That looks really high."

Martin put his hand on the boy's shoulder. "We went that high up inside the lighthouse at Montauk last summer, remember? You didn't have any trouble with that. You'll be fine." Martin also realized his son probably hadn't looked down when they climbed the circular lighthouse stairs; here, that would be harder not to do. "I'll be right behind you, sport."

At the base of the stairs, he sent Marty up first, followed by Jackie, and then Stevie; he took up the rear. "Hold the rail," he told them, needlessly, since they already were.

About halfway up, the two youngest lost steam and slowed way down. Martin could picture impatient scowls on the faces of the people coming up behind him. The stairs were just steep enough that he didn't want to climb without holding the rail with one hand, so that made it impossible to carry both of them. After a moment's hesitation, he picked Stevie up in one arm and carried him the rest of the way, and told Marty to help his sister.

The view from the top made the climb worthwhile.

"Wow!" Marty said, and was promptly echoed by Stevie.

Martin put his arm around Marty and squeezed his shoulder. "Happy birthday, buddy."

"Look, Daddy!" Jackie said, pointing at the multitude of falls spreading before them. "Look at all the rainbows."

"That's a lot of rainbows," Martin agreed. "How many do you see? Can you count them?"

That kept them occupied for a moment, while the two youngest pointed and counted out loud. Martin stared in awe at the seemingly endless crescent of waterfalls. Most of them were massive, divided by small rocky islands covered in short trees, but a few were small branches that split off from the main river. The cries of jungle birds in the forest surrounding them pierced the air over the roar of water. Below them, he could see the boat heading back downriver, crossing diagonally toward the Argentine side.

To their left was a trailhead, and hikers moved up and down the trail through the trees, which skirted the edge of the cliff at a distance of a few yards. "Come on, kiddos, let's go this way."

"Are there tigers in that forest, Daddy?" Jackie asked.

"No tigers."

"You promise?"

"I promise."

Gustav Fiedler held back, following at a distance. The American was playing it cool, acting the part of the tourist. Fiedler would have to be patient.

They were moving the right direction, at least. Fiedler checked his watch; the trucks would be nearing the smugglers' crossing about five kilometers above the falls. He wondered when the American would stash the children somewhere and dash for the Brazilian landing point.

And who would be there to meet him.

Javier hurried east along the riverfront of Puerto Aguirre, past the ferry to the city of Foz do Iguaçu on the Brazilian side. He needed to get to Brazil, but he'd never had a passport, so the ferry wasn't an option. He also didn't want to take the tourist boats to the falls, some nineteen kilometers upriver, and waste precious time.

No, he needed a fisherman without strict scruples to take him across unofficially, and drop him off at some secluded portage on the Brazilian side. Preferably just below the falls.

Fortunately, the old Guaraní cleaning lady at the inn had a brother who didn't mind a little unofficial work.

He found the docks of the indigenous fishermen nearly half a kilometer upriver from the main docks of the town. Their boats looked like giant dug-out canoes, as if they had been pulled from the illustrations of his old school history books, but with outboard motors fastened to the backs.

It took a lot of asking among men whose first language was not Spanish, but he finally located the cleaning lady's brother.

"Are you Mr. Guerrero?" he asked. When the old man regarded him suspiciously and didn't reply, he added, "I was sent here by your sister, Jeruti Rivas. She said you might help me. I can pay."

The old man came toward him. His dark skin was deeply creased, and his black eyes stared at Javier, unblinking. "I am Kauan Guerrero," he said in heavily-accented Spanish. "What do you want?"

"I need to get to Brazil, but not be seen arriving."

Guerrero stared at him unblinking for several seconds. "I can do that, sir, for one hundred pesos."

Javier almost smiled at the more-than-reasonable price. He handed the amount to Guerrero and asked, "How soon can we leave?"

**

The trail was semi-rugged, trending mostly uphill, and after less than a kilometer Martin realized this might be too much for his youngest children, though Marty seemed to be having the time of his life. He'd found a walking stick, and was outpacing everyone, so that Martin had to warn him multiple times to slow down and wait for everyone else.

Martin picked Jackie up and put her on his shoulders, placing both hands on her knees to hold her while he kept walking. "Hey Stevie, why don't you ask your brother to give you a piggyback ride?"

"Yay, piggyback ride!" Stevie shouted, and ran toward Marty with a sudden burst of energy.

Marty turned back toward his father with an impatient look. "Aww, Dad! That'll slow me down."

"You can still use your stick, you won't slow down that much," Martin said. "Now go on, give your brother a piggy-back."

"O-kay," Marty said in that elongated way that said it really wasn't. But he knelt down to let Stevie jump on his back, and looped his arms under his little brother's legs.

"Come on," Martin said to his eldest, nodding ahead of them toward a large rocky overlook just on the upriver side of the falls. "That looks like a pretty swell place to rest up there. Maybe you can throw some sticks in the river and watch them go over."

"That would be fun," Marty agreed.

Martin smiled at him. "Then let's go. Not much farther."

Fiedler's patience was growing thin.

The truck caravan should have reached the crossing now, and the local smugglers they had hired would be loading the crates onto their boats. There wasn't much time left. What was this American playing at?

Fiedler supposed if he had to take out this enemy with the children present, he would do what he had to. They were clearly Aryan children, and he'd hoped the American would deposit them somewhere safe—as he surely must, before he rushed east to intercept their illegal cargo. But time was of the essence, and Fiedler couldn't afford to wait until the last possible second, as this American seemed to be doing. He couldn't risk losing him at the critical moment.

Fiedler put his hand in his pants pocket and felt for the Maxim Silencer. He glanced around to make sure no other hikers were close enough to see what he was doing, and he quickly installed it on the end of his pistol before once more stashing the gun under his shirt.

The old Guaraní fisherman had deposited Javier at a secluded anchorage about a kilometer west of the falls, well hidden by the jungle canopy. He had pointed Javier toward a bare, rocky outcropping, where the cliff face was less steep, with multiple hand-and-footholds for climbing.

Javier's stomach dropped when he looked up at it.

"Our ancestors used this portage long before white men came," Guerrero explained. "They climbed barefoot, with baskets strapped to their backs. With shoes and nothing on your back, it is easy. Go!"

This is for Mr. Schuller. Javier swallowed his fear and started climbing. It seemed to take hours to reach the top, and his heart pounded in his ears the entire way.

When he reached the top, a trail through the dense forest led directly from this spot toward the falls. He looked back down to wave at his courier, but Guerrero and his boat had already disappeared.

He checked his watch and realized there wasn't much time. He started running at full speed.

Martin put Jackie back on the ground when they reached the rocky overlook, and Marty slipped Stevie off his back. An iron railing had been installed around the overlook, about two feet back from the edge, and signs at regular intervals warned *"Perigo."* Danger.

335

Martin nodded at some dead wood littering the edge of the forest around the rock. "Go get some of those, then stand right here, and you can throw them in the water."

Marty and Stevie collected sticks, while Jackie stood beside Martin and grabbed his hand.

"There it goes!" Marty shouted when the first big piece of wood went over the edge.

Martin laughed. He looked down at Jackie, holding his hand and staring at the water. "You want to do it, too?"

She shook her head.

"Just wanna watch?"

She nodded.

He leaned down to kiss the top of her head. "It's still fun to watch."

Marty and Stevie heaved pieces of wood into the river with grunts, then shouted and jumped when they went over the falls.

Fiedler crouched in the brush at the edge of the path. To get a clear shot at the American, he'd had to get within twenty meters of the open overlook; it was closer than he would have liked, but the forest provided minimal cover if he needed it.

At least the American had taken the little girl off of his shoulders. Now Fiedler would be able to aim for the middle of his back. If he caught him square between the shoulder blades, he would only need one shot.

A pair of hikers went by, a dark-haired young man and woman in their early twenties, and cast curious glances at Fielder crouched beside the path. "Resting," he said in Spanish, certain they couldn't see the gun he held against his right hip, which was turned away from the path. The young man nodded, and they moved on, not stopping at the overlook.

Fiedler waited a couple of minutes to make sure there was no one else around. Then he brought his gun slowly into position.

Javier felt like his lungs were about to explode. He was not used to running, and after three kilometers the muscles in his legs burned, his feet screamed with pain, and he had to fight to keep going at any speed.

The ancient portage trail had merged into a wider tourist trail just below the falls, which made the going a tiny bit easier, though he had to sidestep the occasional hikers.

He'd passed the falls a while ago, and he was starting to get concerned that he hadn't found Mr. Schuller yet. He rounded a corner, and his ragged breath caught in his throat.

A thin-haired middle-aged white man crouched in the brush at the edge of the trail, slowly raising a gun.

To his left, Javier spotted Mr. Schuller standing in the open at an overlook. Three children stood nearby.

Javier willed his legs to move him faster, and he plunged forward even though his muscles screamed in protest.

The man's gun came into position, and his finger wound around the trigger.

"Mr. Schuller!" The warning shout escaped Javier's lips as he threw himself into the air, and a second later he crashed into the side of the crouching man.

The crack of gunfire rang in his ears as he and the gunner tumbled into the broad, waxy leaves of the tropical bush, but it was more like a muffled boom than a loud shot.

The gun clattered onto the rock, and Javier glanced over to see it skidding away, flying between the two little boys, and disappearing over the edge into the rushing water.

39

Martin spun around. Time seemed to slow to a crawl when he heard the gunshot. He watched the pistol skid across the rocks toward them as if in a dream. It moved inexorably toward Marty and Stevie, and he felt his heart stop.

He moved in slow motion, but the gun slid neatly between the boys and tumbled over the edge of the rock into the turbulent river.

Then the world snapped back into normal speed, and without a second thought he stepped between his children and the direction from which the gun had come. "Get into the bush! Go, hide in the bush!"

He pushed Marty and Jackie a little too roughly, and they stumbled as they moved into the thick leaves, Marty bumping into Stevie and pushing him along in front.

As soon as they were under cover, Martin spun toward the shooter, certain he'd disappeared into the jungle in the intervening seconds.

Instead he saw the humorless man from the boat struggling on the ground with Javier Velasco.

His eyes had to be playing tricks on him.

The gunman was stronger than Javier anticipated, given that he had to be almost forty. He recovered quickly from the shock of being attacked, pushing his knees against Javier's midsection to create distance between them.

He reached for Javier's throat, but as his fingers curled around his windpipe, Javier plunged his fist into the man's gut.

The man grunted and grimaced with the blow, but didn't loosen his grip. Javier began to see stars.

But then a foot slammed into the man's ribs from Javier's right. The man dropped his hold on Javier and tumbled to the side.

Mr. Schuller grabbed Javier by the arm and tugged him up. Javier watched as Mr. Schuller slammed his foot down onto the gunman's gut, causing the man to scream and fold into a ball. Then Mr. Schuller spun Javier by the shoulder to face him, and his green eyes were wild.

"Get my children out of here!" Mr. Schuller shouted. It was in English, but Javier understood. He turned and ran toward the overlook.

Martin squared his stance as the man rose from the ground several feet away. His only thought was to be a human wall between the assailant and his children until Javier could get them far away.

He noticed when the man stood, that his posture was decidedly crooked now. He was favoring his right side, where Martin had kicked his ribs.

"What do you want?" Martin asked, first in English, then in Spanish.

The man stared at him with undisguised hatred. "Don't pretend to be ignorant," he hissed in German. "I know why you are in Iguazú today. I will not let you interfere with our cargo transport. It is needed in the Fatherland for our attack on the English, and I will see that it gets there."

Cargo transport. Of course. Martin glanced around at the dense rainforest surrounding them, remembering the lack of Brazilian Customs at the boat landing earlier. It made perfect sense.

The Abwehr had heard about the increased FBI presence in Buenos Aires, he was certain, and they were taking evasive action. Across the porous border into Brazil, and then to Santos or Rio de Janeiro where there were no American FBI agents snooping.

Martin had no idea how he could possibly stop their shipment single-handedly, but this man clearly thought he was already trying to. And now he had to try.

"You have already lost," Martin bluffed. He saw the look of doubt that flitted across the man's eyes, and plunged ahead. "You can't stop us all."

He hoped the man didn't have another gun.

The man's face flushed with fury. "Foolish Americans. Why would you think we need to stop all of you?" He pulled a small leather sheath from his pocket and removed a stiletto.

Martin reached into his own pocket. It might not be a match for a stiletto, but his pocket knife was better than no weapon at all.

His opponent barked a laugh when Martin opened his pocket knife. Then he lunged forward with a cry of effort, pointing his stiletto at Martin's gut.

Martin sidestepped the attack, which was weakened by the man's broken ribs. He took a shallow swipe at the man's forearm with the blade of his pocket knife as he passed, hoping he'd drop the stiletto.

The cut wasn't deep enough to do damage, and the man continued to grip the handle of his knife—though Martin noticed the grip was now white-knuckled.

They faced off again, this time Martin with his back to the forest, and the man's back to the river.

"Why do you Americans insist on meddling in affairs that do not concern you?" the man asked through gritted teeth, breathing heavily now. He started inching toward Martin. "That pompous windbag Churchill convinced you that the Limeys have familial feelings toward their American cousins? Ha!" He spat on the ground. "I have spent time in London; they look down their haughty noses at you as much as they look down on us Germans. They think they are better than everyone else. Once they have gotten what they want from you, they will brush you off as so much nuisance and go back to their empire."

The irony was not lost on Martin of an Abwehr agent accusing the British of thinking they were better than everyone else. Pot calling the kettle black indeed.

"We are not meddling in your affairs," Martin said. "You are meddling in our hemisphere, which makes it our affair."

A sinister grin spread across the man's face, and he laughed without mirth. "Fools. Soon every hemisphere will be our hemisphere."

He lunged toward Martin again, having shortened the distance between them to a few feet. Martin barely had time to get out of the way, but as the man brushed by Martin brought his elbow down on the man's right wrist.

The stiletto flew off into the brush.

The Abwehr man's cry of pain lasted only a second, and then turned to rage. He jumped at Martin and clawed at his eyes, and Martin tumbled backward onto the path.

The man was on top of him in an instant, and though he grunted and grimaced at the impact, his hands reached for Martin's throat.

Martin grabbed his shoulders and rolled them both over. The man cried out as his broken ribs pressed into the exposed rock on their way over. Somehow, he managed to keep his head enough to halt their momentum when he was on top of Martin, and he brought his legs up to clamp his knees around Martin's hips.

His hands encircled Martin's throat.

Martin's mind raced. He knew he had one chance to throw the man off before he constricted his air. He gathered his strength, and with his hands on the man's shoulders and bringing his knees up to surround the man's sides, he heaved with every muscle in his body and tossed the man to the side like a bale of hay.

His attacker landed against a post of the guardrail, arms and legs flailing. He struggled to stand while Martin backed away crab-style, but lost his balance midway up.

He fell back against the guardrail. His arms pinwheeled wildly. That was the fatal error—the motion of the pinwheel tipped him backward. He hung there, suspended across the guardrail for one interminable second—

And then he tumbled headfirst into the rushing river.

Martin pushed himself up in time to see the man's body jettison over the edge of the falls.

Hutson

40

Javier paced the overlook at the top of the stairs, where the old portage trail merged into the larger tourist trail. Mr. Schuller hadn't arrived yet, and he was starting to really worry. The three children were quiet, somber even, and stood in a cluster near the top of the stairs.

He stopped in front of them, hesitated, and then knelt down. He forced a smile. "Have you had fun at the falls today?" he asked, trying to sound cheerful and only succeeding in being overly loud.

The older boy and the girl nodded, but their eyes were wary. The little boy played with his hands and looked down at them.

He wasn't good with children. He had nieces and nephews about this age, but he only saw them a few times a year. At least on Christmas, he could kick a soccer ball with them around the park after dinner. He didn't have a ball now, of course; and these American children didn't play soccer, anyway.

He started to pace again.

When he finally saw Mr. Schuller coming down the path, with a slight limp, he exhaled hard with relief. He looked back at the Schuller children and grinned for real. "Your father is here!" he said, his own excitement obvious.

Martin's heart had been in his throat the entire way back down the trail toward the stairs where they'd started. When he rounded that last bend and saw his children standing with Javier Velasco, he felt a tremendous weight lift off his shoulders and chest, and he hurried forward to meet them.

"Daddy!" they shouted in unison, and ran toward him.

He leaned down and took them all in his arms, squeezing them tightly to him, and kissing their cheeks.

"Dad?" Marty asked, quietly, after Martin had stood.

"Yeah, sport?"

"That man back there—was he a robber? I mean, a bandit?"

Martin couldn't think of a better explanation his kids would understand. "That's right. That bad man was a bandit, and he was trying to rob my friend here."

"And you stopped him, Dad?" Marty's eyes had grown wide, and a sparkle of excitement gleamed there.

A faint smile cracked Martin's lips, and he nodded down at his son. "Yes, I stopped him."

"How? Did you punch him?"

Martin cringed. They had tried to teach Marty not to fight. But he sighed and nodded again. "Yes, I punched him. Sometimes you have to fight, to protect good people from bad ones."

"Just like The Batman," Marty said, almost in awe.

Martin couldn't help but laugh. Then he rumpled his son's hair. "That's right, just like The Batman. C'mon, kiddos, let's go back and get cleaned up for dinner."

Javier found Thaddeus Acker sitting alone in a dark booth in the back corner of a restaurant, checking his watch. It hadn't been hard to find him—Puerto Aguirre was a small provincial town, there were only two restaurants here.

Thaddeus's eyes widened when he saw Javier approach.

"How...how did you know...?"

"I knew you were in the north," Javier said, taking a seat opposite Thaddeus. "I also knew some operation was happening here. I was needed, and so I came. I suspected you were here."

"I'm meeting a man from the German embassy. A Navy commander. I have a message to pass along to him. It's routine."

Javier shook his head.

There was fright in Thaddeus's pale eyes, and he glanced around. "You shouldn't be here. It's dangerous." He leaned forward, and whispered, "The Shepherd is dead. They tortured and killed him. He didn't reveal our names—by the time they got him to talk, he wasn't making sense—but you should leave. If the commander sees you here—"

"He won't see me," Javier said. "The man you are waiting for is dead."

A look of awe came to Thaddeus's eyes, but didn't replace the fear. "How involved have you become?"

Javier didn't answer that. "The man you are waiting for tried to kill my American friend. He's dead now." He didn't elaborate.

Thaddeus's eyes widened again, and he leaned back, seeming in shock. "The American? You've been working with the American? But I..." his voice trailed off, and he looked down at his lap. "I never should have talked to the Shepherd. You played me."

Javier scowled. "The Shepherd brought you to the right side."

Thaddeus was silent for several seconds. When he looked up, his eyes were wet. "How do you know which is the right side?"

Javier looked at Thaddeus with compassion. These were not easy questions, he knew—but this time, the answer was clear.

"The side fighting against oppression."

There was a small bar at the inn, and Martin joined Javier Velasco for a drink after he put his kids to bed.

"First, thank you for saving my life," Martin said. "Second—how did you know the German agent was going to try to kill me?"

Javier gave him a Cheshire cat grin. "Spies do not name their sources. I would think you would know that, Mr. Schuller."

Martin shook his head. "I'm not a spy." *I catch them*.

Javier laughed. Then he waved a hand in the air dismissively. "Of course you aren't."

Martin scrutinized him for a moment. "Would it have something to do with a certain Basque Intelligence officer known as Shepherd?"

Javier looked surprised for a moment, but then he laughed. "You are a fascinating man, Mr. Schuller. I cannot fool you."

Martin was embarrassed by the compliment, but nodded in acknowledgement.

Javier leaned forward and lowered his voice. "I learned this afternoon that Shepherd was killed by German agents. A reliable source says that he didn't betray us."

Martin nodded, somber. It was a dangerous business. Shepherd killed Raúl Peña, and now the Abwehr had killed him. He drank his beer in silence.

They were both caught by surprise a few minutes later when Roberto Calderon strode into the bar, walked right up to their table, and took a seat. "Good evening, friends."

Javier's mouth hung open for a few seconds. "Roberto? What are you doing here?"

Roberto leaned back in his chair, crossed his thick arms over his chest, and stared back at Javier with a proud smile. "Today I helped the Federal Police catch a band of smugglers who were trying to take platinum across the Iguazú River to Brazil. Your friend the Shepherd sent me, and I got hired as a laborer to move the goods."

Martin shook his head in awe. These remnants of the Basque Intelligence Service had quite a network. He knew he could learn a thing or two.

And with Dietrich Niebuhr running multiple smuggling operations here, Martin was certain he would need to.

41

Monday, August 5 – Buenos Aires

Martin felt as if a vice were closing around his heart when he was introduced to the new typist, who was already ensconced in Rosa Linda's former desk. He forced a smile, shook her hand, and welcomed her to the embassy.

Once inside his office, he collapsed into his chair, looking in despair at the stack of papers and folders that had accumulated in his inbox over the two weeks he'd been away.

Instead of beginning work on them, however, he opened his desk drawer and removed a piece of plain stationery. He flipped through his card file to find the address Harriet Sloan had given him before they left last month.

He wrote a letter in ink.

Dear Miss Corely,

I have recently returned to Buenos Aires from the region around Iguazu Falls. While there, my children and I visited the Brazilian side of the river, and I became aware of something with which you might be able to assist me.

If you would be interested in performing an occasional task for me, please find a private place to telephone me. I will provide the phone number separately. You may reverse the charges.

I look forward to your affirmative reply.
Sincerely,

Martin Schuller

Thursday, August 15

"Mommy! Mommy!" the kids shouted when Martin pointed out Becky coming down the gangplank. They all ran toward her when she reached the bottom, and threw their arms around her legs and waist.

Martin noticed she didn't reprimand them for running, the way she had when they'd arrived two months before. Instead she beamed at them, touching their faces and kissing the tops of their heads.

"My darlings, I missed you."

They took hold of her hands, and regaled her with their adventures.

"We got to ski down a big mountain with my friends, and I was super fast," Marty said. "Then we rode horses at an estancia out on the pampas. And I learned how to throw a lasso and everything. I almost roped a calf once. Dad bought us gaucho hats, too, so now I can play cowboys and Indians for real."

"I rode my own pony!" Stevie shouted.

"Did you?" Becky patted Stevie's head, but didn't scold him for shouting. "My, but you're getting awfully big."

Stevie beamed, and bounced on the balls of his feet.

"We went to see the orchestra play, Mommy," Jackie said, tugging Becky's dress. "Daddy said you would like it, too."

Martin couldn't help a grin when he looked at Becky and shrugged. "She and Stevie fell asleep halfway through the symphony. But you didn't, did you, sport?" He reached over and rumpled Marty's hair.

Becky handed Marty a ticket. "Why don't you take your brother and sister and give your luggage to the porter for Mommy, hmm? Hand him this ticket."

"O.K." Marty nodded, and took Jackie and Stevie with him.

Becky watched them walk away, and sighed contentedly. Then she looked at Martin.

"Well! Sounds like you and the kids had a fun summer—or winter, I suppose," she said, cooly. "It doesn't feel much like winter, at least."

Martin didn't take the bait. "Winter here is like fall in Washington."

Becky fixed him with an icy half-smile. "And now the children get to have fall in Philadelphia. Six months of fall for them, it seems."

He felt himself stiffen, and made an effort not to snap at her. "It'll still be plenty hot there on Labor Day; and for a couple of weeks after that, at least."

The kids were coming back, and he smiled at them and said, "You're sailing north, so it'll be hot on the ship in a couple of days—by the time you get to Brazil, it'll feel like summer."

"Mom, we went to this giant waterfall, called Iguazú," Marty told Becky, grinning from ear to ear. "It felt like summer when we were there."

Becky smiled for Marty's benefit, but looked at Martin, and he could see the annoyance in her eyes. "Well, I guess you got to do about everything. You'll have lots to tell your teacher on the first day of school."

"Can I take my gaucho hat to show-and-tell?" Stevie asked, bouncing.

"I don't see why not," Becky said, and Stevie cheered. She shushed him for the first time since she arrived. "Not so loud, please."

"You enrolled him in kindergarten, I presume?" Martin asked.

"Yes. You'd have known that already if you were in Philadelphia," Becky said.

"That's not fair."

"What's not fair? That your kids don't live in the same city as you?"

He glanced at the kids, put his arm on Becky's shoulder and turned them away. He lowered his voice. "And whose fault is that? Huh? You were the one who left, Becky, not me."

She shook her head. "You left us long before then. Always having to be off somewhere, 'saving the world.' Like one of those stupid superheroes in Marty's comic books. You're thirty-two years old, Martin."

The superheroes in Marty's comic books. Martin grinned from ear to ear. He saw Becky's arched eyebrow, and let it go.

EPILOGUE

Wednesday, June 11, 1941

"You wanted to see me, sir?" Martin asked after being ushered into the ambassador's office.

"Have a seat, Schuller," the ambassador said. "I have some news for you. Big news."

Martin couldn't help the apprehension he felt as he took a chair. It was unusual to be called to see the ambassador himself without any pretext, and Martin couldn't think of anything he had done recently that would warrant extraordinary praise or rebuke.

"You've been recalled to Washington, effective immediately," the ambassador said, a touch of bemusement barely hidden in his tone. "Leadership has given us very little information—only that it's a permanent recall, the purpose is classified, and you are to return to the States *post haste* on the SS Brazil."

Martin took a second to let the news sink in. "But my children are arriving on that very ship next week."

"Yes, the cable mentions that," the ambassador said, lifting a corner of a communique on his desk for show. "They'll turn right around and go back with you. The tickets have already been arranged. This has all been ordered by Assistant Secretary Berle."

The Assistant Secretary of State for Intelligence. A few puzzle pieces came together in Martin's head, but in a random pattern.

"That gives me just enough time to get ready. Thank you, sir."

"We're sorry to see you leave early, Schuller," the ambassador said, friendly but formal. "You'll finish out the work week as normal, and leave any loose ends with the First Secretary."

"Yes, sir. Thank you, sir." Martin rose and shook the ambassador's hand, and a vague sense of anticipation filled him.

Thursday, July 3 – Washington, D.C.

Three men occupied the conference room on the top floor of the Old Executive Office Building when a middle-aged secretary ushered Martin in and silently closed the heavy wooden door behind him. Martin recognized Under Secretary Sumner Wells and Assistant Secretary for Intelligence Adolf Berle from their photographs, but the third man was unknown to him.

"Welcome back, Mr. Schuller," Assistant Secretary Berle said, shaking his hand. "It's a pleasure to meet you in person. This is Under Secretary Wells. And this is Colonel William Donovan, retired military."

Martin shook hands all around, intrigued. Berle motioned toward a leather chair at the long mahogany table, across from Donovan. Everyone took a seat.

"President Roosevelt is appointing Colonel Donovan to a newly created post, with the title Coordinator of Information," Wells said from the head of the table, taking charge of the meeting. "Everything we are about to say is classified."

"Understood, sir," Martin said, and excited butterflies filled his stomach.

He was back in it.

"Last summer, Colonel Donovan completed a secret mission to London for the president, and assessed the ability of the British to continue the fight against Nazi Germany without support from the French after their unfortunate capitulation," Wells continued. "Since then, he has liaised on behalf of the president in an unofficial capacity with John Godfrey of British Naval Intelligence; and with William Stephenson, the head of British Security Coordination.

"Colonel Donovan's role will soon no longer be unofficial. A new Office of the COI will be tasked with overcoming the lack of cooperation between existing intelligence agencies—military and civilian—and to cooperate when necessary with British and Chinese intelligence agencies."

"In anticipation of war with Germany or Japan," Martin filled in.

"Precisely," Donovan replied with a nod, and Martin turned toward him. "I have several positions to fill, and in preparation for opening this office we reviewed your file. You have some impressive credentials, Mr. Schuller."

"Thank you, Colonel," Martin said, anticipation growing.

"I'd like for you to come work for me," Donovan announced, putting his arms on the table and leaning forward. "You will continue officially as an employee of the State Department, but you'll report to me and take orders from me. You'll assist in analyzing intelligence on the German war machine and propaganda, and prepare for eventual clandestine operations. What do you say?"

Martin almost felt like he was floating. He couldn't have dreamed up a better offer. And as a bonus, he would be back in the same country as his children. Philadelphia was only an hour from Washington by train.

He stood and offered Donovan his hand. "When do I start?"

END

Thank you for reading Spy Tango. If you enjoyed this book, please tell a friend, update your social media, and/or write a review on Amazon, Goodreads, or other forum.

Questions or comments? Feel free to contact me at www.garretthutson.com

Also by Garrett Hutson:

In A Safe Town

The Jade Dragon (Death in Shanghai, Book 1)

Assassin's Hood (Death in Shanghai, Book 2)

Hidden Among Us (Martin Schuller Spy Catcher, Book 1)

About the Author

Garrett Hutson writes upmarket mysteries and historical spy fiction. He lives in Indianapolis with his husband, four dogs, and two cats, and more fish that you can count. He has one grown daughter. You may contact him at his website, www.garretthutson.com.

Historical Note

This is a work of fiction. All characters, with the exception of a few historical figures noted below, are fictional.

Among the historical figures included in reference only are President Franklin Roosevelt; Secretary of State Cordell Hull; British Prime Ministers Neville Chamberlain and Winston Churchill; Argentine President Ortiz and Vice President Castillo; German chancellor Adolf Hitler; Major Mark A. Devine, Jr., U.S. Military Attaché to Argentina; and Captain William D. Brereton, Jr., U.S. Naval Attaché to Argentina.

I try to avoid casting real people as characters, but on occasion it is necessary for the story—some historical figures that appear briefly in the narrative include Ambassador Armour; First Secretary Monnett Davis; Under Secretary of State Sumner Wells; Assistant Secretary of State for Intelligence Adolf Berle; and Colonel William Donovan, Coordinator of Information (COI).

The period from 1939 to 1941 was an interesting time for American intelligence gathering. Aside from domestic counterintelligence, no formal intelligence organization existed outside of the narrow purview of the Army and Navy. With war now a reality in Europe—albeit a distant reality to most Americans—the U.S. government saw the need to step up its political intelligence gathering, but without any concrete plans. As a result, American embassy and consular staff around the world were given little direction and had to make things up as they went along. This has left me plenty of room to use my imagination in regards to Martin's activities in Argentina in 1940.

I've endeavored to be as accurate as possible in describing the political and social environment of the story, and the complicated interlocking games of diplomacy and espionage in the first year of World War Two. I have taken only a few liberties, such as the presence of Reginald Sloan in Buenos Aires many months before the first FBI agents were assigned there in June of 1940. In doing so, I felt that this change was in keeping with the overall spirit of U.S. involvement in Latin America during the early war years, which focused heavily on enforcing the neutrality of the Americas Security Zone.

The novel's description of the legal status of gay men in Argentina is accurate—sexual activity between men had indeed been decriminalized in the Argentine republic, unique in the Western Hemisphere; though there was the interesting disparity that heterosexual prostitution was legal while homosexual prostitution was still criminal.

In spite of this liberal legal stance, Argentina was a conservative society, largely Catholic, and as a result the LGBT community there was hardly open by today's standards. The country's first gay bars were still decades in the future at this point, and there was no cohesive gay rights movement.

Public decency laws prohibited overt displays of affection, and there is evidence that the police enforced this with greater vigor when the display was homoromantic rather than heteroromantic. I feel that my depiction of Javier and Antonio's arrest reflects this reality.

One of the biggest challenges to writing historical fiction with gay characters is to portray a realistic stance for those heterosexual individuals who—like Martin—did not subscribe to the pervasive homophobic attitude of the time. What passed for a "liberal" attitude in those days would not seem so very liberal—or even moderate—in the twenty-first century. But it would be an error to expect a social liberal in 1940 to hold modern views. I believe that Martin's attitude—accepting the individual as long as (or even because) he kept his sexuality private—is the correct attitude for a straight ally at the time, however short it may fall from our modern standards. I feel this is important to show.

Like many large cities at the time, Buenos Aires had a bohemian subculture that challenged established mores. While not as large and visible as the more famous bohemian enclaves in Paris and New York, the literary and artistic community centered around the *Barrio Almagro* did fit the description. I have attempted to depict them as they would have been in 1940. Bohemian subcultures tended to accept alternatives to heteronormative sexuality regardless of the attitude of the larger culture, which is why I placed Javier Velasco and Antonio Rivera within that bohemian society.

As always, I have done my best to be as historically accurate as possible, except where noted above. Any errors are mine alone.

Acknowledgements

Contrary to appearances, writing and publishing a novel is never a solitary endeavor. I have many people to thank for their contributions to this book.

First, as always, my thanks go to the talented writers in the IndyScribes critique group—Laura VanArondonk Baugh, Stephanie Cain, Stephanie Ferguson, Marcia Kelly, Peggy Larkin, Jim Meeks-Johnson, Chelsea Sanders, and Jim Thompson—who patiently read and critiqued many sections of the first and second drafts, and provided excellent feedback. They've had a hand in improving every book I've published, and the stories are better for it. You all are the best!

My sincere thanks to my wonderful team of beta readers—Lisa Wheeler, Ann Griffin, and Peggy Larkin—who took the time to read the entire manuscript, and provided valuable insights and feedback. You all helped to bring out the best in this story, and I can't thank you enough.

Many thanks to Tiffany Cabrera, PhD from the U.S. Department of State's Office of the Historian. The documents you provided helped illuminate Martin's role in countless ways. The Office of the Historian's extensive archive of memoranda was invaluable in piecing together our country's aims and diplomatic efforts in Latin America, and Argentina specifically, in 1940.

Thanks to Steven Novak for another amazing cover. It really captures the essence of the story.

And last, but never least, my deepest gratitude, love, and devotion to my husband David Lee. You put up with countless hours during which I immerse myself in my stories, with nary a complaint. You give me the freedom to live this amazing and sometimes infuriating life of a fiction writer, and you are always supportive through all of its ups and downs. I love you more than words can express.

-Garrett B. Hutson, March 2020